DANGEROUS

"Fast paced and action packed, bubbling over with ideas and full of heart, *Dangerous* is a dangerously addictive read." —**Scott Westerfeld**, *New York Times* bestselling author of the Leviathan and Uglies series

"One of the best books I've ever read. Ever." —**James Dashner**, *New York Times* bestselling author of *The Maze Runner*

"Master storyteller Hale takes readers to dizzying new heights. Layered with gritty action and heartfelt characters, *Dangerous* is a can't-miss adventure." —**Kiersten White**, *New York Times* bestselling author of *Paranormalcy*

"Girl power abounds. . . . Hale's range is wider than her readers might have expected." —***Kirkus Reviews***

"An action-packed SF thriller with plenty of surprises." —***Publishers Weekly***

"A must-read for fans of superhero adventures." —***SLJ***

"Hale writes her first suspenseful science fiction novel with great success. Maisie Danger Brown is a strong, smart, unique character." —***VOYA***

"This novel is a whirlwind of excitement." —***RT Book Reviews***

BOOKS BY SHANNON HALE

DANGEROUS

SHANNON HALE

BLOOMSBURY

NEW YORK   LONDON   NEW DELHI   SYDNEY

First published in the United States of America in March 2014
by Bloomsbury Children's Books
Paperback edition published in May 2015
www.bloomsbury.com

Bloomsbury is a registered trademark of Bloomsbury Publishing Plc

For information about permission to reproduce selections from this book, write to
Permissions, Bloomsbury Children's Books, 1385 Broadway, New York, New York 10018
Bloomsbury books may be purchased for business or promotional use. For information on bulk
purchases please contact Macmillan Corporate and Premium Sales Department at
specialmarkets@macmillan.com

"Desert Places" from the book THE POETRY OF ROBERT FROST edited by Edward Connery Lathem.
Copyright © 1969 by Henry Holt and Company, LLC. Copyright © 1936 by Robert Frost. Copyright © 1964
by Lesley Frost Ballantine. Used by permission of Henry Holt and Company, LLC. All rights reserved.

The Library of Congress has cataloged the hardcover edition as follows:
Hale, Shannon.
Dangerous / Shannon Hale.
pages   cm
Summary: When aspiring astronaut Maisie Danger Brown, who was born without a right hand, and
the other space camp students get the opportunity to do something amazing in space, Maisie must prove
how dangerous she can be and how far she is willing to go to protect everything she has ever loved.
ISBN 978-1-59990-168-8 (hardcover) • ISBN 978-1-61963-155-7 (e-book)
[1. Astronautics—Fiction. 2. Love—Fiction. 3. People with disabilities—Fiction. 4. Adventure and
adventurers—Fiction. 5. Science fiction.] I. Title.
PZ7.H13824Dan 2014   [Fic]—dc23   2013034322

ISBN 978-1-61963-819-8 (paperback)

Book design by DDesigns
Typeset by Westchester Book Composition
Printed and bound in the U.S.A. by Thomson-Shore Inc., Dexter, Michigan
2 4 6 8 10 9 7 5 3 1

All papers used by Bloomsbury Publishing, Inc., are natural, recyclable products
made from wood grown in well-managed forests. The manufacturing processes
conform to the environmental regulations of the country of origin.

For Wren,
who is a superhero

PROLOGUE

The warehouse was coffin dark. I put out a hand, feeling my way up the stairs.

I knew I wasn't alone.

I strained to hear movement. A scuffed foot, the rustle of clothing. The clink of ammunition. Anything.

There was nothing. Just the sound of my own labored breathing.

If I had known all that would happen these past months, would I still have entered that stupid sweepstakes?

No, I thought. Never.

But my hand pressed against the tokens in my chest, protective. I climbed faster.

Our team was shattered. Two of us left. Only one would walk away from this encounter. But I didn't want to kill again. And I didn't want to die.

PART ONE
FIRETEAM

CHAPTER 1

Every superhero has an origin story. Mine began with a box of cereal.

"Mom?" I said, pulling a box of Blueberry Bonanza out of a grocery sack. "Really?"

I'd like to say I was helping her unload the groceries because I'm that wonderful. In fact it was an excuse to escape. When she'd returned from the store, I'd been working on Accursed Geometry.

"They were on sale," Mom said. "I thought you'd like to try something different."

I opened the box and poured some "Fruitish Nuggets and Marshmallow Fun" into my hand to show her.

"Oh!" she said. "I didn't realize they were so blue."

"*Guácala*," I said. The Spanish word for gross sounded so perfectly gross.

"*Guácala*," she agreed.

I was going to put the cereal in solitary confinement on a high shelf when I noticed the words "Astronaut Boot Camp" on the back of the box:

SWEEPSTAKES OPEN TO U.S. RESIDENTS AGES
12–18. GRAND PRIZE INCLUDES THREE WEEKS
AT HOWELL ASTRONAUT BOOT CAMP.

"Thanks for the spontaneous help," Mom was saying as she put away the fridge items. "Am I correct in assuming I'm saving you from geometry?"

"Now, Mom, you know I find nothing so thrilling as calculating the area of a triangle."

I shelved the box, too ashamed to show Mom the sweepstakes. Since I was five I wanted to be an astronaut. But little kids always dream of being astronauts, princesses, or spies and then grow up to realize that's impossible. I should have outgrown my space fantasy by now.

"Hey, Maisie," Dad said, coming in from the garage. "Did you hear about the dog that gave birth to puppies in the park? She was arrested for littering."

"Heard it," I said. "Can you really not remember which puns you've tried on me?"

"I have a photographic memory, but it was never developed."

"Heard that one too."

Newly motivated, I hurried through math so I could get on the Astronaut Boot Camp website. In order to enter the sweepstakes online, I had to fill out a survey. It was crazy long.

"Wow, there's something shockingly unnatural about bright-blue food, isn't there?" Dad called from the kitchen. How had he even found the cereal? "Did you know there's no FDA-approved natural source for blue food dye?"

"Yep."

"The color blue is an appetite suppressant, our body's primal instinct to warn us away from poisonous things," he went on, in full lecture mode. "Blueberries are actually purple skin around green pulp. And red foods like maraschino cherries owe their color to the ground-up bodies of female cochineal insects."

"Mom bought the cereal," I called back. I started to feel guilty, as if I were lying to my parents, so I added, "Um, read the back of the box."

"Oh!" Dad leaned around the kitchen wall. "Maisie, you know the odds of winning the sweepstakes must be astronomical, no pun intended. For once."

"I know. I just thought, why not enter, right?"

"Okay then. When you grow up to be a famous astronaut, don't forget your humble roots. Those who get too big for their britches will be exposed in the end."

"Enough already!"

And the survey went on and on.

"This is weird . . ."

"What?" Dad was sitting on the couch now, reading a science journal and absently rubbing his bald spot. These past few years, the spot had degraded into more of a bald territory. He had only a rim of puffy hair left. I was afraid I'd hurt his feelings if I suggested he just shave it all off.

"It's a marketing survey," I said, "but listen to these questions: 'How would you rate your memorization ability? How many languages do you speak at home?' Here's my favorite: 'What would you do if you were in an elevator on the fiftieth floor of a building, the brakes broke, and you began to plummet?'"

Dad put down the journal. "What *would* you do?"

"I'd climb through the hatch in the elevator's ceiling, take off my pants, wrap them around one of the cables and tighten until I slowed my fall, and then I'd swing onto a ledge and wait for rescue."

"And put your pants back on, of course."

I frowned at him. "I just escaped a runaway elevator, and you're worried that someone will see me without pants?"

"Are you kidding? My baby girl is a teenager—I worry about everything. *¡Cariña!*" he shouted toward Mom in their bedroom, which doubled as her office. "Can we hire someone to guard Maisie for the next several years? Maybe a Navy SEAL?"

"*¡Adelante!*" she shouted back. Mom was Paraguayan. Even though she'd been living in the States since she was eighteen, she still had an awesome accent. "Get a cute one with a full head of hair."

"Hey!" he said, and she giggled at her own joke.

I thought my plan would work—that is, if I had two hands to grab the pants. In my mom's uterus, amniotic bands had wrapped around my forearm, and I was born without a right hand.

It was my right arm's fault I was into space. When I was old enough to dress myself, Dad replaced buttons on my clothes with Velcro, saying, "Velcro—just like the astronauts." I'd wanted to know more, and a few library books later, I was a space geek.

"Howell Astronaut Boot Camp?" he said, reading over my shoulder. "I didn't know Bonnie Howell ran a summer camp."

Bonnie Howell was, of course, the billionaire who built the Beanstalk—the world's only space elevator. Library books published less than ten years ago still called a space elevator "decades away." But the Beanstalk's very real ribbon of carbon nanotubes connected an ocean platform to an asteroid in geostationary orbit, thirty-six thousand kilometers up. (That's twenty-two thousand miles, but I was raised on the metric system. A side effect of having scientist parents.)

"She said she started the boot camp to 'ignite the love of science in the teenage mind,'" I said, scanning a Wikipedia article. "Hey, did you know she has a full space station on the Beanstalk's anchoring asteroid? She uses the station for mining operations and unspecified research."

Dad perked up. To him, "research" meant "hours of nonstop fun, and all in the comfort of a white lab coat!" He went off to call his science buddies for more details.

There was a single knock at the door, and Luther let himself in. *"Buenas tardes,"* he said.

"Buenas, mijo," Mom greeted him from her room. "Get something to eat!"

Luther shuffled to the kitchen and returned with graham crackers smeared with chocolate hazelnut spread. He was wearing his typical white button-down shirt, khaki pants, and black dress shoes. He sat in Dad's vacated spot on the couch, setting his plate on the threadbare armrest.

"Did you finish Accursed Geometry so we can talk science project?" Luther scowled at me, but he didn't mean it. He just needed glasses, but he refused to succumb to another stereotype of the nerd.

"Yeah, hang on a sec . . ." I answered the last question on the marketing survey and clicked SUBMIT. "Okay, your turn."

I grabbed Luther's arm and pulled him into the computer chair.

"Maisie, what are—"

"Wow, you're all muscly." My hand was on his upper arm, and when he'd tried to fight me off, he flexed his biceps. We'd been homeschooling together for five years. When had he gone and grown muscles?

I squeezed again. "Seriously, you're not scrawny anymore."

He pulled away, his face turning red. I pretended not to notice, filling him in on the sweepstakes. He laughed when I told him my answer to the elevator question.

"That only works in the movies. Never mind. Think science project. Could a lightweight car function as a kind of electromagnet, repelling the Earth's magnetic force so it could hover—"

"Reducing friction, and therefore using less energy to propel itself? Definitely!"

Luther started sketching out ideas. I smiled and pretended enthusiasm, as I had been for the past year. Pretending.

My world felt like it was shrinking—my tiny house, my tiny life. Mom and Dad. Luther. Riding my bike in the neighborhood. Studying space but going nowhere. Why did everyone else seem fine but I felt as if I were living in a cage I'd outgrown two shoe sizes ago?

Luther had a big extended family with reunions and camping trips and dinners. They went to church, joined homeschool clubs, played sports.

My parents believed in staying home.

I told myself I could survive without change. Things weren't *that* bad. College wasn't so far away. Then astronaut boot camp taunted me. It could be a fascinating experiment: take Maisie out of her natural habitat, put her in a new place with astronomical possibilities (some pun intended), and see what happens.

◆

You could say I regularly checked the website for updates, if regularly means twenty times a day. For weeks and weeks.

"Dad and I were talking," Mom said one day, "and when—*if* you don't win, maybe we can save up to send you next summer."

"Thanks, Mom," I said, but I knew there was no way they could afford it.

I had to win. The degree of my wanting alarmed me. I'd always been certain of four things:

1. I wanted to be an astronaut.
2. Space programs recruited the "able-bodied" types.
3. I had to be so good at science my limb lack wouldn't matter.
4. Science requires objectivity, and emotions create errors. To be the best scientist, I needed to rid myself of cumbersome human emotions.

I winced my way through the spring, trying to become Maisie Robot. I thought I'd prepared myself for the inevitable disappointment when I came home from Luther's one day to a year's supply of Blueberry Bonanza on our front porch. The accompanying letter left no doubts:

YOU WON!
YOU WON YOU WON YOU WON YOU WON!

It was happening. That huge, whooshing engine of anticipation wasn't going to zoom past and leave me in the dust. I lay back on the stoop, hugging one of those boxes of nasty cereal, and stared up at the sky. At a glance, the blue seemed solid, but the longer I stared, the more it revealed its true nature as a shifting thing, not solid and barely real.

The sky seemed as artificial as the cereal in my arms. It wasn't a cage. I wasn't really trapped. I was about to break free.

CHAPTER 2

You'll be gone three weeks?"

"Yeah."

"Oh." Luther stared at his feet, tilting his shoe so his laces slopped to one side and then the other. "That seems like a long time."

"Generally speaking, when your best friend wins a sweepstakes, you're supposed to say congratulations."

"Best friend . . ." He said it softly, and I realized that we'd never used that term before.

After that, he avoided the topic of my departure till my last day at home.

We were working on a history project. Luther had thought we could compare mortality rates with urban cleanliness: the Poo Project. It had sounded more interesting before astronaut boot camp dangled so sparkly and enchanting in my periphery.

Luther shut his notebook. "I guess I'll go home."

"Hey—we can chat during my free hours, Sundays and Wednesdays at ten." Cell phones weren't allowed at astronaut boot camp, and Luther despised talking on the phone anyway, so my only option would be chatting online in the computer lab.

"Okay, so good-bye, I guess," he said.

He reached out, and I thought he wanted to give me a hug, so I leaned in. It was only when I glimpsed the surprise in his eyes that I realized he'd probably been about to pat my shoulder or something. But stopping a hug almost enacted would be like trying to stop a jump when your feet were already in the air.

So I leaned in the last ten percent.

"Take care," I mumbled against his shoulder, patting his back.

He hesitated, then his arms rose around me too. I still thought of him as the short, pudgy kid I'd met riding bikes five years ago. When had he grown taller than me? I could feel the pulse in his neck beating against my head, his heart slamming in his chest. I panicked, my entire middle from stomach to throat turning icy, and I let go.

"Don't you dare finish the Poo Project without me," I said casually.

"Okay," he said.

That night I thought more about Luther than astronaut boot camp.

My parents drove me to the Salt Lake City airport early the next morning. We all got sniffly sad hugging by the security line.

I was missing them even more when I had to take off Ms. Pincher (as we called my prosthetic arm) to put it through the X-ray machine. A little boy behind me howled with fright.

I knew I was too old to be so attached to my parents. But as the plane took off, I imagined there was a string connecting my heart to theirs that stretched and stretched. I used my rough beverage napkin to blow my nose and kept my face turned toward the window. I was in the false blue sky.

In Texas, a shuttle took me from the airport far beyond the city. Howell Aeronautics Lab was completely walled in, guard turrets at each corner. Why did it look more like a military compound than a tech company? Inside the walls, the clean, white buildings resembled a hospital. A creepy hospital in the middle of nowhere.

For the first time, I wondered if this was an enormous mistake.

In Girls Dorm B, my dorm mates were changing into the jumpsuits we got at registration, bras in pink and white flashing around the room. I undressed in a bathroom stall. The jumpsuit had Velcro. I sighed relief.

I looked pale in the mirror. Just what would this girl in the orange jumpsuit do?

I was entering the auditorium for the introductory session when I heard a redheaded boy whisper, "Man, did you see her arm?"

The jumpsuits had short sleeves. My arm was swollen from the airplane ride, so I hadn't put Ms. Pincher back on. I had some regrets.

The redhead repeated the question before the dark-haired guy beside him asked, "What about her arm?"

"It's *gone*."

"Then the answer is obvious—no, I didn't see her arm."

"Look at her, Wilder. She's missing half her arm, man."

The dark one looked back at me, his eyes flicking from my naked stump to my eyes. He smiled and said, "Cool."

Cool? Was that offensive or kind?

He wore a braided leather wristband, sturdy flip-flops, and

appeared to be comfortable even in an orange jumpsuit. I wanted more information.

After the session, he looked like he might be a while chatting with some blond girls, so I picked up his folder from his chair.

> **NAME:** Jonathan Ingalls Wilder
> **ADDRESS:** 21 Longhurt Park, Philadelphia, Pennsylvania
> **FATHER:** George Theodore Wilder
> **OCCUPATION:** President, Wilder Enterprises
> **MOTHER:** Alena Gusyeva-Wilder
> **OCCUPATION:** Philanthropist

He cleared his throat dramatically. I noticed that the blondes were gone.

"Just getting to know you," I said, flipping to the next page.

"'Hello, what's your name?' is customary." He had an interesting voice, kind of gravelly.

"Does philanthropist count as an occupation? Oh—" I said as I realized. "You're rich." He wasn't one of the sweepstakes winners. His parents could afford this place.

He sighed melodramatically. "Poor me, burdened with billions, shackled to my father's shadow."

The room was empty but for us, everyone else headed for dinner.

"Jonathan *Ingalls* Wilder?"

"My mom read the *Little House on the Prairie* books in Russian when she was a kid. I think she married my dad for his last name." He grabbed my folder and started to read. His eyebrows went up.

"Yes, that's my real middle name," I said preemptively.

"Maisie Danger Brown. What's the story there?"

I sighed. "My parents were going to name me after my deceased grandmothers—Maisie Amalia—then in the hospital, it occurred to them that the middle name Danger would be funny."

"So you can literally say, Danger is my middle—"

"No! I mean, I avoid it. It's too ridiculous. It's not like anyone actually calls me Danger. Well, my mom sometimes calls me *la Peligrosa*, which is Spanish for Danger Girl. But it's just a joke, or it's meant to be. My parents have to work really hard to be funny. They're scientists."

"Father, Dr. Nicholas Brown, microbiologist," he said, reading from my info sheet. "Mother, Dr. Inocencia Rodriguez-Brown, physicist. Researchers?"

"Dad is. Mom works from home editing a physics journal and homeschooling me."

"A homeschooled, black-eyed Latina." He whistled. "You are turning into a very ripe fruit for the plucking."

I blinked. No one talks like that. But he was so casual about it, so self-assured, as if he owned the world. And for all I knew, maybe he did.

We walked toward the cafeteria, reading.

"Your elective is . . ." I searched his class schedule. "Short-field soccer."

"You almost managed to keep a judging tone out of your voice."

"Why would you come to astronaut boot camp to play soccer?"

"Because I'm unbelievably good at it. And yours is . . . advanced aerospace engineering?"

"I'm not wasting my time here. I'm in training."

"Wilder!" The redheaded boy came charging from the cafeteria. His name tag read FOWLER, and I wondered if it was vogue for all rich boys to go by their last names. "Hey, I saved you a seat at our table."

"In a sec," said Wilder. "It's not every day I meet a future astronaut."

"Who? Her?"

Wilder nodded, his attention returning to my papers.

"Are you delusional?" Fowler asked me. "You have *one hand*."

"Then I guess I'll be the first one-handed freak in space."

"Whatever." He turned back to Wilder. "So, if you want to join us . . ."

Wilder started into the cafeteria, still reading, and Fowler followed.

"Hey, you'll need this back." I held out his folder, but he shook his head.

"Yours is more interesting."

That was probably true. Wilder's papers had the barest info. He hadn't filled out the survey or included a personal essay, and his academic records only showed he'd attended five schools in the past three years. I wondered what he was hiding.

CHAPTER 3

The folder switch forced me to track down Wilder at breakfast and ask him where I was supposed to be first hour.

He looked at me leisurely before opening my folder. "Astrophysics in 2-C. That sounds like a party in a jar."

It did. If a party in a jar was a good thing. Would setting a party inside a glass container make it more amusing? Or was he being sarcastic?

"And you have navigation in 4-F," I said, though he didn't ask.

"I can't just follow you to astrophysics? Sit in the back, pass you notes, sketch your profile on my desk?"

I was sure he was kidding. Almost sure. I should have done some homeschool projects on Teenage Social Life or Boys in General.

Wilder did not follow me to astrophysics. I looked around a few times, just to be sure.

For second hour everyone migrated to the auditorium again. The crowd hushed when a short white woman with frizzy hair clomped onto the stage. She was wearing a floral dress that was a little too big and a pair of heavy, wide sandals.

"I'm Dr. Bonnie Howell," she said, her hair bobbing, her skirt swishing.

I started to clap, getting in three awkward slaps of my hand against my thigh before I realized no one else was clapping. I sunk lower in my seat. Maybe they didn't realize that this was *the* Bonnie Howell, as in Howell Aerospace.

"I hope you weren't expecting kiddie camp," she said. "I don't employ veteran astronauts and the top minds in science so you can eat marshmallows and sing songs. Did you know," she bounced on the balls of her feet, "your teenage brain is a work in progress? If you want big, beefy brains as adults, you must learn to organize your thoughts, control your impulses, and explore different ideas and subjects while you're still a teenager. Challenge yourselves, for pity's sake! By adulthood, any neglected areas in your brain will shut down. So sit back and stick to what you know, and you'll be condemned to being flimsy, pathetic little piñatas, frozen in form with no hope of establishing the connections you ignored as teenagers. Okay?"

And she left the stage.

If Luther had been there, I would have whispered to him, "I give her an A for Brain Trivia, B for Bounciness, and D for Closure."

A large black man in a suit took the podium. Well, he stood behind the podium—but he did look capable of actually picking it up if he wanted.

"I'm Dr. Dragon Barnes, Howell Aerospace Chief of Operations."

His name was Dragon? That was almost as embarrassing as Danger.

"In addition to your classes each day, you will meet in groups of four we call fireteams. Your fireteam will complete timed and graded missions. The fireteam with the best cumulative score will win an exciting opportunity." His voice was leaden. I doubted he knew what "exciting" meant. "The last week of your stay, Dr. Howell and I are flying to the ocean platform that is the planet-side base for the Beanstalk. Usually only the Howell Aeronautics crew is permitted aboard the base. But this time—"

Dr. Howell suddenly ran back onto the stage and yelled into the microphone, "Some of you will get to come and watch!"

Everyone winced at the shriek of feedback from the speakers. Silence followed. I didn't seem to be the only one unsure of what she meant. Dragon nudged her aside—I was already calling him by his first name in my head. It was just too memorable.

"To clarify," he said, "the members of the winning fireteam will visit the Beanstalk's base and observe the space elevator ascend. From sea level. The Beanstalk doesn't take tourists."

There were a few moans of disappointment.

"Nevertheless, you will tour a site few have set foot on. Recently the president of the United States requested a visit, and she was refused." Dragon glanced sideways at Dr. Howell, his mouth stern. "*Ahem*. Know that this is a great privilege."

He didn't have to tell me. I hadn't taken a breath in at least sixty seconds.

Dr. Howell nodded vigorously, her frizz bouncing. "So work hard, my little hamsters. We will be watching!"

She bobbed off the stage. Dragon added a quick "thank you" before hurrying after her.

The head counselors got onstage and assigned us to our fireteams. Wilder's name was not read next to mine.

I found my assigned meeting spot by a fountain in the

blazing-hot courtyard, my thoughts dancing up a Beanstalk cable into space.

A skinny Asian girl sat cross-legged on the lip of the fountain, drinking a blue slushie she must have carried out of the cafeteria. She introduced herself as Mi-sun. Her name sounded Korean, but her accent was fully American.

"So is this all weird or fun?" she asked.

"Both, I think," I said.

She nodded sagely and slurped her drink.

An older girl with loads of curly red hair approached but wouldn't sit or make eye contact. Just as a boy joined us, a counselor with a megaphone told all the groups, "You have five minutes to get to know your fireteam members. Go."

"Okay, I'll go first," said the boy. He had a short, tight Afro and black geek-chic glasses, and when he talked, dimples pressed into his cheeks. In less than a minute we learned:

1. His name was Jacques.
2. He grew up in Paris with his African-French father and American mother. When his parents divorced, he moved with his mom to the Chicago area.
3. He was an Illinois state chess champ for three years, and he spent a week on Junior Jeopardy.
4. He was a Blueberry Bonanza sweepstakes winner.

"I filled out that *bleeping* survey," he said. "Marketing surveys are always digging for something, and I *bleepity-bleep* gave it to them."

If you can't tell, I changed some of his words. My mom only

swore in Spanish. My dad's worst insult was "chump." Luther's expletives included "Balefire!" and "Frak!" So I was a bit sheltered from R-rated language, and Jacques unnerved me. I tried not to show it.

The redhead went next. She had a curvy body and was super tall if she stood straight, but her shoulders rounded, hiding her chest. "I'm Ruth. I'm from Louisiana. I'm a sweepstaker too, and I hate the heat." She threw her long hair over one shoulder.

After Ruth's hasty intro, I worried I'd sound needy if I said too much. "I'm Maisie, I'm from Salt Lake City, and I . . . uh, I like cheese." I angled my body away from them, Ms. Pincher behind me.

Mi-sun was more forthcoming about living in Alaska, her two little brothers whom she missed "so, so much," and her crafty hobbies. Mi-sun was a sweepstakes winner too, even though she was only eleven.

"But the contest was for ages twelve to eighteen," I said.

"I filled out the survey, and they called me and told me I'd won." Her lips were stained blue from her slushie, and with her dark hair and pale skin, she looked undead.

A counselor fetched our fireteam for our first mission, gesturing us into a small outbuilding and shutting the door behind us.

We were in a bare white room, darkly lit. We waited. Was something supposed to happen?

"Cry havoc!" Jacques said suddenly, making me jump.

"What?" said Ruth.

He folded his arms. "It's my battle cry."

A man's voice spoke from a hidden speaker. *"Do not share details of this exercise with anyone outside your fireteam. Your ability to keep a secret will be considered in your final score."*

Metal doors rolled down each wall, encaging us with a loud

screech and a clang. Mi-sun cried out. My body buzzed with adrenaline.

The man's voice said, "*Get out of the room.*"

I tried to lift the metal doors. They were locked down.

"Could we reach that?" Mi-sun asked, looking up.

There was a hatch in the ceiling. Ruth was the tallest, so Mi-sun climbed on her shoulders. Not tall enough.

"Hey, check this out!" I said. The tiles on the floor were a little loose. I could unsnap them and pull them free.

Jacques turned a tile over in his hands. "Look at these notches. They're building blocks."

The girls started pulling up tiles as fast as we could and clicking them into boxes while Jacques figured out the best configuration to stack them. The process seemed to take forever. I kept glancing at the walls, sure they were closing in.

Finally we'd built a narrow staircase. As soon as we climbed up through the hatch and onto a ledge above a private courtyard, the man's voice said, "*Find the treasure.*"

A zip line, coded map, and buried chest of chocolate coins later, a buzzer went off.

A gate opened, and Bonnie Howell stepped in. She looked us over. "Well, you just set an astronaut boot camp record."

A rush of elation shot up through me, hitting my throat and strangely making me want to cry.

Jacques and Mi-sun high-fived. Ruth was beside me—tall, beautiful, so fearsome seeming. I held up my left hand.

"Yes, Ruth! Record time!"

"Don't spaz. You'll hurt yourself worse." She looked at where my right hand wasn't and shuddered.

Unsure what I had next hour, I made my way toward Wilder's class, noticing for the first time just how many security cameras spied from the ceiling.

The zip line adventure had irritated my arm, so Ms. Pincher was in my bag. A couple of boys bumped into me, and when they noticed my arm, one jumped back.

"Gross, her meat stump touched me!" he said, wiping off the sludge of my touch.

Ruth's reaction already had me on edge, I guess, because instead of pretending I hadn't heard, I waggled my bare arm at the boys and shouted "WAAAH!" like I was some fearsome, spell-casting hag. "Foul creatures of the night! WAAH, I SAY!"

They ran away. I kid you not—*ran*, as if I were the chainsaw guy at the end of a haunted house.

Wilder was coming down the hall, and he smiled at me, appreciative, as though we'd been in on the joke together. As though we were the only two sane people amid this rabble.

He has intelligent eyes, I noticed.

And all afternoon I kept on noticing.

That night at lights out, I got my mini flashlight and read through his folder again. When his fireteam entered that weird room, would he discover the tiles were pieces of a puzzle? Would he find it all as strange and alarming and exciting as I did?

I closed my eyes and saw his. Sleep felt like the loneliest place in the world.

CHAPTER 4

On day five, I woke up grateful that at last I'd have a free hour. After morning scuba class, I hurried to the computer lab, checked out a tablet, and curled up in a corner chair. A few years before, Luther and I had discovered a Japanese website that appeared to promote teeth whitening. It had a message board no one ever used because, honestly, who sits around discussing white teeth? So we colonized it.

Luther was already logged in, his user name LEX blinking green. Homesickness pulsed in my belly.

Luther wouldn't tolerate any emoticons or messaging shortcuts, but it didn't slow me down much. I'd been typing one-handed since I was four.

MAIZ: Greetings, friend of Wookiees everywhere.
How's the weather?
LEX: Cloudy with a chance of stupidity. My cousins are staying over and they want to play "war" every day. I'm thinking of removing our "no kill" rule.

MAIZ: Enough with the quotation marks. I can hear your sarcasm from four states away.

LEX: Fine. How is "astronaut boot camp"? I mean … ASTRONAUT BOOT CAMP.

MAIZ: You'd go crazy happy for all the gadgets but throw up in the takeoff simulator.

LEX: I would not.

MAIZ: Remember the tilt-a-whirl?

LEX: That was an aberration. I had consumed a hot dog.

MAIZ: Anyway, nonhuman stuff is awesome. Human stuff is to be expected.

LEX: What are the flatscans doing?

MAIZ: Freaking out about the arm.

LEX: Frakking flatscans.

MAIZ: I'll weather it.

LEX: When will you be home?

MAIZ: The 20th.

LEX: In the morning, afternoon, or evening?

MAIZ: I don't know.

LEX: Find out.

MAIZ: Why?

LEX: I just want to know when Maisie Brown is in her house again.

MAIZ: You miss me, don't you?

LEX: Yes.

I'd expected a snide rebuttal, but I saw no sarcasm in his yes. I thought of our accidental hug, the tick of his pulse against my cheek.

LEX: Are you still there?

MAIZ: Yeah. Sorry.

LEX: The 20th?

MAIZ: I'll probably be home after dinner but not too late. I should go. I need to call my parents still.

LEX: You wrote to me first?

MAIZ: You're my best friend.

I waited. Luther didn't respond. I suddenly felt shy.

MAIZ: Signing off...

LEX: Okay. Write again, okay?

MAIZ: Sure. Till Wednesday.

Just three more days felt like forever.

I phoned my parents from the lab's landline. When my mom started to gush in Spanish, I felt a pricking in the corners of my eyes.

"*Te extraño, Mami*," I said, telling her I missed her. "Three weeks is a long time, isn't it?"

Dad sighed agreement. I didn't tell them about the teasing. I suspected the reason they kept me isolated at home was to protect me from people like Ruth and the running boys.

As I left the lab, I overheard two girls talking. "I sneaked my cell phone in, but every time I turn it on, there are no bars."

Weird. Were cell phone signals blocked entirely out here?

I shuffled toward my next class, watching my feet as I walked. I noticed grooves in the floors where steel doors could lock down, cutting off parts of the building. I didn't notice that Wilder was next to me.

"You're curling into a question mark," he said.

I snapped back upright. He was without his usual satellites of blond girls and guys sporting last names.

"I just got off the phone with my parents," I said by way of explanation.

"And they're all a bunch of eejits?"

"No . . . I miss them."

He tilted his head, trying to figure out if I was serious.

"How was your call?" I asked. I had his schedule memorized.

"Brief to nonexistent."

"But numbers were dialed?"

"And words were spoken, so thin and flimsy as to barely count at all."

"Words like, hello, how are you, I miss you, good-bye?"

"Like that, but mostly good-bye." He sounded apathetic.

I held an invisible phone to my ear and made a ringing noise. He blinked.

"Answer the phone," I whispered helpfully.

His squint was suspicious, but he answered his own invisible phone. "Hello?"

"Hello, honey bear! How are you?"

"Um . . . I guess I'm fine. And you?"

"Bright-eyed and bushy-tailed. How's that cute little space camp of yours?"

"Campy, spacey, what you'd expect."

"You have a good time now. Good-bye, sweetie pie!" I hung up my pretend phone.

A faint smile was inching across his lips. "And that was for . . . ?"

"On your call day, someone should speak those words to you. You know—hello, how are you. The ones besides just good-bye."

"I think you skipped one."

"I did?"

"Yeah, you'd promised an I-miss-you."

"Right." I dutifully returned my phone hand to my ear, and I looked up to meet his eyes as I said, "I miss you."

My heart revved like a lawn mower. It was supposed to be a joke. But speaking those words made me feel them, believe them. I missed him, as if he were Luther or my family, someone I cared for who was far away.

He held my gaze, and his smile tipped up, full of suggestion. He said quietly, "I miss you too."

When faced with danger, our bodies experience the Primary Threat Response. Muscles contract, ready for flight or fight. Blood drains from extremities, making feet and hands feel cold, and from less-essential systems like the stomach, causing that butterflies sensation. The blood swarms into the head and organs, creating heat (and sweat). Heart pumps faster, blood pressure rises, and breathing turns rapid. All this to prepare the body for possible injury.

But there was no saber-toothed tiger, crouched and hissing. Just Wilder, smiling. I tried to smile back as if my heart weren't thumping and my breaths weren't shallow gasps.

Had he noticed that I watched him in the cafeteria? Had he guessed that I reread his file? That some nights when I closed my eyes, I saw his?

I'd thought I wanted to live free of my mundane little cage, but the world outside was feeling more and more hazardous.

"Why did you keep my folder?" I asked.

"Because I noticed you, Peligrosa. And I liked it."

Actually my nickname is *la Peligrosa*, or "Danger Girl." *Peligrosa* just means "dangerous." But I didn't correct him.

I left Wilder to go kick some butt in our fireteam's fourth mission.

"Cry havoc!" Jacques shouted as we charged into a room featuring a model spacecraft. I got to wear a harness that simulated the weightlessness of space and pretend-fix a satellite.

After that was aerospace engineering and the day wrapped up with medical exams. The doctors put us through the same physicals and brain scans and so on that they did on actual astronauts.

Only late that night in bed, when it was so quiet my thoughts were louder than my breathing, did I allow my mind to return to Wilder.

1. He kept my folder.
2. He remembered my nickname (more or less).
3. He noticed me.

I wanted to list these things, examine them under a microscope, order them into their proper family, genus, and species. Understand them. Were Wilder and I friends? Did I have a crush? Did he?

I rejected the temptation to daydream about Wilder, and so I was completely unprepared.

CHAPTER 5

The night before Howell would announce the winning fireteam, I was lying in bed awake when our dorm door opened and a paper airplane flew through the crack. "Maisie Danger Brown" was written across the top in thick black marker. I picked it off the floor and unfolded it.

> Peligrosa,
> I hear there's a comet tonight.
> Come out and play?
>   W.

Curse the curiosity of the scientific mind, but I went out.

In the hall, Wilder was reading notices on a bulletin board, his hands in his pockets. I examined him objectively; he didn't have the kind of face you'd see on a magazine cover, yet his confidence made him seem especially attractive. I told myself I was unaffected.

"You rang?" I said.

He turned, taking in my T-shirt and sweats. He'd changed into jeans and a gray shirt. It was nice not to be glaring orange at each other.

"What good is a comet overhead when no one admires it?" He inclined his head upward toward the roof.

I'd been complaining about missing the comet earlier to Mi-sun, but I shook my head. "If we're caught, they might send us home early."

"They're not going to kick out a sweepstakes winner. Bad publicity. That's why I want you with me, Danger Girl."

"I don't know if your logic is sound," I said, though I took two steps toward him.

When I was twelve, Dad had showed me scans and charts, proof that a teenager's brain is underdeveloped. We're missing connections and parts adults have that help them analyze situations and take appropriate caution. That's why teens need rules and guidance, he told me. We're not biologically capable of being fully rational. I swore right then that I'd be a smart, cautious teenager.

Now those underdeveloped parts of my brain were perking up and looking around.

I kept my head down as we hurried through the corridor, aware of the security camera's gaze. We took a dark staircase up, the butterflies awake in my belly. Wilder picked a lock and opened a door.

The air on the roof was cool yet humid enough to feel cozy, the stars splashed out and sizzling on a Teflon sky. He'd already spread a blanket on the roof's gravel top, left a pair of binoculars waiting.

I could see one of the guard turrets from here. Its windows were black. I hoped no one was inside looking out.

Wilder and I sat about ten centimeters apart and took turns gazing at the bright dot blazing through the constellation Cassiopeia.

I loved comets, engines of nearly endless motion and reminders that the sky wasn't a flat, static surface but a window into vastness.

Afraid of the silence, I blurted the first thing on my mind. "You know, the Lyra comet was born beyond our solar system, which makes it an alien here, the nearest exotic thing."

"Besides the foxy Latina on my right," Wilder said.

"Do girls usually respond to that kind of talk?" I asked.

He frowned. "You'd be easier to woo if you were dumb."

"Then don't woo me," I said.

I didn't mean it.

I sort of meant it.

I didn't know what I meant.

We were quiet, two tiny specks glued down by gravity, peering at a universe that didn't notice us back. The quiet and dark made me feel mysterious and stilled, a thing that glints in the dark, an object that can only be understood by careful study. Something like a poem.

I said, "'All that we see or seem / Is but a dream within a dream.'"

I had a bunch of poems memorized, and whenever something reminded me of one, out it came. Spewing dead poets at my parents was one thing, but I knew immediately I'd made a mistake with Wilder.

Hide your geekiness, Maisie.

But Wilder asked, "What does that mean?"

If Luther didn't know, he'd pretend he did.

"It's Poe," I said. "I think of it whenever the world seems especially mysterious."

"Memorizing poets doesn't seem a practical hobby for the first one-handed freak in space."

I know it sounds odd, but from Wilder that seemed like a compliment. I honestly considered blushing.

"Poets seem to know things that scientists don't. And vice versa. Maybe they balance each other out somehow. If I'm going to get to space, I'll need all the help I can get," I said, lifting Ms. Pincher. "Poe included."

"What do you want up there anyway?"

"To learn things you can only study in a weightless environment. And besides that, space is the place. Nebulas and novas and galaxies and massive expanses of endlessness. My brain can't think about it without having a heart attack."

"Your brain has a heart?"

I laughed because I was sounding ridiculous, and for some reason, I was loving it. "Sure, and it suffers a massive coronary any time I try to comprehend the hugeness and possibilities of space. I mean, just think about Jupiter's moon Europa. With its oxygen-based atmosphere and liquid ocean beneath a sea of ice, it's very likely a home to extraterrestrial life, which would be the biggest discovery since . . . since . . . *ever.*"

"Someday we'll spend trillions to get to Europa only to discover very expensive bacteria," he said.

"By examining what's different from us, we understand ourselves better." Why wouldn't I shut up already? "Um, what lured you to astronaut boot camp?"

"I have a crush on Cassiopeia."

"Cassiopeia."

Wilder nodded, eyes wide, eyebrows raised. "She is *stacked.* Have you seen the size of her stars?"

"Right. And besides the bodacious and boastful Cassiopeia, anything else drawing your attention to the big black yonder?"

Wilder's teasing tone weakened. "I get bored easily. But I can't *know* space, so it keeps me wondering. Maybe there's something worth finding out there, something that's missing down here. Life feels like half of itself."

"'A dream within a dream.'"

"And I want to wake up."

For the first time, I felt like Wilder was saying something he really believed. But I couldn't think of anything to say back that wouldn't sound nerdy.

"Maybe this is stupid, but do you ever feel like you're doomed?" He laughed. "Never mind. Anytime the word 'doomed' is involved, it's definitely stupid. But it's like I'm chasing nothing, and I can't stop until . . ."

"Until what?" I said.

His gaze was up, almost as if he'd forgotten I was there. "'Till the stars run away, and the shadows eat the moon.'"

I knew that line. He was quoting William Butler Yeats.

"'Ah, penny, brown penny, brown penny,'" I finished the poem, "'One cannot begin it too soon.'"

He looked at me. His lips parted. Then he studied my face as he quoted, "'Oh, love is the crooked thing.'"

For the barest moment, I became aware of every part of my body. Not only the pressure of my legs on the roof, the wishy breeze tickling the hairs on my arm, the rise of my chest as I inhaled, the click of my eyelids as I blinked. Not just those places of touch and motion, but all of it. Everything. Everywhere. I thrilled with life. And I looked at Wilder.

"I said I didn't want you to woo me." My voice sounded foreign to my own ears.

"I wasn't."

"Oh. So . . . what does that mean, 'love is the crooked thing'?"

"I don't know." He was still looking at me. "I just like the way it sounds."

I looked down, twisting a loose thread on my T-shirt.

"Poetry kind of reminds me of looking at things through a microscope." I didn't know what I was saying—I just started to talk. "I got a microscope when I turned six. You know, physicist mom, biologist dad. I examined things I thought I knew—a strand of my hair, a feather, an onion peel. Seeing them up close, they changed. I started to guess how, you know, things are more complicated than they seem, but that they have patterns, and the patterns are beautiful. Space has all those patterns and intricacies and mysteries, but not tiny under a microscope. So big, so expansive, when I think about it, I feel like the solid parts of me are dissolving and I'm out there in the blackness and light, moving with the whole universe."

I glanced up to see if he was bored. Instead I felt his hand on my cheek and his lips on mine. Just a touch, a softness, a greeting. One kiss that lasted seven rapid heartbeats. His other hand lifted, both holding my face. A second kiss—one, two, three, four, five beats. It was easy to count by my heart. I could feel it thud through my whole body. My left hand clutched my right arm, afraid to touch him or to not. His lips moved again (how did mine know how to move with his?). A third kiss—one, two, three, four. Only four beats before the fourth kiss. Either the kisses were speeding up or my heart was. A fifth kiss, a sixth, and I counted each beat. It seemed the only way to keep from drowning. Numbers were solid things I could grip, a buoy in a flood.

Seventh, eighth, one beat, two beats, three—

He pulled back (or I did?) but his right thumb stayed on my cheek, his fingers on my jaw. His eyes were still closed.

"You'd better not talk about microscopes anymore," he whispered, "or I don't know if I can control myself."

I laughed. It was good to end a kiss (my first kiss—my first eight kisses) with a laugh, because I didn't know what I was supposed to say. Thanks for the kiss? Um, nice lips? Did you know there are over seven hundred species of bacteria living in the human mouth?

So I laughed again. "I'm pretty sure there are rules against this sort of thing at astronaut boot camp."

"I sure hope so," said Wilder, "or it wouldn't be nearly as fun."

He's dangerous, I reminded myself. And this is not the experience you left home for. You should run away.

I didn't move.

CHAPTER 6

Would he have kissed me again?

I lay in my bunk staring at the tiny black dents in the white ceiling tiles, wondering how anyone can sleep after her first kiss. Or first eight.

It might have been more, but we'd heard a noise (a security guard?), and I hurried back to the dorm. Though once the risk of capture was past, I wondered what wouldn't be worth another kiss. I rolled over, pressing my fingers against a smile, and that was the kiss. My bare feet searching for cool, untouched spots at the bottom of the bed, my hand full of blanket, the press of my collarbone into the pillow. Every touch, every motion was a reminder of Wilder's kiss.

I didn't want to fall asleep and miss a single hour of remembering. But once I did, sleep was lively with dreams.

Wilder wasn't at breakfast. I'm positive about that, since I checked a few times. (Maybe forty-eight.) He came to the tail end of calibration looking sleepy, his hair wet. He winked at the instructor and took the chair beside me.

"Hey," he whispered to the guy sitting on my other side. "Are you checking out my girl?"

"Wha-what?" the kid stuttered.

"Not that I blame you," Wilder said, "but have some respect for the lady."

I hid my face with my hand.

When the bell rang for lunch, I hurried off so Wilder wouldn't think I expected to eat with him. But then he was walking beside me.

"May I escort you to lunch, Danger Girl? I noticed you have a penchant for cheese—"

Wilder stopped, staring at a man in the atrium wearing flip-flops, long cargo shorts, and a washed-out Hawaiian shirt, his hair a little long, his beard a little bushy. He was juxtaposed by three large suited men, buds in their ears.

Dr. Howell approached the Hawaiian-shirt guy. "Hello, GT. Shall we talk in my office?"

He nodded at Wilder before following Dr. Howell.

"Who was that?" I asked.

"My dad," said Wilder.

Dr. Howell had called him GT. I remembered the name George Theodore Wilder from Wilder's papers.

"Does he always dress like that?" GT was not what I imagined when I thought billionaire.

"Yeah, it's a power play. Come on," he whispered, taking my hand.

Another first. It felt like a surrender to let someone take charge of my one hand, but the surrender came with a thrill.

He walked quickly away from the cafeteria. "I need out of all this for an hour, and I want you with me, okay?"

"Okay," I said.

We ran into the parking lot. Wilder opened the driver-side door of an expensive-looking red convertible. He gestured me in, and I scooted down the bench.

"And this car is . . ."

"Dad's." Wilder reached under the dash for a magnetic box, pulled out a spare key, and started the engine.

"I don't do stuff like this, you know."

"That's what makes you so enticing. One of the things anyway. There's also your black magic eyes."

"And my cunning mind and rapier wit, right?"

"Hey, baby," he said, chucking my chin, "all the guys want you for your mind. Isn't it refreshing to be with someone who only cares about your body?"

I laughed. It was becoming my default response. "You know, I'm not going to be that girl who gets pulled in by your cheap lines."

"*My* lines? You're the one who gets things steamy discussing microscopes."

"Are you only capable of talking to me as if an audience were listening?"

"Okay, Peligrosa. Okay."

I felt him relax as he put his arm around my shoulder, looking back as he reversed.

"So what do you usually do to escape?" he asked.

"Escape? I . . . I guess I ride my bike to Luther's." Man, that sounded pathetic to me now.

"And Luther is?"

"A guy. A friend. My best friend."

Wilder glared as we zipped out of the parking lot, and I suspected he wasn't just squinting against the sunlight.

I'm not an expert on manners, but I think he was rude.

Wilder was waiting just inside.

"What is your dad doing here?"

"He's a control freak. He stops by once a week to make sure the security is vigilant in protecting an important man's son." Wilder traced my lower lip with his finger. "I like your mouth."

"I'm not that girl," I reminded him, but I wondered if maybe I was.

So much knowledge gained in the past two weeks, I couldn't contain it all. I started to organize it into a tidy list:

1. Turbulence is characterized by chaotic, random property changes in air flow.
2. The most dangerous part of scuba is the buildup of nitrogen molecules in your body and those gases expanding if you rise up through the water too quickly.
3. You can like a person's mouth.
4. You can feel your heart beat not just in your chest, but everywhere at once.

"Let's skip the next session," he whispered, his hand finding my lower back. "We could find an empty room and talk about microscopes."

I shook my head. "No. No way."

"You're a good girl." He frowned. "Your middle name lies."

I didn't want to be rude like his father. So I took his hand and said, "Jonathan Ingalls Wilder, you have become one of my top five favorite people in the world. Now come on."

We found seats and watched a documentary about the building of the Beanstalk . . . sort of. Wilder kept holding my hand, rubbing my fingernails over his lip. I was field testing a theory that a person's skin emits a scent, and if you're attracted to that person, his scent enters you and releases hormones in your brain that make you disoriented and apt to grin.

After the movie, Bonnie Howell hopped onto the stage, dressed in florals and stripes. She stared at us for a few moments, and then she pulled three green balls out of a bag and juggled. The uncomfortable silence became twitchy.

Howell caught all three balls, pulled the podium's microphone lower with a grating squeak, and spoke with her lips touching it. "I learned how to juggle this year so I could be more entertaining."

She didn't seem to have any other reason for being on stage. Dragon nudged her away from the podium.

"We have the fireteam results," he said.

My stomach made friends with my shoes.

"Congratulations to Fireteam Thirty-six. Jacques Ames, Maisie Brown, Mi-sun Hwang, and Ruth Koelsch."

I had never known before that you can smile so hard your cheeks hurt. But I couldn't stop. It was like my body was in happy mode. My first-ever trip out of the country would be jetting to the equator and getting a front-row seat to a Beanstalk launch.

"In addition, the student with the highest individual rating is invited to join Fireteam Thirty-six as its fifth member. Congratulations to Jonathan Wilder."

Could this moment get any better? Dragon dismissed us, but I couldn't seem to move.

"We're both going." Wilder's words were as heavy as bricks.

"I know it, but I can't get myself to believe it!"

"But . . ." He didn't look at me. "I wasn't expecting this."

Wilder's eyes seemed darker, his whole mood blacker. His gaze slid off me as if I were too lowly to contemplate, and he got up and walked away.

CHAPTER 7

I hurried after Wilder, running into Jacques, Ruth, and Mi-sun in the hall. Wilder stood apart from us, his gaze locked on the ceiling. Ruth and Jacques were celebrating by shoving each other.

"Jacques, you're the man!" I said. Our last couple of victories had been thanks to his awesome strategies.

"Yeah, I know," he said, fake-buffing his nails on his shirt. "You're not half bad yourself, tiger."

"I'm very proud of all of us," said Mi-sun, smiling with lips stained blue.

"That slush can't have enough nutrients for you," I said. She had it for every meal.

"At home I only eat saltines and pickles," she said, "and I'm fine."

She started to talk about the meals she made for her brothers, but my attention kept clicking back to someone and his silence. I walked closer.

"Wilder," I whispered, "what's wrong?"

His expression was blank, yet it affected me like a force. How had I made myself so fragile?

"This," he said, gesturing between the two of us, "was a mistake. I wasn't planning on flying off into the sunset with you or anything, so let's not get tacky about it, okay?"

What?

The troop of blond girls bobbed up to tell him "Congrats!" Wilder put his arm around the nearest and pulled her closer, whispering something. His lips brushed her earlobe. She blushed and giggled.

For the rest of the day I felt like I'd been hit by a train, cartoon birds twittering around my head. I'd just gotten the best news of my life, but I was wasting it moping after an asinine boy.

We rushed from the medic to supplies to suit fitting. At dinnertime we ate the cafeteria food on leather sofas in Dr. Howell's office—malibu chicken, green beans, mashed potatoes, peach cobbler. Wilder was a dead space in my periphery. Did all boys turn weirdo-zombie after kissing a girl? Had I done something wrong? I should have stuck to my plan—work toward becoming an astronaut, eschew emotions, become Maisie Robot.

When Bonnie Howell asked if we had any questions, I jumped in.

"How did you get the Speetle to work on liquid hydrogen?" I asked, referring to the spacecraft Howell Aerospace had launched years before the Beanstalk.

"Speetle?"

"The . . . uh, the Space Beetle. I've been calling it the Speetle in my head. By the way, I'm surprised you don't shorten Howell Aeronautics Lab to HAL."

She sniffed. "I will now. Anyhow, you wouldn't understand if I told you."

"I might," I said.

She obliged me with an explanation that had me lost by the

first sentence. Howell had hazel eyes, neither warm nor cold, but they pierced me.

She's not just a crazy old bat, I thought. She's scary-smart.

"We should wrap this up, Dragon. I want the fireteam back here at 0500." And she bounced out of the room.

"Good night, um, Dr. Howell," I said.

"Everyone just calls her Howell," said Dragon.

"Like she's some cool teenage boy?" I said. I glanced at Wilder and wished I hadn't said "cool."

Dragon escorted us to small private bedrooms, mine next to Wilder's. I locked my door and fell into bed. I could hear Wilder moving around for a long time, so I didn't move at all. I wanted to be soundless, invisible.

I woke with a jolt, terrified I'd overslept, but the clock read 3:14 a.m. My heart was pounding. No chance I was getting back to sleep.

The luxury of having my own shower made everything feel hopeful, the heat scraping the lack of sleep from my skin, yelling at my muscles to wake up. I was an hour early, but I headed to Howell's office. It felt closer to midnight than dawn. My nerves danced on dagger shoes.

Someone was singing. I stopped, peeking in the door. Dragon, his back to me, was doing paperwork and singing opera in a faux soprano. I couldn't believe that squeaky voice came from such a massive, muscular body. And most surprisingly, he wasn't horrible.

He saw me and stopped. "Busted," he said, laughing a bouncy, high laugh. "Don't tell anyone and spoil my formidable image?"

I zipped my lips. "Dr. Barnes, can I borrow a phone? I want to let my parents know about the trip."

"It's too early to call, but they signed a release form with your initial registration, so everything's set."

When the others arrived, we took a van to Howell's private airstrip. Wilder claimed one of the comfy leather seats in the back of the jet, so I sat in front.

Jacques leaped aboard, shouting, "Cry havoc!"

"Why do you always say that?" asked Mi-sun.

"It's an old military command, instructing soldiers to pillage and generally make chaos," he said. "Besides, it sounds kicky."

Ruth snorted.

Two days ago, I couldn't have imagined regretting those eight kisses. The first one that lasted seven heartbeats, and that second one lasting five. The third when his knee touched mine, the fourth when his thumb twitched on my cheek. The fifth when he breathed in through his nose, the sixth when a whisper of a moan escaped his throat. The seventh and eighth that had slowed, lingering.

My mom said that my mind is a scanning machine that makes a copy of everything I see or read or hear. I wished I could delete those kiss files. But the memory sat over me, mocking, like that mouthy raven in Poe's poem. *Nevermore.*

Stupid bird.

We watched a couple of movies before landing on a little island off the coast of Ecuador. The scenery was scrubby and bare, the sun relentlessly hot. But we only stayed long enough to put on astronaut suits. I felt kind of dorky, like a teenager still going trick-or-treating. But Howell wanted us to have an astronaut experience. We even had to wear astronaut diapers.

"This is a stupid place to build something expensive," Ruth said, looking over the sea. "I'm from Louisiana, yo. I've seen what hurricanes can do."

"Actually this is the safest place," I said. "Due to the Coriolis force, hurricanes don't develop on the equator."

Ruth smacked me on the shoulder—for correcting her, I guessed.

"Back off, Ruthless," I said, rubbing my arm.

Jacques smirked at the nickname.

"How's about I call you One-Arm?" she said.

I shrugged. "If it's a good name, it'll stick."

"Let's call her One-Arm," Ruth whispered to Jacques.

"That's stale, *Ruthless*," he said.

So she hit Jacques.

"Ruth, keep your hands to yourself," Mi-sun said in a perfect gentle-but-firm tone. "I won't tell you again."

Ruth rolled her eyes but stopped hitting.

From the island we took a helicopter out to sea. The sun was high—a hot brand melting through the blue. The helicopter was silent under the deafening stutter of the blades. Every face pressed to a window. Slowly the Beanstalk's base came into view.

The ocean platform resembled an oil rig with an Eiffel-like tower. Invisible from this distance was the six-centimeter-wide ribbon made of carbon nanotubes—lightweight and stronger than steel, the only known substance that could support the tension and pressure of climbing into space. The Earth end ran through the tower and attached to the ocean platform. The space end was attached to an orbiting asteroid thousands of kilometers away.

We landed, and I was the first out. At the top of the tower waited the elevator car—a silver pod with wings of solar panels. I could make out the glint of the ribbon. I looked up, following the line into the sky, and got vertigo.

"Hello, gorgeous," I said.

Wilder's face swung toward me.

I smiled. "I wasn't talking to you."

"I didn't think—" He shook his head and walked on.

"Howell, can we get a peek inside the pod?" I asked.

Howell considered. "Well, since you're here . . ."

Jacques gave me the thumbs-up.

A metal lift took us to the top of the tower where the pod rested, looking as dangerous as a boulder on a cliff. Howell and Dragon went into the pod first, and the rest of us followed. From the outside, the solar panels had made it look deceptively large, like long legs on a small-bodied spider. Inside it felt downright cozy. If the interior of a metal ball can be cozy.

Six seats with harnesses were bolted to the floor around one half of the pod. Each faced a small window—just a slit, really, like the ones on old castles that archers would shoot through. The cargo area took up the other half of the pod. In the center was a hollow metal pillar. The ribbon ran through it, and the pod used robotic lifters to climb the ribbon.

"Companies pay us to transport their satellites," Dragon was saying, "which in turn pays for the expense of building and running the Beanstalk. This trip we're only carrying food and supplies for the Beanstalk's two space stations: Midway Station and Asteroid Station."

"So you don't have a lot of cargo this trip," Wilder said, resting his arm on one of the chairs. "You're not overweight. You could take, say, five passengers on a quick jaunt?"

For a few seconds, no one spoke. Then Howell said, "Well . . ."

My legs turned cold.

"Howell," said Dragon in a warning tone.

"We're *not* overweight," she said.

"Howell," said Dragon again.

"Why not? It's for education's sake."

"Howell, it's not safe for children. Their parents—"

"Why would they protest? This is a singular opportunity!"

She clapped her hands and gave a command. A horde of crew in white jumpsuits squeezed into the pod, fitting the fireteam with headsets under soft helmets, leading us to chairs, and harnessing us in. My stomach squelched.

"Howell," Dragon said with exasperation.

"Don't be such a wet blanket. We'll only go up a bit."

Howell sat in the sixth and last chair. Dragon grumbled and sat on the floor, pulling his arms through some straps of the cargo bags.

Howell *tsked* her tongue. "*You're* the one not being safe."

That phrase caught in my mind, stuck on repeat: *not being safe, not being safe . . .*

"If you're going, I'm going," he said.

The pod door sealed with a hiss.

"Wait." Jacques started fumbling with his harness. "What is 'up a bit'? How far is a bit?"

"Isn't this exciting?" Howell said in a happy, singsong voice. "Next stop: space!"

CHAPTER 8

Stay strapped in and remember your training," Dragon said.

"What training?" Ruth yelled. "You mean kiddie camp? You've gotta be kidding me!"

I was smiling but it was that freaky kind of smile, hard and frozen, as if my facial muscles couldn't decide between ecstatic glee and eyeball-clawing horror.

"If any of you want to turn down this chance, speak up now," said Dragon. "Just say the word and we'll open the door."

Ruth stopped squirming. No one answered.

The pod rose slowly for a few meters and then stopped with a loud *click*. I heard control counting down on my headset.

Ten . . . nine . . . eight . . . seven . . .

My parents would so not be okay with this. Was I okay with this? Space travel is not a field trip, and I was not an astronaut. Three Beanstalk astronauts were killed a couple of years ago. Their pod just cracked open on descent. I didn't want to go to space like this, unprepared, unearned, rushed off in a possibly faulty space elevator. It was too dangerous.

And then I thought, Danger is my middle name.

I thought those very words.

Six . . . five . . . four . . .

Prove it, Maisie Danger Brown, I dared myself. Your name was supposed to be a joke. Prove it's not.

Three . . . two . . .

I didn't say no. I didn't say anything at all.

One . . .

The pod pushed up with a force that left my stomach on the ground. There was a lot of screaming. Mostly Jacques.

"AAH! AAH! I DO NOT LIKE HEIGHTS! I DO *NOT* LIKE HEIGHTS!"

"Say it, Jacques," I said.

"Ican'tIcan'tIcan't—"

"Come on," I said. "Your war whoop, your rebel yell, your battle—"

"Cry havoc," he said, his voice trembling. "Cry havoc! CRY! HAVOC!"

It was better than his screaming. I began muttering prayers in Spanish as my mother did when she was worried or scared.

Padre nuestro, que estás en el cielo. Santificado sea tu nombre . . .

We rose so fast, in seconds the ocean waves looked motionless, a great expanse of cake frosting. I glimpsed red—lasers pointed up at the photovoltaic cells on the pod's wings, powering the elevator's ascent. The whole pod was vibrating, a plucked elastic band. The vibration chattered my teeth. My vision wiggled. My bones felt too close together. Gravity would not let us go without a fight.

I was thinking of those rides at amusement parks that lift you terrifyingly high and then drop you in a rush of butterflies and squeals. My body kept expecting the drop. A ribbon of carbon nano-tubes had sounded so sciencey cool. Now climbing a string into space was the most ludicrous thing I could imagine. I shut my eyes. I hugged my chest. I wondered if I was about to die.

Then everything turned off. The whole world, as if someone had hit the switch. I felt strange. Lifted. Out the window the sky was changing from summer noon to midnight.

"Really?" I whispered. "Really?"

My stomach tingled in the middle of my body. My toes curled up in my boots. I watched my knees rise.

Beside me, Mi-sun smiled at a lock of her black hair that had escaped her helmet and was floating in front of her face. Jacques was shaking. Wilder was looking out his window, his face turned away.

"Ladies and gentlemen," said Howell, "welcome to space. It's a long trip to our anchoring asteroid, Big Barda, so today we'll only go as far as Midway Station. Remain in your seats with seat belts fastened and tray tables up . . ." She broke off, giggling.

"What is she talking about?" Mi-sun asked.

"That we're not going all the way up." I was proud of the lack of emotion in my voice, but I couldn't seem to shut up. "Most human-space activity takes place at two hundred and twenty kilometers, but at that level, a satellite orbits the Earth in ninety minutes. The physics of the space elevator require the anchoring end of the tether to be in geostationary orbit, so it moves at the same rate as the Earth itself and remains straight above its equatorial platform. So the ribbon extends thirty-six thousand kilometers to the asteroid Big Barda, which is about ten percent of the distance to the moon. If it were any closer—"

"Enough, Maisie," said Jacques. "I don't like heights."

"Yeah, I think you mentioned that," I said. "Or screamed it."

"So stop rattling off those big numbers or I'm going to *bleep* this *bleeping* diaper."

Dragon and Howell floated past us, doing astronaut stuff. Without gravity to tame her frizzy hair, it looked like a clown wig.

Jacques started to undo his harness.

"Hey!" Dragon's voice seemed to shake the whole craft. "If I snap your neck out here, no one will hear you scream."

Jacques did his harness back up. I suspect that sometime during our trip, he made use of his allotted diaper.

I spent most of the trip staring at the planet and its misty cloak, all those gas molecules drawn to Earth's gravity. Around its curve, we saw the white glow of sunlight, no atmosphere to trap the light and trick us into thinking the sun was yellow. No atmosphere to soak up and scatter the blue light, fill the heavens with that safe, robin-egg hue. No tricks. Black space, white light. A place without ambiguity.

I'd never understood before so clearly that we don't live in a Ziploc bag that kept the air in and the freezing vacuum of space out. It made the world seem vulnerable. Precious.

I wish I could explain better. NASA's next urgent mission should be to send good poets into space so they can describe what it's really like.

" 'Stars, hide your fires,' " Jacques said, looking not down at the Earth but out. " 'Let not light see my black and deep desires.' "

He was quoting *Macbeth*, I was pretty sure.

While keeping our gazes on the spectacular Out There, we chatted and played "Name That Tune." Jacques was unbeatable.

"Trivia is my pattycake," he said.

Ruth snorted. " 'Trivia is my pattycake'? What does that—"

"Just think about it," Jacques said.

"That doesn't even mean anything," she said.

Jacques spouted something in French. All French sounds vaguely insulting to me, so I told him in Spanish to watch his tongue. Mi-sun spoke a sequence of crisp Korean. Wilder said something obviously crude in Russian. Ruth spoke two hard words in German.

"We're all bilingual?" I said. The way they spoke, it wasn't Foreign Language 101. It was raised-from-birth.

Chatter on the headset silenced us, the Midway crew communicating with Howell. The pod sealed to the station, and the hatch opened. When Dragon unlatched my straps, they hung in the air as if underwater. I was so distracted by them, Dragon had to lift me by my sleeve and pull me toward the airlock. There were three station crew members wearing shorts and T-shirts, and they helped me strip down to my orange jumpsuit.

"Go ahead and find your space legs," said Howell. "Just don't push any big red buttons."

I grabbed the handle along the narrow corridor and pulled myself up, kicking my legs before reminding myself that I wasn't swimming. I emerged into an open chamber, caught another handle, and hung in the air.

My head was dizzy as if I were spinning, and my stomach rolled with mild nausea. I was still but felt as if I were rising through the ceiling and into space. My arms flailed, my legs thrashed. I felt like I was suffocating, my brain confusing little gravity with little oxygen.

I remembered our training and focused on breathing in,

breathing out. I calmed. Looked. Lifted my arm, turned slowly, and let go.

It didn't feel like flying did in my dreams. The universe was just holding me up. Gravity had been chaining me for my whole life. But here I was everything I could be. I was Maisie Danger Brown.

Jacques was tumbling, Mi-sun was doing spiral spins as she launched herself between this chamber and the next. Ruth pushed off and let herself zoom down the passage, her red hair streaking like flames. Her high laugh sparked one in my own chest.

Wilder eased himself into the chamber until he was suspended in the center, touching nothing. My ponytail snaked around my neck, tickling me unexpectedly and pulling out goose bumps.

"Isn't this it?" I was so happy, I didn't want to remember that he had turned into evil zombie Wilder. "You said we'd find it here. This is a start, isn't it?"

I laughed and spun around.

He smiled just enough that it touched his eyes, and he said, "You're beautiful."

He said it like he hadn't meant to, like it just slipped out. Which, I believe, is the very best way to say those words to anyone. I felt as if all the oxygen in the module had been sucked out into space. There was an enormous moon out the window just over his shoulder, but I couldn't take my eyes off Wilder.

He looked around. Mi-sun was gone, Jacques was spinning into the next chamber, and Ruth was staring at the moon, so for a few seconds, we were alone.

I reached out my left hand. Wilder took it. I flew into him. His arms were around me. I closed my eyes while we hung there, spinning, kissing. I didn't count. It all seemed part of the same long, tingling kiss. His lips were cool, but mine seemed to burn. I didn't want to take it slowly—it felt like any moment it would end and never come back. I held him tighter, and I heard him inhale sharply. His arms circled my waist, our knees touching, our feet too. Weightless, we were upright and lying down at the same time.

Compatible, I thought. We were negatively and positively charged ions, irresistibly attracted to each other. It was simple physics.

We hit the wall, propelled by the impact of me flying into his arms. We pressed there for just a moment, kiss paused, lips still touching, and then he let go, pushing against a wall to flee into the next module. Jacques floated back in, Ruth turned around, Mi-sun called out that she'd discovered the astronaut ice cream, all of them oblivious to the fact that my world had just cracked open. I hovered where he'd left me, spinning just a little, my arms floating at my sides. I didn't flex a muscle. I held my breath. I wanted to remember that moment.

Through a porthole I could see the Earth turning, very slowly, just like me. Green and blue, brown and white, big fat gorgeous Earth. My whole body tingled. At that moment, I truly believed that the rest of my life would be glorious and happy and easy as sipping soda through a straw because I'd gone to space, witnessed the whole world, and Wilder had kissed me again.

CHAPTER 9

Now this is what I call astronaut boot camp!" Howell shouted.

"Yeah!" said Ruth. Space had greatly improved her mood.

Howell gave us a tour of Midway Station. Module 2 was the crew's living quarters with workout machine and kitchen. Module 3 was storage, where bags of food and water floated, tethered to walls, and rows of drawers held tools and supplies.

"It's cheaper to send water from the asteroid to Midway than from Earth," said Howell. "Big Barda is unusually rich in both precious metals and ice. We mine ice from the asteroid, and a machine melts water for drinking and cleaning as well as breaking it down into oxygen for breathing and hydrogen for fuel."

"How is the asteroid yours?" said Ruth. "Did you buy it?"

"I got to it first," said Howell. "Finders keepers. Astronomers thought Big Barda would pass us by, but she got caught in Earth's gravitation pull and entered orbit. At the time, my craft the Space Beetle was already prepped for the first private-sector mission to the moon, but we changed our destination and got to Big Barda first. I can tell you, several countries and corporations were P.O.'d, but, you know, losers weepers."

And back to Module 1, which was the lab. Howell showed us how they unfolded tabletops from the walls and stuck things to them with Velcro. We novices were all trying to maintain ourselves vertically while the crew hung horizontally or upside down. Of course, all those designations were meaningless now.

"Without gravity, everything we do is ten times more challenging," one of the crew was saying. "Really, an astronaut needs four hands."

Ruth and Jacques glanced at me, and I became keenly aware of Ms. Pincher, dead plastic floating on the end of my arm.

We used the restroom (peeing into a vacuum hose—weird but effective) and ate, sucking chicken noodle soup out of bags. I was floating near Howell, reaching for a bag of juice, when I heard her whisper to Dragon, "Should I show them?"

Dragon shook his head.

"Show us what?" I said.

"Nothing," said Dragon.

Everyone went silent. I hadn't noticed before how noisy the station was—the whir of fans, creaks and clanks and ticks. All that equipment working to keep us warm and breathing and safe from the freezing vacuum on the other side of the curved wall.

"What is it?" Mi-sun asked.

"Well, now you *have* to show us," said Ruth.

Howell's fingers strummed the air with eagerness. "Come now, Dragon, we've been planning to reveal them soon anyway," she said. "Why not let the kiddies take the first peek? They were brave enough to climb the Beanstalk. They deserve a treat."

Dragon didn't protest again. The five of us gathered closer to Howell. My feet felt cold.

"As lucrative as mining Big Barda has been," she said, "we

uncovered something inside the asteroid even more valuable than platinum: a container, undoubtedly crafted by an intelligent species."

I snorted. This was clearly a joke.

"The container held several items of different shape but similar substance," said Howell. "They are the first proof of alien life ever discovered. And you are about to become five of only about thirty human beings to see them and touch them."

Howell handed small wooden boxes to the other four adults, keeping one for herself.

Dragon hovered near me. I noticed he was balding on top, but he shaved his whole head down to its shine. Dad would look better like that.

"What's really in the box," I whispered. "Pez dispenser? Star Wars action figure?"

He shook his head and returned his attention to Howell.

"Go ahead," Howell said, opening her own box. Dragon lifted the lid, tilting his box and moving it down so the thing hung in the air between him and me. It was pale and about as long and thick as my index finger, curved without a definitive shape.

What a shame, I thought. They could have planned something genuinely funny.

Howell picked up her item and showed it to Wilder.

"Unusual, isn't it? Unlike any other matter I've encountered."

Dragon plucked his out of the air, holding it to his palm with his thumb.

"We call them tokens, for lack of a better signifier," Howell said. "They are cool against the skin and tingle a little. Go ahead, you can touch them."

"It isn't dangerous?" Ruth asked, eyeing the token in her astronaut's hand.

"My team and I have been holding and studying these for years," said Howell. "As you can see, we're perfectly fine."

That might be a matter of opinion, I thought.

Dragon offered the token to me between his thumb and forefinger. It was like liquid that could hold form. I pinched it between my fingers, and it brightened as if turning on.

"This is not a Pez dispenser," I whispered. The token felt crazy cold. I was leaning in to get a closer look when it slid, settling into my palm. The lack of gravity should have made that impossible.

I started to ask Dragon, "What is this really?" But then the pain struck.

White-hot cold piercing my hand, stealing my breath. I heard someone scream and someone else say, "Owie, owie, owie . . . ," but I couldn't look away from the token thing submerging as if my palm were water. I clawed at it with Ms. Pincher's plastic fingers.

The ripping pain stabbed into my wrist and crawled up my arm, tearing through my shoulder and thudding into my chest, where it flared to a point of agony that killed every thought from my head.

The torture lasted seconds that felt like hours, and then the pain just ended.

I became conscious of myself again. I seemed to be upside down from where I'd been, huddled against the ceiling in the corridor outside the lab, my knees against my chest, my hand pressed to my heart. Dragon was holding me, one arm around my back, his other under my knees, as if I were a baby.

"Are you okay, are you okay?" he was asking over and over again.

"No," I said. My voice was cracked from screaming. I touched my palm. There was no mark. "I saw that thing go into my hand. Did I hallucinate it? Am I crazy?"

"You're not crazy," said Dragon. "Don't worry, we'll figure this out."

The way he held me reminded me again of my dad, and a pang of homesickness twitched in my chest. When you're a thousand kilometers above Earth and an alien sausage burrows into your arm, all you really want is Mommy and Daddy.

"Dragon—I'm just going to call you Dragon, okay?" I figured the whole alien torture-token thing had earned me a first-name basis. He nodded. "Dragon, did something lethally bad just happen?"

He was taking my pulse. "I don't know. I don't think so, but I don't know."

In the lab, the others looked as bad as I felt, crouched against walls, shuddering. Ruth was yelling at Howell.

"You just infected us with an alien parasite! Are you insane?"

"But it's not a parasite. It's . . . it's technology. Of some sort," Howell said. Beads of sweat shivered on her brow, no gravity to slide them down.

Dragon checked my pupils and fit me with a blood pressure cuff.

"His blood pressure is a little high," said the astronaut checking out Jacques, "but that's normal, considering . . ."

Was there something on Wilder's chest? Pale brown, peering over the V-neck of his jumpsuit. I pushed off to him so hard, we crashed and spun while I held his collar and investigated the tattoo-like mark. A circle with four squiggles, two sticking out of the circle, two sticking in.

"Whoa, Maisie," he said.

Technically I *had* been rubbing his chest. I let go and looked at the same spot on my own chest. Starting four finger-widths from the hollow of my throat, a deep-brown crooked X. The others loosened their collars—Jacques's mark was as dark as mine. Ruth's and Mi-sun's were henna brown, each shape unique, reminding me a little of Arabic symbols.

"That's it, isn't it?" said Mi-sun. "That thing that went into my palm. It's still inside me."

"Why did it attack me but not you?" Ruth asked her astronaut.

"I don't know." She was a dark-haired woman, petite with large, scared eyes.

"Mine got brighter when I held it," I said.

"So did mine," said Jacques.

"You affected these tokens differently than we did." Howell held onto a wall and bobbed up and down, as if wishing she could pace. "Was this the first time five people touched the tokens all at the same time? Are they linked to act together? Were there environmental factors? Or do you all have something in common that we lacked—genetics or age?"

"You should have known," I said. My arm burned with the memory of pain. "We're *minors*, and you just threw us into space and assailed us with unknown alien technology!"

"How could I have known?" A drop of sweat lifted from Howell's brow and floated in the air. "I couldn't have known. I . . . I . . ."

"You're reckless and crazy and you're going to get us killed!" I yelled.

"I told you it was alien. No one made you touch it."

The talking went on. There were lots of "What's happening?" followed by "I don't know" in various forms. It's amazing how often people will repeat the same opinions in case no one heard them the first three times.

Howell said we'd find out more back at HAL, where they could do tests, but that we wouldn't risk the trip till she was sure we were stable. Mi-sun started in with a dry wail. Ruth locked herself in the toilet closet. If the token was sucking my life away and would leave me an empty husk, there wasn't anything I could do about it, so I decided there was no reason to waste the few hours I had left in space.

I helped Dragon unload supplies from the pod, tossing around huge bags of food as if they were feather pillows. When Wilder joined us, I opened my mouth to ask him why he'd been so weird before, but the words melted on my tongue. Nothing seemed to matter compared with the things in our chests.

Every once in a while (i.e., a hundred times an hour) I checked to see if the mark was still there. My skin over the mark was warm, a localized fever.

The crew got us dinner and tucked us into the crew beds, which were like sleeping bags attached to the walls.

I shut my eyes, trying to shut off my thoughts, and the darkness seemed to shift into something tangible, something real and huge, something that I could fall into. I was already falling. Fear of what the token might do to me made my heart feel leaden, and yet excitement tickled my belly.

I shifted in my sack, afraid and excited and too tired to sleep.

CHAPTER 10

After a few hours of darkness-staring, I pulled free from the Velcro bag and went back to the lab. A headache had been swelling ever since the token crawled up my arm. I found pain relievers in a med kit and took them with a squirt of water.

The moon was out of sight, but a thick band of speckled light showed one sweep of the Milky Way. For years I'd known its stats—a spiral galaxy housing 300 billion stars, just one of billions of galaxies in the universe. But until that moment, I'd never really absorbed the fact that the Milky Way galaxy wasn't something far away—I was *in* it.

Earth seemed alien, eerie in its darkness, a black orb marred with the orange electricity of cities in splutters and cracks like bleeding lava. I could no longer imagine what my life would be like when I returned there.

Wilder emerged from the crew quarters, rubbing his head. Jacques and Ruth started rummaging around the kitchen area.

"I don't feel good," said Ruth, holding her stomach.

"Then maybe you shouldn't eat," I said.

"I can't help it," she said, her fists full of protein bars.

Jacques nodded agreement, sucking in his fifth bag of yogurt.

I went back to Mi-sun's sack and found her awake and twitching.

I rubbed my sternum. Was the token a kind of computer? A bomb? An egg sac? Maybe soon robot babies would tear out of me and take over the world.

Howell came up from the pod.

"The tokens are doing something to us," I said.

She nodded. "We're going back, and we'll figure it out."

She and the other crew readied the pod while the five of us waited in the lab. I noticed that we sort of clumped together, shoulders and knees bumping and touching. We watched the moon rise.

"I don't like being afraid," Ruth whispered.

No one responded. I think the others were as startled as I was to hear those words from Ruth. She kept talking, glancing from the window to Wilder.

"My sister hits me," she went on. "Usually on my head so my hair will hide the marks. Grandma won't tolerate crybabies, so I stopped crying. I shouldn't let Sabine hit me, right? That's what I think, until I go home after school and there she is, and I'm scared and don't say a word." She glared at us. "This doesn't mean you can feel sorry for me. I just wanted to say it out loud."

"Thanks," I said.

Ruth shrugged. "We can't let them hurt us. *Any* of us."

"We won't," said Wilder. "That's what a team is for."

Ruth looked at Wilder, considering, then said, "Okay."

Mi-sun put her hand out. Wilder put his hand on top of hers and the rest of us followed, as if we were a Little League team. It did make me feel safer somehow.

"Did you guys know that 'fireteam' is a military term?" Mi-sun's voice was so trembly from her shaking I had to strain to understand. "My mom's military. A fireteam is the smallest unit of s-s-soldiers."

"Fitting, since we're probably being reprogrammed into the advance force of an alien invasion," said Jacques.

"I highly doubt that," Wilder said.

"Why would the tokens seize us and ignore the adults?" asked Mi-sun.

"I don't know." Jacques stared at his hand. "Does my skin look weird to you?"

"Your everything looks weird to me," said Ruth, eating a protein bar.

Jacques peered closer at his arm. "It feels weird . . ."

Mi-sun bumped into me, and I could feel how hard she was shaking. She reminded me of Baron Harkonnen, Luther's pet bunny. The baron wasn't exactly a calming influence. Every time anyone held him, that rabbit literally vibrated with panic, his pink eyes open wide, fuzzy white nose going like a jackhammer.

Mi-sun's just a kid, I reminded myself, and I wished my mom were there to take care of her.

"So, is your dad military too?" I asked, hoping to distract her.

"No. He's crazy," said Mi-sun.

Wilder and Jacques looked up. Mi-sun's gaze was full of stars, but her mouth was serious.

"He hasn't hurt anyone yet, so insurance won't send him to an institution. He just stays home and g-g-grumbles. After school, when my mom's at work, I take care of my little brothers. Sometimes I have to take my dad food. When I open his door, the grumbles turn into yells. Usually that's all he does, but sometimes—"

"Mi-sun," I said, interrupting her in case she wanted to stop talking.

"Sometimes he's on top of the dresser or in the closet or—"

"Mi-sun," Jacques said, as if afraid to hear any more.

"Or in the bathroom. One time I found him with our stuffed animals. He must have sneaked out of his room when we were asleep and taken them. He had them in the ba-bathtub, pushing them under the water, and . . . and I don't want to go home."

"What does he say?" Wilder asked. "When he grumbles."

"*Herma, harma, herma*," Mi-sun said in a scratchy low imitation of her father. "*Herma arrgh toast soup. Toast soup crunchy toast eat it.*"

Jacques and Ruth laughed. Mi-sun's pale cheeks turned bright with a pleased blush.

Wilder rubbed the back of his head.

"You've got a headache too," I said.

"Feels like there's a rat with steel claws trapped in there," he said, touching the top of his neck, "trying to dig free."

That was exactly what it felt like, except the rat was clawing at my forehead. I laughed a little, and Wilder smiled, then we both laughed because what else are you supposed to do when you're orbiting the Earth and alien technology is making your head feel like a cage for violent vermin?

I couldn't keep laughing for long. By the time I climbed back into the pod, I could barely see for the pain.

"Wait," I said as Dragon harnessed me in. "What if we really *are* the advance force of an alien army sent to destroy Earth—"

"You're nobody's puppet, Brown," he said, patting my head. "And if I'm wrong, I'll take you out myself and save the world."

I couldn't focus on his expression through the pain, but I was almost sure he was kidding.

We started the long descent, and I could feel force again as my shoulders pressed against the harness. Jacques was saying, "Oh *bleep*, oh *bleep*, oh *bleep* . . ." Apparently for his fear of heights, going down was worse than going up. I barely registered the planet enlarging outside my slit window. Pain screamed in my brain.

Suddenly space was gone, and we were in a barely blue sky, early in the morning. The pod stopped with a sigh, followed by a snap. The door hushed open, and warm, humid air gushed in.

I climbed onto the ocean platform, gravity a giant's hand pushing down. My arms were like logs, my neck felt too weak to hold my head.

Ruth shoved past me, announcing to all of Earth that she was starving.

A breeze tickled the hairs on my face and hand and seemed to tie the world together—rough morning sun, swishing air, salty scent, and huge spaces of quiet. I gazed at the sliding color of the sky while my feet pressed hard against the ground and almost said, "Where do I belong?" Aloud, the question would have sounded cheesy and immature. But quiet in my head, it was small and hard and perfect, like a seashell. *Where do I belong?*

Ruth sat on the pocked metal floor and ripped open a bag of potato chips.

As soon as we were back in Texas on the shuttle van to HAL, I asked to borrow Howell's phone.

"Flapping mouths will prove dangerous," she said. "You'll be able to contact your parents shortly, but first, let's figure out as much as we can."

I hugged my chest and stared out the window. The world pulsed with pain.

We spent the rest of the day in a large lab being examined by

Howell's MDs and PhDs. Pain meds did nothing. One bonus of the crippling headache was that I barely noticed the spinal tap.

When the doctors sent us to bed, I flailed through sleep, the headache riding with me into dreams and out again. It was easier to just give up trying.

All my stuff had been moved into my cozy room, so I tossed aside the boot camp jumpsuit and dressed in my normal Maisie uniform: hightop sneakers, jeans, peach cotton blouse, a clay bead necklace, and silver hoop earrings. I brushed my hair back into my usual ponytail.

I had a sudden conviction that Wilder was leaving his room. I squeaked open my door, and there he was, just shutting his own.

He glanced at me. He took a double take. "You changed."

I touched my face. "Is the alien worm rewriting my DNA?"

"No, I mean . . ." He gestured to my clothing.

I couldn't read his expression. "So are you still going to be zombie-weird or are you normal-weird again?"

He frowned. "Sorry. Kinda. I don't know. Can we just start over?" He stuck out his left hand. "Hi, I'm Jonathan Ingalls Wilder. And you are?"

"Being eaten from the inside out by a rabid hamster."

He didn't respond.

"Maisie Brown," I said and shook his hand. And that was it. He'd chosen to erase everything that had happened between us.

"Nice to meet you," he said, businesslike.

I didn't answer—the words on my tongue were borrowed from Jacques's lexicon.

I followed Wilder to the lab, where the whitecoats were pleased to subject us to more tests. In between my duties as a lab rat, I started to take apart the centrifuge. No one stopped me.

A crash startled me to my feet. Ruth stood beside the metal ruins of an examination table, her face redder than her hair.

"I didn't mean to." She stared at her hands. "This morning I tore off the faucet at my sink. I feel so weird, as if . . ." Her gaze wandered to the food table in the adjoining conference room. "Ooh, ham!"

Jacques and Mi-sun had arrived too. Jacques wasn't wearing his black geek glasses, and his face seemed smaller, younger. Mi-sun was shaking away.

"Have the rest of you noticed increased strength?" Wilder asked.

Mi-sun and I shook our heads.

"No, but . . ." Jacques scooted in closer and whispered. "I clogged the shower drain."

"Gross!" Ruth said.

"It wasn't me! I mean . . ." Jacques held out his hand, palm down. "Watch."

The back of his hand seemed a little shinier than before, and then his knuckles smoothed over as if being airbrushed. Something the color of his skin was growing over his hand. He removed a perfect mold and handed it to Wilder.

"Jacques is molting," Mi-sun said.

"It's not skin," said Wilder.

There was another crash. Ruth stood over a broken conference table, a sandwich in each hand.

"Oops," Ruth mumbled, her mouth full.

"Ruth, are your clothes pinching on you?" Wilder asked.

"What? No! I'm not gaining weight. I'm just . . . really hungry."

But one of the doctors put Ruth on a scale and reported she'd gained thirty pounds since before our space trip.

"She looks the same to me," I said.

"And thirty pounds can't explain all that strength . . ." Wilder glanced at me as if I'd know why.

"Maybe she's denser," I said.

"Maybe *you're* denser," said Ruth.

So I shut up. But I was thinking about how everything is mostly empty space. If you compacted all the atoms in the planet, Earth would be the size of a golf ball and yet still weigh the same and have the same gravitational pull. What if the atoms of Ruth's skin, muscles, and bones were compacting, even a little? With less space between the protons and electrons, her atoms would weigh the same but be so much denser. The repulsion between the protons and electrons would have to be masked somehow, and scientifically, that was *impossible*. But that word was rapidly losing meaning to me.

My headache was easier to bear when I was busy, so I kept fiddling with the centrifuge while Wilder talked with Mi-sun. She was gripping her hands together, but when he pulled them apart and touched her hand to his, he said he felt a prickling.

It was too hard to follow the conversation from under my cloud of pain. I put the centrifuge back together. Sometime later I heard a scream.

There was a small hole in the conference room wall, and on the other side Ruth was laid flat. She jumped back up, plucking a metal tack out of her shirt.

"Are you guys mental?" she said, hurling it back at the floor.

"I have a feeling," Wilder said quietly, "that tack would have gone straight through anyone besides Ruth. Let's try something less lethal."

Mi-sun pinched Cheerios between her thumb and forefinger and aimed at the wall. The cereal shot from her fingers in an electric-blue streak, hit the wall, and shattered.

This was getting too bizarre. I started taking apart a defibrillator. I knew Wilder was standing next to me before I looked up.

"What are you up to?" Wilder asked me.

"Just . . . you know . . . preparing a defibrillator in case someone gets heart failure from Code Blue over there," I said, nodding at Mi-sun.

One of the whitecoats returned with a piece of Jacques's shedding and spoke to Howell. "I couldn't cut through it with anything we have here. My best guess? It's a polymer—"

"Of carbon, oxygen, and hydrogen," said another whitecoat, swaying side-to-side, too excited to stand still. "Or maybe nitrogen!"

"What is it?" Mi-sun asked.

"Plastic," I said.

Strong plastic, grown like armor. These changes weren't disease symptoms. These were very specific alterations to our bodies.

Or to Ruth, Mi-sun, and Jacques anyway. What about me and Wilder, the headache twins?

"Are we dying?" I asked Dragon.

"Your vitals are good." He showed me scans of my brain, and I could see the color blobs were different prespace and postspace. "That red streak is usually a dormant area, but yours is hot."

I was trying to read Dragon's notes when a loud *clang* knocked my headache. Howell was shaking a brass bell like an old-time town crier.

"Time for talking, my chickadees," said Howell. "Time for deciding."

CHAPTER 11

Dragon led the five of us to Howell's office, plush with carpet, garish wallpaper, and floral-patterned sofas.

Wilder's dad, GT, was leaning against Howell's desk at the head of the room. His hair was combed back under a baseball cap, and he wore a plain T-shirt and cutoff jeans, but his eyes were all Wilder—blue and cunning. Wilder hesitated before standing at his shoulder.

Howell sat on the coffee table, her back to GT. She rooted in a bag and pulled out three red balls.

No way is she going to juggle, I thought.

She juggled.

There was a disbelieving kind of silence. At the end she threw one ball high and caught it behind her back. Mi-sun clapped politely.

"Thank you!" said Howell. "So, I can't let you go home."

"What?" said Ruth. "We're, like, prisoners?"

"Oh, Miss Koelsch," Howell said with an indulgent smile and then didn't answer the question. "After this meeting, you might call your parents to say you earned a bonus week of specialized training."

"We need to keep together," said Wilder, "figure out what the tokens are doing to us and why."

I blinked. This tone was new for Wilder.

"So far we've learned that each token contained likely trillions of nanites," said Howell.

"Trillions of what?" asked Ruth.

"Nanorobots," I said. "Microscopic robots engineered to perform functions at a molecular level."

Howell beamed at me. "Exactly. We found nanites in your spinal fluid. As soon as we extract them, they shut down, so it appears they only function while in the body their token inhabits. It would be impossible to extract them all. They take up residence in the brain and other organ systems, altering the cells of your body."

Ruth went to sit on the arm of the sofa, tripped, and shattered a metal-and-glass side table.

"Oops," she said, crawling out of the pile of broken glass. She looked at her hands and knees. Not a scratch.

During my sleepless night, I'd wondered if Howell had lied to us—if somehow she herself had manufactured the tokens and deliberately infected us with them. But this technology was beyond space elevators. I looked at my palm, where the token had passed through my skin without a mark. The technology was so alien, I got goose bumps.

"You should remain here until we figure out what the nanites do and how to remove them," Howell was saying.

"Can you cut out the token?" Mi-sun asked, but even as she said it, she put a protective hand over her chest. I knew how she felt.

My token was starting to feel unnaturally right in my chest, like an organ I couldn't live without.

"Removing the token would not remove the nanites loose in your body, Miss Hwang. Besides, the scans show that the token is linked with your heart. Any attempt at retrieval would put you at risk for heart failure."

"I would take my son home right now and have my own doctor remove the thingie," said GT. He unwrapped a stick of gum, broke off half, and slipped it into his mouth. "But I believe there's no way to remove it without killing you. And you should know, there are plenty of people who would be willing to do just that to get your token."

"So you want us to keep this on the down low," said Ruth.

"No, I don't want you to keep it on the 'down low.' I don't want you to keep it anywhere. If you tell *anyone*, that rumor will spread until those people I'm talking about decide to make the big score by treasure hunting in your body. My son is at risk by association. If any of you talks, I will make sure you face the consequences."

GT had such a comfortable tone of voice, so relaxed and trustworthy, it took me a minute to realize he'd just implied that if we weren't murdered for blabbing about the tokens, then he'd see to it himself. My heartbeat pounded pain in my brain.

Howell cleared her throat, reached for her juggling balls, then reconsidered. "Perhaps it will help if we make a promise to keep this secret?"

We all took turns affirming our solidarity.

" 'To be thus is nothing,' " Jacques added. " 'But to be safely thus.' "

"What was that, son?" GT tilted his head as if he thought he'd been insulted.

Jacques flushed and mumbled something.

"It's from *Macbeth*," I said.

GT looked between us, chewing his gum thoughtfully.

"Why is Wilder's dad here?" Ruth asked.

"He happened to visit, and I felt an obligation to bring him into early confidence," said Howell. "Now, each of the tokens took deliberate residence on top of your hearts. We're not sure why—"

"I bet Maisie's figured it out," Wilder said.

"What is your hypothesis, Miss Brown?" asked Howell.

I did kind of have one. "Well, maybe the token isn't just a nanite bag. It's a machine too, and it's powered by something heart-related—blood flow or the repetitive beats. That's why the tokens were drawn there."

"But how could something created for an other-planet species work as intended inside us?" asked Jacques.

"I don't know," Howell said. "But we did find sloughed-off skin-like cells on the tokens. I believe the species that made these are also complex, intelligent, carbon-based oxygen-breathers."

The adults were speculating on the tokens' function and adaptability when Wilder interrupted again. "What else, Maisie?"

Why was he picking on me? I cut my eyes at him.

"Well . . . ," I started. "Howell found the nanites in our spinal fluid. Maybe the nanites are powered by the electricity in the nervous system, and they've turned our nervous systems into a network with the token as the router."

Dragon blinked. "That's quite a detailed hypothesis."

I shrugged. "It was just an idea."

Wilder was strolling to the door.

"What made you think to ask Miss Brown?" asked Howell.

He turned. "This morning she stripped a centrifuge down to its parts and rebuilt it. A lab guy says it works better than before."

"Mr. Wilder has become very observant," said Howell. "He suggested that we examine Mr. Ames's skin for unusual bacterial growth, and his guess was right on. The nanites from Mr. Ames's token appear to trigger mutation in the bacteria living on his skin. The new bacteria produce a polymer. Unfortunately, when removed from him, the bacteria die immediately."

"So maybe the nanites not only trigger the bacteria's mutation," I said, "but turn Jacques's skin into a micro-atmosphere perfectly suited for keeping those bacteria alive."

Wilder pointed a gun finger at me.

I pretended indifference to my blush. "What are the nanites changing us into, Wilder?"

"I don't think we're changing into something so much as *for* something."

"For what, then?"

"For action. So we'd better be prepared." And he left.

As if called, Ruth, Jacques, and Mi-sun followed him. It felt risky—wrong even—to be away from Wilder, and I actually gripped the sofa arm to keep myself from going too. I wasn't experiencing any inclination to start taking over the world in advance of an alien army. The only change I felt, beyond the headache, was an increased awareness, I guess, of Wilder. Or was that my own idiotic girl self?

The other staff and GT left as well, leaving me and Howell.

"I'd like to call my parents now," I said.

"Interesting that you are the only one who recalled to ask," she said.

She indicated the landline on her desk.

My mom answered.

"*¿Es la Peligrosa? ¡Hija mí, cómo te extraño!*"

There was a few seconds' delay between when I spoke and when she responded, as if I were calling from across an ocean. Maybe it was a buffer—someone was listening, ready to cut me off if I spoke out of turn. The thought made my back prickle.

"Is Dad there?" I spoke softly, afraid my voice would crack and then there'd be no stopping the tears.

She conferenced in my dad at work.

"Our group took first place in the team competitions," I said. "Howell—Dr. Bonnie Howell—she wants to keep the five of us here for more specialized training."

"Do you want to?" Mom asked.

"It's the most interesting thing that's ever happened to me."

"Maisie, you haven't been . . . *contenta* lately." She used the Spanish word for content or happy, as if it were too stark, too uncomfortable to say it in English. I hadn't realized that she'd noticed. "Are you now? How do you feel?"

"I'm okay."

"You sound exhausted."

"When you were a baby, we had to call the police on you," said Dad. "You were constantly resisting a rest."

"Heard it," I said.

"Come home the minute you want to," Mom said.

My old, comfortable, small life was waiting. Part of me was tempted to run back to it, pull a bedspread over my head, and pretend that nothing had changed.

"I need to stay. I want to." And I meant it.

I trusted my parents way more than GT, but I didn't break my promise. Speaking about all the drama to *Mami y Papi* would make it feel dangerously real. Besides, if they knew, they would come for me at once.

When I hung up, Howell came back in and unloaded a long box into my hand. She sat on her desk and began reflecting a mirror onto the ceiling.

"Um, did you want me to put this somewhere?" I asked.

"It's for you. *I* have no use for it," she said as if I'd said something foolish.

I opened it. I gasped.

"A Rover," I whispered.

It was a robotic arm, nicknamed Rover because the inventor had called it "a one-armed man's best friend." Raw metal, skeletal and fierce looking, it was not meant to just resemble a human arm like Ms. Pincher—it was meant to be *awesome*.

And yet I had an inkling that it could be better.

◆

For the next two days, I felt a hot, crazy, whirling sensation, as if the whole world were on fast-forward and I had to keep thinking fast enough just to survive. The diversion seemed to separate me from both my headache and my freakish yearning for Wilder. Every item I requested, one of my new whitecoat groupies would go fetch. I imagined a basement in HAL where Rumplestiltskin spun straw into spools of gold wire and titanium dioxide nanotubes.

I programmed a computer inside the arm to recognize, amplify, and interpret my brain patterns so I could control the arm with my thoughts. It should have been impossible to train my nervous system into believing I had an arm, but maybe all those nanites were working for me on the inside.

I'd say, "What's an experimental, low-weight, renewable power source?" or "I need to understand the nervous system," and my groupies would talk me through it. Pieces of what they said would click, and I'd build from the idea. Or they helped me build, since my ideas raged faster than my one-handed ability.

Howell's engineers had been working on a strong, stretchy fabric to use as the "muscles" for the space station's robotic arm, so we looped some of that inside Rover and covered the titanium tungsten skeleton with flesh-colored plastic for waterproofing.

"This little pump pulls in water vapor from the air," I showed my groupies when the upgrades were complete. "The water functions as an electron battery. This bracelet is made of photovoltaic cells, and in concert with the titanium dioxide nanotubes, they catalyze a directed electron drift. On demand those electrons can be snatched up and used for electricity."

"Um . . . how?" Dragon asked, unblinking.

"I . . . I can't seem to find the words. I tried writing it down and I couldn't. I just . . . *know.*"

It reminded me of the time I'd tried to describe an astounding dream to Luther, but in the retelling it turned into a boring, senseless story. Dreams have their own language, we decided, and you are fluent only while you're asleep. In the same way, it seemed my token had taught me a language of technology, and I was fluent only inside my head.

I couldn't tell them, but I could show them. I slipped the arm over my right elbow, sensing where each pincher would connect with certain nerves. I opened and closed the fingers. *My* fingers. I raised my hand and waved.

"Meet Fido," I said.

Everyone applauded. Except Wilder. I could sense him standing behind me.

"How's your head?" he asked.

"Pain's gone," I said. "Whatever my nanites were trying to do in there seems to have been resolved."

"Then let's go play," he said. "We've got some things to show you."

CHAPTER 12

I followed Wilder outside. Now that the boot campers were gone, Wilder had claimed the acres of scrub surrounding HAL as the fireteam's playground. Ruth was tossing a half-destroyed SUV as if it were a doggie toy.

"Whoa," I said.

"I know, right?" She set it down with a grating squeak and came over by me in the shade. I sat up straighter. Her attention felt like an honor.

"Ugh, I hate the heat," she said, batting at her long red hair.

"Why don't you pull your hair back? Or cut it? That must weigh a ton."

She took a bottle of polish out of her pocket and began to paint her nails. "'What pretty hair,' people always say. If I lost the hair, what would I have left?"

"Superhuman strength and invulnerability?" I said.

"Yeah. This is kinda awesome, isn't it?" she whispered. "I mean, unknown, dangerous, blah, blah, blah, but kinda—"

"Awesome," I said, wiggling my Fido fingers.

Ruth nudged me with her shoulder. "Look at you, Two-Arms. Look at *us*."

I fought the temptation to hug her. I would not act like the immature weirdo she already thought I was.

"I wish my psychopath sister would try to smack me now." Ruth laughed, standing to stretch. She didn't stoop. She seemed aware of her extraordinary height and shape, her long hair loose. She was beautiful.

I walked over to Mi-sun, who had finally stopped shaking. She picked up a lug nut and pointed her fingers at a two-inch-thick plate of depleted uranium set up a hundred yards away. *Crack!* Faster than I could track, the lug nut shot from her hands, leaving an electric-blue trail and slicing clean through the target.

"Not to brag, but I'm getting good," she said.

"Yeah you are," I said.

CRACK!

Between Howell's cadre of PhDs, Wilder's instincts, and my techno-brain, we hypothesized that Mi-sun's skin attracted spare electrons and her token acted like a battery and stored them. With a thought she could send the electrons from her token down to the nerve endings in her hands and expel them in bursts. When she was holding ammunition in those hands, look out.

Jacques could cover his entire body in armor. He made a shield that was impervious to Dragon's gunfire, and Mi-sun's lug nuts could only dent it.

"We thought the bacteria died upon leaving his skin," Howell explained, "but it looks like many remain in a dormant state on the armor he discards. After about ten hours they wake up and gorge themselves on the plastic, expelling nitrogen, hydrogen, oxygen, and carbon, effectively undoing the work that they'd done."

"So his stuff has a built-in recycling system," I said.

"Here's what's left after two days." Howell showed me a petri dish with a heap of shiny black dust. "Carbon. The rest of it changed to gasses."

Mi-sun squinted at the dust. "Where did that come from?"

"From Jacques," I said. "The bacteria build the plastic from what he breathes, drinks, and eats."

Ruth laughed. "Jacques, you're eating all that black stuff?"

"So are you," said Dragon. "Plants 'eat' carbon dioxide and water, and then we eat plants. Or we eat animals that have eaten plants. Besides vitamins and minerals, our food is just hydrocarbons."

"I'll stick to slushies," said Mi-sun.

"Why don't you do anything cool?" Jacques asked me.

"I make stuff. That's cooler than being host to bacteria that poop plastic," I said.

"I'm *bleeping* amazing," Jacques said, putting his fists on his hips. "I'm Plastic Man."

"That name's taken." Dad had a comics collection. I knew these things.

"I'm Super Plastic," said Jacques. "Super Man—"

"That one's taken too," I said.

"I KNOW!" Jacques said with a laugh. "I meant Super Jacques—"

"Jack Havoc, Creator of Chaos," I said.

"Be nice, you two," Mi-sun said.

Ruth whispered to me, "Mi-sun is *so* bossy."

"What about Wilder?" said Jacques.

"He's the thinker, right?" I said. "He figured out what each of us can do. Have you guys felt . . . um, weirdly tied to him lately?"

Jacques snorted, but Ruth and Mi-sun nodded. I fiddled with Fido to hide my relief.

"Yeah, I'd like to test that out." Wilder looked out over the open brush. "Anyone want to play hide-and-seek?"

Howell gave us each an ATV to drive. Wilder had half an hour to hide. The four of us started at different points on the compass, and then we had to find him using instinct.

By then it was night. My ATV's headlights lit up pale circles on the ground, ghost eyes staring back. I'd been trying not to think about Wilder with emotion ever since he weirded out on me, and I'd done okay, except for that kissing relapse in space. But now as I hunted him, wanting to win the game, the barrier in my mind thinned. I wanted *him*.

The need to find him became an ache. Maybe if I got there first. Maybe if I found him before the others were near, he might look at me the way he used to—

A roar to my left startled me.

"Have you seen him?" Jacques shouted from his ATV.

"No," I said. Go away, I thought. But he rode beside me.

It was creepy, not comforting, sensing Wilder out in the dark. I found myself thinking about a species of caterpillar Luther and I had studied. A wasp stings the caterpillar to turn it into its zombie slave. The caterpillar will spend the rest of its life protecting the wasp's larvae, neglecting to eat or rest or do anything else until it dies. I wondered now if the caterpillar was content in its zombification.

We spotted Wilder just as Mi-sun and Ruth came up behind

us. He was staring at a line of smoke on the distant highway, illuminated by a car's headlights pointing up.

"Come on," Wilder said.

As we sped over the bouncy terrain toward the asphalt highway, I realized we weren't just following Wilder. The four of us had formed a web around him, Ruth in the lead, Jacques and Mi-sun on his flanks, and I in the rear. The formation felt natural, safe even. I was a part of something important.

A livestock truck lay broken-backed on its side. Smoke crept out of the engine. Cows were bawling. A passenger car was off the road in a ditch, lights blindly staring at the sky.

Wilder yelled back at us, using nicknames. "Ruthless, Havoc, help the people out of the car before something blows up. Peligrosa, Blue, get the animals out. Does anyone have a phone?"

Personal phones had been forbidden at astronaut boot camp, but technology was my department. I should have come prepared.

"I'll ride into town to get help," Wilder said.

I watched Wilder go, and that safe-web feeling was torn. We all looked at each other.

"Um," said Ruth.

Jacques was staring after Wilder as if he would follow.

I pointed at the passenger car. "You two help them?"

Mi-sun and I went to the back of the trailer. The calls from the cattle were forlorn and desperate. The door had twisted in the crash. I grabbed a handful of gravel from the road.

"If you shoot these around the door at an angle, careful not to hit the animals inside, maybe you can weaken the door till it comes off."

I ran back to the cab. The driver was conscious but woozy, his forehead bleeding. He was belted in, the driver's side up in the tilted truck. I hauled myself on top and opened the door.

"I can't reach the seat belt release," I called to Jacques. "Can you work your havoc magic and make something sharp enough to cut with?"

His eyes widened as he thought about it, and then on the tip of his finger he formed havoc armor—that's how I thought of it, anyway. It grew longer than his finger with a sharp edge. He sliced through the seat belt and helped pull the guy out.

I thought I saw a phone lying against the passenger-side door. I tried to lower myself in, but my hand slipped. I fell, my impact causing the cab to roll a little more. The door above me slammed shut, the crushed seat folded, and I found myself curled up and pinned against the far side of the cab.

"And it's not even a phone," I said, pulling a tin of mints from under my back. "Jacques! Ruth!"

The door behind me was smashed against the pavement, the door above obscured by the bench. I heaved at the bench with my legs. It barely budged.

My eyes stung. Smoke from the engine was drizzling into the cab. Both doors closed, windows closed, glass intact, no outlet. Pulling my shirt over my mouth, I took one last deep breath, gagging on the tainted air. I reached up, thumping on the windshield with my fist. My brain was firing, designing a dozen different devices that could free me. If only I had the materials and tools handy.

My legs shook, exhausted from pushing against the crumpled bench. How long until in panic I'd take a smoky breath and suffocate?

Minutes seemed to pass. I was somehow still conscious, unless there was no distinguishable difference between life and death, which I found unlikely, not to mention anticlimactic.

Then I thought: smoke means fire. Fire plus gas means—

I twisted around and banged the windshield with my Fido fist till the glass cracked.

The door ripped off above me and the bench went flying out. I took Ruth's hands and a moment later I was running away. Behind me, a sputtering explosion. The boom shoved me in the back, heat whooshing past, knocking me to my knees. I took a breath. The night air was hot and singed.

Ruth had carried the driver away, and he was lying near the car's dazed passengers—a woman and a boy.

Wilder roared up on his ATV. "The cattle?" he asked.

A loud moo in my ear made me jump. A cow was snuffling my shoulder.

"Got it," said Mi-sun.

We could see lights down the highway.

"The good guys will take over from here," said Wilder.

"Wait . . ." The woman propped herself up on her elbows. "Who are you kids?"

Wilder turned back, his helmet under his arm, his figure dark and dramatic against the piercing headlight.

"We're the Fireteam," he said, as if this were a trailer for an action movie. "Come on, let's ride!" He revved his ATV and zoomed off the road and into the open field. We ran for our vehicles and followed, the whine of sirens chasing us away.

With relief I fell into my position in Wilder's web. It hadn't felt right when he was gone. It was like he was the nucleus, and without him the four of us were spare electrons, bouncing around without purpose.

He told us to keep our headlights off so no one could follow. It was scary driving back in darkness, never sure when we would hit a bump or a rut. Jacques kept himself armored. Ruth hit a rock and fell off her ATV. She kicked it, sending it vaulting into the air. It exploded.

"Nice," said Jacques.

"Ruthless, calm down or—" Wilder started.

"Shut up," she said, and ran beside us all the way back.

I could hear the pounding of her feet off to my left. I was thinking of the old warning—never make eye contact with a predator. Running in the dark, Ruth seemed more animal than person. I didn't dare meet her eyes.

CHAPTER 13

How was it?" Howell asked as we entered the lab, Jacques and Ruth making for the table with its never-ending supply of snacks.

Wilder told Howell about the crash. "We need lifelike training situations."

"I got trapped in the truck's cab for several minutes," I said. "There was smoke, and I think I held my breath the whole time."

Wilder looked at me, and then he was shouting orders. The doctors hooked us up to heart rate and oxygen monitors, Wilder set the clock, and the five of us held our breath.

It got boring fast. No talking. Just sitting. Watching the monitors. Five minutes. Ten minutes. I had to concentrate so I wouldn't breathe out of habit. Fifteen minutes.

Are we actually dead? I began to wonder. This is creepy.

I found it comforting to imagine I was a dolphin diving into the blue—merely another mammal, not an alien freak.

Nineteen minutes.

I started to feel pressure in my chest, anxiety clawing at my lungs. My eyes watered. At twenty minutes we all gasped.

"That's not something you see every day," said Dragon.

"Their cells must be naturally oxygen rich," Howell said.

"Like dolphins," I said. "But . . . why?"

"I don't know, but I'm sure we need to stay together and keep preparing for . . ." Wilder scowled, rubbing his forehead. "Whatever it is that we were made for."

"Conquering the planet on behalf of a hostile alien force," Jacques mumbled.

"Or putting on shows for kiddie birthday parties!" I said with a fake grin.

While they debated our mysterious purpose, Mi-sun wandered over to the slushie machine. I noticed GT approach her, and I went to a desk behind them, pretending to look at some papers.

"Hey tiger, I brought you a present." GT opened a small velvet bag and poured silver rings onto the table. "Titanium, one for each finger. You can wear your ammunition. How awesome are you, huh?"

Mi-sun's eyes widened and she took a loud, grating slurp of her slushie.

GT noticed me. His gum chewing got louder.

"Maisie Danger Brown." He shook his head and smiled, and I got the feeling he was accustomed to charming people with his smile. "You could change Earth's technology forever. What do you say we work on something really valuable? Cold fusion? Faster-than-light travel?"

I laughed. "I'm not a gumball machine of inventions, just put in your coin and out comes a prize!"

GT's smile vanished.

"I mean," I said softer, "the techno token doesn't work that way. Mostly I just have an understanding of how some machines work.

When I come up with a new idea, it's not something random I want but something I *need* . . . or . . . I don't know how to explain."

He nodded as if interested, but I guessed he still hadn't recovered from being laughed at.

"I have noticed your regard for my boy."

"He's our fireteam leader, that's all," I said, busying myself with Fido.

"I think it's sweet that a girl like you caught his eye." He held out an unwrapped stick of gum. I shook my head. "You're not his usual type, but of course you figured that out. I'm sure he's confided in you about his expulsions, his time in juvenile detention, his dozens of disappointed ex-girlfriends. Thanks for overlooking all that." He put an arm around my shoulders and whispered close to my head, "I know he can be frustrating sometimes. If you ever need to talk, think of me as a second father?"

I glanced across the lab and found Wilder watching us. He didn't look away until his father had left the room.

"I don't like him either," Mi-sun whispered, and it took me a moment to realize she meant GT.

"It's like he wants to recruit us to work for him," I said.

Mi-sun shook her head. I knew she felt as I did, that we wouldn't leave the team for anything. Couldn't, perhaps. If I was a prisoner—or a zombified caterpillar—for the moment I was a willing one.

She stirred her slushie, the straw making a rustling sound as quiet as her whisper. "I think I'm going crazy. Maybe what my dad has is catching."

"Or maybe it's the token."

"Have you been having crazy dreams too?" Her eyes looked hopeful. "I dream about pink things. All the time."

"Pink things?"

"Pink floaty things. You don't dream of them?"

"I don't think—"

"They don't like me, the pink floaty things. They want to take my body."

I patted her shoulder and hoped that would count as comforting.

◆

At least we didn't have to deal with GT much longer. He flew out the next morning.

Wilder started us on a schedule that made astronaut boot camp look frivolous. Up at dawn for a group run. Ruth ran circles around us. Literally.

Back to HAL for breakfast (Ruth and Jacques ate an entire ham each) and then fireteam training. We began to redo all the fireteam exercises from boot camp, shattering every previous record. Wilder's strategies were scary-good. I wasn't too shabby myself. Our model rocket flew eight thousand meters and broke the sound barrier.

In the afternoon we had time to hone our individual skills. I installed the guts of a GPS and satellite phone into Fido that I could control the same way I controlled the arm, dialing with a thought. But I wanted to offer more help than the ability to call 911. So like any reasonable teenager in my situation, I designed a robot suit.

A few days into the build, Wilder rushed into the workshop my lab groupies and I had taken over.

"We've got a training mission. Come on."

He took off, and I dutifully followed.

"Some of the security guys were Special Forces," Wilder explained over our headsets as Dragon flew us in a helicopter to the site. "They set up a simulated rescue. All we know is there are two VIPs trapped by enemy gunmen. They're instructed to fall down as if dead when Ruth taps them or Mi-sun shoots them. Mi-sun, you'll be shooting paint balls."

While he went over tactics for a rescue operation, I strapped on my robot suit's arm and leg pieces, the power pack and tool kit on my back. It was raw and skeletal, metal bars running alongside my limbs, a breastplate over my torso.

Soon Ruth was moaning in boredom, so Wilder scrapped the lecture and we started telling jokes. My dad's puns were *not* a hit. Jacques told the showstopper:

> All year Tommy looked forward to his birthday. He couldn't wait for the party and presents. He especially couldn't wait for the cake.
>
> At last Tommy sat at the table, surrounded by all his friends, and his mom brought in a huge, frosted birthday cake. Tommy cheered!
>
> "Cut the cake," said his mom.
>
> "I can't," said Tommy.
>
> "Birthday boys always cut the cake," she said.
>
> "But I can't," said Tommy. "I don't have any arms."
>
> Tommy's mother sighed. "Sorry, Tommy. No arms, no cake."

Jacques was laughing so hard by the time he got to the punch line, he nearly sobbed. Even Wilder laughed.

"You *can't* think that's funny," I said.

"A bit, yeah," said Wilder.

"It's not even a joke."

"It's a joke because it isn't a joke."

I suggested we play "Stump Jacques" instead. Jacques used to get every song we sang at him, but he missed again and again. When Wilder did an obvious Beatles tune, Jacques said, "It . . . *sounds* familiar."

I frowned at Wilder. He wouldn't meet my eyes.

"Why did you guys agree to go up?" I asked. "In the Beanstalk, we could have said no."

"I was curious," said Mi-sun.

"If someone offers you a gun," Ruth said to me, "are you going to say, 'No thanks, I'm scared of guns'? No, you take the gun, 'cause then you're prepared for whatever."

"I wouldn't take a gun," said Mi-sun.

"Yeah, well, you *are* a gun," said Ruth.

"I'm not a coward," Jacques mumbled.

"No one called you a coward," said Wilder.

"My dad used to because sometimes I'd duck when he'd throw a ball at me. I didn't want my glasses to break, so what? I don't know why I even cared what the *bleeper* thought. *Je ne suis pas un lâche.* I hate heights. *Hate.*" He was sitting beside the window, his body angled away from it. "But I still climbed that *bleeping* string hundreds of miles straight up, so *mon pére* can eat my *bleeping bleep.*"

Ruth lifted her fist, and Jacques bumped knuckles with her.

"Why didn't you say no?" Wilder asked me.

I wasn't sure if he really wanted to know, but he waited for an answer, so I said, "Because Danger is my middle name."

No one laughed.

We stepped out of the helicopter and onto sagebrush and rocks. In the distance, broken windows on an abandoned building looked chiseled by sunlight.

Jacques took up his familiar pregame stance, one fist raised, and he shouted, "Cry havoc!"

Mi-sun, Wilder, Ruth, and I were all thinking the same thing, I guess, because as one we shouted, "Havoc!"

Jacques beamed. "I *love* you guys."

"Yay us," Mi-sun said quietly.

"I mean it," said Jacques. "We gotta stay in touch after all this is over."

Wilder met my eyes, and I gathered that he already knew what I suspected: there might be no "over" for us—no going home, no leaving one another, no normal anything ever again. My heart cramped a little, but at that moment I was more afraid that it *would* end.

"Don't hurt my guys," Dragon said from the pilot's seat.

At Wilder's signal, we ran forward in our usual formation. Jacques was covered in his havoc armor, a motorcycle helmet to protect his exposed face. Mi-sun carried a havoc shield, and a bag of paint balls bounced on her hip.

The afternoon sunlight was coming down at an angle like a swinging blade. My heart picked up its pace; my limbs felt long and strong. I was becoming used to this delicious sensation, the motion of the fireteam, Wilder at the center, the four of us connected to each other through him. A word popped into my mind: "home." Was this bizarre web my home now?

Mi-sun had the best vision of all of us and spotted snipers on the roof. At Wilder's command she began shooting paint balls. Ruth ran out in front, fluorescent splatters of paint balls exploding against her chest and legs. If one hit me, I'd have to play dead. I ran low. I didn't want Wilder to think I was useless.

Just as we gained the building, a gas cloud erupted around us. We held our breath, shut our eyes, and followed where we felt Wilder lead.

When I could open my eyes again, we were inside the building. Wilder gave instructions to the other three to scout out the surrounding rooms while I climbed up to a security camera, took it apart, and connected my tablet to the security system.

"Turn off—" he started.

"The cameras. Got it," I said.

"And any—"

"Alarms are now off. There's—"

"A lockdown area? That'll be the prisoners. Can you shut down—"

"Yeah, just give me ten—"

"Havoc," Wilder said on the headset, "detention block in center stage. Ruthless, back him up. Code Blue to me. Let's get an escape route ready."

Something exploded, and our back door was blocked with concrete chunks. Wilder and I ducked as paint balls fired through the broken windows.

I crawled to the doorway, slid the metal flats of my robot suit hands under the chunks, and lifted, sending our barricade tumbling.

"You're awesome," Wilder said.

"Thanks," I said. "I work out."

He gave me that appreciative smile, and I returned it. And maybe we held the moment a few seconds too long.

A crash and a boom from outside startled us.

"Sorry," he said. "You're distracting. I have to ignore you better."

"Gee, thanks."

Mi-sun arrived and began firing out the door, driving back our attackers. She took a paint ball on the leg.

"Blue, you're hobbled now," Wilder told Mi-sun.

"Climb on," I said, and she sat on my robotic shoulders, still firing paint balls.

Outside Ruth was exiting the far side of the building, tapping guys and watching them sit down.

She'd just cleared the area for Jacques when an explosion bit my ears and briefly blinded me.

When the smoke cleared, Ruth was standing in a crater made by the blast. Her clothes were completely gone. It looked like someone—probably Wilder—had anticipated that because Ruth was wearing what I can only describe as havoc underwear, and her hair was wound up inside her havoc helmet. One lock had slipped out. Ruth noticed the charred-off chunk and screamed.

I set down Mi-sun and ran forward, shouting to Ruth to see if she was okay. She shoved me back just as another group of gunmen rounded the corner. Gunfire pinged her, splattering in carnival colors. Ruth yanked a paint ball rifle out of a shooter's hands and threw it back at him, still screaming. The gunmen fled, and I don't think they were faking their fear.

One didn't flee. He kept firing, his eyes hidden behind mirrored sunglasses. Ruth grabbed him by his head and picked him off the ground.

"Ruth, stop! Stop! Stop!" Wilder was running forward.

Ruth looked at Wilder. She released the guy, turned, and punched through the building.

"We said we wouldn't let them hurt us," said Ruth. "We promised."

"I okayed the grenade," said Wilder. "I didn't think it would hurt. You're not even bruised, see?"

He lifted her arm, and she yanked it away from him.

"Ruth, you can't hurt anyone else. Okay? You promise me."

She shook her head, then lifted one shoulder. "Okay, just . . . don't touch me."

Jacques ran out of the building carrying cardboard cutouts in people shapes holding signs that read: RESCUE ME. "Yes, we did it! We rock so hard!"

Howell's security guys stood up and gathered around us, slapping us on our backs and shaking their heads. A huge, hairy ex-Marine kept saying, "Whoa. Seriously, kids—whoa."

Dragon approached, checking his tablet. "Two minutes, six seconds. It was supposed to be *hard*."

We started back to the helicopter. The exclamations and applause from the security guys felt like physical pats on my back. If I hadn't been weighed down by a robot suit, I might have skipped.

"I bet there are real people in the world we could save like that," I said.

"Rescuing kidnapped victims not our job," said Wilder.

"Then what is?"

He shrugged, his face twisted with frustration. "Whatever we're meant for, it's bigger than anything."

Jacques was humming the Beatles tune Wilder had sung earlier. "Is it the Rolling Stones?" he asked.

I no longer felt like skipping.

CHAPTER 14

Mom and Dad asked when I was coming home.

"Howell invited the five of us to stay longer, and all the other parents agreed," I said.

"You're studying directly with Bonnie Howell?" Dad asked.

"Every day. You want to talk to her?"

They did, and from the sciencese Howell was spewing, I knew Dad would be convinced I was safe in the hands of another scientist.

We said the I-miss-yous and *te-quieros*. I hung up the phone, and my chest felt hollow.

"Maisie," Wilder said.

"What?" I said, suddenly so tired. "What now, what do you want?"

He didn't say anything, just stood in the doorway of Howell's office, his hands in his pockets.

I rubbed my forehead. "I hate lying to my parents."

"You okay?"

"None of us are," I said. "Ruth picked up that guy *by his head*. Jacques failed at name-that-tune. And Mi-sun—did she tell you that she's dreaming about pink things? Is there something wrong with me that I'm not aware of? What if the nanites are toxic to humans, damaging parts of our brains, making us—"

"No, we're—" His voice cracked. He took a breath. "We're a team, and if we stay together, we're okay."

I nodded. Perhaps it was nanite poisoning, but I believed him.

Wilder leaned against the threshold. "I'm glad you're here, you know," he said, and his words were like water to me.

"I want to be here, with you—you guys," I said. "I'm scared, but at the same time I can't imagine ever leaving."

"I know what you mean."

Mom and Dad wouldn't understand. Luther either.

"I've never won a trophy or anything like that." I found myself talking to him again like I used to, words pouring out, saying things I didn't think through first. "It always seemed like a cool thing, to be part of a championship soccer team or win the school spelling bee. Earn a trophy for doing something great, proof of worth that I could hold. But my family doesn't do stuff like that. Which is okay, but I guess I just felt . . . small. And here—with the token, with you guys—I don't anymore."

He nodded, no judgment in his expression. His lips smiled slightly. Approval? An invitation?

The space separating us seemed nearly unreachable, the vacuum between Earth and the moon. I wanted to cross it, to let him hold me. To re-create that night on the roof, that car ride. His attention had been addicting. I didn't want to miss it, but I did.

I stood there, thinking about microscopes but saying nothing. He looked down at his feet, slowly turned, and walked away.

I fled to my workshop and made impact boots.

Inside the soles of black leather boots, I packed an array of carbon nanotube springs, so every step I took stored potential energy. Besides allowing me to spring about, they would absorb impact. Theoretically. I wanted to practice before showing Wilder in case I flubbed it and landed on my butt.

The day was cloudy. The cafeteria was dark, the light from the windows gray and mealy. I jumped off a table and felt as if I were landing after a tiny hop. Good. Now to climb higher.

Fido was stronger than my left hand, so I had no trouble scaling the whitewashed bricks in the wall and hitching myself onto a ledge that housed wicker baskets full of fake greenery. Weird decorating choice. Who thinks, "Hey, plastic plants in dusty baskets. Now that's what I call beauty!"

I was about to jump down the four or so meters when I heard the door open.

Ruth entered and made for the kitchen. When she found the door locked, she punched a hole, reached through, and ripped the entire thing out of its frame.

I was about to speak up when a voice called out from the corridor. It was a security guy I'd nicknamed Collie because his hair was shaggy and goldish-brown.

Ruth was tearing open a box of crackers with her teeth.

"There's plenty of food for you in the lab," said Collie.

"And plenty of people staring at me while I eat. I've had it. You know what that means? Had it? Sick of it? Done? That's me." She kicked the amputated door.

"*I've* had it with you destroying property."

Collie pulled out his walkie-talkie as if he would call the security chief, but Ruth took it away, crushing it between her palms.

"I'm stronger than you," she said. "I'm stronger than . . . than *everybody*. And that means I don't have to do what anyone says."

He stared at her. "You will come with me. Now."

He put his hand on her arm and pulled. She grabbed his arm, considered it, and twisted her hands. I heard a crack.

The weird thing was that he didn't scream. He just stared at his arm hanging wrong. Maybe the shock was too great. Maybe that's why I didn't speak either.

Ruth was breathing hard. Her face seemed pained. She mumbled, "I can't hurt anyone, I said I wouldn't—"

She glanced at the door, then back at Collie. His eyes were wide. He opened his mouth, perhaps at last finding that scream.

Her fist came down on his head. He dropped to the floor.

I pushed myself back against the wall, pressed myself there, my heart pounding at my gut, my gut rolling over, my head feeling full of helium.

Do not look up at me, I pleaded. Do not look.

Through the plants I could see Ruth sitting on her heels beside the body, her arms around her knees, rocking back and forth.

She got up, paced, and then stalked to the door as if she would leave the cafeteria. I almost took a breath of relief, but instead she shut the door and locked it. She peeled a strip of metal from the broken kitchen door and used it to tie the cafeteria door handles together, locking us in.

She paced, rubbing her hair, squatting down with her hands over her face, then rising to pace again. She pulled a taser from Collie's utility belt and zapped herself. It didn't seem to affect her. I guessed she was trying to make it look like Collie had attacked her.

I began to lower myself down, trying to hide myself completely behind the baskets. I moved so slowly, I could hear my knees adjusting. I was setting my hands down when her eyes flicked up. I froze. She scanned the baskets, studying the grimy fake plants before her eyes spotted mine. I felt as if all warmth left my body in one mad rush.

"Maisie." Ruth took a startled step backward, then blurted, "It was an accident."

It wasn't. I'd seen her eyes.

When I was four or so, my mom had left the groceries on the counter while she'd gone to the bathroom, and I opened a carton of eggs. They were so beautiful. I squeezed one in my hand, punching through with my thumb, felt the shell give, the goo ooze out. I cracked another, because one time just wasn't enough to understand. I let some fall onto the kitchen floor to hear the pleasant crunch and watch the splatter patterns. I knew that I was doing something wrong, but it wasn't until I picked up the very last egg that I paused to really think about it. My mom returned, and I held out the last egg.

"Here," I said, as if it were a present.

Suddenly I felt awful. I tried to run to my room, but she grabbed me and crouched down by me and said that she'd always wanted to do that too. She helped me clean up the mess and then do chores to earn money for another dozen eggs. But she never got mad.

Had Ruth broken his arm out of curiosity, like dropping eggs onto the floor? But then she'd tried to hide the deed, and there was no way to clean this up.

"Ruth," I said. It was all I could say, all I could be sure of—her name. Though her old, short name didn't seem to apply anymore. She was Ruthless.

Her eyes were fierce. "An accident."

"I saw."

"An accident," she said again, more insistent.

"I saw, Ruth. I saw." She'd done a big, scary, very bad thing, and the only way to keep it from getting worse was to face up.

Her mind was whirring as she thought it through, weighed her options.

Apparently she settled on the option that included killing me.

She launched herself, jumping right up to my platform, grabbing it with her rock-solid hands, the concrete cracking. I stumbled away, just managing to seize the edge of the platform as I fell to orient myself so I landed on my feet. The impact boots worked, but they didn't just take the drop—they shot me up again.

Wrong setting, wrong setting, I thought as I ripped through the air, my arms spiraling. I must have accidentally switched "impact" to "hop." The wall came rushing at me. I grabbed a windowsill with my Fido hand. Ruth jumped down, picked up a table, and hurled it at me. I let go, falling just as the table slammed into the wall where I'd been. Windows shattered around me. No chance to reset my impact boots. Once again as soon as I landed, they launched me into the air. Another thrown table whooshed past me. The force of its passing spun me around in midair. I struggled to land on my feet, only managing to get one down flat. I would have been rocketed back into the air again but I scrambled for a hold on the nearest table and pulled myself back down.

"How are you doing that?" Ruth yelled.

"How are you going to explain two deaths?" I yelled back, stooping to turn off "hop" before the boots could launch me headfirst into a wall. I ran toward the door, and another table smashed in my path. I pulled up short. "Come on, Ruth! There's no way to make all this look like an accident."

She lunged again, and I dived under a table, scrambling out the other side. She grabbed for me, just missing my foot and cracking the floor tiles with her hand. She knocked the table out of her way. Nothing separated me now from the furniture-tossing monstrosity. My heartbeats were so painful, I thought my chest would explode. Three more seconds and I would be paste.

CHAPTER 15

The cameras!" I pointed at one of the security cameras bolted to the ceiling. There was no pulsing red power light, but I gambled that Ruth hadn't noticed.

She leaped for one, tearing it loose before twisting it into metal scrap. She must have realized that if the camera had been filming, there would be a recording somewhere. Her face twisted like the metal, regret touching her eyes for the first time.

"What should I do?" She wailed the words.

"Just explain what happened. You wouldn't have done this before that token crawled inside you. It's not all your fault. The police will take it easy on you for that, and because you're a minor too."

Ruth laughed, and she looked at me with hot contempt.

"You think Howell will turn me over to the police when I have her precious alien technology?" Ruth put a hand over her chest, her eyes wild. "She'll carve it out first."

We heard boots on tile, the doors shaking as people tried to open them. Ruth swiped at me, but I'd been backing away. I palmed a table with Fido and sprang over it. Her hand cracked down on the floor, busting a tile into shards. The shaking at the door was more intense.

"I'm not afraid," said Ruth. "I don't have to be afraid anymore."

She squared her shoulders, facing whoever was trying to enter. The sparking light of a blow torch buzzed through the door. They would come in—Dragon, Howell, Wilder—and Ruth would kill them all.

"They can't take your token if you're not here," I said.

She turned to me quick, and her eyes burned. I looked down, afraid of returning the predator's gaze.

"You can go anywhere, do anything," I whispered. And I looked at the window.

The door screeched against the blow torch. Ruth startled.

She barreled through the bedlam of tables and shattered through the large window. I saw her sideswipe a truck in the parking lot before she was lost from view.

Your turn, Maisie, I told myself. Run.

But adrenaline had drained me dry. Not all dry, though, as I was sweating like a cold can of soda.

I forced myself to stay on my feet and shambled forward, refusing to look at the body in the kitchen.

"I'm here," I shouted through the door. The blow torch stopped its work. My arms seemed to have forgotten how to function, so I kicked the rest of the metal band loose and pushed the door open with my hip, letting in Dragon, Howell, and a few others.

"What's going on?" Howell asked, scanning the room. "Miss Brown, perhaps you could test your gadgets outside—"

I was suddenly on the floor. My legs felt like cooked noodles, cold and floppy and useless.

Must've been the strain of the impact boots, I thought, before noticing that my arms were shaking too.

Wilder was there. He crouched, looking into my face.

"Ruthless," I said. I pointed toward the kitchen and the body she'd left behind.

After that things happened quickly. Someone carried me to the lab and the doctors. There was nothing they could do for Duarte (Collie's real name had been Duarte). Dragon ran for a helicopter, and the security guys chased after him and Ruth in a swarm of black SUVs.

"You've had a shock. Stay put and rest," a doctor told me, but I was too restless to rest, so when his back was turned I went to Howell's office. She was talking to Dragon on a headset, tracking Ruth on her computer. Wilder paced.

"Shouldn't we call the police?" I asked.

"No point," Wilder said. "I'm not sure the army could stop Ruth. And if they know what's going on, they might take you and me and Mi-sun and Jacques and put us in little cages with sawdust and gerbil food."

"Don't be dramatic," I said. "Surely they'd give us bread and water."

I stood behind Howell's chair, looking over her shoulder until I remembered how annoyed Luther would get when I did that to him. *Luther.* I felt a jab of homesickness. I'd messaged him that I was staying longer for a special project. He'd wanted to know how much longer, and I'd waited to reply until I knew. Was he logged onto the Japanese teeth-whitening site right now?

Howell's monitor displayed a map of Texas and a red blip moving south.

"That's Ruth," said Howell.

"She has a locator chip," Wilder explained.

If Ruth did, then I bet we all did. I thought over each poke and prod over the past weeks. One shot had seemed odd—in my ankle. I felt around, discovering a tiny lump on my left ankle that wasn't on my right. I sat on the floor in the corner, where Howell and Wilder couldn't see me. I took off an outlet cover, pulled out some wires, and, using a screwdriver, rubber door stopper, and paper clip, sent some pointed electricity into that spot on my ankle, frying the locator chip.

"I'm telling you," Wilder was saying to Howell, "the other four members of the fireteam are equipped to stop her."

Howell rubbed her head in frustration, kicking up a mass of curly hair. "I couldn't predict this."

I could hear a crackle on Howell's headset.

"Keep her in your sights, Dragon," said Howell.

"Attacking will set her off. Offer her food," Wilder said and Howell repeated.

Dragon was shouting. I could hear the panic, even though I couldn't understand the words.

After a minute the sound stopped. Howell stared at the floor, taking deep breaths. She looked at Wilder.

"Get the rest of your team," she said.

I offered to stay behind and build some Ruthless-proof hand-cuffs, but Wilder had me quickly sketch the plans for Howell's team to build.

"The fireteam has to stay together," he said.

Jacques had been in the pool and Mi-sun target shooting outside, so they both had to be caught up to speed in the helicopter.

"This is bad," Mi-sun whispered.

"So if I ran off like Ruth," said Jacques, "you all would, what, hunt me down? Take me out?"

"You're not going to run off," said Wilder.

"Jacques, she killed Duarte on purpose," I said.

"And just now she picked up one of the SUVs the security guys were driving and threw it at the helicopter," Wilder said. "Three men in the SUV died. Of the four in the helicopter, only Dragon survived. Ruth escaped."

Jacques gnawed on an energy bar.

Mi-sun started to cry. "It feels like it's ending, and I don't want it to end."

I put my arm around her and kind of rubbed her shoulder. Wilder said her name until Mi-sun looked at him.

"We're still a team, okay? I need Code Blue. We have to take care of Ruthless, we have to make it safe for everyone. Are you still with me?"

She nodded.

Wilder had brought Mi-sun a belt with two bags that hung on her hips like holsters. No paint balls this time—one held screws, the other cut pipes. I doubted they'd even bruise Ruth.

I spotted Ruth below us, running across a two-lane highway. A few kilometers away there was a town, and beyond that, the Gulf of Mexico. The helicopter passed her, and we landed between her and the town. Jacques was wearing havoc armor like a shiny brown body suit under his clothes. He and Mi-sun went first, Mi-sun holding a havoc shield. Wilder and I came up behind. I wore my robot suit but had changed out of the impact boots. I didn't want to go hopping when I only meant to walk.

"Ruth!" Wilder called.

She stopped, squinting at us in the sun that had seared away the clouds. Her posture was tense, her leg crooked, ready to bolt.

"Hey, sorry about all the mess." He took off his sunglasses, squinting in the strong light, and shrugged boyishly. "Howell and everybody don't get it. We don't play by their rules anymore."

"I promised you," said Ruth. "I told you I wouldn't hurt any-one. But I . . . I . . ."

"It happened," he said. "It's over. I'll take care of it."

Ruth put a hand on her chest. "They're going to try to cut it out."

Wilder rolled his eyes. "Like we'll let them. Come on, we're a team."

He sounded so sincere. Did he mean it? Or was he that great of an actor?

Ruth rubbed her forehead with the back of her hand. "One-Arm there said I had to turn myself over to the police."

"Maisie!" Wilder gave me an incredulous expression. "Seriously, Maisie. You should apologize."

"S-sorry, Ruth." This was ridiculous.

"I'm sick of having all those doctors examining us and watch-ing us like we're freaks," Wilder said. "I got Howell to give us our own place—this huge house off in the country, where we can figure out what we want to do. The kitchen is amazing. All the food we want. We'll eat, hang out, play video games. Eat."

Ruth was still several meters away, but she took a step closer. "Stocked kitchen?"

"Oh yeah, fully. It's amazing. Steaks and pizza, burgers, hot dogs. You should see the waffle machine. Epic! We've got an entire freezer just for cheesecake. I want one of those soft ice cream machines—you know, the twisty kind, chocolate and vanilla? It's on order, so hopefully we'll get it soon."

"Who's in the helicopter?"

"Pilot." Wilder's expression stiffened.

"And he's going to just let me get in the helicopter and fly us to our private clubhouse?"

"Maisie's going to pilot from now on so we can go it alone," Wilder said.

I was?

"Oh, I forgot a slushie machine for Mi-sun! Sorry, Mi-sun, I'll order that too. Anything else you want, Ruth? Like a deep fryer? We could make doughnuts."

Ruth stared at the helicopter as if trying to see past the glass to the pilot's face. She rubbed her arms and looked into the sky.

"Those guys aren't going to let me just come back. I did some stuff. Not going to let me, not going to—"

"We *need* you, Ruth. You're part of the team. You won't be safe without us."

"No, *you* won't be safe! I should be in charge. I'm strong!"

"You are," he agreed. "You're strong, Ruth. You and I—we won't let anyone hurt our team."

"Wait . . ." Ruth's suspicious squint turned on Wilder. "Are you lying to me?"

Her face lengthened with a profound sadness, and then fire filled her eyes. She stalked toward Wilder. She was fast. Wilder didn't give any command, but Jacques stepped forward anyway, blocking her with his armored self. Ruth shoved him aside. Mi-sun squelched a little scream, scrambled for a pipe chunk from the bag, and shot it at Ruth. A flash of blue and Ruth was shoved back through the air, hitting the ground and rolling backward.

No way to come back from that, I thought, my stomach tightening.

Wilder must have thought the same because he said, low and fierce, "Run."

CHAPTER 16

He didn't wait, turning and making for the helicopter. I could hear thuds behind us. Ruth was running too.

"Get us out of here!" Wilder shouted to the pilot.

I took four strides for every thud I heard. She was close. The helicopter was closer. I got there just after Wilder and hauled myself in, Jacques shoving his way in behind me. Mi-sun had only grabbed the door when the helicopter started to lift. Jacques and I held her wrists, pulling her up.

Below us, Ruth jumped. I watched her rise, leaping impossibly high, her arm outstretched.

We're going to die, I realized with a strange calm. She's going to grab the foot of the helicopter and pull us down and slam us into the ground and we'll explode into a huge flaming ball, and Jacques is the only one who will survive the explosion until Ruthless gets her hands on him, cracks his armor, and breaks his neck.

But the pilot jerked the helicopter to the side, and Ruth managed only to swipe it with her fingertips before falling back. The vehicle tumbled. The four of us weren't seat-belted, and we rolled to the other side, thankfully away from the open door. The pilot pulled us higher just as Ruth hurled a rock, barely missing us.

Wilder had a megaphone, and he shouted out the door.

"You stupid brute, we're going to hunt you down and cut that token out of your chest and give it to someone smarter, and you're not strong enough to stop all four of us!"

She screamed something. Jacques stared at Wilder as if he'd morphed into a giant cockroach.

"Smooth," I said. "That talked her right down."

"I'm trying to get her to chase us," said Wilder. "If she goes off and hides, it'll be impossible to stop her before she does more damage. We've got to capture her now."

"She'll go home," I said. "She'll kill her sister."

"She's chasing," said Mi-sun.

I leaned over to look down. Ruth didn't run so much as bound, her powerful legs thrusting her forward in huge, arcing strides.

Wilder scanned the horizon. "We need to keep her away from populated areas, and we need something heavy to slow her down."

I pointed to the harbor. "There's the water."

"Howell," he spoke to his headset, "there's a ship out there, looks like a cargo vessel. Can you clear the people off?"

And just like that, she could.

Our pilot flew us toward the water, skirting the city. A few minutes into our flight, Ruth started to slow.

"She doesn't seem as excited to kill us as she was a few minutes ago," I said.

"Swoop us back around," Wilder told the pilot. "Blue, pelt her with some screws."

A handful of screws screamed from Mi-sun's hands like

buckshot. That would have ripped another person apart but only knocked Ruth off her feet. Once she gained them, she was after us.

Near the water's edge, Wilder employed the megaphone again. "Nice running, lard bottom, but you can't run on water."

She dived in.

We got to the ship ahead of her. I could see a couple of motorboats carrying away the crew. Wilder asked our pilot to drop us on the upper deck and then leave. "No need to give her another target."

The ship was eerie in its vacancy. Wilder had me inspect the anchor and a crane used to lift cargo pallets.

Working with technology was instinct to me, in the way that, once you know how to read, you don't sound out words anymore. You just see and know. I examined the clunky thing, hefted my toolkit off the back of my robot suit, and got to work—faster, stronger, quicker, better.

I didn't have much time. The white splashes Ruth made while swimming were getting closer.

Wilder was talking to Mi-sun and Jacques. "We can't let her knock holes in the ship and sink it. We need to lure her up here, make her want to kill us."

"You're freaking me out, man," said Jacques.

"Jacques, you're going to have to get close to her."

Jacques was patting himself all over, as if testing for weakness in his armor. "I can take a couple of her hits, but—"

"We'll dunk her. When she comes back up, she'll be easier to cuff."

"And then what? It'd be safer just to kill her," said Jacques, but I didn't think he meant it. His hands were twitchy, eyes wide, too afraid to think straight.

"No one could kill Ruthless," said Wilder. "All we can do is slow her down until Howell gets here with the cuffs."

"She won't fall for it," I said. "Who would climb up here to fight us when it's so clearly a trap?"

"Ruthless," Wilder said, staring at the water. "She feels indestructible. It makes her careless. Besides, if she really wants to break free from this team, she'll want me dead."

I knew what he meant. It'd be no easy task for any of us to run away from the living thinker.

Wilder positioned us around the ship while he stayed on the bow as the bait. I tried to imagine what would happen if he died. I wiped my palm on my jeans. At least my Fido hand didn't sweat.

The white splashes kept coming closer.

On Wilder's cue, Mi-sun shot a pipe. It hit Ruth's forehead, dunking her under. She came back up and swam closer to the boat. Mi-sun hit her again. Ruth was furious. She was too easy a target in the water, where she couldn't move as fast. She could have gone underwater and punched through the boat. But Wilder had guessed right—Ruth wanted to get her hands on us. On *him*. She started to climb the anchor chain.

"Go away!" Wilder shouted. "Leave us alone!"

He sounded desperate. Man, he really could act.

Ruth leaped from the top of the chain onto the deck, and Wilder scrambled back so fast, no way it was acting. If she touched him, she would kill him. And we'd be next.

The four of us worked fast. Mi-sun struck Ruth from behind, knocking her over a length of anchor chain while I maneuvered the crane to lift the anchor and drop it on Ruth. Several tons of steel anchor held her down for a moment. Then the crane picked up the chain, crossing it around her.

Wilder had Mi-sun distract Ruth with pelted screws while Jacques sealed Ruth to the chain with havoc bands. She thrashed, and I worried she would break free before we had a chance to dunk her.

I pulled the chain up, dangling Ruth and the anchor. She screamed in anger. I had the crane release its cargo, and while Ruth fell, Mi-sun shot a large pipe at Ruth's chest. The force knocked Ruth-and-anchor over the water before they slammed down. The chain sped after her underwater, meter after meter, clanking angrily as it unwound from its massive spool.

The clicking stopped. Surely Ruth was wrestling with her bonds in the depths. She could hold her breath for twenty minutes and had enough strength to either break the havoc bonds or swim with an anchor strapped to her back. I didn't see how this trick would stop her.

"Howell's on her way," Wilder said.

Hopefully Ruth's underwater struggle would tire her enough that we could get the cuffs on her. And then, fingers crossed, those temporary restraints would hold her till I could design and build a Ruthless-proof prison.

I imagined Ruth hitting the bottom of the ocean and in a fury pushing back up. Like a torpedo. Coming straight for us.

I backed away from the railing. So did Jacques.

"She's going to be one *bleeping* mad hornet," said Jacques.

I had a sudden thought. "She took the scuba course, right? She knows about the bends?"

The bends—decompression sickness. What happens when you go deep underwater, then come up too fast. The deeper you are in water, the higher the pressure, and the gas molecules in your body compress. But then as you come up, all those little bubbles of nitrogen expand again. Rising too fast, the nitrogen molecules act like little bombs. To avoid the bends, scuba divers take decompression stops on ascent and wait while the nitrogen naturally seeps out of their bodies.

Wilder was staring at bubbles starting to form in the water. "She's coming up fast."

"The bends can't kill her, right?" I said. "I mean, her skin and bones are strong, her muscles dense. Surely her veins and organs have toughened up too."

Actually, Ruth with the bends seemed like a great idea. If she was in a little pain, she might be too weak to immediately kill us. But perhaps our oxygen-enriched cells prevented the bends altogether. After all, dolphins and whales don't suffer from decompression sickness.

The bubbles thickened to a hard boil. Jacques was adding layers to his havoc skin and cramming down an energy bar. Mi-sun was gripping handfuls of screws. I jumped into the seat of the crane, my sweaty palm slipping on the controls.

There was a white explosion, and Ruth nearly cleared the surface before splashing down. Waves slapped against the side of the ship. Bubbles flicked the surface like a swarm of insects. Ruth lay floating on her back.

CHAPTER 17

Maisie, get her in!" Wilder called.

I steered the crane into the water and picked up Ruth in a vice grip that would have broken a normal person's bones. I let the robot arm drop her onto the boat's deck. Her groans were constant, unaffected by the fall. Maybe she wouldn't need restraints after all. Maybe she needed a doctor.

Howell's incoming helicopter churned the air above us. If we took her back to HAL, we'd put everyone there in jeopardy of a crushed skull when she recovered. I couldn't think of a solution. Hopefully Wilder had.

Jacques approached Ruth, but he stepped back when she started coughing and clutching herself, her back arching. She seemed unaware of anything but her own pain.

"Wilder," I started, "I don't think—"

Ruth gasped, gagged, and her loud breathing stopped.

Jacques and I bolted forward, but Wilder pulled us away.

"Don't touch her. Everyone stay back."

No.

My instincts that taught me how to breathe, how to stand, how to be, also said to trust Wilder. Every nanite-enhanced cell of me was bound to him. But my brain said when someone is dying, you help. We'd all certified in CPR at astronaut boot camp. I could help, so I should.

Everything seemed to stop—the wind, the motion of the boat, the cells dividing in my body.

I met eyes with Mi-sun and Jacques. If we were the ones who fell, if our hearts stopped, would Wilder let us die too? A kind of understanding ran between the three of us, a plan that didn't include Wilder, and that felt strange and dangerous but right.

I made for Ruth, and it took Wilder a fraction of a second to realize what I was doing. He darted for me, but Jacques and Mi-sun stopped him. That simple action, two people putting themselves in the way of another, felt like an earthquake.

The team is broken, I thought, and then I tried not to think, dropping to my knees beside Ruth and releasing my arms from the robot suit.

"What are you doing?" Wilder yelled, struggling against Jacques. "Let me go!"

Ruth's skin was cold from the ocean water and felt rubbery to my fingers. No pulse. I tilted her head back to clear her airway and began chest compressions, Fido on the bottom so I didn't crush my left hand with my cyborg strength.

"Maisie, don't touch her."

"I have to try," I said. He was wrong, but at least he cared enough to worry about what Ruth would do to me if she came to.

Suddenly I was yanked back. I struggled out of Wilder's grip, Jacques and Mi-sun grabbed him again, and I returned to Ruth.

My Fido hand wasn't as pressure-sensitive as my left hand, so I switched, my left hand over her heart. I was concentrating so hard on making sure Fido didn't push my human hand too hard that I didn't notice at first. The different sensation on my palm. The extraordinary cold.

I didn't notice until the pain.

I heard my scream before I felt it. I pushed away and my back hit the deck. My head ached with the fall before all other sensation was swallowed in the agony I'd felt on Midway Station. Ruth's token had entered my palm.

I knew that once the pain shot up my arm and flared in my chest it would ease. I clung to that promise during those few seconds that seemed hours, a path of agonizing fire, bitterest cold, pain like muscles torn in half, bones crushed to bits. There was an explosion near my heart like an electric blackout—no sight, no breath, no hearing, nothing but white-hot pain. I wanted to die. If I'd been able to move, I would have done anything, anything to end the pain . . .

I became aware again.

My breath was hitting my lungs in slow, hard gasps, my forehead prickling with sweat. I was looking up into a sky a shockingly calm blue. Wilder was kneeling beside me, his arms around me. He was saying, "Maisie, Maisie, what did you do . . . ?"

He touched my palm. He touched the mark on my chest.

"You have Ruth's token," he whispered. He shut his eyes, hard, as if squinting against a glaring headache.

I sat up, pushed away, backed away, looking at him, at Ruth's body, at Jacques shiny in his armor, at the helicopter landing on the upper deck, as if everything was part of a swarm of bees I should swat. Ruth had died. Her heart stopped, the nanites swooped back into the token, the token released and was drawn into my palm.

Howell leaped out of her helicopter and ran toward us. "Ruth?"

"Dead," said Jacques, stripping off his armor like an orange peel and tossing it onto the deck. "We were just trying to capture her. *Bleep, bleep, bleep.*"

"Don't mess this up, Maisie," said Wilder. "Don't freak out. Take deep breaths."

I took deep breaths, but I was definitely starting to freak out. Ruth was dead. And part of my brain was dimming. I had become accustomed to the sharpened thought, the way I could look at things and understand what was beneath them, like having X-ray vision for machines. Now it was as if I'd lost the prescription glasses I hadn't realized I'd been wearing. The ship's robot arm, the helicopter, my Fido arm and robot suit—I could see their outsides but I could barely imagine their insides.

I looked at my chest. There was the bright-brown double swoop of Ruth's brute token. My techno token was paler, washed out beneath it.

My insides rumbled. It was like hunger pains but not localized to my stomach. I was starving *everywhere*.

Wilder was looking at me as if I were an escaped grizzly bear. "Hungry?"

I nodded. Really hungry. I wanted a steak. I wanted a cow.

Wilder shouted to Jacques, and he tossed a few energy bars on the deck. I ate them without breathing, gulped down a couple liters of water Howell offered, and said, "The techno token is dying."

"Dying?" Howell's eyes widened.

"I guess the brute token is burying it." I stared at Fido, flexing my fingers, twisting my wrist. "It's almost gone."

Wilder shouted something in Russian that sounded like a curse, tore off his headset, and threw it onto the deck. "The newest token must trump the oldest. Maisie, why'd you have to do it?"

His words were getting harder to hear over the pounding of my heart, the sweeping breaths in my lungs. Men were sliding Ruth's body into a long white bag.

I sobbed, remnants of an energy bar flying out of my mouth. "Did we . . . did we just *murder* her?" My eyes and nose were wet and running, sobs wracking my chest. "Am I going to turn into her now? Am I going to hurt people and end up anchored to the bottom of the ocean?"

"Maisie . . ." Wilder held up calming hands.

That was all he could say, no promises.

"Oh no, oh no, oh no . . ." I started to back away. Heartbeats ravaged my chest, and even though I knew I could hold my breath for twenty minutes, I felt like I couldn't get enough air. I ripped off the robot suit and clawed at my own skin as if I could cast that off too. I wanted to peel away everything, every part of me. I dug my fingernails into my arm and couldn't make a mark.

Wilder was speaking again, his hands in taming-the-wild-beast attitude. I could hear him making noise, but his words just scratched at me, not entering my brain. Men were carrying Ruth's body bag to the helicopter. The wind struck at me like Mi-sun's buckshot. I felt trapped on every side—Wilder and Howell, this strange, empty ship, Ruth's body. My own body was hardening, tightening, unfamiliar. I was clutched in the fist of a giant.

Something clamped my wrist. It was a massive metal cuff. I reached with my Fido hand to pull it off, and Dragon snapped a second cuff over my robotic wrist, both connected by a short, thick chain. I'd designed these cuffs but no longer remembered exactly how. Restrained, my left hand couldn't reach to remove Fido and get free.

Dragon said something as he took a few steps back. Was he afraid that I would crush his skull? And would I?

I turned, looking for Wilder. There was a streak of blue and a sting on my lip. I smelled powder. Wilder was standing beside Mi-sun. He'd had her try to shoot a pill into my mouth. Something to knock me out? Something to kill me?

I pressed my lips shut and backed away.

Wilder approached, hands up again, talking. If I focused beyond my heartbeats, maybe I could hear him. I tried but heard instead the sound of the water below, like television static, crackling, angry, insistent.

We're a team, I imagined Wilder saying, and I felt that stronger than my own heartbeat. But Ruth was dead, and Wilder had tried to drug me, and I wasn't even sure who Maisie Danger Brown was anymore.

Wilder was still talking, Mi-sun was crying. I stepped to the edge of the deck.

The water spread out before me, calm, undemanding. The water looked like freedom. I wasn't strong enough to run away from Wilder, but I was strong enough to fall.

So I fell.

PART TWO
RUNAWAYS

CHAPTER 18

I hit the water like a bomb, knocked off my shoes, and kicked. My hands were chained, so my legs did all the work. The chilly water didn't bother me, though I was intensely aware of it, every molecule of H_2O brushing over my fingers and toes and the tiny hairs of my skin. The water felt hard to push against, but a good kind of hard. Satisfying, the speed liberating.

A helicopter clacked above me, spraying water. Didn't Ruth bring down a helicopter? Maybe she didn't mean to. Maybe I wouldn't mean to either.

Wilder was calling to me with the megaphone, and I ached to give in. He was the thinker; I shouldn't leave him, I wouldn't be okay without—

Ruthless, her fist coming down on Duarte's head. The memory shocked me like a live wire, and I dived under, burying myself and my thoughts with five meters of water. I kicked, leaving a trail of bubbles. Some time later I came up for a breath and spied the helicopter a ways off. They couldn't find me. Pain bit at my heart, but I could take it. I went down again.

The whole world was blue, as if it had absorbed the sky. Currents rushed past me like wind, fish like birds darted over my head. I seemed to fly.

The next time I surfaced, the helicopter was out of sight. I fought the waves into shore, dragged myself onto an empty beach, and lay facedown on the sand. I wanted to be dead. I fantasized about a huge crane raising me into space and then dropping me. If I went home to Mom and Dad—*Ruthless, her fist . . .*

Although I could no longer remember exactly how the cuffs worked, I did recall worrying that Ruth might discover a certain weak spot. I hammered there with my heel and eventually the cuffs came free.

I heard voices on the beach and spooked, fleeing back into the water and swimming away. My speed and the strength was more than Fido could bear, so I tucked my Fido arm against my chest and swam on my left side. I sped, I zoomed. I gasped. I was getting even stronger.

Blind, I swam through the night. I was so hungry, my entire body throbbed like a wound, aching, aching, needing.

Dawn came like a seizure. I dived, trying to escape the sun, and stayed in the deep for twenty minutes at a time. I had no plan except the idea that I should get as far away from Wilder as I could. Thoughts came in slow, thick drips, the way cold honey pours. I didn't seem able to think the truth—*I'm too dangerous now, I can never go home*—but the idea was there, burning. I swam away from it.

My muscles trembled, anxious for nourishment, and my bones creaked, demanding it. When I could no longer bear the pain, I crawled ashore, scavenging for food and finding nothing. I saw cars nearby, and I was terrified that if I got near people, I would do something horrible. I turned away from the cars and the sea, and I ran.

My bare feet were alert to everything I stepped on, from the jab of broken glass to sand grains on asphalt. I left the paved road, ripping through clots of dark vines that hung between trees like webs of massive spiders. A couple of times, I ran straight through a tree.

At an empty rest area, I gulped water out of the bathroom sink, went back outside and slumped on the ground next to the vending machine. I was so hungry, the world seemed to vibrate to the rhythm of my need—*food, food, food* . . .

My body trembled with tiny, hard shivers. I splayed my hand on the vending machine glass. I pressed. The glass cracked, making a web around the spider of my hand. It was beautiful. I knew there was a reason why I shouldn't break the glass, but at the moment no reason made sense to me. I pressed harder. The glass clicked and groaned. I gripped a shattered edge and tore a hunk away. Exposed now were the neat, careful rows of candy bars, nuts, chips, granola bars, crackers, fruit leather.

I ate it all.

When the frenzy passed, I was sitting in a pile of broken glass and wrappers. I noticed the sound of a chittering bird in a tree nearby, the windy zoom of cars on the highway. Perhaps Ruth's token hadn't turned me into a mindless brute—perhaps my brain had just been too underfed to think clearly.

I picked up a shard of glass and tried to press it into my palm. I could feel the edge of the glass, but my skin didn't cut. I pressed harder. The glass broke.

A car pulled off the highway toward the rest stop, and I stood and ran like a kid abandoning a broken cookie jar.

If I didn't go home to my parents, I would either steal to live or starve to death. But if I did go home, would I hurt them?

Maybe I wouldn't turn into Ruth. Maybe I could be careful. Even with Ruth's blood on my hands, her volatile token in my chest, I knew my parents would welcome me. I closed my eyes, so grateful I thought I might cry.

With a thought, I activated the phone in Fido and dialed.

I was sobbing as I spoke. "Dad? Dad, can I come home?"

CHAPTER 19

Dad wired me money for a bus ticket and food. Mom and Dad drove south, I rode north, and we met at a bus station in the middle.

"I'm sorry," I said.

Mom hugged me and I held still, raising my hand to almost touch her back. I was mindful of what I could do to her with just a squeeze, and it made me feel sick beneath the constant hunger.

"*¿Qué pasó?*" she whispered, asking me what had happened.

I looked around the bus station. Some people were staring. My clothes were stiff with salt. I felt like garbage swept up with the tide.

Dad said, "Let's talk in the car."

On the long drive home, between bites of food, I told them everything. The Beanstalk ride and space, the techno token and Fido, the car crash and robot suit, Ruth's death and the brute token, the fear and the long swim. I spoke until my tongue was sticky.

"Howell's people haven't figured out yet if the tokens are harming us or how to get them out, and I don't think they're going to."

"So stay home," Dad said, "and we go on as we always have."

"They might come after me," I said.

"Then we'll deal with it," said Mom.

How? Hours later when Dad turned onto our street, we still hadn't come up with a plan. Everything looked so small—the bungalow houses, the rectangular front yards, the skinny road, as if since leaving I'd grown into a giant.

Luther was sitting on the front porch. He looked the same.

"You know what's longer than three weeks?" Luther said when I got out of the car. "Six."

"I haven't gotten to advanced math yet, but I'll take your word for it."

"Well hello there, Luther," Dad said in an overly casual tone. He pointed to Luther's bike lying on the lawn. "You know why a bicycle can't stand up on its own? Because it's two-tired."

There was a pause. Dad turned to Mom and mumbled, "I thought it was funny."

Luther's gaze dropped to my right arm. "That's not Ms. Pincher. Did you get a new one?"

Instinctively I curled my fingers into a ball, my wrist twisting, a gesture too intricate for a normal prosthetic.

"Whoa. What is that?" Luther whispered. He took in our startled faces, and his eyes narrowed. "What's happened?"

"Nothing," I said. "I mean, I got a new prosthetic at astronaut boot camp. Whoever got the . . . the highest score on the final exams won a prize."

"Frak, Maisie, in what universe can you win a robotic arm at summer camp?"

We'd decided to keep my change a secret, but Luther was too smart to fool. Mom and Dad gave me significant looks and left us alone on the front steps.

"Before I tell you what's going on, make a guess," I said.

Luther sighed, careful to look indulgent. "Bonnie Howell met you and said, 'I can rebuild her. I have the technology.'"

"The truth is so much weirder than that."

"Double good," he said, plopping down on a step.

So I spilled—parts, anyway. I had Luther at "extraterrestrial nanorobots."

"You have to keep this to yourself, Luthe."

"Of course. My parental units are not like yours. They would so not be okay with my being shot into space and implanted with alien hardware."

"So mum's the word?"

"I hate that phrase, but yes, of course I'll keep your secret. So are you going to go out on the mean streets and fight crime?"

"I'm going to take a shower. My hair smells like the fish department at Food 4 Less."

"Maisie, you're Luke Cage. You're Wonder Woman. You *have* to be a superhero."

"Shower," I said as I went inside.

When I came out, clean and dressed, Luther was on the tablet, searching "police scanners."

"Won't work," I said. "There's no way we can get to a bank robbery or high-speed chase before the police."

"In Gotham, Batman just stumbles onto crime," said Luther. "Salt Lake is annoyingly tame."

"I can't get noticed," I said, doing some pushups. My muscles were going crazy after the inactivity of the drive. "It'd be off to a government cage or the trophy case of a crazed supervillain. If you've read any comics you know."

"Just how tough are you?" he asked, picking up a pair of scissors. I laughed derisively.

"Really?" he said.

I shrugged. "Go ahead."

He stabbed my leg lightly. Then harder. I wasn't numb. In fact, the brute token seemed to heighten sensitivity along with strength. But nothing broke my skin, though he did make a hole in my jeans.

"Hey!" I said.

I got bored with being stabbed, so I went into the kitchen in search of anything edible. There was a tug on my hair and a click.

I swirled around fast. Luther dropped the scissors and leaped back, hitting the wall. My heart sped.

"Don't . . . okay?" I said. "Don't do anything too close to me. Or surprise me. Don't."

His eyes went really big. He glanced at the door out, and I felt way more pain than being hammered at with a pair of shears.

"You won't hurt me," he said.

"You can't be sure."

I took a step back. He came closer.

"I'm sure."

I nodded. "Okay. Okay, Luther."

He nodded too, then held up a small lock of my hair. "And now we know that the nanites don't care about protecting your hair."

"Great." I fingered the hole in my jeans. "Whatever purpose I was made for, apparently I can do it bald and naked."

Luther turned red and quickly opened the fridge.

Seriously? Was he imagining me bald and naked? In retaliation I tried to imagine *him* bald and naked . . . and then quickly busied myself making a few cheese sandwiches.

Don't do that again, Maisie. Ever.

Too late. My brain filled up with the image of Luther again, naked but not bald. How come it was easier to imagine him without clothes than without hair?

Stop it!

We ate and made rapid conversation that had nothing to do with nudity till Luther had to go home.

I stood by the door and watched him ride his bike away. It felt so normal having him around, like I was still just Maisie Brown, working with my study buddy. I wondered if I was happy now. I'd left home and come back changed. In a way, wasn't that what I'd wanted?

My stomach squelched. I was probably just hungry because, hey, I hadn't eaten in ten whole minutes. But the squelch seemed like fear.

I carefully shut the front door and locked it. The deadbolt felt cheap under my fingers. I wasn't sure what I was locking the house against, but I suspected the act was useless. Something or someone would find its way in.

CHAPTER 20

I was awakened by hunger the next morning. Mom had gone grocery shopping and hard-boiled three dozen eggs. The increase to my skin's sensitivity as well as my strength enabled me to walk without stomping through the floor, pick up a cup without cracking the glass, and peel an egg without damaging the white flesh.

"I'm coming into the kitchen," Dad said, narrating his actions as my parents had begun to do around their brute daughter. He yawned and rubbed his bald spot. "First thing in the morning, a hard-boiled egg is hard to beat."

"Uh-huh."

He pointed to the last egg in my hand. "Are you going to eat that?"

I plopped it into my mouth unpeeled. Crunchy.

"Good for you. Eggshells are rich in calcium," he said, cracking a banana off the bunch.

"Ruth took a few days to gain and control her strength, but the effects of the second token were faster for me."

"Because your nanite network was already laid?" said Dad.

"Maybe. I also wonder if the first couple of days the nanites were scoping out our internals and reporting to the token, and the token was reprogramming the nanites for human specifics. The second time around, the brute token already knew the inner workings of my species."

"Have you noticed changes to any other bodily functions?" Dad asked.

"Well, I don't seem to produce very much, um, waste."

My body was so efficient now, nearly everything I ate was used to enhance energy and strength.

"Fascinating," said Dad.

Yes, my father was fascinated by my poop schedule. Biologists.

Dad shambled off again, so I was alone when I became aware of *him*. Heat and cold poured through my middle; my heart beat so that I heard it. I pressed against a wall away from the windows, which was pointless since I knew he could sense me too.

Then a dog barked.

I peeked out the blinds. A gorgeous German shepherd was sitting on my front lawn. The guy holding the leash wasn't hard on the eyes either. I wanted to run away. Hold him. Scream. Hide. Die.

I opened the door.

Wilder was leaning against a yellow convertible.

"Maisie. How are you? You look good. You look great, actually."

"I'm okay." My chin started quivering as if I would cry, so I focused on the dog. "What's his name?"

"Laelaps," said Wilder. "Happy birthday."

"How did you know it's—"

"I still have your astronaut boot camp papers."

I had his memorized. I jumped down the steps and knelt by the dog, letting him sniff my hand before I petted his head. My skin sensed every hair of his thick coat.

"Since your rhapsody about Europa the moon, I read up on Europa the queen," he said. "Did you know Jupiter gave her four gifts? There was the dog Laelaps, a javelin that never missed—I'll have to work on that one—and a bodyguard named Talos. But you don't need a Talos. You are the bodyguard."

Laelaps nuzzled my hand. My pets over the years had included a turtle, hamster, and hermit crab. Let me say that German shepherd trumps hermit crab. But I wished it was just the dog that was making me feel all jump-up-and-down-ish. I wondered if drugs did for addicts what Wilder's nearness did for me.

"Jupiter also gave her a necklace," Wilder said, pulling one out of his pocket. It looked handcrafted, beads in white, black, and several shades of brown, woven as a choker with a separate strand dangling a brown tanzanite. I would have taken Wilder for the gold-and-pearls type, but this looked like something I would wear. If I were rich.

He gestured to my neck, asking for permission. I stood up.

He stood close to me, facing me, leaning around to see the back of my neck as he did it up. Taking his time. His hands touched my neck, his chest pressed against my arm, his breath tickled my ear. My eyes closed.

"I could do it up faster with one arm," I said.

I could hear him exhale a small laugh. I wanted to cling to him and tear in half anyone who got too close. Was I a giddy girl or a wasp-stung caterpillar?

I heard the clasp click, felt the necklace settle, but still he didn't move. The side of his head rested against mine, his hand pressed the back of my neck.

"Come back with me," he whispered. "We need each other to get through this, and whatever else is coming. I know you feel that."

Like a bonfire in my chest I felt it. But I also remembered Wilder talking to Ruth beside the helicopter, so suave, so sincere—all lies. An hour later, she was dead.

"These nanites mess with our heads," I said. "And they're probably filling us with instincts that don't make sense and a premonition of a danger that will never appear."

Laelaps nudged my leg. I pulled away from Wilder and crouched to scratch the dog's neck. His pink tongue lolled out the side of his mouth. Wilder sat beside me, petting the dog's other side. I glanced at Wilder's profile, his chin, his lips. I suspected that the dog was the only thing keeping me sane in that boy's presence.

"I've missed you, Danger Girl." Wilder's hand crossed over the dog's neck, and his fingers hooked mine. "Missed you a lot."

I wanted that to be true. I wanted him to like me so much, it hurt. I opened my mouth, not sure what I was about to say.

"Who is this trog?" Luther asked.

I stood up fast, moving away from Wilder, and blushed as if I'd been doing something bad. Luther was standing on the sidewalk, his arms folded.

"This is Jonathan Wilder, a . . . friend I met at astronaut boot camp. Wilder, this is my best friend, Luther."

The boys looked at each other. The mood was Arctic Circle.

"Okay, break up the love fest." I took Luther by the arm (gently) and escorted him to the front door. "I'll be in soon." I shut the door after him.

Wilder was staring with pleased incredulity. "*That* was Luther, your BFF, your top gun, your Tweedledum?"

"He's a good guy. Some can actually manage the good-guy thing."

Wilder blinked, then shrugged. "I'm sorry." He took a couple steps forward, holding out his hands as if asking to hold mine.

I wanted the whole world to shut off, rush to night, and leave me and Wilder with a starred sky and maybe a moon, no one else around. And I wanted his thinker self to answer all my questions and make everything make sense. But the more I talked with Wilder, the harder it would be to cut him loose, so all I said was, "Thanks for the dog."

His hands dropped. "I wanted you to have someone to watch your back, if that someone couldn't be me."

"Thanks," I said again. "Good luck." And I went inside. Because if I didn't go quickly, I wouldn't go at all. I leaned against the closed door, taking deep breaths.

Luther was sitting on the stool, fingers drumming his knees.

"Report," he said.

I peered through the blinds. Wilder was screwing a stake into the front lawn. He attached Laelaps's leash and unloaded a few sacks of dog food from his car before driving away.

I sighed. "It's a nice dog."

"What dog?" Luther peered through the blinds beside me. "Did you get a dog?"

"Seriously, Luthe, you're as observant as a hibernating bear."

He grilled me as I went back outside, filling up water and food bowls for Laelaps.

"That guy knows what you are? Why was he all Betazoid on you?"

It never helped to ask Luther questions like, "What does Betazoid mean?" He would just mock me and not answer.

"I don't like him. He kept calling you by your middle name."

"He calls me Danger Girl sometimes, but it's not a big deal."

Luther folded his arms. "You think your middle name is a feeble joke. If I'd called you Danger Girl, you would have hated it. But he does and you think it's all girlie cute?"

"Luther, you're freaking out about nothing."

"Oh, am I? Then let me freak out of your way."

He got on his bike and rode off. Laelaps and I watched.

"I think he forgot it's my birthday," I told Laelaps.

Mom came out, saw the dog, and muttered in Spanish that if Dad was going to get me a mammal for my birthday he might have checked with her first.

She drove us to the west desert where I could exercise and punch rocks. That dog could run. I was falling in love. When we got back the phone was ringing. I answered.

"Miss Brown? Is that you?"

"Oh. Hi, Howell." I sat down.

"You made it home then. I've tried calling you on your Fido phone but never have success."

"Yeah, you won't. I had set it up so the number was constantly rotating. Can't be tracked or traced. How . . . how are you all?"

"Well, we're not riding unicycles and juggling at the moment. Actually, I *am* juggling, but just for practice. I've worked up to four balls now."

"Wow. Congrats on that. Um . . . so, how's the rest of the fireteam?"

"I'd like to know. They all left after you did."

"Left?"

Come back with me, Wilder had said. Back where?

"Mi-sun didn't want to go home, but when Jacques ran off she changed her mind. How am I to protect you when your behavior is so unpredictable as . . . is that a doughnut? No, just the shadow my lamp made on my desk. Anyway, if your secret gets out, the government will come after you, Miss Brown—maybe not even ours. And heaven knows who else. You're not safe."

I looked around. I couldn't see my mom.

CHAPTER 21

I hung up on Howell and ran to Mom's bedroom. She glanced up from her desk, her expression turning to alarm when she saw my face.

"I have to go," she said on her phone and clicked it off.

"I can't leave you alone anymore." I was weirdly out of breath. "The others . . . they're not with Howell. We're all separated. That feels wrong. The fireteam was supposed to stay together. It was dangerous to be apart. We all felt that."

Mom called Dad, asking him to come home, her eyes never leaving my face. A line from a Yeats poem was going around and around in my head: "Things fall apart; the center cannot hold."

"Ruth died and broke the team," I said. "Maybe I helped break it by leaving, and I bet none of us function right anymore." Sitting was impossible. I paced. "Four powerful people who were tied to a leader. I think . . . I think bad things can happen to us when we're apart. Lions loose in the circus without the tamer, or maybe sheep without a shepherd. Or both. Am I making sense? We're vulnerable or the tokens won't work right or maybe we'll go bad like Ruth or just crazy when we're alone—"

"You're not alone," Mom interrupted.

"But the team . . ."

She took my hand and said it in Spanish, so I'd know she meant it. *"No estás sola."*

Laelaps started barking. I told my mom to lock her room behind me, and I inched open the front door.

GT, in a frayed Hawaiian shirt and cargo shorts, was coming up our walk, two men in black suits following. I'd read up on GT—high school dropout, moved up from bag boy to supermarket owner to filthy rich corporate mogul. Three times acquitted on federal charges of corporate espionage, embezzlement, and conspiracy to commit murder. In an interview, when asked to explain his shocking success, GT said, "Clean living. I don't smoke, drink, gamble, carouse. I'm at peace with the world. But I'm relentless. When I have my eyes on a prize I never, ever give up."

Right then, his eyes were on me.

"Maisie Brown," he said, his voice warm, his smile charming. "How are you? May I come in?"

He seemed so tranquil and harmless, maybe I would have let him in, but Laelaps kept barking. It kept me on edge.

One of the suits looked at Laelaps through his dark glasses, his hand going into his suit coat. "Want me to shut up the mutt?"

I pulled the guy to me by his lapels and stuck my hand into his jacket. I was aware of his tender ribs that could break with a flick, of all the tiny bones in his hand as he tried to push me away. But I got my fingers on the gun I'd suspected was there and yanked it free from its holster. It took two squeezes of my left hand to squish it into a ball, careful to avoid pressure on the bullets. The steel made a nice grating sound, satisfying, like popping packing bubbles.

The guy's eyes lifted in alarm above his sunglasses frames, and he stepped back, falling down three steps to the concrete walk.

I put the metal ball into GT's hand. "Maybe we should just talk on the stoop."

GT laughed, his smile crinkling his eyes. "Maisie Brown, you are extraordinary. Your fearlessness, your decisiveness. If I had twenty employees like you, I'd own the world. I have to speak honestly . . ." His voice lowered, he leaned against the doorjamb, and he gave me a crooked smile. "I am *enchanted*."

Laelaps was still barking.

"You are *so* your son's father," I said. "I have to know—do you, um, surf or is this a fashion choice?"

He winked. "I have an opportunity that could be worth a great deal of money to you."

I wrinkled my nose.

GT's expression shifted, and I thought he could tell that he'd gotten me wrong. "But of course you're not interested in money. You want . . . protection for your family."

"Are you threatening my family?"

GT chewed his gum. "No. Not me, of course, but—"

"I understand that the police are interested in your general doings, GT. Maybe I'll let them know you're trying to blackmail a minor."

GT looked down at his flip-flopped feet. "Detective Brand . . ."

The man who had fallen down the steps was on his feet again. He flashed an FBI badge.

"The officers and agents I don't own will be happy to exploit you for their purposes," said GT, "only they don't pay as well as I do."

I felt sick. I started to shut the door, but GT put a hand on it. I could have broken his hand off, but he must have known I wouldn't.

"You think Howell is content losing her treasure to a bunch of kids? Her people will discover a way to extract them, and then she'll come for you. Maisie, I *want* you to keep what's yours, and you can use it to your full potential in my employ. I can help you, and I'm the only person who can."

Howell's warnings were still pricking goose bumps on my skin. Dad would be home soon. I wanted to crouch over my parents, protect them. I wanted GT gone.

"Look, you seem like a *really* nice guy," I said with a fake, toothy smile. "But you're way too old for me."

I shut the door. And I watched through the blinds. If any of them had touched Laelaps, I would have jumped through the front window and gone Hulk on them. But they just looked around the side of the house and went back to their expensive-looking black car.

After GT got in, someone else got out.

I opened the door. "Jacques!"

He waved at me, his cheeks full of dimples. I still wasn't used to his face without his thick black glasses frames. His eyes looked smaller, his face thinner.

"Maisie, Maisie, one-armed crazy," he said, strolling to my stoop.

"Get off my lawn, you pesky kid," I said happily.

"Go *bleep* yourself."

"Go teach evolution in Tennessee."

"Go . . ." He squinted. "Go . . ."

Pre-token Jacques would have countered with "go wear a fur coat to a PETA fundraiser" or "go wear a thong on a nude beach" or something. But now he just rubbed his forehead.

"Jacques, what are you doing with *him*?" I whispered.

"Seeing what the tide brings in." Jacques fished a pack of peanuts out of his pocket.

"If you want to get away from him, I'll help you."

"No thanks," he said, crunching on peanuts. "I'm in the big time, baby."

"Are you sure? Has he threatened your parents?"

Jacques made an expression of disgust. "I went home yesterday. Mom said hi, I missed you, and by the way, an honorable businessman has offered you a *bleepload* of money to start working for him immediately. Told me it'd do me some good to work for a guy like that. Do *her* some good. She's getting sick of working two jobs to pay for my private school. *Bleep* her, I don't care."

I couldn't imagine my mom pushing me to go with GT. "What about your dad?"

"*Mon père*? Oh, you mean the guy who calls on my birthdays and sent me a *bleeping* LEGO set at Christmas? No. It was GT who got me away from HAL and . . . and the thinker."

I knew why he stumbled. Just a few days ago, leaving the thinker had been unthinkable. I wondered if it'd been as hard for Jacques to run away from Wilder as it had for me. I wondered if his heart still hurt.

"Wilder made some mistakes with Ruth, but GT can't be better. Is Mi-sun with him too?"

"What if she is? Think of it—you, me, and Mi-sun. The fireteam, on tour and ready to conquer!"

"You and Mi-sun should come here. My parents are cool, they'll take care of us."

He dropped the empty bag of peanuts to the ground and rubbed his nose, his eyes never leaving mine.

"How. *Bleepin'*. Tender. Okay, fine, you stay here in your shoe box of a house. Does it feel good, imagining yourself smart and superior and cozy with your very special mommy and daddy? Does that feel extra fine?"

He started to the car.

"Jacques," I said.

He turned back. "He won't stop trying to own you. Neither will Howell or Wilder or any of them. We're too valuable." He smiled. "Pick a side, Peligrosa."

CHAPTER 22

When Dad got home, we sat in the family room, too nervous to eat dinner. Laelaps took up half the couch, his head on my lap. I stroked his ears.

"What do you think the techno and brute tokens are worth?"

"Hundreds of millions," said Dad.

"More." Mom rubbed her neck. "This isn't a safe place for you, Maisie."

"We need to stay together or I can't protect you," I said.

Perhaps we were falling into GT's Plan B. He intimidates us, Dad stops going to work so I can watch over him, we get desperate for money, and GT's "business proposition" starts sounding really good.

The phone rang. Laelaps sat upright.

Mom glanced at us, then answered. She listened for some time before saying, "Thank you, we'll consider that," and hung up. "GT offered to hire Maisie as a consultant and pay her a one-million-dollar signing bonus. He implied . . ." She faltered and then finished in Spanish. He'd implied that if I didn't, there would be consequences.

Things fall apart, I thought.

A breeze came in through the open window, rattling the blinds. The evening warmth was distilling into the coming dark. I could feel the cool promise of it on my skin, raising the hairs of my arms. The world was softening toward autumn. I put my hand on my mom's knee and was aware of her heartbeat, fast as a rabbit's.

The phone rang again. Mom stiffened.

"Don't answer it," she said.

Dad said, "It's better to know as much as we can."

I said, "From now on, no one gets to you guys without going through me."

I answered.

"Do you know where Mi-sun is?" It was a woman's voice.

"Is this Mrs. Hwang?"

"Bonnie Howell said Mi-sun left. She said to call you."

"I'm sorry, I haven't seen Mi-sun since I left Texas."

"She never came home," said Mrs. Hwang. She had a mild Asian accent, her tone frantic, breathy. "Bonnie Howell took her to the airport, but Mi-sun must not have gotten on her flight. She called me from somewhere, said she didn't want to come back. I have two other children. How can I handle a daughter who runs off?"

I really wished my mom had answered the phone.

"Mrs. Hwang, if I see Mi-sun—"

"Tell her not to come home if she's too good for us now."

She hung up.

I put down the receiver, almost missing the cradle because my hand was shaking. I made sure for the tenth time that the blinds were shut. It felt like the whole world was peering in.

"GT or Howell took Mi-sun. Or the police or FBI or some token hunter . . . I don't know who is safe."

"Do you trust Dr. Howell?" Mom asked.

"I want to, but—" I tapped my chest. I didn't need to say it—Howell had discovered perhaps the most valuable treasure in the world, a bunch of teenagers ran off with it, and who knew what she would do to get it back.

"We have to go," Dad said.

"They can't hurt me," I said. "I won't make Ruth's mistakes. And . . . and I could fight them, I think."

"No," said Mom. "Don't fight them."

"But I can—"

"I've seen people live a fighting life, *nenita*. I don't want that for you."

Dad nodded. "We go. Together."

"No. No! Just . . . just abandon our house and your jobs and everything?" I started pacing again, and I could hear the floorboards protest beneath me. I felt a bone-deep anger, a boiling that made me want to punch something. "This sucks. It *sucks*. I didn't even do anything wrong."

"Maisie . . . ," Mom started.

I didn't want to hear it. Guilt was a knife in my gut, twisting.

"It's partly your fault," I said. "You gave me this stupid middle name, so I had to prove that I'm not a joke."

I stepped too hard. There was a crunch of wood, and my leg was knee-deep through the floor. I stomped again and again, feeling strong and mean enough to break the entire earth and let the rocks bury me. And that was where I wanted to be—down and far away, hidden from everybody.

Laelaps whined. I was hip-deep in a hole in the middle of our living room. I glanced up. My parents didn't look mad or scared. Just sad.

Mom said, "*No es culpa tuya, nenita.*" It's not your fault.

I put my hands over my face and cried. I felt Mom and Dad pulling me in, and I let them hold me. Because if Mom hadn't said what she did, I think I would have run through the front door. I would have gone into the night and never stopped running.

"Luther," I said through my hands.

"The best protection we can give our friends is if they know nothing at all," said Mom. "We pack up what we need, and we go."

"Where?" I whispered.

They hesitated, and I snapped my mouth shut. What if the house was bugged? Anyone could be listening.

We stood in silence for a couple of minutes, full of thoughts that didn't need speaking. I could see the pencil marks on the door-jamb measuring my height every birthday, the dent in the wall where I'd knocked over a chair, the lighter bit on the hardwood where Dad had sanded away the purple splotch from my spilled grape juice.

Everything felt slippery, life too slick to hold, tipping forward fast. Hadn't I ached for change? What a huge joke the universe was playing on me.

There was a knock at the door. We all startled, my own heart thumping. Why didn't Laelaps bark?

"Don't answer it," I whispered. But the door started to open on its own. I tiptoed closer, my hand in a fist.

"Is the residence occupied?" Luther called out. He froze mid-step, seeing us standing in the dark. "Um, inconvenient time?"

My mom took his face in her hands and kissed both his cheeks. "*Mi hijo,*" she said. My son. She often called him that, but this time she said it with such affection, my eyes watered. Dad and Mom left the room, and I knew they were going to pack.

Luther looked at the hole in the floor. "Whoa, what happened there?"

"Groundhogs."

He squinted at me. "What's going on?"

I'd never talked to him about GT, Ruth's death, or told him much of anything about Wilder, Mi-sun, and Jacques. If questioned, he could be genuinely ignorant.

"Dad's taking a sabbatical," I said. "We're going to be traveling, doing research. For the semester. And maybe the entire year."

"Where?"

"All over," I said, my expression hard.

"And I'm coming too?"

"Luther..."

He looked at me with a pleading expression. I shook my head.

He sighed and sat on the couch. "Happy birthday," he said, pulling a T-shirt out of his backpack and tossing it at me.

He'd printed his own design: BLUEBERRY BONANZA: NOW WITH SUPERPOWERS IN EVERY BOX!

"Thanks," I said.

"Should I go?"

I wanted Luther away from here and safe with his oblivious parents in their tidy house. The Earth was spinning at a crazy angle and way too fast, and I needed to pack or think or run, do something to force it back in control again. But I also knew that this might be the last I'd see Luther for a long time. Or ever.

"Can we try this again?" I held my arms out.

"What have I done to deserve such a fate," he said, though he came closer. He was taller than me, and as his arms went around my back, his chin touched my temple. He didn't hold me close at first, but I squeezed him tighter. And I thought the words, I love you, Luther. His arms relaxed after a couple of seconds as if signaling an end, but I didn't let go. So he sighed and hugged me for real. One of his hands opened on my back, pressing me closer, his head leaning against mine. I turned my head so my face fit into his neck and squeezed my eyes tight to keep from crying.

I love you, Luther, I thought again, more fiercely this time.

When he let go, his arms fell as if they were really heavy. He turned and then stopped at the door.

"I could—"

"No," I said. "Don't do anything."

"But—"

"No."

"Who?" he asked.

I shook my head.

His shoulders slumped, and he walked out the door. Into the night. Into our neighborhood that suddenly felt as safe as a coal mine on fire.

"Wait!" I wanted to walk him home, but I wouldn't leave my parents. Laelaps trotted along at my ankle. "Wait . . . I want you to have Laelaps."

Luther's eyes got wide, and he looked six years old. "You lie."

"He barks whenever strangers come to our house, but he didn't bark at you. And he's way cooler than your freaky shivering rabbit."

"My parents will have a conniption," Luther said, but he was already kneeling on the lawn, scratching the dog's neck.

I watched from the front porch until I couldn't see Luther and Laelaps anymore. My heart pinched in on itself. At least Luther would have some kind of guard.

My parents were in their room. They'd packed a bag for me too. "It's late," said Mom. "Let's get some sleep."

If the house wasn't bugged, it'd be better to leave in the morning when it wouldn't look suspicious and get far away before anyone realized we were gone for good. Besides, we might need the rest.

Mom invited me to sleep in their bed, between them like I used to when I was little. No way I would risk waking up flailing from a bad dream. I sat on the floor, listening to their breathing and folding a gum wrapper into squares.

A couple of hours into my watch my eyelids felt weighted. I was about to give up and sleep when I noticed that the tips of my fingers were tingling. Little black dots danced in my periphery. My parents' breathing had slowed.

Maisie Brown, I asked myself, if Ruthless were asleep in a house, what would be the safest way to catch her?

Why, flooding the house with odorless gas. The kind that knocks you out. Permanently.

CHAPTER 23

I flung Mom and Dad over my shoulders, and they didn't stir. I grabbed the bags as I passed, hoping one of them had the car keys, and ran for the garage, kicking a door off its hinges on my way. I could feel their hearts beating against my shoulder blades and their diaphragms slowly contracting as they inhaled. Alive still. I needed to get them into clean air.

I placed them in the backseat, got in the driver's seat, locked the doors, and clicked the button to open the garage door. It groaned and creaked. Slow. Painfully loud and slow. But at least it gave me time to ruffle through my mom's purse and find her keys. Success. I hadn't taken my driver's license test yet, but I was pretty sure my parents would approve this infraction.

I'd just started the motor when a car zoomed into our driveway, blocking us in, the headlights blinding. This was definitely not the friendly neighborhood watch.

I jumped out, grabbed the car's chassis under the front bumper, and flipped it upside down into the street. I hoped the occupants were wearing seat belts. Kind of.

"You trying to kill my parents?" I shouted at the night. "Kill me first!"

I backed out Mom's Camry and screeched down the street. At the last moment, I remembered to hit the remote button, shutting the garage door. As if we were just going to run an errand and would be back soon. As if that house was still our home.

"*¿Qué pasa?*" Mom asked, what's happening?

"Someone gassed us in our sleep," I said, the car stuttering as I braked around corners. I was not a great driver.

Dad was groaning, and I guessed they'd woken to headaches. At least they'd woken.

There were car headlights behind us. I sped up. The car sped up. I made a fast left. So did they. I wasn't sure if I was scared or mad, but my chest felt like red-hot metal and my mouth wanted to scream.

"Who wants to drive?" I asked.

"I can," Dad said.

I screeched to a stop, jumped out, and ran toward the oncoming car. The tires squealed as the driver braked and turned at the same time, its side slamming into my side. I rolled, Fido tucked to my chest, got back to my feet, and ran forward again.

A couple of bullets stung my shoulder. Not cool. My parents were close by.

I punched the hood of the car. Not quite enough. I jumped up and came down on it with my elbow, like those brightly Spandexed wrestlers. Now the engine was a bowl of spaghetti.

"Holy crap!" I yelled, because suddenly there was a really big gun pointing out the window—the kind that shoots rockets. I yanked it out of the guy's hands and bent it into a circle, tossing it back into the car with them.

"Who are you?" I asked, sticking my head through the window. They stared back, wide eyes in unfamiliar faces. Not the Howell or GT guys I'd seen. "Who?"

I pulled the closest one out of the window and held him over my head. I felt a rush of energy, as if every cell in my body was *awake*, and I could do anything.

Ruthless believed she could do anything, I thought.

Another car sped around the corner, the yellow headlights burning straight for our Camry. I dropped the guy on the roof of his car and ran.

"Drive!" I told Dad. He hit the gas and took off. I veered straight for the new car. It sped up as it approached me. I stomped, planting my feet in dents I'd made in the asphalt, and I leaned my shoulder into the oncoming car. The tires screeched, the metal groaned, and half the car went accordion before I fell into a backward somersault. I didn't pause to interrogate this time. I ran after the Camry, reaching it in a dozen huge strides. Dad slowed as I opened the front passenger door and hopped in, and then we sped off.

◆

Dad took back streets, eventually merging onto the interstate a hundred miles to the south. The highway was only two lanes here, the landscape brush and low hills.

Mom had been keeping boxes of protein bars in the back of her car since I'd Hulked out. I lay in the backseat, eating and watching for cars and helicopters. I was sleepy, but I couldn't sleep.

In Phoenix, Mom found a chop shop and sold the Camry for parts. We walked to the bus station.

It was early afternoon, the streets were crowded, the buildings too shiny, nearly melting in the sun. Everything felt sharp and fast, like a dream of falling.

In the back of the bus, I made phone calls on Fido. It was the only safe phone to use, but only I could use it. I called both my parents' work managers and told them we had to leave town for an unexpected emergency. I asked the post office to hold our mail, canceled our utilities, and called the bank to arrange ongoing automatic transfers from my parents' savings for the mortgage.

"How much money do you have saved?" I asked.

"Enough to pay the mortgage for four months," said Dad.

"And if we're gone longer than that?"

Mom closed her eyes. The bank would take our house. And everything in it. My mom loved that house. My dad loved his job. I pressed my knees to my chest, imagining that I could get smaller and smaller until I disappeared.

And we just kept going. Sleeping on buses, eating in truck stops, washing our faces and underarms in gas station bathrooms. We didn't stop till we'd reached the Atlantic Ocean. Florida. Mom and Dad had withdrawn the maximum cash from ATMs in Arizona, and we used all that for a deposit and first month's rent on a one-bedroom furnished apartment.

Traffic screeched outside our window. There was no air-conditioning. We ate street tacos by the open window, listening to Cuban and Puerto Rican–accented Spanish, the hard slap of basketballs from the weedy court.

The whole world was orange-hot and loud as a train. I looked at the scalding sky and wished for something. That my parents wouldn't die. That we could go back to our small house and small life. I was invulnerable. And I was scared.

CHAPTER 24

Wake up. Breakfast. Shower and dress. It was still gray every morning when Dad and I took a bus to the golf course. We'd discovered a wild area behind the manicured links, perhaps reserved for a future expansion. No one was ever around. I scouted out lightning-struck palm trees—headless and dead-standing—and pulled them up by their roots. I cracked the trunks into sections and left them in piles.

And sometimes I just ran.

In moments my skin was as hot and sticky as the air. Dirt I kicked up stuck to my skin, the shower undone. It was the only hour of the day I actually felt alive.

When we got back, Mom was already gone to work at the convenience store. We'd learned that people would hire a Latina woman without an ID but not a white guy.

Dad did the shopping and cooking. I did the cleaning. In the afternoon, he went to the library. I had to avoid public spaces. With or without Fido, I was too recognizable.

One month. Two months. Three.

When the fourth-month anniversary struck us, I curled up on my sofa and cried quieter than the sounds of night traffic. Back home, the savings account was empty. Foreclosure imminent. Very soon, our house would no longer be our house.

It was Christmastime when we started getting careless. I couldn't sit in that apartment one more day, reading library books to the tune of electric piano music that marched through the walls. Dad didn't argue when I followed him to the local library. I started in the poetry stacks. Hungry for the kind of winter Robert Frost knew, I added him to my internal anthology:

> *And lonely as it is that loneliness*
> *Will be more lonely ere it will be less*

I glanced at the computer bank and back at Dad. He was lost in the history stacks. It felt like a crime, but I eased into a computer chair and got online.

The news sites read like incredible fiction. Parliament in India was shut down, rioting in Beijing, an entire town of people disappeared in Australia, some new scary flu in South America. Maybe the world was always this crazy. Maybe it felt more dangerous because I felt dangerous, cut off and raw, untethered.

I didn't dare e-mail Luther. I wouldn't paint a target on his back by letting any big bads know I cared about him. But like my brute body constantly craved food, my whole self craved Luther. Somebody. A friend.

I checked the Japanese teeth-whitening site for the most recent post from user LEX. It was a month after I'd fled Utah, and all it said was: "I'll save the Poo Project for you." Nothing since.

But there was a recent post in English from a user named Talos—
the same name as Europa's guard, a gift from Jupiter. My adrenaline
spiked like needles in my heart and wrists. I read the post.

> Poe would come in handy right now because I can't
> use my own words.

My whole body shivered as if Wilder were there beside me,
breathing against my ear. How had he found out about that site?

If I responded, Wilder would know that I was alive and on a
computer. What if he was loyal to GT or Howell or whoever gassed
our house?

Blame the faulty adolescent brain. I logged in as new user "DG"
and replied.

> Poe said, "I wish I could write as mysterious as a cat." I
> wish I could do a lot of things.

By the next week, Dad had agreed to weekly library visits if I
wore a long-sleeved shirt and one of those surgeon-type masks many
had started wearing to guard against the mystery flu. I sat at the
computer, forcing myself to check the news sites first. The flu from
South America had a name: the Jumper Virus, so called because of
how it seemed to jump around the world. Entire towns on four
continents were known to have contracted it and were placed in
complete quarantine.

The news was all depressing. I went to the Japanese site. There
was a post from Talos. My skin felt cold as if I'd just dived into
the unexpected waters of the ocean.

It's snowing outside, and the day is dark. I want to
slow down and contemplate those lovely and dark and
deep woods, like the Robert Frost poem. But I have this
token. And I can't rest. Not for winter, not for anything.
But I take a breath. And I feel how much I miss you.

How do I respond to those last words? Apparently with a heart
that slammed against my ribs and a face that burned. So what's it
going to be, Maisie—flight or fight? I read his message over and
over, letting each word take as much power as a shout, as a touch.

I decided to ignore his last line and respond to the weather
chitchat. A library window was open, the breeze warm as bath-
water, the sky dazzling. I closed my eyes and tried to remember
what those Utah Decembers were like.

I love nestling into the dark days of snow. I love how
the afternoon feels days long, the prolonged feeling of
Cozy, that wistful slowness, how the energy of doing is
buried under the heavy, soft layers of watching.

The exchanges with Wilder were hot bright spots in a long
wash of gray. Mom, Dad, and I ate oranges and oatmeal, sat by
open windows and read books, all the time watching for black
cars and tensing for the sound of helicopter blades. Crying at
night, smiling by day. It was a time of clenched jaws and fists and
feeling muggy and tired and adrift. Little to distinguish one day
from another, besides a weekly message from Wilder. His words
gave me something to hope for, an outcome other than fear and
absence.

I am thinking about you, though I know it makes things
harder. I am thinking about you, your hair in a ponytail.
You're wearing blue. And you don't smile at me.

His messages often left me wordless, but I had to keep the conversation going or I was afraid I'd disappear.

Today I'm imagining you wearing an orange sweater
vest, because it's so wrong and it makes me laugh.

His responses would come within the hour, though I wouldn't
see them until the following week.

I happen to have a closet full of sweater vests. I wear
them at every opportunity—to dress up or dress
down, over collared shirts or nothing at all (I dare you
to imagine that). I wear them while swimming, while
bathing, while sleeping. I rock sweater vests like a
rock star.

Each week I expected to see Luther's LEX join the conversation,
but he must have given up on looking there. Maybe he'd given up altogether. Wilder seemed to be the only being out in the world who
remembered me. And all I could do was wait for something to change.

Waiting felt like holding my breath longer than twenty minutes. Waiting felt like being buried alive. Each day that I sat and did
nothing, my body throbbed harder. My dad staring at a wall, his
mouth turned down. My mom lying on the bed after a night shift,
her body a sigh.

At night when I tried to sleep, I would fidget and thrash against the real, physical pain of inactivity. Morning runs and felled tree trunks weren't distracting my brute body anymore. I was made to do *something*. I could almost feel the nanites nipping at me, as if I'd swallowed a nest of fire ants.

"We can't live like this forever," I whispered into my pillow, and I knew at last that it was true.

CHAPTER 25

The next trip to the library gave me the excuse I'd been craving.

I was reading news online. Schools in Florida and other states with quarantined towns were shut down until scientists could figure out how the Jumper Virus was spreading and contain it. Universities and churches too, and even Congress. Craziness.

An unrelated article from three months before caught my attention: BILLIONAIRE SHOT WITHOUT A GUN.

Businessman Alexander Islinger was killed on Wednesday while he delivered the keynote address at a Chicago charity banquet. He was shot twice in the chest and died instantly. No bullets were found.

"We had metal detectors, X-ray machines, so I don't know how anyone got a gun in," reported the head of security.

The building was locked down. Police searched every guest and employee and

> then combed the premises. Witnesses say
> whatever weapon was used was completely
> silent.
>
> This is the fourth mysterious assassination
> in the past month, leading to speculation—

The story was interrupted by a photo of the guests leaving the building. There were dozens in the photo, but I made out a slight figure with dark hair and a pale face. Were her lips stained blue? What had she shot at the guy—one of the platinum rings GT had given her? Could she simply shoot an ice cube from her water glass, leaving no evidence at all?

I searched Alexander Islinger: onetime business partner of GT; their relationship soured when Islinger accused GT of unethical business practices. Was GT holding the safety of Mi-sun's family over her head? Guilt like a hatchet cracked my chest. I'd abandoned Mi-sun to wolves.

I messaged Talos.

> I've read the news. Keeping still is killing me.

His response appeared a minute later.

> Yeah, it's not good. If the team stays together, we can
> protect one another.

I was disturbed by how happy that thought made me, but I wrote:

> I feel sick about Blue, but I shouldn't abandon my den.

Wilder replied so quickly, he'd been typing his rebuttal before he even received my decline.

> They are safer away from you. Besides, we have a
> responsibility to help our teammates.

I hadn't responded when Wilder sent another message.

> Do you remember what those two can do? They're
> with him, and I can't get to them on my own. I need
> you. And Blue most definitely needs us.

If GT had gotten Mi-sun to kill for him, then Jacques was in no better shape. It was pointless to try to break away from the team. We'd been re-formed by the tokens, and we would be linked together until we accomplished the Great and Mysterious Purpose. Or if there was no purpose, then until we died.

> Okay.

Again, his response was nearly instantaneous.

> Call me.

He gave me a phone number in code, for example, "the number of onion rings you ate in our stolen car" instead of one (one was enough—it was my first and last onion ring) and "the number of strands in the necklace" instead of three. At the moment, I couldn't remember why I'd been avoiding him. It didn't matter, not with

Mi-sun and Jacques working as GT's assassins. Not with my parents languishing in perpetual danger.

I went into the library bathroom and dialed mentally. The phone rang only once.

"We need to meet," he said. I'd forgotten his voice already, how it was a little rough and caught on some words.

"Are you working for your father?" I had to know.

"There's been a pretty aggressive estrangement in the family. He tried to kill me."

"Okay. That's good. I mean, I'm sorry, of course, but I'm glad to know you're not with him."

"I know what you mean."

"I feel terrible about what's happening, but I don't know if—"

"I've tried to get to her, but I can't," he said, and I knew he meant Mi-sun. "I can't figure out a way to break her out of there without your help."

Any doubt dissolved. I had to help Mi-sun, and Jacques too if he needed me. "I don't have money for travel."

"I'll wire you some."

"I'll call you in five days with the details."

That would give me some time to get out of Florida. I thought I trusted Wilder, but suspicion kept me wary. Even more, I didn't trust anyone who might be listening in, and I would not lead anyone to my parents.

"So . . ." He paused again. "How are you?"

"I have to stretch. I'm supposed to *work*, you know?"

"Yeah, I do." He paused. "Call me in five days. I'll be on this phone."

"Okay." *You confuse me and I'm suspicious and logic says to keep away*, I might say, *but I can't anymore. Maybe the token is nothing but a wasp stinger, but I need you so much, more than anyone else in the world.* But I said, "Good-bye."

"Good-bye," he said, sadly it seemed.

"Wait," I said, remembering our conversation at boot camp. "I also meant to say, Hello. And how are you? And . . . and, I miss you. Because, you know, someone should speak those words to you."

"And mean them," he said.

"Right. And mean them."

He said, "I miss you too."

It sounded like good-bye, so after a few moments of silence, I disconnected.

Five days. I had to get as far away from my parents as I could.

That night I updated them over dinner. Mom brought rotisserie chickens from work. I ate two, bones and all. Food was too expensive for me to throw parts away. Besides, bones were delightfully crunchy. Mom said watching me eat was like being trapped in the scary parts of fairy tales, but she said it nicely.

"Wilder is right," I said. "It's our responsibility to help Mi-sun and Jacques get away from GT and stop them from hurting anyone else."

Dad's shoulders slumped. "So you're leaving."

"I don't like feeling dependent on Wilder. He lied so easily to Ruth. But I have to fix this," I waved to the apartment that still didn't feel like home, Dad's frown, Mom's gray convenience store shirt with a name tag that read MARIA.

"You're my baby," Mom said. "I should be taking care of you."

"You are," I whispered. "But if I can help, then I should."

We were quiet. I ground a chicken leg bone into powder between my molars. Mom and Dad looked at each other. Dad nodded.

"Well," Mom said, slapping the table, "this is perfect for your schooling. We've never done a project on the social systems developed by those who are infected with alien technology!"

Dad groaned and put a hand over his face. "My baby girl . . ."

"Don't worry," Mom said, rubbing his back. *"La Peligrosa es fuerte."* Danger Girl is strong.

I handed my dad a knife, handle first. "Here, break this against my hand. It'll make you feel better."

He smiled at me through his fingers. "Someday you may grow up and have kids of your own and understand why breaking a knife against your hand will not make me feel better."

Mom soothed the back of my neck. "Go save the world, *la Peligrosa.*"

There was little chance of that. I felt so pathetic when I thought of Luther's superhero plans. The brute token was wasted on me.

We had just enough cash to buy Mom and Dad prepaid cell phones. They wouldn't be able to call my Fido phone, but at least I could reach them, and I promised to call twice a day—morning and night.

I hugged them good-bye. I could feel everything about this embrace, so aware of their bones, their skin, their hair, the thump of their hearts and inhale of their lungs. They were fragile.

But we couldn't hide forever. And I couldn't ignore the tugging that insisted Mi-sun was partly my responsibility. And Jacques too. And Wilder out there, reeling me in.

CHAPTER 26

I walked to a marina, the sunset at my back pushing my shadow forward, a spindly monster always just ahead.

I'd prepared shoes and a change of clothes in three layers of plastic bags. Adding Fido, I tied the baggage to my chest and dived in. I seized the underside of a cruising boat, hitching a ride away from the oily marina waters and into the Gulf Stream. The current was swifter there, and I swam on alone, exhilarated by the added speed.

After buying the cell phones, my parents had no cash to send with me, but I wouldn't have taken from their meager funds anyhow. I had a plan to appease my elephant's appetite: sushi.

I dived under, clocked a large fish over its head, and floated on my back while eating the soft white meat. Better than chicken bones.

All night I swam on my back, kicking and staring at a flawless starry sky. I felt *between*. My parents behind, Wilder ahead. I wondered, in a poem kind of way, if I existed at all.

Day two I was swimming deep, feeling weightless and strange, when I was knocked hard in the side. Silver against black water, a dorsal fin sharp as a blade, it circled and came back. Adrenaline flared in my heart. Shark! Big, toothy, scary shark!

Then I remembered who I was. And I ate it.

I coursed through days three and four. The movement of my muscles felt like humming, the kick of my legs a song. I dived under whenever I saw a boat and also just for the joy of it, zooming deep, spiraling, arching, leaving a wake of bubbles to boil away. I was no longer a static thing.

Sometimes I went on land to call my parents and drink fresh water, napping under the sun. On the fifth day I dragged myself ashore for good. My clothes were destroyed by salt and the speed of my swim. Hiding in tall marsh grasses, I tore off the rags and put on fresh clothes from my waterproof packet.

I phoned Wilder. The swim had been like grabbing a nap in the midst of a chaotic day. Now my heart returned to playing washboard on my ribs.

He answered. "That felt like five very long days."

"Sped right by for me."

"Humph. Where are you?"

I checked Fido's GPS. "Near Atlantic City."

"Great. I'll be there in an hour."

"An hour? Wait, where are *you*?"

"Philadelphia, baby. You're right on my doorstep."

I shivered, unsure if it was coincidence or if our tokens could have called to each other across hundreds of miles.

It was January in New Jersey and every cell of my skin seemed to harden against the cold. I ran out of the marsh grasses onto a road and found a gas station, washing my hair in the sink with the goopy pink hand soap.

It took me the rest of the hour to jog to the crossroads he'd named. Following the pull on my chest, I found him in a beat-up gray car with the engine running. I slid into the passenger seat and, without glancing at me, he pulled out.

I felt so right just being near him. My heart seemed to hum happily—or was it my nanites? I leaned back against the seat and sighed without meaning to.

He was wearing sunglasses, jeans, and an orange sweater vest with no shirt under it. I laughed.

"Nice sweater vest," I said.

"What, this old thing?"

I patted my hair, hoping there was no obvious sign that I'd been in the ocean for days. I didn't want any trail leading back to my parents. "Where are we going?"

"I've got a place—"

"Tell me it's a secret lair. I've always wanted to hang out in a secret lair."

"Of course it's a secret lair."

"Yes!" I glanced at his bare arms and then quickly away. "So, where are you getting your money?"

"I'm not working for him, Maisie. I promise."

I nodded.

"It's ridiculously easy to get a credit card under another name, now that I've figured out how."

"Seems a tad unethical."

"Better than assassinating people."

His posture was stiff, left arm resting on the driver-side door, his body angled away from me. I told myself the emotional content of his e-mails had played no part in my decision to come here.

Mi-sun and Jacques needed me, and working with Wilder was logical. I hadn't expected him to revert to his pre-Beanstalk, pick-up-line, over-the-top self. And I didn't want him to.

I told myself lots of things.

He pulled into a drive-through before I could ask, ordering everything on the menu. I went straight for a fish burger. The cooked variety was a whole new experience.

"Where'd you get this?" I asked, touching the woven leather wristband he never seemed to take off.

"From one of those gumball-type machines," he said. "Years ago at some pokey zoo, my mom gave me two quarters for the machine and this was the prize."

"Does your mom know about the tokens?" I asked, realizing I knew nothing about her.

"Doubtful. She's been missing for three years."

He said it so casually, I choked on a tater tot.

"Missing?"

"GT said she moved back to Russia and was too busy running her charity stuff to call me." He twisted the wristband. "Apparently I needed billions of nanorobots enhancing my brain before I could figure out the most obvious truth. GT knocked off his wife. Maybe she asked for a divorce. He would never allow that."

"Wilder, that's . . ." I couldn't think of any adjective strong enough for what that was.

"That's the wacky Wilder clan!" he said. "Imagine the reality TV possibilities. I didn't figure it out until I got to using my thinker brain on something other than the fireteam—so, after you left. GT and I have parted ways forever. You know that car accident we stumbled on when we were playing seek-the-thinker? That was

Dad's work. He caused it so he could observe the fireteam in action."

"And now he's turning Mi-sun into an assassin."

"And Jacques. Their weapons are undetectable. They can get in anywhere. And have."

I was feeling ill, and it wasn't the second cheeseburger. "How many people have they killed?"

"Twelve that I know of."

"Oh, poor Mi-sun!"

Wilder nodded.

I leaned back. His presence was like coming into an air-conditioned house on a sweltering day. His pull eclipsed worry for my parents, for Mi-sun and Jacques, for anything.

We were in a neighborhood cut in half by railroad tracks and celebrated by graffiti artists. Wilder parked in a little garage with a pull-down door and led me up some wooden stairs. He unlocked an apartment door.

"How long have you been living here?"

"A couple months."

Whitewashed walls losing their wash, bare bulbs dangling, carpet rubbed bare in spots like a mangy dog's coat. And what exactly leaked from the apartment upstairs to leave those brown stains on the ceiling? There was a mattress on the floor, loose blankets, a computer, a little fridge and a hot plate, and some bags of food.

He watched me take in the place.

"I've been lonely," he said.

"I can see that."

"Dad won't look for me here." Wilder turned his back, took off the sweater vest, and put on a gray sweatshirt and a navy sailor coat.

So he'd worn the vest just to make me laugh. "He thinks I'm like him and would never choose to live in squalor. Besides, it's cheap. I'd rather not steal more than I have to."

A tablet in a keyboard attachment sat poised atop a cardboard box. We knelt on the floor, and he showed me the files he'd been keeping, tracking Jacques's movements, his father's, likely places to find them next.

"What about Mi-sun?"

"She's been off-radar for a bit, but Jacques never leaves Dad's side."

"Maybe we should combine forces with Howell," I said. "Someone tried to gas me and my parents in our house, but it's seeming likely that it was GT."

"I don't know what Howell's plan is in all this, but I have no doubt she's shady."

He showed me patents Howell had recently filed for an energy source powered by titanium dioxide nanotubes, an improved defibrillator, parts for a robotic exoskeleton—things I had invented with the techno token. I was about to get seriously annoyed until I yawned.

"You should sleep."

"It's still day," I said, though the afternoon was yellowing around the edges like old paper. Those days of swimming had depleted me.

"Go ahead," he said, nodding toward the mattress without looking away from his computer. "I've got work to do."

I pulled a blanket over my face to block out the light that slithered in through the ratty blinds and dreamed I could fly.

CHAPTER 27

I roused to hunger, morning light, and the clicking of the keyboard.

"If we're going to find Jacques, we've got to get moving," Wilder said without looking up from his tablet.

The space beside me on the mattress was warm. I glanced around: no sofa, no second bed.

"Did you sleep next to me?" I asked.

The keyboard clicking paused. "Sorry. I've been lonely," he said again, still looking down.

I took a shower and didn't want to put back on my slightly briny clothes, so I borrowed a pair of Wilder's jeans, rolled up the cuffs, and belted the waist. I wore a sweatshirt that hung past my hips.

When I came out of the bathroom, Wilder smiled at me. His expression caught my breath. We didn't talk about it.

Philadelphia was locked up in a bitter cold that January, high noon rarely peeking above negative ten degrees Celsius. No one was out except Wilder and me. We put on coats and hats just so we wouldn't draw notice.

"Didn't realize it till winter hit," he said, "but I'm pretty indifferent to cold."

"These *improvements* aren't random."

"So, what task requires five people with brute strength, techno know-how, spontaneous armor, and long-distance shooting, all tied together by a thinker, who can withstand the cold generally and oxygen deprivation for up to twenty minutes?"

I shook my head.

"Yeah, I don't know either. But given the tokens' likely origin from beyond our solar system, it must have to do with . . . with . . ."

"Aliens?" I knew why he hesitated. I felt ridiculous even saying it.

"I assume our purpose is noble," he said, "but what if we *are* the advance guard of alien invaders, and at their signal, we'll start rampaging—"

"You think we're wasp-stung caterpillars?" I said, explaining about the zombified bugs enslaved to watch over wasp larvae.

"No, that doesn't feel right."

"Wilder, I don't think there is any mission. Most likely that asteroid with its alien time capsule had been wandering the universe for millions of years before randomly drifting past Earth."

"I know that's the most logical conclusion, but I . . . I feel like we . . . like the fireteam has a real and imminent purpose, and if I wake up slowly enough I'll remember the dream that tells me what it is, or if I turn the right way I'll see it, or . . ." He shook his head.

We were sitting on a rooftop across from a building where Wilder thought Jacques and GT might be working. So far no sign. Below us, wind chased loose snow low across the asphalt, writhing and swimming like horizontal candle smoke.

"I *can* break through walls, you know," I said. "We don't need a key to get inside."

"I won't risk going into any place my father has claimed as home turf. We wait till they're in the open. This is why I need you, Danger Girl. I can find Jacques, but I can't force him to come with me."

My breath came out in a cloud. "So what is his weakness?"

"Food, just like you. If I wanted to stop you, I'd stick you in a Maisie-proof box with no food, and when I let you out you'd be too weak to fight. Not that I would ever do that."

"Of course not. You're a gentleman."

"If you force Jacques to keep creating new armor, he'll weaken."

"And once he's defenseless . . ."

"Carry him back to the car. I'll meet you there. We'll take him to the apartment—"

"Lair."

"Right, lair. If I can just get Jacques away from GT, I know I can persuade him to rejoin the team. Jacques could give enough evidence that even a crooked FBI agent would have to convict Dad."

"So," I said, "he mentioned you'd done things, gotten kicked out of schools . . ."

"Yeah," he said.

I looked down to avoid his gaze, inspecting my fingernails. I understood why Ruth had been obsessed about keeping her nails painted. The brute token grew them so thick they had a yellowish tint. I'd started keeping mine painted in Florida. This week they were coral pink.

"What did you do?" I asked.

"Car theft, dealing prescription drugs, vandalism, fighting. Mostly to impress my dad."

"Yeah, that kind of stuff dazzles my dad too," I said.

Wilder smiled. "Dad worked his way from grocery store bagger to the top. The corporate mogul part was a lot of work, but the megalomaniac part came naturally. He put me in expensive private schools but wouldn't buy me clothes. Anything I wanted, I had to earn, just like he did. So I started side businesses. His approval seemed to increase the more creative I got. He wanted me to make myself wealthy and successful, no matter how I got there."

"So you tried to become a criminal to follow in his footsteps."

"I guess. And because it was funny. And because I was bored."

"Is that why you suddenly didn't like me anymore after they announced we both would visit the Beanstalk? You were bored with me?"

His exhale was so heavy, I couldn't see his eyes behind that puff of breath.

"No, I just—I panicked. We were getting close fast, and I was afraid after the week of training alone together—"

A door opened down below. Three people exited the building just as a black SUV pulled up for them. Two were bundled up in the cold, but one was hatless. I could see his short, curly hair.

"Go," Wilder whispered.

I pushed the power button on my earpiece, put a hand on the ledge of the roof, and leaped over. It was five stories down. I tried to keep straight, my legs fighting the air to keep my body from twisting. I landed feet first, and the sidewalk cracked beneath me. My bones seemed to vibrate, and never had the soles of my feet been so aware of the ground.

GT stumbled away from me. The other guy had pulled out a gun, but I heard GT say, "Don't bother."

"Jacques," I said. "Please come back."

Jacques looked up to where Wilder sat hidden.

"The *bleeper* returns," Jacques whispered. He swept back his brown leather trenchcoat. He was wearing a gray turtleneck, jeans, and silver-studded motorcycle boots. And I was pretty certain that underneath it all were his bulletproof long johns.

"We need to be a team again."

"A lot's changed, One-Arm."

"Wilder says we're strongest together. We need each other to figure out—"

"I'm not going back with Wilder—are you crazy? It was hard enough to pull myself away from that spider's web the first time."

"Take her out," GT said.

Jacques's eyes seemed uncertain.

"Like you told me, the fireteam should be together," I said. "Me, you, Mi-sun . . ."

Jacques's laugh was as bitter as a sob.

"Mi-sun's gone. Wilder took care of that himself. Now I have a new directive."

Blades of sharp havoc grew out from Jacques's hands and his armor extended over his head, everywhere but his eyes.

I went for his eyes.

CHAPTER 28

Jacques ducked, rolled to the side, and came at me with arms windmilling. I jumped back, just missing his attack. So, it would appear he'd spent the past months training.

I heard the car start behind me.

"Ignore GT," Wilder said in my earpiece. "Keep Jacques on defense, push him away from the car."

I threw a garbage can at Jacques, and he sliced it in half with one of his arm blades.

"Are you going to let GT treat you like his pool boy?" I said.

Jacques emphatically lifted one of his blade hands, and I was pretty sure he was giving me the bird.

I ran in for a tackle, and he dodged to the side. The force of my run sent me sprawling into a building. Now he was behind me and running toward the car. GT had just climbed inside, the other guy getting into the driver's seat.

"Knock him down!" Wilder's voice cried in my earpiece.

I threw half the steel garbage can, striking Jacques in the back. He fell face forward, quickly regaining his feet and turning to block my punch with one of his blades. It sliced through my sweatshirt and grazed my arm.

"Ouch," I said. "You're prickly."

His eyes smiled. I had a weakness.

He attacked with vigor, slicing at me with his razor arms. I grabbed the garbage can half and used it as a shield, but Jacques carved it up. One of his blades found my shoulder, coming down hard.

"Ow!" I said, backing away. Nothing had ever hurt my brute hide before. And the increased sensitivity of my skin made it ten times worse.

His eyes glittered with pleasure, but instead of slicing at me with those havoc blades again, he got excited with his fancy new skills and tried to roundhouse me. The arrogant little bacteria farm.

"Grab him," Wilder said in my earpiece as Jacques's armored leg caught me in my gut. I snatched his ankle and threw him against a wall.

"His armor," Wilder said.

I was trying, but I couldn't get my hands on him, let alone crack it and pull it off. I went in for a punch to knock him down at least, but Jack Havoc was both nimble and quick, and I ended up punching bricks.

"Come on, Jacques! This is silly. Just come talk to us."

His response was to try to slice my leg.

"Getting stuffy in there?" I said. "Doesn't that bacteria poo make you sweat?"

Jacques's eyes narrowed and he tried to stab me, but I was not letting that thing get me again. I grabbed his arm at the wrist, twirled him above my head, and threw.

He rolled across the pavement and stood up, releasing the armor over his mouth.

"You think I'm the bad guy? You're the one who *bleeping* left. You left, Maisie, just like Ruth."

I felt struck, and I just stood there when he came at me again, blade arms swinging.

"Maisie!" Wilder shouted.

I moved, just ducking under a swipe, grabbed his arm, and threw him again.

"Wrong way!" Wilder said, but too late. I'd thrown Jacques toward the SUV.

Jacques sprang to his feet, and GT pulled him inside before I caught up. The car peeled out as I grabbed a handful of bumper. I threw the bumper like a spear through the back window, but the car didn't slow.

"Chase it, Maisie. Grab the first big thing you find and throw it at the car!"

I was chasing. I bounded as fast as the car could drive, but no faster.

They turned a corner, and the first thing I saw that wasn't bricked and mortared to the ground was an empty minivan. I grabbed the chassis, getting it up on my left shoulder to fling it forward. The vehicle groaned like a robot in pain.

In less than a second, I did the calculation. I could hurl the minivan and smack it right on the roof, but not beyond. I throw this two-ton car onto that two-ton car, and most of the people inside are crushed.

Ruth's token throbbed in my chest.

"I can't," I said.

"Do it!" Wilder said.

"I can't . . . ," I said, trembling to defy the thinker. But I put it down.

Two seconds later, the SUV was out of sight.

I began to chase it, but Wilder crackled in my ear. "Forget them. You can't catch up now."

It had taken Wilder weeks to find Jacques, and I let him get away. If the techno token was still working, I could have built something to tap into Jacques's tracking device. By taking Ruth's token and losing access to the techno token, I'd weakened the team.

I jogged back to the building and met up with Wilder as he came down the fire escape.

"I managed to throw a tracker onto the roof of their SUV at least," he said.

"I'm sorry, Wilder. I didn't realize that I couldn't . . . do something that might be fatal. I should have realized earlier, so you could have planned for that."

He paused, as if the most important thing in the world right then was just to look at me. "Maisie Danger Brown, you are—"

His hand rose, and for a moment I thought he would touch my face or my hair, but his hand paused at my shoulder. He examined the cut in my shirt.

"Jacques marked you. He left a wound. I didn't know he could . . ."

I opened the rip wider and traced the thin red welt made with a havoc blade. It stung to the touch.

Wilder was so close to me, the air warmed between us. He frowned, took a step back, and turned away.

Back in our car, Wilder tracked their movements on his tablet. Sometimes he'd stop and rub his hands together.

"Are you cold?" I asked.

He paused to think. "No. Must just be habit."

"Or else you're practicing your evil genius hand rub."

"Mwa-ha-ha," he said unconvincingly.

"Jacques said Mi-sun was gone, that you took care of that."

"Gone . . . ," he said, tasting the word. "I wonder if Mi-sun got away from GT, and Jacques thinks she's with me. Maybe she's with Howell."

We followed the signal into another neighborhood and found the tracker in a gutter on a tree-lined street, the limbs heavy with ice.

"Probably knocked off by a branch," Wilder said. "Where are you, Jack Havoc?"

We drove around the rich, dusky streets, houses hidden far behind walls, parks open and empty.

"Have you always given nicknames?" he asked suddenly.

"What do you mean?"

"Ruthless, Jack Havoc, Code Blue, Speetle, HAL. You name things, and they stick."

"I don't know. I've always just called you Wilder."

"Should I be hurt?"

I didn't nickname Luther either, or Mom or Dad. It was the rest of the riffraff, the huge teeming world. My brain wanted to remember it all, so it invented shortcuts.

But I didn't need any help remembering Wilder. I didn't tell him that.

"Do you wish Ruth were your partner instead of me? Someone who wouldn't have hesitated to crush GT's car?"

"Maisie Danger, I don't want anyone else—" He stopped. "Sorry, I . . . I'm trying not to talk like I used to."

I turned away to watch the world darken outside my window. Wilder cleared his throat.

"I should have been clearer, told you to throw it *past* the car, blocking their escape."

"No way I could have thrown the van that far. Since getting this token, I can usually tell how far I can throw, how much I can lift."

He squinted at me a moment before returning his gaze to the street before us. "Ruth could have done it. Maybe the nanites are more potent when it's one token per person. I hadn't realized . . ."

He parked in our little garage. I'd just pulled the garage door down when Wilder grabbed my hand and pulled me at a quick but casual pace to the side of the building behind the stairs. Across the street was a man in a suit, brown coat, and knit cap walking, scanning the buildings. A black SUV drove by, the driver slowing to talk to the man.

"Is that them?" I whispered.

"I don't sense Jacques, but they could be some of GT's guys."

Wilder still hadn't let go of my hand. I pretended not to notice.

"Do you want me to capture them?"

"No . . . see, the guy's talking on an earpiece. If Dad's on the other end, he'll find out where we are and have the advantage."

"They must know where we are, or they wouldn't be here."

Wilder shook his head, his eyes tracking the man. "They wouldn't be so obvious. If they're looking for our lair, they don't know they've found it."

He rubbed his thumb across the back of my hand. My heart responded, thudding out frantic Morse code messages. S-O-S, S-O-S.

We stayed pressed to the wall, watching through the breaks in the stairs as the man looked over our building, the one next to it. Wilder's fingers intertwined with mine. And though my gaze never left the guy, I barely noticed when he climbed into the SUV and drove off. Ninety percent of my brain power was focused on that touch. I took a deep breath, and my breath shuddered.

"I think they're gone," I whispered.

"Maybe," he said, though he didn't move either.

I could hear his breathing speed up too, though all we did was stand there, our hands touching. I had to get away or my chest would explode with the increasingly violent beats of my heart.

"We should go while it's clear," I said.

So we ran up to the apartment. Wilder still didn't let go. He fumbled with the key while I watched the street. We closed the door and locked it. The broken blinds were partially open, the light on in the bathroom, and I felt visible to the whole world. Another man walked the sidewalk outside. He turned, looking up, as if noticing our window. Wilder ducked, diving onto the mattress and pulling me beside him.

Calmáte, tonta, I scolded myself.

I felt so aware of Wilder, his weight on the mattress, his warmth, his hand. Aware too of my own body. I was way overreacting to a harmless touch.

"Maisie?" he said.

Don't answer, I told myself. Pretend you're not here. Even though you're holding his hand, feeling his palm with your thumb, timing your breaths to his, lying beside him—just pretend that you're far away and alone and—

"Yeah?" I breathed back.

Traitor, I called myself.

"Maisie . . ." He turned onto his side so he was looking at me. I didn't look back. For a long, long time . . . like, several minutes. Or one. Because when his voice got soft like that, his eyes would be brighter, his just-plain-touchable face would be so close and his attention locked onto me, and I would feel swoony and vulnerable and completely giddy-brained. So I didn't look. For several seconds.

Then I looked.

"I'm not supposed to feel like this about you." His right hand was still tangled with mine, his left rose to my face, his thumb barely touching the corner of my mouth. His blue eyes were hot like a hydrogen flame.

"I shouldn't," he whispered, leaning closer, glancing at my lips.

"Okay," was all I said. Words were smooth as glass and slick in my hands. The only thing I could seem to hold was the rough ache of longing.

CHAPTER 29

Wilder was as close as an exhale. It wasn't far to lean, but it felt like a journey. I hesitated till resisting made my skin ache. Then I moved, he moved, and we met in the middle. Our mouths touched, a soft greeting. Relief poured through me, cold followed by hot. He pulled me closer. And we kissed.

We kissed, and I was back in space, my arms around Wilder, our bodies spinning. But there was no hurry here, no Ruth about to turn around, no Mi-sun or Jacques or Howell. Nowhere to be but here.

There was time between the kisses to trace the line on his jaw, discover that slight roughness. I wanted him to understand, as I kissed his cheekbone, that I'd missed him. So many places to kiss. And be kissed. And I wanted to know them all, like I wanted to breathe.

And his hands explored my back, my neck, my hair. He held me closer, and his kisses sped up. I wanted them to. I wanted the rough skin of his jaw against my chin, his mouth against the hollow of my throat. I wanted everything. My body rang with an exquisite kind of joy. This, this, is what it was made to do.

His hands went up my back beneath my shirt, soothing finger-tips against my bare skin. He kissed the pulse under my jaw. His hands found my waist, circled front, and pressed against my belly. How simple that was, and yet what an astonishing sensation.

Then his thumb popped the button of my jeans. My eyes flicked open. Thoughts thudded back into my head.

"Uh-uh," I said.

He stopped, but his eyes pleaded with me. His hands caressed my face.

"Maisie ... you're so beautiful ... I can't help myself ..." His fingers traced my chin and then found my lips.

He started to kiss me again, and I relented, kissing back.

But his words haunted me—*I can't help myself*, as if he were constrained to want me. I wanted him to *choose* me, not kiss me mindlessly. Even so, a part of me would give up any choice to just let things happen. And that shocked me. I'd decided long ago what I would do and would not do, and here at the first opportunity, I was tossing out reason for instinct. If I couldn't make a decision using my brain, then was I even Maisie anymore? Better to ache with want than to become an illogical girl I didn't know, I thought.

So I whispered, "Stop."

He leaned his forehead against my neck, frustration in the grip of his hands.

"Please," he said.

But my brain wasn't going to let my body win. I felt like I'd been dropped in a vat of icy water.

"When you kiss me, my brain stops working. I don't want to make a choice without my brain. And if I cease to be rational, then I've lost myself."

He leaned over me slightly, his finger tracing my bottom lip. "If you're worried about being safe, I'm prepared."

That set me sitting straight up. "You—what?"

"You know, I have—"

"I know what you meant. You carry one with you at all times?"

He blinked, as if trying to catch my train of thought.

"So this is a regular occurrence for you," I said. "Alone with a girl—doesn't matter who, really—and you get to kissing, and she's willing to go further but wary of the risk, and thank goodness! You save the day by being prepared!" I suspected that I was being a little bit ridiculous, but I didn't care. I was remembering him with his arm around that blonde at boot camp, whispering against her ear.

His smile was incredulous. "It's a good thing, right? I'm being respectful. I was thinking about you."

This did not appease. "So you planned this. You thought, 'I'll bet I can get Maisie to succumb to my practiced seductions against her better judgment, so I'd better be prepared.'"

I could see that rapid-fire thinking going on behind his eyes. "There's no way to get out of this gracefully, is there?"

"We should get back to work," I said, starting to get up.

"Wait . . ." He put a hand on my arm, then removed it. "Can we just lie here for a minute?"

I hesitated.

"Please. I haven't . . . *felt* much of anything for a while. It's such a relief just to be near you."

I lay back down, relieved too. I didn't want to work right then. I was feeling too much and not understanding all of it.

He was on his side, returning my gaze. Suddenly he laughed.

"My brain is infused with billions of clever-making nanites.

You'd think I could come up with a strategy to get a pretty girl to sleep with me."

"Nice use of 'pretty' there. Still working the old strategy?"

"I never stop."

It was flattering and disturbing and exciting to be wanted. And to want in return. But I don't think I've ever felt so strong—not even with the brute token—as when I said no, not yet.

So we lay there, not touching, just wanting. And it was a feeling I didn't mind prolonging. The best part of Christmas is the dark side of morning, staring at the clock, anticipating the day.

I drifted to sleep, and when I woke it was night. I was panicking even before I'd opened my eyes because I'd forgotten to call my parents. So I crept to the bathroom and phoned. My dad's voice was anxious.

"You're keeping safe?" he asked.

"Sure," I said.

"I mean . . ." He cleared his throat. "If you and Wilder are sharing a room together . . . alone . . . I want to make sure that you remember all the reasons why—"

The Sex Talk my scientist parents had given me came complete with diagrams, brain charts, and science journal articles. They'd presented a solid argument about why teens should wait. Dazzled by the data, I'd agreed.

"Dad!" But why did he have to ask me about that right now? "I remember, Dad."

"I know. I trust you, Maisie."

My throat tightened.

I chatted with Mom and headed back to bed. It seemed suspicious that Wilder purchased boxes of protein bars in anticipation of my arrival but not a second mattress. When I lay down, Wilder pulled me closer, my head against his chest, his right arm curled around me.

"I'll be good," he whispered. "I'm a good boy . . ."

I swallowed a laugh because I suspected he was talking in his sleep. But lying close felt nice, like I had a place, that I wasn't homeless, weighted with a dead girl's token, and doing things that scared me.

We woke like that in the morning, still intertwined. When I opened my eyes, his were open too.

"I wouldn't share a bed with my parents," I said. "Too worried I'd flail at a dream and chop off their heads."

"I like that you're not worried with me," he said, touching my cheek.

"Oh, it's not that so much. If I accidentally killed you in my sleep, just think of all the problems solved."

"With that kind of power logic, you should be the thinker."

We were both slow to get up. Holding someone in the morning can be a lazy and euphoric way to start the day. I did kiss him again. Not like the night before, partly because he kept grinning.

"Am I the cause of all this amusement?" I asked him.

"I'm just happy. Really happy. And so relieved."

"Because of me?"

He nodded, still grinning, and kissed my forehead. "For the first time, I feel like everything's going to work out, because I know what to do."

"And what's that?"

"At the moment, just this," he said, touching my hair. "'I am looped in the loops of her hair,'" he said, going back to Yeats.

For the next two weeks we slept beside each other at night. By day we held hands. If he was on my right side, he held my Fido hand as if it were no different. And though I missed feeling his warmth and those electric pulses that shivered across my skin, I'd never felt so accepted, so wholly me, than when Wilder was holding the hand I'd made.

He worked on his computer while I bench-pressed the car in the garage or grocery shopped. We did a lot of stakeouts and ate dinner in the backseat. We stared at each other.

I'd drawn a line. And he didn't push it. There was just holding and touching and breathing and yearning. And there was some kissing. A lovely bit.

A tiny worm of worry burrowed into me that Wilder would be bored soon. But I didn't want doubt to taint this strange, magical interlude.

When I called Mom to check in, she said, "You sound happy."

"I guess I am."

I didn't tell her why, and that made me feel all the miles between us. Guilt nibbled at me for not yet saving her from the convenience store and her Maria name tag. But Wilder and I wouldn't give up till we'd set everything right.

And so I floated along, blissfully happy and hormonally insane. I wasn't scared that it would end. It seemed inevitable.

CHAPTER 30

I got on Wilder's tablet to surf the news and then wished I hadn't. Scientists still didn't have a clue how the Jumper Virus was spreading across continents in such random patterns. Over a hundred towns were quarantined worldwide. Elections disrupted, some countries under marshal law, and the world economy taking a dive in all the uncertainty.

The mess seemed to bring out the crazies. I watched a security camera video of a man walking up the Delaware state capitol steps, sipping a drink through a straw and holding a gun. The officer spoke to him; the man lunged. Another officer rushed out and shot the man down.

"Whoa," I said, and clicked on a new link.

"Wait, go back." Wilder watched it again. Then again. And again. It'd been disturbing the first time. By the fifth I wanted to smack myself with a frying pan.

"Are you worried Mi-sun was involved?" I asked.

"Huh? Oh, no, I just found it . . . weird." He turned off the tablet and jumped up. "Let's get them. Today."

He'd found another lead. Some of GT's guys were in a house outside Philly. We watched with binoculars from an alley.

"Most of Dad's businesses are legit, but he keeps a thug contingent to handle the dirty side of things."

"Dude's got power issues," I said.

"You have no idea. I don't sense any fireteam members here."

"But maybe GT's guys can lead us to them."

"Since it seems like they're going to be a while . . ."

Wilder startled me, pushing me against the brick wall. My instinct was to hold still so I wouldn't hurt him. Clearly unconcerned about his own safety, he leaned down to bite my neck.

"We're working," I said, resuming my watch through the binoculars.

"You are brutal."

"You wanna see brutal?" I leaned over and picked up a steel Dumpster.

"If that's an attempt to turn me off, it's having exactly the opposite effect."

Neither of us noticed a guy in a huge parka coming around the corner till he was right in front of us. He stopped short. I put down the Dumpster.

"Hey," said Wilder, uber-casual.

The guy fumbled for his cell phone. Wilder knocked it out of his hand. The guy wound up to punch, but I grabbed him from behind. He had ahold of Wilder's shirt, and as I pulled him back, Wilder's shirt ripped at the neck.

The guy elbowed me, knocked his head back, kicked his heels against my shins.

"Why don't you feel pain?" he whined.

He clawed at Fido and felt what wasn't skin.

"Oh no. You're a robot, aren't you? Some super-advanced Japanese attack robot. Leggo, leggo, I can't stand freaky robots. Seriously, I've got a bona fide phobia, I can't . . . I can't . . ."

"I've seen you before," Wilder said. "You work for my father. What's your name?"

"Brutus," the guy said, still in full panic. "Please, just get the freaky robot away from me."

"Brutus, where's my father and his favorite sidekick?"

Brutus shook his head, his legs still kicking.

"Robot girl," Wilder said to me, "scare him."

So I tossed the guy up. Pretty high, actually. I jumped and caught him coming down, my arms dipping with his weight so it wasn't like hitting a concrete floor. Though it probably did hurt a little.

I landed on my feet, and Brutus, who had been screaming, now stopped in favor of rapid gasps, punctuated with breathy squeaks of "Robot . . . robot . . ."

"So . . . we should go," Wilder said.

"Because of the screaming?" I asked.

"Yeah, because of the screaming."

I carried Brutus to the car, joining him in the backseat. Wilder spun around on the gravel, peeling out. Brutus was still trembling when he gave up the address of a warehouse a couple of miles away.

Wilder parked in a vacant lot behind some scrub trees. The sun was low, but the restless clouds smothered anything yellowish and warm looking, bringing night on early.

"Stay here," Wilder said to Brutus, as if I hadn't already duct-taped him to the seat.

We jogged to the closest building. "I'll hide here till you're in,"

Wilder said. "I don't want Jacques to sense the thinker before you have a chance to scout it out. If Brutus is right, GT and Jacques are four buildings west."

No one was out in the freezing temperatures. Wilder lifted his arm to place an earpiece in my ear, and the ripped piece of his shirt lifted. He tucked it back in, but I had glimpsed something.

"Wait." I reached out, moving aside his torn shirt. He flinched but clenched his jaw and let me.

Over his sternum was the henna-brown circle of the thinker token. But there was a second one now, a kind of key shape attached to the circle. I'd seen that mark before, but on someone else's chest.

My heart seemed to stop. In the long, quiet moment between one beat and the next, all I could think was, No. No. Please no.

CHAPTER 31

I backed away fast, knocking a branch off a tree, and I turned to run.

"Wait!" Wilder raced toward me and then stopped. "Wait, Maisie, I didn't kill Mi-sun. You know I wouldn't do that, right?"

My head went fishbowl, the world slurpy and sloshing every which way. I sat down hard before I could fall over and break something else. Like a building.

"Maisie . . ." He came closer.

"Don't!" I yelled.

He jerked back.

Mi-sun was dead. Wilder was wearing her token on top of his own. I thought of warriors keeping the scalps of their kills.

"Stay, please, while I explain. Please."

"Go ahead," I said. My voice was dry.

"Mi-sun was working for my father," he said. "I found her a few days before you came here, and she didn't run when she sensed me. I thought that meant she wanted to escape with me, but she went crazy. She took off one of her rings, and she shot it at the token in her chest.

So fast. She fell over. I pressed my hands to the wound ... to stop the bleeding, not sure if she was still alive, but ..." He shuddered.

"The token entered you, against your will."

"Yeah."

I waited for more. He didn't explain.

"And you didn't tell me before because ..."

He lifted his hands helplessly. "Because I felt guilty. Because I thought you'd doubt me. And if you doubted me, we couldn't work together."

In the lair, Wilder had turned his back to me when he changed his shirt. I'd thought he was being modest.

Mi-sun—like Ruth—gone. Two out of five.

I wanted to run through some brick walls screaming. But my brain refused to get freaked out, biting down hard on the facts that I had. Wilder had hidden something really terrible from me, but I did trust him. Didn't I? Besides, I'd jumped into the Gulf of Mexico and abandoned Mi-sun to get scooped up by GT. I wasn't without fault here.

"I wish I knew what you were thinking," he whispered.

"I don't think Mi-sun would kill herself unless she felt threatened," I said, my throat sore, my voice cracking. "Why would she feel threatened by you?"

"Because I'm the thinker? Maybe the breaking apart of the team messed her up, I don't know." His eyes teared up. "She just ... it was horrible, Maisie. And she died so fast."

I felt my chin tremble. Mi-sun was eleven, she had two little brothers, she'd been scared to go home ...

"I should have told you, but I was a coward. I'm sorry, Maisie. I'm so sorry."

"Wait . . ." A new realization rumbled through me. "You've got Mi-sun's blue shot, so your thinker token is buried."

He opened the rip of his shirt. "Your techno token faded when you got Ruth's, but both my tokens are equally dark. I guess the thinker token never gets buried."

"I want to see you use the blue shot."

He sighed, picked up a piece of gravel, and shot it at the warehouse wall. Blue shot was faster than a gun and silent. All I heard was the click of the gravel tapping the concrete. The electric-blue trail seemed to appear a split second later, a pulse that faded quickly in the graying evening.

My stomach turned. I'd slept beside him night after night while this huge secret lay against his heart.

And another thought . . . how often he rubbed his hands together. And the way his touch felt, my skin tingling under his fingers. How I fancifully and stupidly decided it was a manifestation of our attraction. But it was just the spare electrons dancing down his fingertips, a side effect of the shooter token. Anger dried my eyes.

"So has your thinker brain figured out what we're for? Another secret you're keeping from me?"

"No," he said, not reacting to my gibe. "But I've traced several assassinations back to Jacques, and for the moment it's the fireteam's responsibility to stop him and bring him back."

I didn't want to be some alien's zombie servant, doing things against my will. But it seemed logical that we had to protect people from ourselves if we could. And I felt what Wilder did—that the surviving fireteam members needed to stay together.

"I should have told you," he said. "I'm an idiot, I know. How can you trust me? But please believe I was just trying to do what I thought best to re-form the team. And now that you know, I don't have to stupidly hide the blue shot. I might actually be of some use backing you up in there."

GT and Jacques might be in that building right now. If I failed, GT could make it impossible to find Jacques again. Now was not the time to mourn Wilder's lies. Now was the time to strike.

"Okay, I'm going in," I said, standing. Wilder exhaled relief, but I glared. "And we'll talk after."

He nodded, putting his hands back in his pockets.

At astronaut boot camp, when he'd turned suddenly cold, I'd felt vulnerable because of our eight kisses on the roof. If I was vulnerable then, what was I now?

I gestured to the building with a nod of my head. "Get going, Wild Card. I need to phone home, then I'll be there."

"Wild Card?" he said.

"Yeah, maybe it's time you had a nickname."

He frowned. "Don't forget to turn on your earpiece when you're done. Stay in contact, and as soon as you're in, let me know the situation and I'll come in shooting. Don't let Jacques cut you. Hit him hard and fast. Between the two of us, we'll wrap this up nice and easy."

"Sure." I was losing faith in nice and easy.

He picked a padlock and broke into the near building while I headed toward GT's building, dialing my mom's phone. It went right to voice mail, so I left a short message, saying I was fine. All had been well when we spoke that morning, so I tried not to worry. I called Dad next.

"Maisie?" he said. His voice was breathy as if I'd caught him in the middle of exercising.

"Yeah, hey Dad. How's stuff?"

The line cut out. I stopped walking.

Low on battery? Bad signal? I called back five times. Nothing. My stomach knotted. Driving to Florida would take at least fifteen hours. No reason to panic without evidence. I'd keep phoning, and in the meantime, I'd go get Jacques.

Frosted weeds cracked like glass under my feet, reminding me how cold the world was to those unfortunates without tokens. Maybe it was worry for my parents that translated into worry for Brutus sitting in a cold car. I ran back, jumping into the car and shutting the door.

He was shivering. "You going to kill me quick or leave me to die slowly?"

"Option three." I took off my coat and cap and dressed Brutus up as best I could, adding a scarf Wilder had left behind. "I don't want you freezing to death."

"You sure? That seemed like your plan," he said, his teeth chattering.

"I don't make the plans."

"Yeah, I caught that." He squinted. "You're not a robot, are you?"

"No," I said with disappointment.

"So, what, you got all strong—freak accident, genetic testing—and now you think you can run with the boys?"

"Pretty much."

"You don't know anything about these guys. *Kid* killers. I saw your pal Wilder kill that Asian girl with my own eyes."

Everything seemed to tilt—me, the car, the whole world. I felt as if I were sliding fast and hard, scrambling for a hold, because when I hit bottom I'd have to think the words "Wilder killed Mi-sun."

CHAPTER 32

I froze, bent over the seat trying to reach a blanket. "What?"

"Asian girl, little thing. He was mad at her. She wouldn't do something he wanted, and he killed her."

I didn't breathe. I didn't move. "She killed herself. She shot herself."

"Do you hear me talking? I *saw* him. It was right before Halloween. Wilder had the girl on the floor, choking her till the girl was blue in the face. I'm not claiming to be an altar boy, but killing kids? This is what I'm telling you! Not happy company for a girl who comes back to give me her coat, even if you have freaky robot strength."

I carefully stilled my face before turning back around and tucking the blanket over Brutus.

"Thanks for the tip." I got out, shut the door, and ran. It felt good to run.

New data. Brutus could be mistaken or lying. But there was corroborating evidence:

1. Mi-sun's token sat in Wilder's chest.
2. On the boat, Wilder had tried to get to Ruth before me. Had the thinker known when she was dead, her token would come free so he could claim it? When the token entered me, Wilder had been so mad.
3. Jacques said Mi-sun was gone, that Wilder had taken care of that.

Wilder said she died just before I came to Philly. But Brutus said it had been three months. Who was wrong? Who was lying?

"Maybe he wants all the tokens." The words slipped out, hard as the slaps of my feet against the ground. He'd lied again and again and again, but I kept trusting him. Did he deserve my trust? Was I nanite-poisoned—or just blinded by a naive crush?

Perhaps Wilder's thinker brain figured out that he couldn't kill Jacques without my help. Once he added the havoc token to his arsenal, would the brute and techno tokens be next?

Maybe I was overreacting, maybe Brutus was wrong, but I couldn't have Wilder's voice in my head till I figured it out. I pulled out my earpiece and crushed it between two fingers, letting the fragments fall to the wind. I'd go snatch Jacques and deal with the thinker later.

Wilder might have killed Mi-sun. A nudging anger warned me that I was going to feel this later, like a hard workout that screams in the muscles the morning after. My Fido hand clenched as if on its own, and I realized I was a cyborg now anyway, not far from a total, emotionless robot. How liberating that would be.

In moments I was at the building. This far away, I had to strain to sense Wilder. He was where he said he'd be, in that first building, waiting patiently for his queen to get into position and put his father and Jacques into checkmate.

The front doors were unlocked. There was an informal lobby and a guard station. No one there, but the feeds from the warehouse security cameras were live on little black-and-white screens. I looked them over for a sign of Jacques or GT.

A handwritten note was taped to one computer:

PUSH PLAY, MAISIE DANGER BROWN

I backed away, slamming against a wall. Should I run? This was when it would have been handy to have Wilder in my ear.

You're indestructible, I reminded myself. Or nearly.

I touched the screen and it lit up. A video was paused. I pushed play.

The color was grainy, but I recognized my father on a bench in a windowless room. Sitting on his hands. Looking down and slightly away as if ashamed to be there. Instinctively my hands covered my face.

GT was sitting on a chair beside him in a casual pose—leaning back, one ankle propped up on his other knee, his elbow on the chair back.

GT: "Did you ever take her to school?"

Dad: "Just . . . once. One day of kindergarten."

"And the kids were mean?"

Dad spoke quietly, reluctant but too afraid not to speak. "They ran around with their elbows bent, pretending to be . . . retarded. Having one arm and mental retardation was the same to them, and a child damaged in any way became an object of ridicule."

"And Maisie didn't notice, did she?"

Dad shook his head.

"You wanted her to stay like that. Unaware."

Dad nodded.

So the small life I'd outgrown was my fault. My arm's fault. I'd figured, but it still hurt to have it confirmed.

"I get that," said GT. He patted Dad's shoulder, one father comforting another. "So why didn't you have another child? Were you afraid it'd turn out like your first?"

"No. We . . . we love Maisie . . ."

"You were disappointed in your daughter—"

"No."

"Your maimed, handicapped daughter—"

"No!"

"Nick, just tell me. You never meant to have a child at all, right? Maisie was a mistake."

This video was intended to make me emotional and rash. So I knew what I needed to do: Stay calm. Stay smart. Find my dad. I'd turned away to search the camera feeds again when GT's voice said, "You deny it? Nick, can you explain why your wife goes by the name Inocencia Rodriguez-Brown?"

Dad looked up sharply at GT.

GT stood, his hands busy with something—unwrapping gum, no doubt. "She worked from home with an invented name and a stolen Social Security number, she kept her daughter out of the school system, she kept her whole life quiet. *Inocencia*. An ironic choice for her alias, don't you think? Inocencia is anything but innocent. How many years was she a member of the Yellow Flag? How much blood is on her hands?"

I wouldn't listen to GT's lies any longer. I slammed my hand down, splitting the computer in two.

The speakers on the walls spoke to me.

"It just doesn't seem fair that you hobble through life missing a limb while your lying, irresponsible parents enjoy wholeness. Let's even things out. In four minutes your dad loses an arm. Yes, go ahead and call the police. They will take seven and a half minutes to arrive. By then you might not recognize your daddy, because at the five-minute mark, I relieve him of his other arm. Can you guess what happens at six minutes?"

One of the security monitors showed figures, hard to make out. The room had no windows. Large. High ceiling. First floor probably. I started running.

"You want to know how to save him?" GT's tinny voice echoed off concrete. "Just step into my chamber."

I didn't slow to open doors, wood and cinder blocks crashing around me. Three and a half minutes. My heart pounded; my stomach felt full of hornets.

I came through a wall, masonry flying. The room was massive. Maybe it was for storing large things like jets, but now it was mostly empty. It was hard to see up in the rafters and corners of the room. There wasn't a lot of light. But in the center stood a metal box like a large upright coffin. It looked homemade, and not lovingly so. GT's "chamber."

Sitting on a bench beside it was my dad. Mouth gagged, hands tied, he looked at me, his bald head shining, his row of hair poofed up by the gag of black cloth. My heart hurt.

GT was wearing a paint-splattered sweatshirt and jeans, an earbud and microphone on his head. He stood behind Dad, apparently weaponless except for Jacques, beside him in full havoc armor.

"I have sharpshooters positioned all over this room," GT said.

"You can't get to them all, Maisie. And I'm sure you've guessed—they're not aiming at you." He checked his watch. "Two minutes, thirty seconds."

"You want my tokens," I said. Dad was staring back at me as if trying to speak with his stare.

GT smiled that self-aware, charmer smile. "They're a burden anyway, aren't they? My doctors know a safe way to extract them. Just place yourself inside this chamber. The moment the door is locked, I release your father. And I will only keep you until the extraction is complete. Your family will be safe, everything will return to normal."

Your family. Did he have Mom too?

"But how do I know you won't—"

"You *don't* know," GT said, snapping on his gum as if we were chitchatting about the weather. "But you have no other choice. Two minutes, ten seconds."

If I ran to Dad, they would shoot him. I was strong but not large. I couldn't shield him from guns shot from multiple angles. I couldn't see a way through. I needed Wilder.

No, not Wilder.

The fear of losing the tokens made me shudder even as my logical brain calculated that it wasn't a terrible idea. Ruth had killed. Mi-sun and Jacques had killed. And maybe Wilder. Was I next? Maybe GT's influence was incidental. Maybe the tokens compelled us to murder.

Get rid of the alien wasp stingers, I thought. Go into the chamber and let it end.

Even though I didn't trust GT, and the thought of giving up my tokens zapped me with panic as if trillions of nanites were clinging to my every cell, begging for survival, I still might have done it. Except for Mom.

I knew that's who Dad was thinking about. He blinked once, long. Then he shook his head. Maybe Dad would survive this, or maybe I would. But one of us had to. We couldn't take away Mom's entire family in one fell swoop. And if I went into that chamber, GT would have no reason to keep either me or Dad alive.

"Jacques . . . ," I said.

"What, you wanna switch sides now?" he said. "You realize our beloved thinker isn't so hot after all? He killed Ruth, he killed Mi-sun, he tried to kill me—"

"Be quiet," GT said to Jacques.

Jacques took a step back. His nose twitched with a scowl.

Wilder killed Mi-sun . . . No, I would not think about it right now.

Loose cinder blocks from my crash through the wall lay by my feet. I scooped them up.

GT flinched. "Remember, if you harm me in any way, those shooters have orders to kill your father."

"Thanks for the tip." Their order was to shoot if I harmed GT, but it didn't sound like he'd included the chamber in that command. The thing must be brute-proof. On the inside. I chucked a block at its control panel. The cinder block shattered, the panel sparked and popped. Its lights dimmed.

No gunshot.

"So, new orders," I said, shouting to the hidden sharpshooters. "If you hurt my dad, I tear your heads from your bodies. Emphasis on *tear*. None of you will have any mercy from me. But leave us right now and I won't follow."

GT was frowning, uncertain. I don't think he'd planned on my destroying the chamber.

Jacques said, "Don't you know good parenting, GT? Always follow through on a threat. Pretty sure it's been four *bleeping* minutes."

"I told you to shut up!" GT shouted.

Jacques blinked. His arm lengthened with a havoc blade. He grabbed my father's right arm and sliced through.

CHAPTER 33

In a moment I was across the room, backhanding Jacques away
from my father. I heard Jacques hit the far wall. GT jumped back.
Gunfire erupted. I was hunched over my father, covering up his head
and torso with my own body as best I could. As the bullets pinged
my back and head, I calculated where they were coming from.
The gunfire paused. I hurled the two remaining cinder blocks at
the west and north corners. Two grunts. Those shooters were out at
least. I had nothing to throw to the northwest, so I angled my body
between my father and that corner as the shooting started again.

GT was gone. I couldn't leave Dad and go after him. A glance
proved that Jacques had fled too. Just as well. I didn't have time for
a fight.

For the first time, I dared look at my father. He was slumped on
the floor. I was aware now that he had been screaming, something
I'd managed to tune out until he'd stopped. I checked his pulse—
alive. Just fainted. Fainting is what you want to do when someone
cuts off your arm.

The gunfire paused. Sounds of running feet.

My father's wrists were still tied together, though one of the arms . . . My stomach clenched as I tried not to vomit. I tore off my sweatshirt and wrapped my father's arm in it. There was so much blood.

I'm holding my father's arm. It's bleeding. It's bleeding . . .

I slapped myself mentally. Not a good time to freak out.

I picked him up and ran.

I hunched as I ran, holding my father like a baby, protecting him with my body from the bullets.

More gunshots. His legs were bleeding. We left a trail of blood. I clamped shut my jaw and refused to feel anything. I kicked through doors. I ran.

Dad stayed out cold. Why wasn't I fainting? I worried about that, because I felt pretty sure my brain shouldn't be able to handle the fact that I was carrying my bleeding father and his arm.

Don't you dare faint, Danger Girl. Just run.

Outside, down the street, my brute legs propelling me into arcing leaps. Stopping to borrow/steal a car would have taken too long. I wasn't tired. All I could do for my father was run. And I could do that nearly forever.

Navigating the dark warehouse streets, I checked my GPS for the nearest hospital. I could run there faster than an ambulance could get to me. I called 911 on Fido without slowing and told them that there'd been gunfire.

"Also, there's a car in a vacant lot just to the east of those warehouses. A guy named Brutus is tied up in there. He'll freeze to death if you don't get him out."

"What is your name and address?"

I disconnected.

I passed a man crossing the street so quickly, he fell down. I kept running. Thankfully there were almost no people out to see a girl in a T-shirt in negative-degree weather carrying a bleeding man and bounding like a cartoon character.

I must have looked pretty extraordinary bursting through the emergency room doors. My father's blood soaked my white T-shirt, smeared over my neck and chin.

"Amputated arm," I called out. "Forty-six-year-old man, no allergies, no prior medical conditions. Arm severed"—I checked my internal clock—"seven minutes, twenty-two seconds ago. He needs help NOW!"

Orderlies took Dad from my arms and placed him on a rolling bed. They wheeled him and his arm away. Someone tried to check me in too, till she understood that the blood wasn't mine. She wouldn't let me follow Dad.

I dialed Mom. Straight to voice mail. I kept trying every few minutes.

The police arrived. I smiled, resenting that I had to fear them. At least I wasn't bloodstained anymore. The nurses gave me scrubs to replace my bloodied shirt.

The officers were wearing face masks, like most of the people in the emergency room. The trend was becoming increasingly common since the Jumper Virus first emerged. I told the officers GT Wilder and Jacques Ames had just cut off my father's arm. They radioed to get the info on the warehouse. Gunfire confirmed. Brutus found and in police custody. No sign of GT or Jacques. I put my hand over my eyes. I was so tired.

The good-looking cop sat beside me. I wondered if he was a lying murderer too. Seemed to be all the rage.

"Do you know why they did this?"

"They're crazy!" I couldn't remember if looking straight in a person's eyes was a sign of speaking truth or lies, so I ended up meeting his eyes, then looking away, then back again. "GT's son and I were at astronaut boot camp together last summer, and GT freaked out when we sorta dated."

"So he kidnapped your father and cut off his arm?"

"I wasn't there for the kidnapping part. GT called me to that warehouse this evening. He had a creepy video of my father talking about me. Then I found my father and GT there, and GT had Jacques cut off my father's arm." My voice cracked, completely without my permission. But it probably aided the bewildered-teenager schtick. It wasn't too hard to pretend.

One of the cops gave me a glass of water, which I gulped down. My stomach growled.

"I'm real hungry," I said. Yes indeed, just like a little lost orphan child.

"Maisie, how did your father get from the warehouse to the hospital?" the older one asked.

"I carried him." There were witnesses. No fudging this one. "Probably adrenaline helped? Like when people can suddenly lift a van off a trapped child?"

The doctor came in to talk to me, so the cops started to leave.

"Hey, GT's son, Jonathan Wilder?" I said. "He's . . . abnormally smart. And involved somehow. You should keep an eye out for him."

The Wild Card. Brutus said he'd killed Mi-sun. Jacques confirmed it. And he was the thinker—wouldn't he have known that sinking Ruth would kill her? Maybe he designed GT's chamber himself and sent me there to get caught. Maybe the tokens had messed him up as much as Ruth and Jacques and he'd just been better at hiding it.

And where was Mom? There were too many worries banging together in my brain, but I tried to shake some extra space for hearing what the doctor told me about Dad. I felt myself sinking when he used words like "critical" and "blood loss" and "shock." It's pretty sad when "viable limb" and "clean severing" are a conversation's high points.

My body ached and shivered with hunger. I went to the cafeteria. Wilder had given me some emergency cash, and I spent a chunk of it on dinner. The cashier seemed so alarmed by my piled-high tray, I had to offer an explanation.

"I have a parasite," I said.

She looked down as if my eye contact might be contagious.

The cafeteria was mostly dark and empty. I dialed Mom's number over and over. Mom was the one who used to put cool cloths on my head when I had a fever and bring me cold soda and soup. And sing me Spanish songs. And cuddle with me on the couch.

O Mami, me siento tan sola.

By ten in the morning they had reattached Dad's arm, and I was asleep on the hard little couch in his recovery room.

I was dreaming. I was falling. Sleep was not rest.

"Maisie . . ."

I woke up fast. His eyes were barely slits.

"Yeah, Dad, it's me."

"Your mom?"

"Not answering her phone. Did GT have her?"

His eyelids lowered, but he swallowed and spoke. "I don't think so. They got me at the apartment. Your mom was at work. If she went home and found me gone, she would run."

"How do we find her?" I asked.

He grimaced with pain. "I don't know."

His eyes closed for a few seconds and opened again.

"My arm?"

"They're both here."

"Did you . . ." He tried to swallow, his mouth dry. I swabbed his lips and tongue with a sponge-tipped thing the nurse had left. He squinted up at me, his voice a crackling whisper. "Did you hear about the man who lost his left arm? He's all right now."

I smiled. "It was your right arm, Dad. Just like me."

"Oh." His eyes shut. I thought he'd fallen asleep until he spoke again. "Did you hear about the guy who lost his right arm? He's left with the left."

"Yeah, work on that one."

"I will."

His words were barely an exhale when he said, "Maisie, I love you. And this isn't . . . don't worry . . ."

"I love you too, Dad."

I watched him sleep, like maybe he used to watch me. I imagined my infant self, unaware that anything was wrong, and my parents, crying over their baby born without an arm.

Or maybe they really hadn't minded. Maybe they were surprised that first day of kindergarten to see the other kids mocking me. And Mom—or Dad maybe—said, Never mind, then. We'll just keep her home.

And *that* was why I lived a tight little life with nothing much beyond our front yard. Not what GT said, not because my mother was somebody else.

Dad always called Mom *cariña*, which meant sweetheart. He never called her by her name, I realized. He never called her Inocencia.

I lightly touched his bandaged arm. The tips of his fingers were a pale, grayish color and corpse cold. The doctor had said it would take time to see if the reattachment worked.

I dialed Mom again. And again.

CHAPTER 34

Luther.

I woke with his name on my tongue and drool from my open mouth wetting my cheek.

A nurse was coming in to check Dad's blood pressure, so I went into his bathroom. Luther's phone number had sat behind my eyes every day, a forbidden string of numbers. I dialed them now. One of his sisters answered. I tried to disguise my voice when I asked for Luther.

"Hello?"

Luther. My heart buzzed.

"Luthe, don't—"

"Maisie! What the frak—"

"Shut up! Questions later. Listen now. Stuff a backpack with some changes of clothing and as much money as you can—quarters, bills, whatever, but try to get a few hundred dollars. Remember that craft box where your mom hides money? Leave your parents a standard 'don't worry and I'll come home when I can' note with no mention of me, somewhere they won't find it right away. Ride your bike to that one pay phone. I'll call you there."

"Okay," he said.

No argument? No demands? Luther rocked!

"Hurry," I said and hung up.

GT hadn't taken Luther yet. Maybe that meant he didn't know what Luther meant to me. But Wilder did. I'd been vague about the pay phone just in case his phone was bugged. We used to ride our bikes to the corner market to buy Laffy Taffys and would check that pay phone for spare coins.

Seven minutes later I called the pay phone, and he answered.

"Maisie?"

"Oh man, Luthe, it's so great to hear your voice."

"What's going on?"

"Bad guys got my dad and maybe my mom, and I don't want them to get you."

I told him to ride his bike to the downtown bus station, take a bus to Philadelphia, and meet me at the hospital.

"Okay," he said again.

"You're taking this very well," I said.

"Naturally I'd been expecting this sort of a thing ever since you left. Sudden disappearance is the price I pay for being a superhero's best friend."

Best friend. He'd said it. I pinched the top of my nose to keep from crying.

"Be careful, okay? I really don't want you to die."

"Affirmative."

"I missed you, Luthe."

"Yeah, me too."

When I came out of the bathroom, the nurse was gone. Dad was awake.

"Mom?" he asked.

I shook my head. Her phone no longer rang when I called. No way to contact her, and she wouldn't know where to contact us. I only just stopped myself from punching through the wall.

"What is the Yellow Flag?" I asked.

He sighed. "*La Bandera Amarilla*. A militant group. They live in *el Gran Chaco*, a desert wilderness between Paraguay and Bolivia. Your mom grew up with them. Her parents . . ."

"Were soldiers?" I asked.

"In a way." He adjusted in bed, wincing. "Paraguay was controlled by a dictator for a long time. Your grandfather saw his brother tortured. Your grandmother's farm was seized by the government, much of her family shot. They joined an opposition group. That's where your mother was born. Her parents were killed trying to raid an armory when your mom was eighteen. She was wanted too, so she had to leave."

"She'd . . . she'd killed?"

Dad grimaced. "I don't think so. But whatever she did, she was just a kid."

Like me, I thought.

Did that mean I was innocent of Ruth's and Mi-sun's blood? If I, oh, I don't know, murdered Wilder, in twenty years would people say, "Sure she killed the guy, but hey, she was just a kid!"

Dad was saying, "After her parents' death, her community managed to get her falsified papers and into a university in New Mexico. That was where we met. But she was wanted. After we had you, she became even more cautious. She worked from home, made no friends, did nothing to draw notice. She lived in fear of being taken from us and dying in a Paraguayan prison."

"You knew this all along?" I asked.

He nodded. "But I loved her so much." His voice cracked. "I *love* her . . ."

I climbed onto his bed, curling up on his left side, as maybe I used to when I was little. He put his left hand on my cheek, pressing my head to his, and I could feel the wet of his tears.

"We'll find her," I said.

I could feel him nod but he didn't speak. We lay there for a time.

"What's her real name?" I whispered.

"Let's wait until she's back, okay? Let her explain." He shifted in his pillow and groaned with pain. "It can wait."

I hated the word "wait."

I could go to Florida, but how would I find her if she was hiding? Every time I left just to go to the cafeteria, I worried GT's guys would take Dad again, or Jacques would come claim another limb. And who knew what Wilder's plans were? At night I barely slept on my cot, footsteps in the hall bolting me upright.

But at least one knot of worry relaxed when, two days later, Luther stepped into Dad's room.

Late-afternoon sunlight slanted through the window, slicing dust motes in the air. The dust animated with the motion of his entry, dancing around his shoulders, and I imagined they were giddy-happy he was here too.

Personified dust motes, Maisie? I was more tired than I realized.

"Miss," the police sentry started.

"He's okay," I said. "He's family."

The officer shut the door.

Luther was wearing sunglasses. He had Laelaps. I dropped to my knees to pet him. Pet the dog, that is. Not Luther.

"Pretending to be blind so you can bring a dog into a hospital?" I asked.

"And onto a bus. Surprisingly effective."

Dad was asleep. Luther took off his sunglasses, and we stared at each other. I wondered if he thought I looked changed. Luther seemed the same. He wore his puffy orange parka and green knit cap, and with his cheeks ruddy from the cold outside, he looked like an alarmed pumpkin.

He said, "You think I look like a pumpkin."

"No I don't."

"You do. You always make fun of this coat."

I laughed without meaning to.

"Maybe I *want* to look like a pumpkin, did you ever think of that?"

I play-punched him on the shoulder. "I'm glad you're here."

"My parental units are probably freaked out."

"They'd better be."

Luther's mom once told me that even as a baby Luther didn't like to be hugged or kissed. I gathered that once she had some snuggly little girls, she just kind of gave up on her son. He was smart enough to do his homeschool work on his own, and she let him. His dad kept long hours at work, his mom took her girls shopping, and Luther just hung out with me.

My mom wasn't thrilled with Luther's parents. Every time Mom saw Luther, she kissed him on each cheek. She called him *mi hijo*. She stocked our kitchen with his favorite foods.

Thinking about Mom hurt my throat. I blinked rapidly and looked up.

"So tell me what in the frak is going on."

That conversation took us through dinner. We were eating nachos in the back booth of the cafeteria, and I found myself smiling. Despite my dad's arm, my missing mom, my general dead-or-alive status, Luther was here.

The newspaper certainly wasn't giggle-inspiring. A full-color photo of Jacques in a havoc helmet graced the front page under the headline "BLADE RUNNER" ROBS SECOND BANK. The reporter described a young man in a shiny bodysuit who carried two swords. Jacques must have been on his own. GT would never let him be so sloppy.

"Blade Runner," Luther said. "Clever."

"I called him Jack Havoc."

Luther shrugged. "I like Blade Runner better. It's the name of that old sci-fi movie, and you know, Jacques has blades and he's on the run."

"Whatever."

"If we're seeing this, then Wilder is too."

"If Wilder gets to Jacques, he'll either kill him for his token or persuade him to help take me out. I wouldn't have a chance against both of them."

"But cutting off your dad's arm? It seems extreme."

I shivered. "I keep thinking about how Jacques was unbeatable at Name That Tune and then one day he couldn't play it anymore. If the token changed his brain that much, what else did it do to him?"

"But it hasn't changed you. Besides, you know . . ." He stabbed a butter knife against my hand.

"Enough stabbing me!"

"You have to stop that psychopath," he said. "Wilder was right about that much."

"I can't leave Dad to go after Jacques."

Luther held up the newspaper and pointed emphatically at Jacques's face. "Either Wilder will kill him or together they'll kill you. And me. And your dad and mom. At any rate, a lot of killing will go down. You have to go superhero all over this guy."

I raised my eyebrows. "Part of you is loving this."

Luther folded up the paper, keeping his face carefully still, but his eyes were smiling.

CHAPTER 35

I told Dad, made sure the police planned to keep a constant guard, and set out with Luther.

We needed transportation. I resisted calling Howell. Maybe it *was* GT who had gassed our house, but I still couldn't rule her out.

Wilder had left stashes of cash hidden around the city, just in case he ever got cut off from the lair. I chose a location he'd told me about on a busy corner of downtown Philly. I moved in quickly, felt around the backside of an ATM machine, and ripped free a fat envelope.

"A thousand dollars in bills," I told Luther as we headed to a car rental agency. "Not a bad day's work."

Neither of us had a driver's license, so we had to risk using the same rental place Wilder did, where the morning shift guy would take a bribe to look the other way.

We followed new reports of Jacques headed north. It was chilly out but not so bad that we couldn't roll down a window for Laelaps. He'd snap at the wind, his tail thumping the backseat.

Luther bought a police scanner. Jacques's latest assault was a grocery store. He'd filled up his cart, then at the checkout grown a blade from his hand and demanded the cash from the register as well. The store manager stood up to Jacques and got sliced. It sounded like the guy was in pretty critical shape.

"The police can't stop him, Luthe. He's bulletproof when he's armored. If he did get caught somehow, he could grow a blade on his wrists to slice through handcuffs or chop his way out of a jail cell."

"So call the police and warn them."

I looked at Luther hard. He put up his hands.

"I know, I know, you don't have to yell. If someone did believe you, they'd be after your tokens too."

I told him everything as we drove—even Jacques's "no arms, no cake" joke.

"I don't get it," said Luther.

"It's not just me, right? It's not brilliant and witty humor that only the two-handed understand?"

"But then again, I don't get lots of things. Like chicks. And why people say 'chicks.' And why American football isn't called throw-ball. And how come no one's invented a good jet pack yet."

Jet pack! Why hadn't I thought of that when my techno token worked?

The scanner had an update: "Blade Runner" spotted in a stolen car. Soon a police barricade blocked the road. The car was abandoned off road, the front end crumpled against a tree.

"He must be on foot," Luther said.

"What's around here?"

Luther opened a map. He muttered about farms and highways but when he said "Spackman Caverns," I perked up.

"Jacques hates heights. He'd feel safe deep down."

I hopped out. Luther started to get out too.

"Stay with Laelaps. Jacques would use you two against me."

Besides, this was a fireteam matter.

I ran through some woods, keeping away from the police and their dogs. Night was coming on. Against the blue-black sky rose a grand house on a bald hill. A sign read SPACKMAN CAVERNS.

I paused. No sense of Wilder.

The place was closed up and dark. I saw a security guard and hid behind a tree. When the guard ambled around the corner of the house, I ran to the nearest door. The deadbolt was sliced through.

Darkened gift shops, empty corridors. I took the stairs into the cavern's mouth. The rock ceiling started low and then opened up like a basketball arena. Emergency lighting cast a whitish-blue pallor and brown shadows. It was eerie, lonely, and easy to imagine I was the last person on earth.

A massive stalactite hung in the center of the chamber, a spectacular chandelier. I knew from a geology project that stalagmites and stalactites grow only a couple of centimeters every century. A messy fight here would cause irreparable damage. Just in case, I eased the metal bar from a handrail.

Looking over the cavern map, I noted a tunnel leading off from the main chamber that was closed to visitors.

I crawled through the narrow tunnel and into a smaller chamber lit by a single lantern. Jacques was sitting on the far side next to a heap of food, devouring a moon pie. He jumped up when I entered, armor streaking over his limbs, his head. Only his face remained uncovered.

And his face made me angry. I'd come here all set to be calm and convincing, put aside my hostilities in order to lead Jacques away from hurting people. But this was the bleeper who cut off my dad's arm.

I took a deep breath. "Hey Jacques."

"Hey Maisie," he said with no emotion.

I put my hands in my pockets and leaned against the cave wall, trying to imagine what Wilder would say. "Kind of a weird place to hide?"

"I came here on my first trip to the US." His eyes didn't leave me as he finished off his moon pie and tossed the wrapper.

"It sucks that you're doing all this."

"You broke off way before I did *and* took Ruth's token. Nothing could be the same after that."

"And as you recall, you cut off my father's arm."

Panic washed across his face, but he replaced it quickly with a smile.

"How's the old man doing?"

"We're not going to talk about my dad." I stood up straighter, no longer able to affect a casual posture.

"Hey, you brought him up."

"*You're* not going to talk about my dad."

"So what should we talk about? Are you hoping I'll open up, swear to be a good boy, then we'll hug and forget the *bleeping* mortal combat?"

That was pretty much exactly what I was hoping. Except without the *bleeping* part. Or the hug. He did cut off Dad's arm.

"Pre-token Jacques wouldn't do all this," I said.

"Yeah? Well, pre-token Jacques was a *bleepity-bleep* coward."

"There are police crawling through those woods, Jacques, and they'll shoot you in your Achilles' eyeball. Don't you think it'd be better to turn yourself in?"

"What, so they can cut my token out of me and follow up with a lethal injection?" His dimples creased with a painful smile. "There's no going back. And there's no more fireteam. Not after Ruth. Not after I watched our illustrious thinker kill Mi-sun for her token."

Until that moment, I'd been harboring a wish that Wilder was somehow innocent. Jacques's words melted that tiny frozen hope. Wilder had gotten Ruth killed and tried to take her token. He'd killed Mi-sun for hers. And he'd lured me away from my parents to help him kill Jacques.

"The tokens lie," Jacques was saying. "Mine made me feel like I'd be okay if I just stayed with the team, stayed with Wilder. But then Ruth died, and Wilder wouldn't even try to save her. Even after all that, leaving him ripped me in half, Maisie."

I nodded.

"I'm not going to let anyone dunk me with an anchor," he said. "I'm not going to let Wilder kill me and steal my token."

"Well, I don't want your wretched token," I said. "So stop attacking people, calm the bleepity-bleep down, and—"

"Did you just say 'bleepity-bleep'?"

"—and work with me, or we're both toast that Wilder will butter and have for breakfast."

"I *cut off your dad's arm*. You're not going to welcome me into your little house on the prairie."

"Maybe there's a way to . . . to fix it all," I said. I wished I could lie to Jacques as easily as Wilder had to Ruth. And to me. "If you testify against GT, the FBI might let you off. You could start over."

"Start over?" He laughed, though he seemed about to cry too.

"You have no idea all I've done. Last week I tried to go home again. I tried, but I couldn't even . . ." His voice cracked. I hadn't been sure if he was still human enough to feel anything. "Do you remember Ruthless saying she'd done too much? I am in blood. 'Stepped in so far, that, should I wade no more, returning were as tedious as go over.'"

He was quoting *Macbeth* again. He'd forgotten the Beatles but not *Macbeth*.

"Your mom would forgive you," I said. "Moms do that."

He paced, getting closer to the tunnel. I countered, positioning myself before the exit.

"She doesn't know me anymore, and I don't want her to."

Blades formed from both hands, long as scimitars and sharper still. I hefted my iron bar.

"I'm not wasting this power," he said. "I'm never again going to be that kid the school counselor pities or wear clothes that smell like someone else. I'm going to be a GT. I'm going to be the boss."

He took another step forward. I stepped back, my hand tighter on the bar. I could feel molecules of metal readjusting, the bar melding into the shape of my grip.

"What if we're not just killing machines?" I said. "What if there actually is another purpose—"

"GT smartened me up, at least. The only thing my token is good for is making good for me. Let me go, Maisie."

"I can't."

He swiped at me with one of his havoc blades. It made a high, sweet sound as it cut the air, like the ring of a bell.

"Let me out or I'll cut my way out."

"You really think you can take me?" I pretended to laugh, though

I felt sick to my stomach. "You don't remember what it took to stop Ruthless."

"But you're not Ruthless, and I've learned a few things since then."

Jacques's blade came down.

CHAPTER 36

I turned away, his blade just missing Fido and landing instead on my shoulder. The strike stung like the lash of a whip. He came at me slashing, so fast I could barely see the blades. I swung my bar, but he ducked and cut at my side.

I swung my bar again, and he sidestepped. His training showed. I should have joined a dojo or something instead of lying around with Wilder. But of course Wilder didn't want me too powerful. Just powerful enough so I would take Jacques's token before conveniently dying and handing the whole cache over to him.

Anger boiled. I swung harder, swiping just above Jacques's head. He brought his blades down on my outstretched arm, the pain so fierce I dropped the bar.

He was behind me suddenly, a foot on my lower back, climbing to my shoulders and jumping off, using the force of his fall to chop his blades down.

I screamed.

Another useless swipe. He dodged. I wished for Mi-sun's blue shot, for Wilder's plotting.

Keep him fighting, Wilder had said.

I needed to compromise the armor, force Jacques to make new havoc skin. But I couldn't even get a touch. And I was short an arm too, keeping Fido close to my chest. That arm wouldn't survive contact with his scimitar.

I swung with my fist, but his assault was too fast, dodging and cutting, dodging and cutting. My shirt was riddled with slices. He swiped across my middle, getting too close to Fido. Half of the index finger dropped to the ground.

I cried out at the wound done to my cyborg hand, and my attention left Jacques just long enough for him to come in hard. As if he were beating a drum, his blades assailed the back of my neck. Chunks of my ponytail fell around me, the pain so intense my legs buckled. I curled up, my arms wrapped over my middle, shuddering.

Hunched over, shaking from pain, I first realized that Jacques could kill me. I'd felt invulnerable. So had Ruth. Jacques would take my tokens, and then what would he do? Rob more banks? Finish off Dad?

What would Wilder tell me?

Stop trying to hit him. Use your body like a rolling boulder.

I closed my eyes and tried to exchange the pain for anger. When Jacques stepped in for another jab, I threw myself forward. My head caught him in the gut, and he fell on his back. I screamed with the effort of picking him up, and I threw him against the cave wall. The force was enough to crack his armor. He immediately filled in the holes, sealing it up.

He stood up, back on the attack. He was too good at the close game. I retreated and uprooted a stalagmite, thereby undoing thousands of years of slow work with one moment of violence. I kind of hated myself as I threw it at him, striking him in the chest. One of his blades snapped off. Rock beats scissors.

He grew a new blade.

Attacking, he got me on my arm, but I kicked his legs out from under him. I picked him up by a leg and slammed his body against the ground three times before he flipped out of my grasp. One of his blades and a large piece of armor fell off. He formed it anew.

I saw his glance flick to the corner, where he had a stash of food. He was running out of fuel.

My skin was covered with welts and screaming with pain. I screamed back and flew at him. When he sliced at me, I grabbed the blade and broke it off in my hand. My palm was bleeding, the pain as intense as if I'd been stabbed clean through.

He formed another blade, and I broke it off again. I got ahold of his leg and slammed him against the ground, then attacked his armor, clawing off whole sections. He tried to crawl away, but I held him fast. And he kept forming more. And more. The hollows underneath his eyes were sunken, the whites of his eyes yellowed.

He didn't have anything left to draw from. But he kept at it. I tore off his chest armor and he made more.

"Stop it!" I yelled. "Stop! Just give up!"

I got my fingers into the hole in his armor around his eyes and broke it off his face. He gasped. I pulled, and the armor cracked all down his front, weak as shale rock. For the first time, no new havoc skin grew.

"'The yellow leaf,'" he mumbled, his head lolling back and forth. "'The yellow leaf...'"

"What?" I said.

He tried to sit up but slumped back. More armor splintered

and fell away. Jacques was gaunt. His T-shirt sagged, sticking with sweat to his shaking body. His skin was mottled, dried up in patches. I stumbled backward, feeling as if I'd just opened a closet door and discovered a monster. The nanite-enhanced bacteria had run out of fuel to grow more armor and so pulled from his own muscles, bones, and skin. He took a shuddering breath and his eyes rolled, staring at the cave wall but not seeing. He moaned.

"Jacques, why?" I whispered.

He flopped onto his side and looked at the food in the corner. If he ate, would he recover as quickly as he'd broken down? I didn't think I could fight him again. My body felt like grated cheese. I wiped wetness from my cheeks and realized I'd been crying.

The bags were heavy with soda and energy bars. I drizzled soda into his mouth, and he gulped softly. Then I tore off a chunk of a bar and stuck it in his mouth, eating the rest myself. I picked up my iron bar, intending to guard him in case that much food could bring him back to action, but he seemed unable to chew. And I apparently wasn't able to stand. I collapsed, my body trembling as if I were freezing cold.

Jacques whimpered, a sound like Luther's baby sister used to make when falling asleep. I crumpled forward, huddled on the cave floor, washed over with ache. The pain in my hand was louder now that I was still to listen to it, a shrieking that seemed almost audible.

The bite of energy bar settled throughout my body and brought a small, hopeful satisfaction, so I crawled over and fell onto the bags. I ate another bar and drank a soda, wishing it were water. The carbonation irritated my sensitive tongue and went down like a swarm of bees.

"Jacques," I croaked, holding out a bar. "Jacques, can you eat? If you . . . if you promise not to stab me anymore . . ."

He turned his head away, mouth closed. I didn't have the strength to insist. I thumped back down into the mound of wrappers and kept eating. When I felt strong again, I would carry Jacques out to the police and tell them . . . what? Not to feed him? To put him in a cell too thick to cut?

I was wondering over this, trying to imagine what solution Wilder could come up with, when I heard a noise at the cave's entrance and rolled over, expecting to see Luther.

"Hello, Miss Brown," said Howell.

She was wearing a brown canvas shirt, pants, and shoes, as if trying to be a caricature of an explorer. Dragon crawled through the tunnel behind her, followed by three security guys I thought of as the triplets: Hairy, Scary, and Larry. Hairy was the one with the bushy beard, Scary had this wide-eyed stare, and Larry's name really was Larry. They never talked much. Also, they weren't really triplets.

"Jacques still has a tracker in his ankle?" I said thickly.

Howell nodded. "I couldn't get to him when he was with GT." She crouched over him. "What happened?"

"He pulled all the energy out of his own body to make havoc armor," I said.

Howell felt Jacques's pulse, and her eyes widened. I shivered. He wasn't dead. He couldn't be dead. The food in my stomach felt heavy and foreign, and I glanced at the wrappers to prove to myself that I hadn't accidentally eaten rocks.

"Come here." Howell's voice was urgent. "I need you to place your hand on his chest."

Dread thudded into my chest, harder and louder than the pain of my skin. I scooted away, my back to a rock wall.

"His heart has stopped," she said. "He's not coming back. In moments, those nanites will reenter the token and it will leave his body. If that token doesn't bond with you, it will tear out of his body and leave gravity—rise right up through the cave roof, through the atmosphere and into space."

"What? How do you know that?"

"I know."

"But—gravity? Nothing should—"

Howell spoke quickly. "I've spent years studying these. That token will go straight through the rock ceiling like it went through the skin of Jacques's palm. Once it leaves Earth, its momentum will keep it going. Retrieval might be impossible."

Gone? A token gone, gone forever, don't let it, don't let it go—

"Good," I said, but I could barely cough the word out it was such a lie. Along with increased tolerance of cold and other upgrades, the tokens came with an insistence of their own importance. I knew I was just a wasp-stung caterpillar, but I still felt an urgency to protect the tokens, as if they were babies or puppies or something.

"I won't lose any of them, I've worked so hard," said Howell. "Come here."

I shook my head. I felt torn up inside and out—my nanite-infused body wanted me to do it, and whatever was left of me didn't.

"Do you comprehend how precious and important these are?" she said. "Losing a single token would be like ... like losing the Louvre. Or the Great Barrier Reef. Or Cairo."

Howell hadn't experienced the agony of the token ripping through her body. I didn't want the agony. I didn't want Jacques's token. I didn't want proof that he was dead—that I'd helped kill him.

"Maisie—"

"No!"

Dragon picked me up. I pushed him away, sending him to the ground.

Hairy, Larry, and Scary approached, hands in fists.

"Really?" I said.

Dragon glanced back. Howell nodded. He and his guys attacked.

I suppose it was good that I was slowed and tired with pain, so when I backhanded the three guys at once, I didn't crack their skulls. From behind Dragon grabbed me around my waist, picking me up. He was so much bigger than I was, I couldn't get away without hurting him. I elbowed him (gently) in the face. He let go.

"Sorry," I said. I didn't want to break opera-humming Dragon's nose.

"Maisie!" Howell's voice had reached a new pitch of panic.

We all froze, watching as the token rose up through Jacques's chest. The skin didn't split or crack, just lifted a little, while the token, bright and teeming with nanites, crept up. The atoms of the token must have been sliding between the atoms of the skin, reconnecting with one another on the other side. Dragon tried to push me forward, and I knocked him away, my eyes never leaving Jacques.

I imagined the token shooting up through the cave wall, up into the night sky, propelled by its momentum on and on forever, and the idea made my skin hurt worse. My own tokens felt hot in my chest, my thoughts were slippery. I wanted to tell myself it was okay, Jacques's token didn't matter, but I couldn't seem to grab hold of that thought. I was all ache and need and fear, and the vague but fevered certainty that losing that token would be very bad.

Howell trembled. "Maisie, please . . ."

It was almost out, one tip still sliding free of skin.

"No," I whispered.

The token freed itself from Jacques's body, and Howell snatched at it, desperate. She screamed in pain. It was entering her palm. I thought it was bonding with her till I saw its tips rising out the back of her hand. I sucked in a breath.

Suddenly it was free, rising up so fast it seemed to be falling the wrong way, gravity working in reverse. In moments it would be through the cave roof and into the sky. Lost. Gone.

Get it, save it, save it. Now!

I slammed my feet against the ground, jumping as high as the cavern ceiling. I swung my arm, my fingertips barely swiping at the cold, rubbery token. That was all it took—the barest touch. It clung to my fingers. I was falling when it slid into my palm. I tucked my arms against my chest, taking the fall as a roll, slamming into the ground and up against a cave wall.

Now I was screaming. The crash hurt my wounded skin, but that was nothing compared to the icy burn slicing through my palm, up my arm. I clutched my sides and folded in half, sobbing so hard I couldn't close my mouth. I couldn't see, couldn't hear, the sharpness exploding against my heart like a bomb. It couldn't have lasted long, but each second dragged me along hollering in agony.

When it was over, I gasped, sat up, and wiped tears off my cheeks. I was near Jacques. I looked at his gaunt face and remembered—not the worst or the best. Just him. The way he looked when he smiled, cheek dimples and bright-brown eyes. How he could hit the high notes in a song. How he'd close his eyes when taking the first sip of a soda.

I was leaning over myself, crying, and I noticed through my shredded sleeves that the welts on my arms were gone. Even though the new token was healing my wounds, I felt alarmingly weak, covered in paper-thin skin, built of gelatinous muscles and straw bones. I looked at my chest. The brute token had lightened, like the techno token. Jacques's havoc token was dark reddish-brown, a brand-new brand. Bleep, bleep, bleep, what had I done?

The brute token had been inside me for months, indestructibility my norm. Now those nanites were undoing their work to let the new nanites take over.

I had never in all my life been so aware of my skin. So much texture, entire ecosystems between my fingers, inside my ears, between my eyelashes. I couldn't see the new bacteria growing now on my skin, but I felt prickly in a pleasant way.

"I'm hungry," I whispered.

Dragon trolled through the food pile and handed me a moon pie. His nose was bleeding, but he smiled.

"Thank you, Maisie," Howell whispered. She was holding her head, her eyes closed. She'd never called me Maisie before today.

Laelaps padded into the cavern, Luther crawling in after him. Laelaps sniffed Jacques's body and came to me, licking my chin. Laelaps knew me. Maybe I was still essentially Maisie.

"Who?" Luther asked, pointing to our company.

"Howell, etc.," I said.

"Isn't she sort of evil?"

I threw up my hands. "Argh! Who isn't anymore?"

Luther raised his hand with mock timidity. "Me," he mouthed. He pointed at me and mouthed, "You?" with a questioning look.

Laelaps was still licking me. I chose to believe that meant I wasn't evil yet.

CHAPTER 37

We checked Dad out of the hospital, loaded him into one of Howell's planes, and flew to HAL.

I had to ask, "Howell, did you gas our house?"

"No."

"Did your guys chase us in cars with guns?"

"No."

"Promise?"

"Yes."

"I'll come back to Team Howell if you find my mom."

"Done."

"Okay."

I needed someone who could bring my mom home and protect my dad and Luther while I went after the Wild Card. Because that was nonnegotiable. Anyone else he killed before I could lock him up would be my fault.

"What happened to your hair?" Luther asked.

I could feel the ragged edges brushing my cheek.

"Jacques and some havoc scimitars," I said.

"So Wilder will be your next kill?"

I choked. "What? I'm not an assassin! I'm going to capture Wilder and lock him in a HAL thinker-proof cell."

"Maybe you *should* kill him."

"Shut up, Luther." I knew he didn't mean it. He was just mad that I'd lost my brute strength for a power he deemed infinitely less cool.

I stayed at HAL for three days while I practiced being Maisie Havoc. Covering myself with armor was as easy as a thought, my brain sending a signal through my nerves to the bacteria to grow havoc. I quickly learned that, when first growing the armor over my body, I had to move around to keep it nimble. After a few seconds it set, and if I hadn't bent my elbow, for example, my arm would be stuck straight. I'd have to remove the havoc skin and start over, which took a lot of fuel. I could only stand to eat so many energy bars.

To release the armor I simply thought about it, an action like flexing a muscle, and cracks would form. I wasn't sure exactly how that worked. Perhaps it was a coordinated effort with the bacteria to eat through the armor along those lines.

"My mom?" I asked Howell.

"I have a crew already in Florida," she said. "This morning I sent some of my best security guys to help lead the search, but no news yet."

Dad was stable but still recovering, so Howell's doctors took care of him. The triplets taught me to throw knives—I used havoc blades. Hairy taught me some hand-to-hand fighting techniques. And I ate. And ate and ate. And talked with my dad. While eating.

Nights were hard. Often when I closed my eyes, there was Ruth, writhing on the ship's deck. Now wide-eyed Mi-sun joined her, and Jacques, gaunt and shivering.

One night when everyone was asleep, I searched "the yellow leaf" online. Jacques's last words. Macbeth the doomed king spoke them too, in a speech near the end of his life.

I have lived long enough: my way of life
Is fall'n into the sere, the yellow leaf.

I read on till unexpected sadness sharpened into my heart. I didn't have the energy to mourn the person Jacques had become. Not with Dad hurt. Not with Mom missing.

I pled with the ghosts behind my eyes to let me be, and I fell asleep.

I woke in a sweat, my heart pounding. I bolted upright, pulsing with panic that there was something I was supposed to do.

Wilder.

He was willing to kill to get all the tokens, and I had three buried against my heart. He'd come after me. And if I stayed by Dad, he'd be a target too.

I wouldn't wait to be hunted. With two working tokens, Wilder had the advantage, but I wouldn't be facing him alone.

Soon after dawn, I kissed Dad's forehead, bumped knuckles with Luther, and got back in one of Howell's jets.

"You're sure they'll be safe?" I asked Howell for the second time. Or twentieth.

"Who?" she asked.

"My dad and Luther," I said. She'd probably been teasing, but you never knew with Howell.

"HAL is well defended. It would take an army."

Go, go, go, I chanted silently at the air. Though I was dreading meeting Wilder, I needed to be done with it already. To distract myself, I went through my suitcase of stuff I'd left behind at HAL after Ruth died. My old clothes. My orange jumpsuit. My brush and hair elastics (ouch). My impact boots! I put them on.

And Wilder's papers. I read through them again. So little information. His elective: soccer. Why? Because he was good at it. His chosen position: commander. Why? Because there was no point to anything if he wasn't in charge.

We transferred to a helicopter at a private airstrip outside Philadelphia. Wilder had disabled the tracker Howell put in his ankle. The only way to find him was fireteam hide-and-seek. I directed Dragon to start near the lair and then fly over all the places he and I had gone together.

Wilder would want me to find him. He wanted what I had, and he'd be confident he could take it. I remembered his swagger, his brazen smile. And then I started remembering lots of stuff I didn't want to.

I was guzzling a chocolate milk when I felt that twinge of the thinker. I looked out the window and laughed. He was where I'd left him a week ago, still waiting in that empty warehouse. He could have blue shot us out of the sky. Maybe he *didn't* want me dead.

Then again, maybe he just wouldn't risk killing me until my tokens were within arm's reach.

Dragon touched us down at the nearest helipad, far enough away that I could no longer sense Wilder, and therefore Wilder could no longer sense me. We sat and let night come. We'd all seen Mi-sun's blue shot pierce solid steel. The only armor that could stop it was mine, but making body armor for the others would deplete me. Night would hide us at least.

I watched the February sun get messy in the horizon, turning all goldy-rosy, making a show of going down.

"Maybe Wilder is innocent," I said to Dragon.

He nodded. "Maybe."

Jacques could be wrong. Brutus could be wrong. The butterflies in my stomach mutating into angry hornets could be wrong.

Dad called me on Dragon's cell.

"If you see Mom before I do," I said, "tell her the *te-quieros* and *te-extraños*, okay?" The I-love-yous, I-miss-yous. The words that tried and failed to convey pure emotion.

"She knows," he said. "You're doing more than any kid should, Maisie."

"I didn't say no," I said.

"You shouldn't have had to."

The sunset didn't last long. Dragon and the triplets left. They called Howell when they were in position outside the warehouse.

Howell nodded at me. My body felt vibrant and tense, in full fight-or-flight mode. Fight, just fight. I was going to see Wilder for the first time since I'd heard that he killed Mi-sun. But he was still Wilder.

The hornets in my belly turned vicious.

Howell had one of her guys drive me to the warehouse—he stayed on back roads, used no lights. The speed took my breath. The world is a scary place when you used to be invulnerable.

The closer I got, the brighter that beacon. Wilder was there. And now he knew I was here too. No need to be quiet. The driver screeched to a stop and I jumped out, growing armor over my clothes, over Fido, covering everything but my face. I wondered if Wilder could see me running from the car, wiggling every part of me from neck to fingers as I went so the joints would stay supple. I wondered if he'd laugh.

As soon as I reached Dragon, he cut the chain off the back doors and slid them open. The triplets ran forward and took up position in the dark room, never lowering their huge guns.

I peered in. There were stairs going up. Hairy made toward them. He stepped on something that crackled.

Pop.

The room filled with gas. I jumped back, holding my breath, and all four men dropped to the floor.

CHAPTER 38

I ran to Dragon first, felt a timid pulse in his neck, grabbed his ankles, and dragged him back into the freezing night. The effort made me sweat under my armor. I hated myself for being so weak.

"Please, please," I muttered. I felt his pulse again, squeezed his hand. I didn't want to leave him.

I went back for Hairy, calling Howell on Fido.

"Wilder gassed the room. They're all out—alive but unconscious."

How do you out-think the thinker? He guessed which door we would come in. He set a trap to get rid of everyone but me. I'd assumed GT had gassed my parents' house. I needed to stop assuming things.

"Don't go after him alone, Maisie," Howell said in my ear. "That's what he wants."

"I have to," I said, grunting as I dragged out Larry, the final triplet. "I have to get him focused on me instead of these guys, so you can get them to a hospital. Besides, if I don't deal with him now—"

"Maisie—"

"I'm going." I disconnected and ran back in before I lost my nerve.

I missed the strength of my legs propelling me forward. I missed feeling like Supergirl. The havoc skin was thick and dead feeling, a mummy costume.

I slowed at the stairs, scanning for other traps, gas-bomb triggers. The stairs creaked and I turned around, expecting to see Wilder behind me. I was alone.

Well, not alone. I could sense Wilder, though I couldn't hear anything beyond my own shaking breaths.

He's not going to kill you, I told myself. And you don't have to kill him.

It was almost easier to track Wilder in the dark, with nothing to distract me from that agonizingly beautiful pull. Up the stairs. To the right. Through a door. The room was dark and large, cluttered with crates and abandoned office furniture.

I crouched behind an upturned desk, trying to slow my breaths. He'd be able to sense my general direction and nearness, but I didn't want to give him an exact target.

"Man, you took a long time," he said from somewhere.

Through a crack in the desk, I watched him come closer, and the little moonlight from the windows picked his shape out of the dark. He was wearing the same plaid button-down shirt and jeans he had a week ago, and he looked tired and unshowered. His hands were in his pockets, and he leaned against a crate.

I should attack him right now, I thought. Bind him with havoc bands before he has a chance to attack. Fast, Maisie!

I didn't. My muscles felt like clay, my bones like twigs.

"I've been waiting for, like, a week," he said, humor in his voice. Maybe we *could* talk this through. I stood up.

"Hey, Danger Girl," he said.

My stomach turned cold. I loved his voice. I loved his face. He murdered Mi-sun. He apparently pretended to love me so I would help him get Jacques's token. After all that, I'd assumed my feelings for him would just dissolve.

"Hey, Wild Card," I said.

"So . . . I take it Mr. Havoc is dead," he said. "I bet taking a third token stings like the devil."

"Why are you doing all this?" I asked, my voice cracking a little.

He leaned his head back, looking at the ceiling. "Don't be a cliché, Maisie. That's what everyone would ask."

"Poor Mi-sun . . ."

"I figured you must have found out about that when you crushed your earpiece."

"Wilder . . ." I had to say it, though I knew it couldn't possibly help. "You and I *are* the fireteam. We're not competition."

"I'm not here to compete with you," he said. "I'm here to take your tokens. If your death is the only means, then I'm truly sorry."

I'd been prepping myself for his charming assurance that I'd gotten it all wrong and he was still on my side. I'd expected him to flatter, swear his innocence, sweet-talk me, so his words stung like sand thrown in my eyes. Since I was no longer the powerful brute, he didn't need to use chivalry or trickery. Or kisses.

"Seriously, Wilder, were you always such a douche bag?"

"*You* destroyed the fireteam when you took Ruth's token. If I'd gotten it, the four of us would still be together."

"I didn't mean to—"

"Didn't you? You were pretty quick to rush in and save some-one who never liked you."

"I was valuing the sanctity of life," I said grandly. Inside I winced. Hadn't Ruth liked me eventually? A little bit?

"So from your track record, I assume you're here to fight me," he said.

"I didn't kill Ruthless. You—"

"You winched her up and dropped her in the ocean. You're the one who figured out she'd barely paid attention in scuba class and wouldn't make decompression stops."

"But—"

"You hunted down Jacques and killed him for his token. And now here you are, coming after me with a team of heavily armed men."

Enough. My fist clenched, the armor squeaking. I was stalling so I didn't have to fight him. And he was toying with me.

I rushed him, my armor covering my face except for my eyes.

He lunged away, shouting, "Yeah! Bring it!"

He shot me with a handful of screws. I dived behind the desk, but the screws burned holes straight through. I shielded my eyes with my havocked arm, and just in time to feel the pings of screws hit. The armor held.

I waited for him to reach into his bag for more ammo, then stood and threw two havoc knives, aiming for his legs. One grazed his leg, the other stuck in a crate behind him.

He pulled it out, smiling. I'd just given him ammo that could cut through my armor.

I started to run, but he shot the havoc knife. There was a blind-ing streak of blue. The knife cut through the havoc armor over Fido and stuck into the arm itself. In the second I paused to look, Wilder must have scavenged my other knife because he shot again, slicing Fido clean off. The hand and forearm that had felt like my own now dropped dead to the floor. Just a few centimeters remained attached, looking like charred flesh. Phantom pains pierced me.

I dislodged the remainder of my arm and threw it back at Wilder, too angry to think. Angry not just that Fido was broken, but that *he'd* broken it. More than ever, I felt how every kiss had made me vulnerable. I wasn't a fierce warrior. I was a stupid girl who let myself get duped.

He picked up the broken piece of Fido and shot it at me. How fitting if it had torn right through my head and ended it all, but his shot went wide. I couldn't depend on the next one missing me. I had to keep moving.

I switched my impact boots to "hop," slammed my feet down, and shot into the air.

"Whoa," he said, and I knew he hadn't been expecting that. The Great and Powerful Thinker had never seen my impact boots.

I grabbed a metal beam, grew a havoc hook where Fido had been, and using hand and hook swung from rafter to rafter. I hefted myself up and quietly crawled through a few more rafters, huddling in a recess of the ceiling. In his surprise, Wilder had hesitated, so by the time he started to fire again, he'd lost me. His thinker-tracking ability wasn't exact, and the moonlight of the windows didn't reach this high. I prayed the lights were off because the warehouse didn't have power. If he could turn them on, I'd be an easy target.

Blue streaks peppered the ceiling in sweeping arcs, lug nuts and screws ripping through the metal roof. A couple hit the back of my head with bruising power. On his next sweep, something large struck my jaw. I swallowed a whimper of pain. My blood tasted like a mouthful of quarters.

The blue shots slowed. Each strike thinned my armor, and I had to layer new skin over the dents. I grew a blade in my havoc hook arm, turning it into a scythe—so sharp the edge was made up of single molecules. It would cut off Wilder's arm with the gentlest nudge. It would slice through his ribs, right into his heart. My arm trembled.

Wilder was almost under me now, walking as he peered into the rafters to my right.

I switched my boots to "impact" and dropped ten meters down behind him. Wilder started to turn. My blade arm was already lifted, my insides fiery with hatred. I could end Jonathan Wilder. I brought my blade down—

And stopped, the blade millimeters from his neck. *I'm not Jacques. I'm not Ruthless. I'm Maisie Danger Brown.* Instead, I slapped him with the flat of the blade against his head.

He stumbled forward, turning to shoot at me as I ran away. Something large struck me in my back, and I fell facedown. He was shooting cut pipes now, the kind Mi-sun had put through tank armor. My breath was knocked out of me so hard, for a few seconds I wasn't sure I'd ever get it back. And when I did, I almost wished I hadn't. I *hurt*.

I ran again, growing more havoc skin over my back. He struck again, this time in my right leg. I fell flat on my face as another pipe flew just over my head.

Get up. Run, Maisie.

I switched my boots back to "hop" and scrambled to my feet. The pain in my right leg was so bad my stomach twisted, and I wanted to retch. I slammed my left foot down and shot into the air, pitching to one side. My armored head struck the roof as I grabbed a rafter. I swung to a new position and clung there, shaking. Whenever I lifted my arm, pain pierced my left side. Broken ribs?

Blue shot streaked around me, some hitting, but I stifled a cry, holding my breath.

Attack, I told myself. Go attack.

Several of my bones were broken. My Fido arm was gone. I felt cut in half, shattered, and defenseless. I'd had the chance to kill him and I hadn't.

"Come on, Maisie! This is a sorry game of hide-and-seek!"

The roof seemed to tilt, and I clung on, shutting my eyes, too dizzy to see.

An image of Jacques hovered behind my lids, starved beneath his crumbling armor. Not gonna happen.

I'd come equipped with four camelbacks—those backpacks made to carry water for long hikes, though mine were filled with high-calorie energy drinks. I wore them against my skin, under my armor. I removed my mouth armor and put a straw in my mouth, draining one of the camelbacks. My fingers and toes shivered.

Wilder was shooting the ceiling a few meters away. "Throw some more of those homegrown knives, Maisie. That was a brilliant idea."

I removed my scythe hook, hiding it up in the rafters out of his reach. Apparently I couldn't make myself use a lethal weapon. Instead I grew an arm over Fido's absence, ending in a havoc fist.

I jumped down behind him and punched him in the head.

He turned to shoot, off-balance from my strike, and missed as my boots shot me back in the air. My broken right leg screamed at me, so I tucked it up, landing on just my left and hitting Wilder again as I descended, a left-right punch. He shot, but I was back in the air. I switched to "impact" while still arching over his head, and then landed and stayed. He was expecting another hop and aimed high. So while he shot over my shoulder, I struck him in the face.

I'd hit Hairy a few times when he tutored me. Hairy could take a punch. Wilder could not. He stumbled back.

I punched him again, getting him in the mouth. It felt really good. He fumbled for his bag of metal ammo, but I grew a short blade and sliced the bag from his side, throwing it as far as I could.

He faked left, then dived right for a loose pipe. I kneed him in the gut. It hurt my broken leg, but not as much as it hurt Wilder. He coughed and fell over, and I held his wrists together, growing havoc handcuffs over them and sealing in his dangerous fingers. I kneed him again to slow him down so I could call Howell—wait, he'd killed my phone.

How was I going to get him outside? I was hobbled, and he was stronger. His weapon hands were encased in havoc, but could he simply shoot them off? I grabbed his ankles, cuffing those as well.

"Don't you dare truss me up," he said, still coughing from my kick. "Cut me loose and let's end this!"

"No." I bounced on my left foot, my broken leg keeping me from pacing. Could I risk leaving him alone while I went for help? Could I drag him out on my own?

He muttered something in Russian.

"Translation?" I said.

He didn't reply. He was rubbing his chin against his shoulder as if to scratch an itch, but he must have had a little pouch there, because there was a rip and then he was holding something white in his teeth. I leaped for him but he kicked me back, closed his lips over whatever it was, and chewed. His smile was so wicked it made my knees shake.

"Never mess with the thinker," he said. "I always have a backup plan."

Had his thinker-self found some drug that would increase the power of his shooter-self? Any second the bonds over his hands might crack in an electric-blue burst. I took a step back and grew a blade.

He lifted his cuffed hands, still smiling. I hopped behind a pile of crates. I waited. No sound.

I peeked. Wilder was lying down. His hands were still shielded. His eyes were closed.

"Wilder?"

He didn't move. I stepped out.

"Wilder, are you playing possum?"

Blade forward, I walked to him and nudged his foot with my armored boot. Really scientific, Maisie. Might as well poke him with a stick.

"Wilder?" I said again. I knelt over him, releasing the armor from my fingers so I could search for a pulse at his neck, a breath from his nose, any sign of life. Nothing.

Wilder was dead.

CHAPTER 39

My head felt thick, my body so buried in armor I seemed to be falling into it, deep into nothing, away from life and movement and toward numbness.

Wilder had gambled on some trick pill to make him more powerful, but it had backfired and stopped his heart. My own heart was going rapid fire.

I felt in his mouth to make sure his tongue wasn't blocking his throat. But I was more robot than flesh, so I released the havoc skin from my upper body. It clattered to the floor.

Maybe the trick was the pill made him seem dead. He'd wake now that I was unarmored and vulnerable. I stood back.

He didn't wake.

"Not like Ruthless," I said, and started chest compressions with my one hand. If I could keep his heart pumping, his tokens would stay put. I wouldn't have to choose between losing them and claiming them. I started to cry—a crazy-girl, bewildered sobbing.

I winced with every press, afraid to feel his tokens rising, angry that he would really die and put me through this, and then laughing like a *loca* because I was in this nightmare again, killing someone and trying to save him at the same time.

"Wilder!" I slapped him across the face. "Breathe!"

He didn't breathe. I held my hand to his chest, about to do more compressions, but stopped short. The skin of my hand tingled. Was I feeling the electricity of his tokens, nanites zooming in, ready to abandon his body? If they came out, I would have to fight that nanite-inspired urge to keep the tokens safe. Last time I had lost that fight. I couldn't bear the agony again.

The pain of that decision seemed to throb in my crushed leg, my broken ribs, building and tightening in my chest. I leaned over him and gave him mouth-to-mouth. It was pointless. Without compressions his heart would never restart. I wouldn't take his tokens, but I didn't want them lost to outer space either. And I didn't want to let someone else die. I couldn't face Wilder's ghost in my nightmares.

I breathed into his mouth. I breathed and breathed and breathed—

Ow. OW! Fierce pain in my chest. I tried to push away from Wilder, but it had already begun—his tokens, twisting together, white as light, rising from his chest and sinking directly into mine. They were supposed to go through hands! No fair!

I grabbed the ends as they dug into me. That made the pain even more brilliant, like reaching into my own gut and trying to pull out my organs. The freezing heat ripped through my sternum and slammed against my heart with a force that knocked me back and made me briefly blind and deaf to the world. My whole chest was fiercely hot, then ice cold, then numb right before the explosion of pain. The other times seemed gentle to me now. Wilder's tokens burned, as if someone stuck his hand right into my chest, like a bully might grab your shirt, and twisted my heart and lungs in his fist. I wanted to die. I wanted to die, die, die . . .

My broken ribs snapped back into place, my jaw straightened, my leg flamed, nanites fixing up their host body, healing my injuries while my chest was ravaged.

No. I would not be responsible for another death. Wilder did *not* get to haunt me alongside Ruth, Mi-sun, and Jacques. Clawing my way free from the torture, seizing back my strength, I put my hand on his chest and restarted compressions.

Power roared through my muscles as the brute token lit up inside me. I became more aware of Wilder's body, the give of his ribs beneath the heel of my hand. The ease with which I could crack them, even push my hand straight through his chest.

A heartbeat.

Maybe I just sensed my own heartbeat in my hand. I lay my ear against his chest.

Two heartbeats, stuttered and unsure. A raised chest. A breath.

First-aid training at boot camp had neglected to tell us what to do once the CPR actually worked. Did I stop compressions? Or did his heart still need some help to keep going? I held my breath and listened to his; I put my hand on his chest. Train cars of palpitations, one coming after another.

I picked him up and ran.

We were on the third floor. I kicked through a window, jumped, and literally hit the ground running. It was probably jarring for Wilder. I might have saved his life, but I wasn't worried if he got roughed up a bit, seeing as how he'd been trying to kill me.

I was on autopilot, running the same route I'd taken with my father in my arms. The irony made me angrier. Whatever those random aliens made the tokens for, I was pretty sure it wasn't to turn me into a glorified ambulance service. I actually tried to dial Howell on my Fido phone before remembering again.

I glanced down at Wilder's face, unconscious, lying against my shoulder. My heart twitched. I remembered looking forward to waking up every day, knowing he was next to me. I'd never hated anyone before. After Jacques amputated my father's arm, there was anger, disgust, and confusion. Not this boiling, steaming, crushing hate.

A robot wouldn't hate, but a robot, programmed with ethics and justice, would save Wilder. There was some comfort in that. I believed I still made sense if I acted like a robot.

There's something I'm forgetting. Something I need to do, now, now, now . . .

The nagging thought rode me as I ran. Whatever task I was forgetting could wait.

Howell was probably at the hospital with Dragon and the triplets. Waiting for my call. She'd have backup, people to guard her injured men, people who could guard Wilder too.

There's something else I need to do . . . what is it?

I ignored the thought and ran harder, leaping, sometimes cracking the pavement when I came down from a bound. Wilder moaned.

"Stay unconscious or I *will* kill you," I said.

Whether he heard my warning or was genuinely comatose, his eyes didn't open.

"I'm back," I said, rushing through the emergency room doors. "This one chewed a white pill and seconds later his heart stopped. I did CPR, and he came back. Don't know what he ate, but I bet traces will be stuck in his molars. The cuffs on his hands and ankles will dissolve in about ten hours. After that, keep him tied up. He's dangerous and wanted by the police."

Wilder was on a gurney, EMTs wheeling him away, when a gray-haired orderly approached me. She wasn't shy about looking me over—havoc armor covering my feet and legs up to my waist, and my right arm that ended well shy of a wrist.

"You brought in a man a few days ago with an amputated right arm. You had yours then. Where is it now?"

"My right arm? It's—" I looked at my stump, then patted my sides as if checking my pockets. "Now where did I put that?"

She did not look amused. "Police are on their way. You better stay put."

"Sure," I said. "I love police. Who doesn't? Hey, my friend came here about an hour ago, Bonnie Howell, crazy lady with frizzy hair. She had four big guys with her who were unconscious."

"Not here," said watcher lady.

"You're sure?" This was by far the nearest hospital.

"Crazy lady with frizzy hair and four big guys would stand out. You've got a lot of stories. I'm sure the police will love to hear them."

"Yeah, I just need to borrow your phone to call the police and let them know about the *dangerous criminal* you just wheeled away."

She indicated a hospital courtesy phone and then pointed at her eyes and back at me, an "I'm watching you" gesture. I nodded. I'd be suspicious of me too.

I phoned the cute detective who had helped me after Dad's amputation and told him Jonathan Wilder had tried to kill me and then apparently OD'd on something. He said he was on his way and told me to stay put. I didn't have any plans, besides taking over the cafeteria ASAP.

But there's something I need to do . . .

Maybe I was just worried about Dad and Mom. I dialed the first few numbers of Howell's cell, thinking about building a Fido 2. I flinched reflexively. I couldn't rebuild Fido. Techno token had turned off for good.

No. I looked at the phone in my hand and understood how it worked. I glanced around the hospital, all the gadgets beeping and humming as if whispering their secrets to me. Techno token, like brute token, was alive again. And havoc token? I grew a tip to my finger to test it.

I hung up the phone and went to the bathroom. The watcher lady harrumphed so I'd know she was still watching. I waved politely and shut the door.

There was a piece of grout in the corner, loose between two tiles. I picked it up and shot it back at the floor, my hand tingling, a zip of blue marking its path. Four tokens. And the fifth?

Could I think better than normal? It was hard to test. But I stood in front of the mirror and examined my sternum. All five tokens, intertwined, all the same shade of dark brown. I traced the circle of the thinker token, the one that tied the other four together.

I was so busy saving Wilder and hating Wilder that I hadn't thought of it. I had everything. All five tokens. All five powers.

I was sitting on the tile floor before I'd realized I'd fallen. It was a pathetic faint, no dramatic swoon, no out-flung arm and darkness all around. I just wilted and thumped.

I'm sitting on a public bathroom floor, I thought. Ew.

And that made me wonder if I could be harmed by bacteria and viruses like normal, tokenless people. I didn't remember getting sick since our trip up the Beanstalk. Could I get a cold? Or food poisoning? Or that Jumper Virus? And why was I wasting time worrying about this inconsequential crap when Wilder might be brain dead or escaping or—

Something I need to do now, a purpose for all this.

The nagging warning was driving me crazy—a fat fly that buzzes you awake. I stood up and looked in the mirror. The marks were all the same shade of brown. The four tokens fit around the circle of the thinker token, extra spokes and circles tying the five tokens together into a complete symbol.

The design caught my breath. I'd seen it before. But that was impossible. When we'd held the tokens in Midway Station, they'd been as much liquid as solid. How could anyone know what shape each token would take inside a person, let alone the symbol they'd form if all five came together? And yet I felt sure I'd seen something like it.

And then I remembered. At HAL. When we ate dinner in Howell's office the night before the Beanstalk ride, Howell had been doodling on a scrap of paper. She'd made a design a lot like this symbol.

Maybe it was the thinker token, but all those little loose pieces went snapping into place, and I could see so clearly, I felt like a fool for not realizing before.

From Blueberry Bonanza on, Howell had orchestrated everything. She knew what the tokens would do; she exposed us to them on purpose. *She* was responsible for all the deaths.

And she had Luther and Dad.

PART THREE
PELIGROSA

CHAPTER 40

I burst out of the bathroom, past the gray-haired watcher lady, and through the emergency room doors. The police would have to take care of Wilder. I'd trusted my Dad and Luther to a woman as rotten as GT. And Mom too, if Howell really had sent her crew to Florida. I understood now why thinker-Wilder hadn't trusted Howell. Nothing she did made sense unless she was duplicitous, greedy, and power-mad.

I ran to the warehouse and found a car—different from the last one, but I could tell it was the kind of car Wilder would get. No key. I didn't need one. Give me a junkyard and a few hours, and I could probably build a car. I could certainly hot-wire one.

I ripped out of the dirt lot and sped to the private airport.

There's something I'm forgetting about, something urgent . . .

I swatted at the air as if the persistent warning were a swarm of gnats.

At the airstrip, a Howell jet was waiting for me.

"She took Dragon and the others back to Texas," Yosemite Sam told me. (That's what I called him—he had a bushy red beard.)

Yosemite flew me to HAL. I didn't buckle up. I paced. Sometimes I caught him looking back at me and talking to someone on his headset. I felt strong enough to tear apart the plane with five fingers and land safely on the ground five thousand meters below. Though the techno and thinker tokens were live in me, I had no headache. I guessed the pain had been caused by the nanites scrambling to understand a new species, and now that they were reprogrammed for humans—

Something I need to do. Now. Now, now, now . . .

"The Purpose," I whispered. That was the nagging warning, a powerful itch I couldn't find to scratch. An awareness of the Purpose must be a side effect of the thinker token. How had Wilder not gone insane? Then again, perhaps he had.

Before the fireteam broke up, the four fighting members had one directive—follow the thinker. And the thinker had one directive—form a team and prepare for the Purpose. I was the fireteam now. I knew that I needed to prepare like I needed to breathe. But I had no idea for what.

Only focusing on Howell and that immediate mission made it bearable to ignore the pulsing Purpose.

The moment the jet landed, I pushed through the door and ran toward HAL.

I found Luther in the main corridor.

"Where's Dad?" I asked.

Luther described the lab, so I put him over my shoulder and started to run.

"You're . . . brutish . . . again!" Luther said, his stomach thumping against my shoulder.

"And Howell is evil," I said. How had I not realized it before?

"I knew it." Luther clapped his hands as if high-fiving himself.

I peeked into the lab. Dad in a hospital bed. Howell and Dragon and the triplets, looking recovered from the surprise gassing. The lab smell was familiar—disinfectant, grease, food, and the burn of electricity. It reminded me of those first post-Beanstalk days when I was nothing but a walking headache, and my stomach rolled with the memory of nausea.

"I'm going to have to be fast," I told Luther. "You stay here. Stay!"

"Yes, Empress," said Luther with a mock salute.

I ran into the lab. I must have looked pretty aggressive because Hairy, Scary, and Larry moved forward, standing shoulder-to-shoulder before a cowering Howell.

I moved them all aside with a running shove and grabbed Howell by her neck. She squeezed her eyes shut.

"How are you, Dad?" I asked over my shoulder.

"Okay." His voice was sluggish, drugged. "What's going on?"

"I want my parents safe," I said to Howell. "And Luther. Safe from you all. Forever."

"Of course." Dragon's hands were in the air as if this were a stickup. "You're all safe."

"I want a promise—" Frakking flatscans. What good was a promise? I could feel the thump of Howell's pulse against my wrist, the echo of it in her thin bones. It would be so easy to stop her for good. And Dragon. All of them. I thought of biblical Samson, tricked into a haircut and losing his strength, blinded and weak. He got his power back for just a moment and used it to knock down the pillars of a great house, killing everybody who had hurt him. I so got Samson just then. I didn't like being lied to, being blind. I wanted to rip this building to shreds.

Howell whimpered against my arm. I shoved her back and showed her the complete mark on my chest.

"You've seen this somewhere before," I said. "I want to know everything you know. And if you stall or lie or—"

"I'll show you," Howell said, her hands trembling. "I'll show you the whole sh-sh-shebang."

Was she lying again? I positioned myself in front of Dad. It was strange to think there was a time when I wasn't always afraid.

Dragon put out his hand, an offering to shake. "You'll all be safe. On my grandmother's grave, who was a good woman, and on my mother's, who wasn't. None of us here will harm any of you."

"They're my family, Dragon." My voice broke. "They're fragile. I am sick of trusting people who hurt me. I want out of this."

"There's no out anymore," he said. "Not for you."

The words were a hard slap, but I knew at least they were true.

"Is she going to kill me or not, Dragon?" Howell asked.

He studied my face, one eyebrow lifted. "Not yet," he said.

Howell sighed. "Good. Then let's proceed, shall we? A world to save, blah, blah, blah."

I pushed Dad's hospital bed into the private bedroom that had been mine once and asked Luther to watch over him and make sure he slept. I moved a massively heavy steel shelving unit in front of their door. They were temporarily trapped, but at least no one could get in.

Only the boss lady and Dragon were waiting for me in Howell's office.

She entered a code into a wall safe, Dragon entered a second code, then Howell again, followed by voice recognition and an eye scan. She opened the safe, and Dragon brought out a heavy metal box. It was scratched and gouged as if it had been chiseled free of something. The lid bore a symbol of all five tokens, a fancier version of what I wore on my chest.

"Dragon, where do I begin?" she asked, blinking.

"Big Barda, I think," he said.

"Tell me, Miss Brown, how did a previously uncharted asteroid manage to reach Earth at such an angle as to nestle perfectly into Earth's orbit?"

"Because it was sent here on purpose," I guessed.

She nodded. "We were the first to reach Big Barda and discovered she was lousy with platinum—one of the rarest elements in the Earth's crust and yet highly useful and therefore more precious than gold. We built a lab on the asteroid and were able to produce the carbon nanotubes needed for a space elevator much faster in a weightless environment. We tugged Barda into geosynchronous orbit and used her as the anchor point for the ribbon. A Beanstalk ride costs one fiftieth of a Space Beetle launch, allowing us to mine the asteroid. Our profits turned a megalomaniac like GT a nauseating shade of green. So he bought out one of my astronauts to spy for him. And—there's so much to tell. What next, Dragon?"

"There was a metallic mark on the asteroid," said Dragon.

"Yes, and it seemed purposeful, like a character of writing. Buried beneath it in a chunk of ice we found this platinum container. Inside were the five tokens and this disc."

She opened the lid. The box was thick on all sides, the bottom bearing six grooves. Five of the grooves were empty. In the center groove lay a flat, circular object. Howell lifted it out, and I saw that the disc was transparent like glass, smooth on the outside and full of cracks on the inside. Closer, the cracks looked like deliberate cuts, symmetrical facets, like a diamond inside-out.

Dragon took the disc from Howell's palm and placed it under a strong lamp. The direct light pierced the disc and images rose out like colorful candle smoke.

"You are only the third human to view this," said Howell.

"It's basically alien video," said Dragon.

The colors twisted together, shapes emerging.

"We learned you have to relax your vision," Dragon said.

My mind ached trying to form order out of chaos, and I gave myself an eyeball headache.

"Whatever species made that, their eyes don't work like ours," I said.

When I kind of dazed out, I could discern figures. Smoky blue and pink. The marks of the tokens. Some movement. A ball. Figures on the ball. Figures gone. Figures again, smoky blue and pink. What was it trying to communicate? I leaned forward.

My body felt yanked, my muscles burning with whiplash. I couldn't feel any floor beneath my feet. Suddenly I was in space without a pressure suit, and I wanted to scream, but I couldn't breathe. Between me and the stars the smoky images whooshed, urgent, chaotic. I clawed at the air—or lack thereof. I should have been floating, but I felt like I was falling.

I was screaming. And I was on my knees, Howell's carpet beneath my hand.

"Maisie," Dragon was saying. Howell was backed against her desk, her face a mask of alarm.

"I was . . . I was in space," I said.

"You weren't." Dragon was crouched beside me, his arm around my shoulders. "You were here."

"I wasn't expecting that," Howell whispered. "The thinker token?"

"I guess so." I took deep breaths and shut my eyes to avoid looking at the disc. "My tokens must receive the data directly, shout it right at my brain. It seemed so real."

"Maybe you can get more out of it than we could," said Howell.

I nodded, but I didn't open my eyes.

I felt Dragon take my hand. His hand was so large, I felt like a small girl again, my dad walking me across the street to the park.

"I've got you, Brown," he said.

"Don't let go," I whispered.

I opened my eyes and fell once more into the images of the disc.

CHAPTER 41

Again I seemed to be in space, the freezing vacuum pressing against me, piercing into my eyeballs, my eardrums, trying to pull me inside-out into the endless blackness. I tried to ignore my body, to focus just on viewing. It was like being shoved underwater and pretending I wasn't drowning.

I saw two ships, nearly black as space, move toward a green planet. Pink shapes poured out of the boats, and like a creeping mold, blackness consumed the planet. Suddenly I was hurtling into the planet too, toward something—or somebody. Not human. A squat body, limblike parts, something like eyes that were silver and always moving. I seemed to go into an eye, where I felt both terror and urgency.

That image spit me out, and I was streaking through space, past one solar system, into another, toward a second green planet.

The scene there was chaotic, everything so alien nothing made sense, like watching a dozen movies all laid over one another. I wanted nothing more than to shut my eyes. But I forced myself to watch. Finally amid all the images I noticed something familiar—the marks of the tokens on alien bodies. I was seeing the original fireteam.

The fireteam was on that second green planet. Then the fireteam was in space with me. The two ships the color of between-stars were coming. The fireteam went inside one. Maybe I did too. I couldn't comprehend anything that I saw, images pummeling me like fists.

Then there was only one ship. It left. The planet below me was still green. The marks of the tokens went into a box and left too. Ahead, a blue-green planet, spinning, spinning . . .

I shut my eyes. I was curled up on the carpet. I was shaking. Dragon still held my hand. He helped me up into a chair.

"Put it away, please," I said, and I heard a clink and a lid shut.

I took some trembling breaths. "There were two ships. Space-craft. They annihilated Planet A somehow, because it turned black. Before they all died, the inhabitants of Planet A sent a warning to Planet B—a colony planet, I guess, because the inhabitants there looked similar. By the time the spacecraft arrived at Planet B, there was a fireteam waiting. The fireteam destroyed one of the spacecraft, and their planet didn't go black. The other spacecraft fled. The Planet B inhabitants put the tokens into a box, into an asteroid, and sent it to . . . to us. Because that's where the second ship was heading."

"And it'll try to change our planet from green to black," said Howell.

"And you're the fireteam, so you will stop it," said Dragon.

Yes. This was the Purpose. Every cell in my body seemed to sing with it. My eyes teared up with relief like hammer blows that the Purpose was clear. Or somewhat clear. Or not very clear at all, now that I thought about it. A shame the complicated actions of the alien fireteam hadn't been more obvious.

There had been five of them. And there was one of me.

"Brown?" said Dragon. "You okay?"

I looked at the twisted curves I'd squeezed into my chair's armrest.

Robots didn't break chairs when they got scared. Robots didn't get scared. What if the chair had been someone's arm? I shuddered, disgusted with myself.

"You should have told us—"

"I planned to, once you were stable, trained, and unified," Howell said.

"Whatever. Each token grants a specific ability, so all those skills must be needed to stop the spacecraft."

"Which is why I insisted you claim Jacques's token," said Howell.

I glared up at Howell. "What do you want from me?"

"I want you to stop the aliens from killing Earth," she said, her eyes uneasy.

"Why are you involved?"

"Because I've invested a lot in these tokens already. When aliens invade, there's surely money to be made. Rule of war."

"Are you kidding me?" I said.

Howell looked at Dragon as if she hadn't understood the question.

"Maisie finds your motivation in this so shocking, she thinks you're plying her with humor," Dragon said.

Howell nodded slowly. "Would that be funny? I could try that sometime, if it would be funny."

"Howell is making an effort to increase her comic intelligence," Dragon explained to me.

I resisted pulling out what was left of my hair. "Tell me the rest," I said.

"We tested the tokens as best we could on Big Barda," said Howell. "Nothing happened when we handled them. Now we believe that was because we were adults."

Dragon settled into a professor tone. "At puberty, adolescent brains have a growth surge and gain as much gray matter as adult brains, but they still lack some white matter. White matter connects the different brain regions and, eventually, myelin coats the white matter, making it more efficient. We think it's myelin that prevents nanites from entering and altering adult brains."

I thought of those blue figures. "There's no way the species that made the tokens has our same brains."

"Exactly!" said Howell. "But their anatomy must include something akin to our central nervous system to enable them to move, communicate, and build as they have. Perhaps their adults *can* bond with the tokens."

"The tokens must have sensors to tell which hosts would support the nanites," I said. "But how do you know that it has to do with the age of the brain?"

"Kira and Gabe," said Dragon, and Howell rubbed her eyes again.

"Crew members," she said. "When Dragon and I took the disc back to Earth, we left the tokens behind, fearing atmospheric pressure might affect them. While we were at HAL—"

"Let me guess—Gabe and Kira are younger than the rest of your crew?" I said.

Howell nodded. "Twenty-two and twenty-three, both brilliant for their age. When they touched the tokens, well, you experienced firsthand what happened. Soon after, Gabe gained strength and Kira technological clarity. But after a time they became violently ill. I imagine the nanites discovered Gabe's and Kira's brains were too old after all and were rejecting them as hosts. The station commander put them in the emergency pod and accompanied them back down the Beanstalk. We lost contact with the pod at reentry. It broke apart."

I remembered reading news reports about the tragedy. Obviously, there'd been no mention of tokens.

"We believe the tokens removed themselves from Gabe and Kira," said Dragon, "thereby stopping their hearts. Unbonded, tokens cannot exist in higher levels of gravity. As the pod neared Earth's mesosphere and gravity increased, the tokens were repelled. They slide through living flesh without a mark, but metal—"

"The tokens ripped a hole in the elevator pod," I said.

"We never would have located the tiny tokens adrift in space if they hadn't been suspended among the pod debris, orbiting the Earth," said Howell. "We compared Gabe's and Kira's standard prelaunch brain scans with the rest of the crew's. Their frontal lobes were not yet completely encased in myelin, so we concluded we needed younger hosts."

"Teenagers," I said.

"I believe Gabe's and Kira's brains had been *too* developed," said Howell. "There wasn't much myelin, so the nanites could enter and alter the brain, but their synapses were fully formed, their areas of expertise already developed, and other areas going dormant. Adolescent brains are playgrounds, still open to programming. Habits are not yet locked in, personality is in flux, knowledge and skill areas are open. Teenagers are the perfect subjects." Howell sighed. "If I could have my adolescent brain again and start over, I could rebuild myself. I could pursue dozens of different courses of study. I could be brilliant."

"You are brilliant," Dragon said.

"Yeah," said Howell, shrugging. "I meant *more* brilliant."

We were getting off track. "Hey, you put those things into the five of us knowing they might rip out of our bodies."

"GT was confident enough to risk his own son," she said. "And I bet my life on it, didn't I? As you see, you did not die."

"Yet," I said.

"I saw the danger of a ship that turns a green planet black. I thought a little risk was in order."

I frowned and so got them chatting a bit faster, since I'd guessed much of it. Howell started an astronaut boot camp to find a fireteam, using the "marketing survey" of the sweepstakes to profile ideal candidates.

"Children raised hearing two languages have higher-level cognitive abilities. I also wanted subjects who were intelligent, risk takers, and problem solvers. You, Miss Brown, were an unexpected bonus. I examined your DNA after you arrived at boot camp, and as I suspected, you are genetically inclined toward being right-handed but are forced to use your left. Therefore the pathway between your right and left hemispheres is more open than most. Your brain has been forced to compromise and is stronger for it."

"Um . . . yay?" I said.

She evaluated us further by our academic success, rankings in the fireteam competitions, IQ exams, physicals, and brain scans.

"Some of the participants' brains were still too immature, some too mature. Some were already spoiled by alcohol abuse, which damages the forebrain and hippocampus of adolescent brains and halts the production of new nerve cells. Abominable waste of minds!"

Dragon rolled his eyes. Clearly this was a common tirade.

"There were other decent candidates for the fifth position, but

Jonathan Wilder got in because his father blackmailed me." Howell absently rubbed her nose. "On paper, you five were perfect."

Far away, a sentient species created tokens to help five individuals stop the invaders. As a safeguard, if one member died, the thinker could absorb and still use both tokens. I wondered if Ruth and Jacques, and maybe Mi-sun too, might have recovered from their injuries. But when their bodies were weakened, the tokens fled to be ready for a new, healthy host, and in the process stopped their hearts.

There were five potential traitors in my chest. One day they might kill me too. I wondered if I'd have a chance to save the planet first.

CHAPTER 42

I slept for a few hours in the same room as my Dad and Luther, curling up on the floor between them and the door. In the morning, we talked.

"I don't want to have to trust Howell," I said. "But she sent fifty people to scout for Mom. She has resources. If the big bad boat is coming, I want to be ready."

"When? Soon?" Luther asked.

"It feels soon. If the thinker token is uploading the data into my brain, I still can't think in specifics. I'm just aware of a persistent urgency. Not helpful, thinker token!" I shouted at my chest. "Dad, Howell is going to pay off the bank and get our house out of foreclosure, so there's that."

"Don'tworry'boutme," Dad said groggily.

"Uh-huh," I said. "Maybe those docs should lighten up your meds."

We decided to stay. Howell was our best chance to find where Mom was hiding. I kept busy so I wouldn't have to consider bleaker alternatives.

First I built myself a new arm—Lady Robotica the First,

Avenger of Fido. I wasn't able to make Lady quite as extraordinary as Fido had been. Too many nanites in my body elbowing for brain space. The weakness also showed on Ruth's weight machine.

"How do I compare?" I asked after a workout.

Dragon checked the charts. "Ruth was stronger by a fair bit, but you've got her on class."

I tackled the training mission out at the abandoned building. Five months before, the fireteam had rescued the cardboard hostages in two minutes. Alone, I took over fifteen minutes. I thought how disappointed Wilder would be before I remembered that I didn't care what Wilder thought anymore.

Luther kept me company while I worked on Lady, practiced blue shot outside, and lifted weights. He talked to me as I made my way to the scuba pool three times each day. I'd go under for twenty minutes, holding my breath and completing obstacle courses that Howell designed for me. When I came back up, Luther would start talking again.

I loved his company but didn't talk back much. My brain was too busy. Why would aliens go from inhabited planet to planet? How might they attack? What could a fireteam do to stop them that a military with nuclear weapons couldn't?

Luther and I were alone in the lab five days after returning to HAL. I was working on an engine that I hoped to convert to a jet pack.

"I wonder . . ." I didn't mean to say it aloud, but then I had to finish the thought. "I wonder if the police charged Wilder yet. If they can prove he killed Mi-sun, Wilder could go to prison for a long time."

"Which is what he deserves," Luther said without looking at me.

"I'm glad you're here, Luther."

"Of course you are. I'm monumental."

"No, I'm really, really glad."

I smiled at him. He looked at me funny, scratched his nose, straightened his shirt. I was expecting him to say something snarky. Instead, he grabbed me by the shoulders and pressed his mouth to mine.

My instinct was to shove him away, so I froze, afraid to hurt him. Luther seemed to find this encouraging. He gripped my shoulders tighter, kissing harder.

"Luther . . . ," I mumbled against his mouth.

He pulled back, his forehead shiny. "Yeah? What?"

"Luther . . ." What could I say? "That's not something . . . I could hurt you, you should be careful."

Luther began to pace, talking with his hands.

"I have pondered this question for a long time, Maisie, and I have decided that it is awkward, if not impossible, to change from friend to . . . to . . . to *boyfriend*, especially since we were prepubescent when we met . . ."

I wrinkled my nose. Some words I really never wanted to hear from Luther's mouth.

". . . and incapable of honest romantic attraction. But now I realize that you are the most attractive girl I know—"

"Wow, I'm blushing, really, but I'm the *only* girl you know."

He pointed at me emphatically. "That's not true! I see girls everywhere—at the grocery store, at the library. A girl who works at the computer store asks for my phone number *every* time I go in. And then there's TJ's sister Anya, who always says hi."

"Luther . . ."

"Don't use that pitying tone." His voice cracked. "That's a parental tone, not a Maisie one."

"Luther," I said, trying to soften my tone. "Let's pretend that didn't just happen. Let's say you slipped and we accidentally touched lips and it was awkward, so now we laugh about it and go back to being best friends, because that's what we were made for."

"That is so false, it's alchemy. It's phrenology. It's terracentric theory! You aren't wired for mathematics so you don't understand—"

"Wait, are you trying to use math here? Have you assigned us symbols like N and Y and calculated our compatibility?"

He turned red.

"Repeat after me," I said slowly. "Oops, I must have slipped. I didn't mean to smoosh your lips."

Luther looked at the ground. He turned and left.

◆

That night I dreamed about Wilder. He was kissing me, and I wanted him to. When I woke up, I should have been logical again, but my thoughts wanted to linger on a dream moment, Wilder standing behind me, his arm around my waist, his lips against my neck . . .

Stop it.

I was still angry at myself for hanging onto the tattered corner of that dream when I walked into the lab. Howell was talking to a guy with dark hair and a set of shoulders and a chin that looked a lot like Wilder. But it couldn't be.

Then he noticed me. Looked at me.

"Maisie, before you—" he started.

I leaped across the room and formed a havoc bind around his chest, pinning his arms. I turned him upside down, havocked his ankles together, his face pressed to the floor. I gripped one of his ankles, prepared to throw him against the wall.

"No, no, no!" said Howell. "That's unnecessary. He only just got here. I sent Dragon to warn you."

My mouth must have been hanging open. "You *invited* him?"

"I am officially harboring him."

"You're . . . harboring him?"

"Aiding and abetting. Such fun words."

"Maisie," Wilder said, breathless. I might have set his havoc binds a bit tight. "I can help. If you—"

"You recall, Howell, that he's a murderer," I said.

"Even without his token, there is still helpful information meshed with his gray matter."

Wilder was making strangled sounds. I was about to break the havoc band off when I realized that he was laughing.

"Stop it." I shook him.

"You don't think this is a little funny?" he said.

I dropped him and walked out. It would take several hours for his binds to disintegrate. By then Dad, Luther, and I would be long gone.

CHAPTER 43

Dragon was by the front doors talking to the security guys.

"You promised to keep my family safe," I said. "Our agreement is forfeit. We'll be leaving in twenty minutes."

"You saw Wilder."

"I saw Wilder." I turned away.

"Wait. Look, Howell made the call. I don't trust Wilder, but I do trust her."

"Why? How can you?"

"Take a stroll with me?" He opened the door, waited.

I frowned. I had no reason to trust Dragon any more than Howell. A robot wouldn't. Yet I did.

"Please?" he said. Then he sang it in that squeaky falsetto. "Please? Oh please-o?" The security guys raised eyebrows, widened eyes, but Dragon kept singing to me.

"Shush already," I said. "Put these guys on Wilder, make sure he doesn't move."

Dragon gave the order and held the door for me. He let me choose the direction and pace. The sun's forehead rose over the horizon, glaring at us. Dragon took off his sunglasses and offered them to me.

"I've been working with Howell for twenty years," he said. "I was in a boys' home because my grandmother had passed, my parents were dead—probably—and my brother and I had caused some trouble. Howell visited me. She'd seen my test scores and psych profile and said she wanted me to work for her. I was fifteen. She got me released from the boys' home, shipped me off to a prep school, then college, and by the time I graduated I was Howell Aerospace Chief of Operations. I'm not going to pretend she picked me out of the boys' home because she's a charitable angel. She doesn't *mean* to do good, and yet she always does."

"So you stay with the crazy lady because she accidentally does good sometimes?"

"That and she lets me set my own salary. I set it well." He chuckled, and I smiled. Dragon chuckles like a baby, with a squeak at the end. "She's a juggernaut. She misses a lot of the world around her but she also sees stuff no one else does. Big stuff, like an asteroid in orbit, and little stuff, like a smart kid in a boys' home. And she's going to save the world, whether she means to or not. So, yeah, I'd harbor a killer for her. I'd take a bullet for her."

Aw, man! Dragon would take a bullet for her! Those words deflated my righteous indignation. I sighed again.

"You just drink some soda?" he asked. "We used to sigh to hide our belches from Grandma."

So I belched. I could do that on cue now, some biological change *gracias a los* tokens. Dragon laughed, making me laugh too. And then suddenly the laugh turned into a cry. My chest wracked and coughed with a sob. I tensed everywhere, forcing the sobs to stop.

I wiped my face and shook my head, meaning I had no idea what just happened.

But Dragon said, "Hey, you were shot into space and stuck with alien technology. Your body keeps changing in alarming ways. You watched a former friend cut off your father's arm. Your mother is missing. You were an unwilling participant in two deaths. You're carrying the burden of somehow defending the entire world. After all that, you shouldn't have to see Wilder again. Ever."

I nodded and thankfully didn't explode into more sobs.

Dragon's jaw muscle bulged as he bit down hard. "Know this, Maisie Brown—when the drama is over and Wilder's usefulness is extinguished, say the word and I *will* kill him for you."

I coughed a surprised kind of laugh. "I wouldn't recommend killing in general. Devastates a good night's sleep."

He bent over so his face was at my level. "You see these eyes? Do you detect any laugh lines? I ain't foolin', girl."

"Thank you," I said, and I meant it. "I wish . . . I wish I didn't have to feel so much. I'd be better at all this."

For my last birthday, Luther had made me a poster that read ROBOTS MAKE THE BEST SCIENTISTS, and he'd drawn a Dr. Frankenstein–esque robot building a scientist on an operating slab. It was the only thing taped up in my abandoned bedroom.

"You're human," said Dragon, "which is exactly what you should be."

I took off the sunglasses and offered them back, but he lifted his hand. "Keep them. They make you look as fierce as you are."

"Okay," I said, feeling in better spirits than I thought I should. "Tell Howell to keep him locked up, okay?"

He pointed at me as we went back inside. "You're going to do this, Brown. You're going to save the world. And someday I'll sing about it! How about that?"

Dragon moved my dad and Luther to a separate building where they had constant guards. And a large-screen TV with four hundred channels. I slept on their couch, cuddling with Laelaps, and kept the television buzzing all night to drown out the irritating reminder of the Purpose. The nagging was so raw and urgent, there were whole minutes when I forgot about Mom.

Dad was still asleep early the next morning when Luther shuffled out of his bedroom. He stopped when he saw me awake on the couch, and his cheeks and ears turned red. It was the first time we'd made eye contact since our lip-smooshing fiasco.

"Hey," I squeaked.

Luther looked away. He went into the bathroom, slamming the door shut. I slipped outside before he emerged.

Sunlight was already drinking up dew. I closed my eyes and lifted my face to the east. The sting of heat turned everything orange and gold. The breeze smelled of warm soil and sweet grass. Another day when maybe we would find Mom. Another day when aliens might invade. How had this become my life?

I made my way to the lab for breakfast and a workout. Since getting the shooter token, I preferred to go without Lady unless I was building. It'd also become habit to run my left hand along a wall as I walked, my body pulling in spare electrons. I believed that the shooter token acted as a kind of electron battery, storing those gathered electrons. When it was full, the tightness and crackling in my chest became uncomfortable. I'd relieve it by expelling some electrons down the nerves of my arm, where they burst warm from my fingers. As satisfying as scratching an itch—and harmless, if I wasn't holding anything.

I was about to shoot off some electrons when I heard a pounding in the cafeteria. Wilder was alone with a couple dozen soccer balls, kicking them at the mended wall Ruth had once run through. The neck of his shirt was dark with sweat, his face glistening.

"You're not locked up," I said.

He didn't stop kicking. "I was. I picked the lock after your bands disintegrated. So, are you going to kill me?"

"I haven't decided yet."

He turned to me, his arms out, inviting. "Go ahead. I'm gutted anyway."

The thought of losing my own tokens was terrifying. Feeling even a speck of empathy for this deliberate murderer made me uncomfortable. I started to leave.

"You cut your hair," he said, tilting his head.

I'd been wearing a havoc helmet at our warehouse meeting. I fingered the ragged ends at my neck, then dropped my hand.

"Jacques did."

"Oh. Right." He nudged a ball onto his toes and kicked it up into his hands. "I do have some help to offer. If you're not going to kill me immediately, that is."

"You'd better," I said. "I won't let Howell keep you around just so I can admire your calves."

He raised an eyebrow. "You admire my calves?"

Why had I said that? One of the soccer balls lay near my feet. I picked it up and blue shot it past Wilder. It zipped by near his head, its wind lifting his hair, and smacked against the wall. It hissed air and plopped to the floor. Wilder visibly swallowed.

"Let me show you one thing," he said, his voice dry.

I started to shake my head no, but the Purpose nagged.

I followed Wilder into Howell's office. He nudged her away from her computer, opened an Internet news site, and played the video that we'd watched back in the lair. A man in a black suit acting crazy outside a state capitol. He has a gun. A police officer shoots. The man falls.

Only this time, I saw something new. When the man hits the ground, a blurry, pinkish form rises out of him. The newscaster describing the scene, the headline, the text underneath—nothing acknowledges the pink shape that exits the man's body.

"I don't see it anymore," Wilder said. "Only the thinker can."

I stood up fast, knocking my chair over. "They're here. Holy crap, they're already here."

CHAPTER 44

They're here?" said Howell. "As in, *them*?"

"As in, run away screaming—aah, aah, aah," I confirmed. "But . . . but if they're here, why isn't Earth a smoldering black heap?"

"Black heap?" Wilder hadn't seen the alien video.

"I didn't give you permission to ask questions."

I played the video again. Like a lion's DNA spells out gazelle = food, my nanite-tinged cells were screaming, Hunt that thing!

Was the pink stuff an alien? Had it been inside the man's body? I'd assumed the blackened planet meant the aliens had some frightening weapon that would zap life from Earth at the first opportunity. But perhaps the blackness was metaphorical, and the aliens had more subtle means of destruction.

"Their ship may be orbiting Earth right now," I said to Howell. "Sending ghostmen down into people."

"An invisible invasion," she said.

I'd been toying with the idea of a laser mounted to Big Barda to shoot the spacecraft before it got to Earth, but whenever I'd tried to design it in earnest, a jet pack had felt more urgent. Maybe because the subconscious data from the thinker token indicated it was too late for that tactic.

"I don't think the Jumper Virus is really a virus," I said slowly.

Wilder raised his hand a little. I sighed.

"Yes?" I said.

"People assume its name came from the virus's ability to infect one town but jump over others, spreading randomly. But originally 'jumper' referred to the first discovery of the virus in a village in Argentina. A visitor from Buenos Aires found the entire village except the very young and very old converged on a cliff, taking turns jumping off and employing an old parachute at the last moment. Over and over."

"And you know this because . . ."

"I hacked into the CDC director's computer. Back when I did that sort of thing."

"Are they aliens that look like humans or humans who are infected with aliens? And why would they leap off cliffs?"

"I don't know. That was the first quarantined town. Last I checked, there were over three hundred and fifty towns worldwide. One is just a couple of hours away by helicopter."

He looked at me expectantly. It made sense to bring him, if only so I could be sure he was nowhere near my dad.

I put on my improved impact boots, and we ran to the helipad with Howell.

"You don't need to come," I told Howell. "I can figure out how to fly a helicopter. Besides, if it gets sketchy—"

"I'm not leaving you now," she said. "This is all very exciting!"

"Don't talk more than you have to," I told Wilder as we climbed in. "I can't guarantee I won't toss you out the window." I would not allow him to manipulate his way into my affections. I didn't trust myself. Wilder's words had always been evil-wizard dangerous.

Using short sentences, Wilder directed Howell to a small town west of HAL. Then he was quiet for the rest of the two-hour flight.

"Hey, does Ruth's family know what happened?" I asked Howell over the headset.

"That she died in a regrettable scuba accident? Yes, and they were properly distressed and are suing me for negligence. I'll pay them a hefty sum to settle out of court and close down the astronaut boot camp in a show of humble liability."

"Wow, how noble of you," I said. "Jacques and Mi-sun—"

"I've offered their families condolence money as well, but none of that matters, Miss Brown. You saw what is coming. We're talking about the destruction of our entire planet. Green to black."

I remembered Mi-sun had been plagued with dreams of "pink floaty things." Had her nanites tried to upload data about the ghostmen into her brain? Perhaps if the tokens worked right in humans, the fireteam would have known about them from the beginning.

Howell landed the helicopter on a street near the edge of town. A barricade across the road said QUARANTINE.

"Fly off if anything happens," I told Howell.

Wilder sat in back. He smiled at me—a sweet, friendly, go-get-'em smile. I havocked his wrists and ankles together.

"Come on," he said.

"Shut it or I do your mouth too," I said.

"Promise?" he said, almost as if he couldn't help himself.

I havocked his mouth.

Beside the barricade were US GOVERNMENT–branded crates, empty now. Food and supplies dropped for the quarantined town, I guessed. I walked farther in.

Flies twitched over rancid piles of garbage in the gutters, front doors hung open. Dogs trotted around, sniffing the ground. One sat curled up around a bone, gnawing at its old meat. The bone looked a great deal like a human femur.

The dog with a bone growled when another got too close. The second trotted off with purpose. I followed. The sound of flies grew louder—an angry, mobbish buzzing. The gate to a backyard was broken off. I followed the dog through.

There were at least a dozen bodies. Small and large. Clothes eaten by weather and insects. I gasped, the smell struck the back of my throat, and I turned and stumbled off. The way the bodies lay in the dirt reminded me of laundry flung on the floor. Heaped together, cast aside.

I saw no one living till I passed a park where four adults occupied the swings, leaning back as they pumped as high as the chains would allow. I stood staring.

"You shouldn't be here," said a voice behind me.

A white man stood behind the screen door of a house. His face was as wrinkled as a fingerprint, his hair thin, white wisps.

"What happened here?" I asked.

"Viral epidemic. That's what the government says. Overnight people changed. It passed over all us old folk and the youngest ones, but everyone else—"

"They changed how?" I asked.

"Just weren't themselves anymore. Virus eats your brains, I guess. We got quarantined. But the old couldn't take care of the babies by themselves for long, so they picked up the little ones and left."

"You stayed," I said.

"My daughter's here. My grandson too, even if they don't come home anymore." He cried without noise, his eyes seeping water, making tiny rivers of his wrinkles. "But they might get better any day now. Are things out there still *normal*?" He stumbled over the last word, as if he hardly knew what it meant.

"Normalish. Why don't you come with me? I have a helicopter—"

He took a step back. "I'll be here when they get better. I see them when I go to the diner to get my meals. They know me still, I can tell, but they don't talk to me. You should go. In the beginning doctors came into town in those yellow germ suits, but they got infected anyhow."

"I won't stay long."

I followed the main street till I couldn't hear the squeaking park swings anymore. Lights flickered on and off in a diner. I peered through the plate-glass window. The place was packed. Most people were in the kitchen, cooking and eating, some overflowing to the counter, the booths. They smacked their lips over apples and oatmeal, licked the backs of spoons, dipped their fingers into jars of peanut butter. No one talked.

I opened the diner doors and a little bell tinkled. Everyone looked over. No one stopped eating. A petite black woman in an apron approached, half of a hamburger in her hand, her lips outlined in mustard. I saw no obvious mark of a ghost inside, but there was a wrongness in her eyes.

"So . . . do I just sit anywhere?" I asked.

She looked at some of the other people, thoughtful for longer than was comfortable, before directing me to a seat. Away from the windows. Close to a back door.

I talked myself out of nerves. I believed these were regular flesh-and-blood people, even if pink alien ghosts might be stuck inside them, controlling their brains.

Everyone was still chewing and staring. I pointed to a man who was munching a hot dog slathered in peanut butter and said, "I'll have what he's having."

Then I noticed a boy of ten or so, the youngest in the place, though his eyes didn't look young. He kept them trained on me, unblinking, as he shoveled spoonfuls of chocolate cake into his mouth.

No arms, no cake, I thought. And I laughed at that inane joke for the first time, because suddenly its unfunniness made sense. Here I was in a ghost town with a little boy who should be in school or with his parents somewhere, but he was probably possessed by an alien poltergeist, eating enough cake to kill a horse, and I was freaking Supergirl with no idea how to shake that ghost out of him.

"What's your name?" I asked.

The kid watched me but just kept eating.

"Are you still in there?" I whispered. "The kid part, the human part. If the ghost comes out, will you be you again?"

He swallowed. He took another bite.

"I'm sorry," I said. "I don't know how to help you."

The door behind me opened with a *clank*. A white plastic suit of armor in a headless humanoid form was zooming toward me. It was so fast, I'd only managed to get to my feet when a limb-part struck my chest, clawing at my skin through my shirt. But in the fraction of a second before I could bring my arm down on the limb or kick the plastic robot away from me, it zapped back on its own. The people looked at me, their wrong eyes getting wronger.

Someone growled.

The man with the hot dog leaped at me, a steak knife in his hand. I backhanded him midstride, and he hit a wall.

He wiped his forehead, his hand red with blood. I felt swoony. Besides their alien stowaways, these were real people who could get hurt. By me.

I started for the door. The growling intensified and a dozen of them seized my head, neck, arms, pulling, stabbing at me with knives and forks. I tried to shake them off before someone could pull out my already-too-short hair, but they kept coming, howling with frustration.

"Stop it!" I yelled.

I stumbled toward the door, pushing them off as gently as I could, shooting flat havoc pellets with a light touch to knock them back. Maybe among them was that old man's daughter and grandson.

I pushed the last one away and ran out the door and down the street. Howell had the helicopter blades rotating when I jumped in, and we took off.

I was breathing hard.

"Don't fly straight back to HAL," I said. "If their ship is watching—"

A bright, silent beam sliced through half our helicopter, taking off the tail end. We tilted, spun, and fell.

CHAPTER 45

I grabbed Howell and Wilder and jumped out of the remains of the helicopter, kicking it away from us in midair. A second beam flashed and there wasn't much of the helicopter left to hit the ground.

I spun in the air, and my heels clicked together. Had I just set my impact boots to "hop"? I clicked again and hoped they were back on "impact." We were tearing toward the ground in full belly flop position. I kicked my legs, struggling to arrive feetfirst. I hit the ground on my toes, impact boots taking the fall with a jarring that rattled my teeth. Howell and Wilder grunted.

Keeping an arm around their middles, I ran a few paces and clicked my heels, switching the boots to "hop," and took off in huge bounds that left my stomach behind and made my passengers groan. We were easy targets in the open. I made for the cover of trees and switched "hop" off.

A white beam chased us, severing tree branches and hissing through overgrowth. I zigged. I zagged. One beam got close enough to singe my eyebrows.

Wilder was slipping free. I considered dropping him but instead threw him over my shoulder. I could feel his belly slamming against me as I ran.

"Mmm, mmm, mmm," he said, which sort of sounded like "Ow, ow, ow" through his gag. Crybaby.

The canopy sizzled and disappeared, fragments of leaves raining on our heads. I veered a quick left where the trees were denser. Trees disappeared behind me, random potshots from above wiping out groves in near-silent sputters. I veered left again, and this time the firing stayed right. A couple of kilometers later I felt safe enough to stop, dumping my cargo on the forest floor.

Howell's curly hair was tamed by sweat, limp over her ears. Her cheek was bright red from knocking against my shoulder. Wilder's eyes were wide, his face red and shiny. I could see what was coming. I released his havoc gag. He leaned over and dry heaved.

"Bouncy ride?" I said.

I grew a thin havoc blade from one finger and sliced through the bands on his ankles and wrists. He crawled away, collapsing in the dirt.

"Well," said Howell. "Well." She pushed damp hair out of her face and stared straight ahead. "Well."

My stomach growled.

"Wish we could order a pizza," I said.

From behind the tree, I could hear Wilder groan as if he couldn't bear the thought of food.

"Mmm, pizza," I said louder. "Greasy, cheesy pizza, with spicy sausage and crispy pepperoni and black olives as big as beetles."

"You're cruel," he said in a raspy voice.

"I learned from the best."

I didn't actually need a pizza. To decrease my meal dependency, I'd designed concentrated carbon pellets. They looked like rough diamonds, clear as crystals and slightly yellowish. I swallowed them whole, and my amped-up stomach slowly digested them. But I still needed water. I sucked one of my camelbacks dry and stood, anxious to keep moving.

"The diner in town was full of real people who seemed to be possessed by ghostmen," I said. "A plastic robot, kinda like a mini Stormtrooper, came in clicking and clacking. It stuck something on my chest and flew back as if I'd zapped it, as if . . ."

Wilder sat up, looking at me. My thoughts started spinning.

"That's how the ghostmen get into people," I said. "The ghosts are inside those little robot suits. They leave their ship, find a person, stick that probe in the person's chest, and the ghost transfers from the suit into the body. But it didn't work with me."

Wilder tapped his chest.

"Yeah," I said. "Token firewall. I'm safe, though no one else is."

Anxiety gnawed at my bones. Go. Fight. Stop the ghostmen. NOW! I couldn't hear any more puffs of disintegrating trees. Was the spacecraft gone or waiting for me to emerge from the trees before firing again?

"I'm going to go scout out the situation."

"You're leaving us?" Howell tried to stand, but her legs were too shaky. She sat down hard, a lock of damp hair flopping over her forehead.

"Maybe I can take one of those blasts, but you can't. Are you worried about being alone with my attempted murderer?"

"Naw," she said.

I shook my head.

I was just starting to run off when Wilder shouted my name. I turned back and then wished I hadn't. I didn't like responding like a dog to the sound of his voice.

"You might want to armor up," he said.

I hadn't worn havoc armor since getting the brute token back. It seemed superfluous. So no thanks, Wilder, I didn't armor up.

At least, not until I was out of sight.

I ran through the forest and stayed under the cover of trees while bounding back toward the town, following my GPS. It took an hour but eventually I saw some "people."

It was just too random, a group wandering through the trees, silent and gorging themselves on food. Chocolate bars, sodas, sandwiches, carrots.

"Hi there," I said.

They stopped. They looked at me. And kept chewing.

"Nice day, isn't it?"

The nearest one spoke. "You're the one we couldn't pin?" His Texan accent was thick, but the inflection was awkward, emphasizing insignificant words. However the ghosts possessed those bodies, they must have had full access to their hosts' brains—language, memories, sensations. They could speak like humans, but they didn't get it exactly right.

"Sure," I said, guessing "pin" meant "insert ghost alien into a human by means of mini-troopers." I didn't recognize them from the diner, so the ghosts must be able to transmit information to one another. Telepathically? Or via phone? "You guys planning to stay long on my planet?"

"As long as we can, thank you kindly." He reached for another handful of nuts.

"You're pretty fond of nuts?"

"Of course. But apples . . ." His eyes rolled up as he thought of it. "Hot damn, ma'am."

"So . . . you're hijacking human bodies in order to eat apples."

He shrugged.

"You're destroying people, taking away lives."

"Now, now, all we take is your shell."

"But what if the flesh of our bodies is the extent of our matter? What if you take our bodies and there's nothing left?"

He seemed to have never considered the possibility. "Why would such a creature matter at all?"

"You've gotta learn to value the small things. So if I destroy this body you've hijacked, the rest of you—the real part of you—"

"Never ends. If I lose this body, I just claim another." He smiled, and his wrong eyes looked that much wronger. "Let us live out the lives of these bodies. We're gentler on them now that we've learned how to keep them alive. It could be years before we move on to claim new ones, and generations for us to use up all the bodies. You're immune to the pinning. You've got no reason to oppose us, okay?"

Two mini-troopers came whizzing through the trees. They were built of white plastic but had no head or leg parts, hovering over the ground and moving as fast as a car on the highway. The torso part was about the size of a small child, and three arms circled the torso, each tipped with different attachments. I didn't wait to see what they could do. I formed havoc bullets between my fingers and shot the white suits.

With a puff of vapor and a shriek like a braking train, the suits fell over. Amorphous shapes bled out of the holes and rose up like head-sized blobs of pink-tinted smoke. In a second, the ghosts were out of sight in the sky.

The guy was staring hard at me. "You've had communication with the . . . star lickers?"

Did he mean the token-makers?

"There is only one of you," he said, pointing to my chest. "You killed the other four?"

"No! I didn't mean to. I—"

I shut my mouth. I'd thought I was getting all this great info, but this ghost-faced killer was playing me. That's why the ship hadn't taken a pot shot.

A battalion of mini-troopers came through the trees. I shot havoc bullets. They screeched and dropped, pink transparents flowing free. The ghosts rose, falling up instead of down, the same speed as Jacques's token had that night in the cave. Were the ghosts immune to gravity, just like the tokens? I leaped for the nearest rising pink blob, swiping my hand through, feeling nothing but a slight chill. My touch didn't deter it. The ghost kept going up into the sky, then suddenly disappeared.

Almost as if it'd been sucked into something. The idea felt right. Maybe the ship was up there, hovering to catch ghostmen freed of their suits.

I shot sharp havoc discs in the direction the ghost had gone. Their blue trails stopped and the discs disappeared, slicing, I assumed, into the ship alongside the ghosts. But after the last ghost was safely inside, my line of discs stopped disappearing. The ship had moved.

I started to run just as a flash exploded behind me. The ship was shooting at me again. I jumped, catching the edge of the master blast. The havoc armor on my left side was smoking.

I made for the nearest possessed person, thinking that the ship wouldn't fire on its own, but there was a second flash, and I leaped again. I hit the ground hard and screamed out. My back stung as if Jack Havoc had struck me a hundred blows. Behind me, the master blast had left a crater and a heap of charred bodies. Those had been human beings. Now there were twenty corpses on the ground, and twenty rosy ghosts rising in the air.

The only way to find the ship was to see a ghostman enter it.

I kept running, a moving target, but kept my eyes on the ghosts. The first one disappeared—drawn into the ship. I aimed at that spot, shooting chunks of havoc shaped like cut pipes. My ammo disappeared into the sky. And for barely an instant, I saw something kind of twinkle, a huge shape. The last of the twenty ghosts entered the ship, and the shape zipped away.

I felt the air move at its departure. It was massive. And fast. I doubted my shots had seriously damaged something that large, but I was grateful it had retreated.

I fell on my knees, knocked over by the pain. That blast had blasted the fight out of me. The ship might return any second, but I couldn't seem to move.

CHAPTER 46

Resting my head on my arm, I breathed, trying to get control over the pain. I had to move. Now, Maisie.

Humming the *Star Wars* theme to encourage myself, I wobbled onto my feet. Sometimes a girl's gotta provide her own trumpet-heavy heroic soundtrack.

One of the empty white suits had escaped the ship's blast. I picked it up and hobbled back into the trees toward Howell and Wilder.

A little nervous, I felt my back. Chunks of armor fell off in my hand, mixed with pieces of my shirt. No blood at least. I wondered what my back would look like if I hadn't taken Wilder's advice and armored up. Or if I'd have a back at all. Still, no need for him to know he'd been right. I peeled off the remaining armor as I went. When I reached my neck, a crispy hunk of hair came free.

As if I'd had hair left to lose. There would be a pixie cut in my future.

I found Howell and Wilder, and we walked through the woods into the night. Howell did not want to be carried again, and my blasted back was grateful. I spent the walk thinking. If shooting at the ship from a distance was enough to wreck it and solve the alien problem, the fireteam would need only one token.

By midnight we reached a spot I felt was safely far away and called Dragon. He picked us up in a black SUV wafting the scent of french fries.

My mouth watered. "Did you pick up dinner?"

He pointed to the exhaust. "You're smelling the biodiesel. Mm-mmm, good enough to eat."

"Any word on my mom?" I asked, knowing the answer was no or Dragon would have said something immediately. But I couldn't help asking.

He shook his head. "Next time you all do something like this, don't you dare leave me behind."

"The president and vice president never travel together in Air Force One," Howell mumbled. "Either you or I should always survive . . ."

Her knees bent, and Dragon rushed forward to catch her. He picked her up and put her in the front seat, tucking a blanket around her arms and legs. I hadn't noticed before that she was shivering. It would be cold out for someone without tokens.

I almost looked at Wilder to see if he was shivering too but stopped myself. As soon as I started caring about him in any way, I could be vulnerable to his lies and manipulation.

I spent the ride inspecting the mini-trooper suit. The shell was definitely a polymer. I cut it open with a havoc knife.

The polymer shell was completely filled with stiff white gunk, almost like a malt ball inside its chocolate coating.

Nougat, I named it in my head.

The suit must create specific atmospheric conditions for the ghosts. Perhaps the ghostmen couldn't stay put in emptiness. Perhaps they must inhabit and move through solid substance, just as humans can move only through gaseous or liquid environments.

I dug through the white nougaty stuff, searching for anything different, and discovered a polymer sphere in the center. I cracked open the sphere. It housed what had to be a computer and power source, its parts also made up of plastics. So what did that tell me about them? And how I could boot them all off my planet?

I felt like I was in a room with the lights off, and I could almost make out the details—but not quite. I wished I could talk it through with Wilder, then hated myself for the wish.

Dragon hit the first drive-through to get Howell something hot to drink and tossed me a few bags of food. Despite the carbon nuggets slowly digesting in my stomach, I still craved real food. I handed one bag to Wilder, because a robot would.

"Thanks," he said.

"Don't talk to me," I said.

Sharing the back bench with Wilder felt as intimate as a mattress. I could hear his breathing, smell the long walk emanating from his skin.

I leaned forward to talk to Dragon and Howell in the front seats. "How is it possible that gravity won't hold the tokens? Even a single water molecule isn't light enough to escape Earth's gravity."

"Well . . . there's dark energy," said Dragon.

Howell sipped her drink, still shivering. "Yes, that mysterious stuff that repels gravity. We've wondered if the tokens are linked somehow to dark energy."

"Or made of it," I said. "And the ghostmen too." The thought of dark energy inside my chest gave me phantom heart pains.

I could feel Wilder looking at me, and my muscles tensed. If I let him speak, I was afraid he would claim that the nanites had made him crazy and now he was cured, and I couldn't bear to hear it because I'd want to believe him. But it couldn't be true. Not completely. The nanites had affected all of us, but he'd still made choices. Besides, if the Wilder in the warehouse who admitted he killed Mi-sun and tried to kill me too had been nanite-impaired-false-Wilder, then so was the Wilder in the lair who kissed me. He was either all truth or all lies. I knew this logically, but if he spoke—

"Maisie," he said, "I want to—"

I jumped out of the moving car and rolled on the asphalt. Dragon slowed, but I shouted to him that I would run back alone. We were only a few kilometers from HAL.

I left the road, bounding through the brush. The lights of HAL were barely visible, a low, faint star. After hours of trudging, the speed was liberating. I'd loved Wilder, and that confused pain came out of me in a howl as if I were an animal. I remembered Ruth running in the night, and me afraid to make eye contact. She'd seemed fearless. But I was resisting the urge to turn my back to HAL and run far away.

A high, stinging sound cut the night air. I froze to listen—a rabbit's response. I forgot sometimes that I was the predator now.

Move, I thought.

I started to run again, but something tiny pricked my right calf. I didn't slow to investigate. A few steps later, I couldn't feel my leg at all. It just crumpled, and I fell. I looked to make sure my leg hadn't actually disappeared. Sticking out of my calf was a long silver needle. I plucked it free and threw it at the ground.

In the couple of seconds I was down, another needle bit into my left leg. I yanked it out, switched my impact boots to "hop," and slammed my left foot down. Midair, I felt my left leg go numb too. The ground was coming in fast. I twisted, landing on my back, and tumbled down an incline.

I could hear footsteps and a car.

I phoned Howell while crawling through the brush, my legs dragging. "I'm under attack out here. Not aliens. People. Shot me with something, my legs don't work." It wasn't until I heard the panic in my own voice that I understood I was close to toast.

I sent my coordinates from my GPS. Footsteps closer, coming from right, left, behind. I fired havoc pellets into the darkness. I took off my impact boots, put them on my hands, and slammed them down. I hurtled forward, twisting and somersaulting in the air, belly flopping onto a bush. It was a faster means of travel than dragging my body through the dirt, so I kept up the exercise in self-humiliation.

The numbness in my legs was crawling up my pelvis.

Above, three helicopters with searchlights came from HAL. From the darkness, someone shot a missile. The helicopters moved, the rocket missed, exploding on the ground beyond us. Another rocket. The helicopters returned fire. A few bullets struck me in the crossfire, burning holes in my clothes.

Another missile from the dark. A HAL helicopter lurched and crashed. A rocket from a HAL helicopter struck a car on the ground. There were shouts and commands.

A third bite, this time on my right shoulder. Before I lost that arm to numbness, I slammed down my handheld boots as hard as I could and launched myself at the nearest helicopter, flipping through the air, shaking the boots off. I managed to seize the helicopter's foot with my left hand. Someone pulled me in and we took off.

My head rolled back, the prick in my shoulder bleeding cold into my neck and down my right arm.

Dragon was holding me, his bald head shiny with sweat.

"They had needle darts, sharpened to the atom maybe. Pierced my skin." I shouted to be heard over the helicopter noise.

"Are you dying?" he asked.

I shrugged with one shoulder. Every part of me that wasn't numb was cold with fear.

"Don't die," he said. "If you have any choice in the matter, choose not to, okay?"

I nodded once and couldn't lift my head back up again.

We landed inside HAL's courtyard. Doctors met us at the helipad, Howell running alongside as they took me in.

"GT?" Howell asked.

"So it would seem," said Dragon. "Hankering to punch him in the face right about now."

In the lab, Wilder was waiting. I swore in my head. I was paralyzed, helpless. He could corner me and talk his manipulative crap, try to convince me of his reformed nature like he'd convinced Howell. For the moment he was standing out of the way. Waiting.

"Go wake her dad," Dragon told somebody.

I grunted a no. If I wasn't dying, I didn't want to worry him or Luther.

Then I lost the ability to grunt.

CHAPTER 47

Complete paralysis. Even my eyelids froze. One of the doctors slid them shut for me, as if I were dead. My body felt corpse cold, though it didn't shiver. Drool slid out of my mouth down my cheek, a cold wet line like the trail a snail leaves.

I didn't sleep. My mind was microwave popcorn cooked on high. I lay and thought and could do nothing at all. I was waiting for one more change—either my mind would go dark too and that would be that, or something would move.

Hours later, something moved. A finger. A twitch in my toe. My eyelids.

Wilder was still in the lab, waiting like a vulture for me to die and offer up my tokens into his grubby hands. When I managed to sit, he gave up and left. One small victory.

"I'm taking credit for your not dying," Dragon whispered to me, "since it was my idea."

"Fair enough," I whispered back, my throat trying to remember how to talk.

"GT failed to get you out there," Howell said, sitting by my bed. "He'll attack HAL next."

I moved my right leg. My whole body prickled with returning life.

Howell turned to Dragon. "Code Lockdown?"

Dragon wrinkled his nose. "We should have come up with a better name, like Code Armageddon, or Code Imperial Fire . . ."

A few minutes later I eased myself out of the gurney, testing my weight on my legs. My bones felt rubbery, my muscles bags of sand, but I could stand up.

"If GT will attack here, why don't we go somewhere else?" I asked.

"He'd track us wherever we went," said Howell. "And HAL is my best refuge."

"My mom—"

"Will be found and brought here. This is where I have the tools and supplies to support your mission. We'll stand and fight."

I went to find my dad only to see him coming to me under the triplets' guard, Hairy pushing his wheelchair. Dad's legs were bandaged and propped up, the gunshot wounds healing. Luther walked with his hand on Laelaps's head, looking everywhere but at me.

"I don't need so much fuss," Dad said. "I'm feeling fine. Look."

He held up his right hand and made the Star Trek live-long-and-prosper sign.

"Nice," I said. "High five." I made like I was going to slap his hand. He pulled his hand down fast. "Easy, Dad. I was kidding. I won't hurt you."

He smiled as if he'd been kidding too.

Through the plate-glass atrium I could see car after car leaving HAL under guard of helicopters. Dragon got busy on a walkie-talkie, speaking in code. Hallway lights were shutting off.

"*¿Qué pasa?*" Dad asked.

"GT decided we didn't have enough on our hands with the whole alien thing, so he attacked me outside the compound."

"I don't much care for GT," said Dad.

Dragon intoned over the PA system that all remaining complex residents should report to Howell's office immediately. The triplets hurried off with Dad, leaving me and Luther walking together.

"Hey," I said.

"Hey," Luther said.

He put his hands in his pockets. "So, it was weird the other day when we bumped into each other and our faces kind of accidentally smooshed together."

I smiled, but kept my head turned so he didn't see. "Yeah, that was weird."

Luther stopped, so I stopped too. His expression was intense.

"Just promise me it won't be him."

"What?"

"Wilder. Promise me you won't choose him."

If I hadn't had the brute token, I would have slugged him.

"You're disgusting."

"Or I'm discerning and concerned."

"You think I'm vacuous?"

"I think you're a girl, and as far as I can tell, girls do vacuous things for guys like him."

I walked faster, my recently numb legs shaking beneath me. "I thought you knew me better."

"I used to know you," he said, keeping up behind me. "Frak, Maisie, I don't know anything anymore."

Those were words I never thought I'd hear Luther say. Except for the "frak" part. I stopped.

"But we're still best friends, right?" I said.

"Affirmative."

"Then everything's okay."

He smiled as if I'd made perfect sense. I hoped my eyes didn't betray my fear. My mom was lost somewhere. I had all five tokens and was weaker for it. I'd been failing and failing, and it was getting harder to muster up any hope at all.

A mechanical grating noise startled us. A metal wall was unrolling from the ceiling, locking off the rest of the building.

Howell's office was already filled—Dad, Wilder, plus Dragon and a crowd of security guys including Hairy, Scary, and Larry. Just ten of the PhD/MD whitecoats remained after the mass exodus.

"GT will attack us," Howell said without preamble. "It never rains but it's pouring with old men snoring. I've sent away everyone who has children at home, as well as anyone I can't trust with my life."

I glanced at Wilder to see if he showed any shame. He was leaning against the wall, his gaze on the ceiling.

"We've closed down everything but the core of this building," said Dragon. "The lab, a few dormitories, security center, staff kitchen, storage, bunkers, and this office. The gates in the outer walls are locked. The electric fence is live. We are off grid and well supplied. Until GT and aliens are no longer a threat, this is your home."

Luther was pale. Dad cleared his throat before speaking, but his voice still cracked.

"But . . . my wife," he said.

Dragon looked at his hands. "We've had no word—"

"My team in Florida is still looking," said Howell, "and when they find her, they will bring her here. Security, your job is to keep us all alive. Everyone else, your job is to do whatever Maisie Brown needs you to do. Maisie Brown, your job is to save the world."

Howell stood, catching us all in her fierce gaze. She picked up three red balls off her desk and juggled them with just her right hand, spiraling them in high ellipses. She caught two in her hand and the third in her mouth. Her people sprang to their feet, applauding.

"Very nice, Bonnie," Dragon said. "Team Basilisk, I want your eyes on the monitors. Team Griffin to the turrets. Team Yeti, take a rest. You'll be on duty tonight."

"Who named the teams, Dragon?" I asked.

He lowered his sunglasses to look at me as he left. "Team Danger, you're general of the civilians." He shut the door.

"I'm general?"

"You're the thinker now," said Howell.

All eyes were on me. Even Luther's. He was fussing with the zipper on his sweatshirt, its *zing* the only sound in the room. I cleared my throat.

"So, I think I know some things." I was aware of Wilder still leaning against the wall, but I didn't look at him. Luther's *zip-zip-zip* made me want to pace. "The ghostmen are old. Not tortoise-old. Planet-old. They don't die."

Someone whimpered. I agreed that wasn't good news.

"This is just a hypothesis," I told my dad as an apology.

"I'd say hypotheses are in order," he said.

"Okay. So the ghostmen are adversely affected by gravity and need robot suits in order to move outside their ship. When the robot suit arm attaches to a human, the ghost can leave the suit, shooting through the arm and into the person. An intangible parasite, it takes over all the human body's functions. After people are possessed by the aliens, it looks like they mostly spend their time eating and seeking out adrenaline rushes."

"Seriously?" said Luther.

"They're here to enjoy physical bodies," said Wilder.

"That's what I've observed," I said. "Here's my best guess about the rest. The ghostmen evolved from something like dark energy. Maybe they came across technology from another species and adapted what they found for their own uses." This was all feeling right, the thinker token seeming content inside me, so I went on. "They didn't know what pleasure was until they inhabited another species' bodies. Once they experienced a tangible existence, it became their obsession, and now they cross the galaxy seeking new hosts so they can experience sensations again.

"At some point their two ships arrived at what I'll call Planet A and started taking over bodies. Planet A inhabitants probably discovered them, fought them, and failed, but managed to send info about the enemy to Planet B, another planet they were in contact with, probably their sister colony in another solar system. After the ghosts used up the last of Planet A's dwellers, their ships traveled to Planet B.

"By the time the ships arrived, Planet B had made the tokens that gave five individuals the necessary skills to destroy the ships. They succeeded with one, but the other ship got away, heading, most likely, for the next nearest planet with sentient life: Earth.

The token-makers packaged up the tokens and sent them to us, presumably to spare us the fate of Planet A and help us destroy the second ship.

"The ghostmen will want to stay here as long as possible. I think they try to be careful to avoid notice, inserting themselves into people who live in isolated places."

I glanced at Wilder. He nodded once as if he'd thought the same thing, then looked back at the ceiling.

"When possessed humans die, the ghosts are booted out," I said. "I think if the ship isn't nearby to suck them back in, the ghostmen would keep floating right out of Earth's atmosphere into space's vacuum, where they'd be helpless. That's where we want them."

I paused. Everyone waited.

"And so, in conclusion, I need to destroy their ship."

"And . . . how?" asked Luther.

"I was able to fight off the mini-troopers pretty easily," I said. "But as soon as they realized I was the fireteam, the infected humans must have alerted the big ship to my location, and it master-blasted me. I don't . . . I don't know if a direct blast could *kill* me, but maybe. I think the fireteam's purpose is to destroy the ship. That has to be where they store their robot suits, and without them, they can't enter any new bodies. And without the ship to recapture them, disembodied ghostmen will enter space and have no way to return to take any more bodies."

"Okay, so let's get some heavy firepower and obliterate the sucker out of the sky," Luther said.

"Well, it's superfast and invisible," I said. "The only way to locate it is to watch where the disembodied ghostmen go, and only I can see them. So here's the plan: we need to gather together a bunch of possessed people and somehow kick the little pink aliens out of them. The ship will come to rescue them, and I'll follow the ghosts to the ship, break into it, and destroy it from the inside."

CHAPTER 48

It felt great to have a plan at last. I looked at Luther, expecting his approval of my superhero scheme. But he was just staring at me. Everyone else looked away—at the floor, at their hands. I felt the doubt in the silence like a vise.

"Do you know how smart the token-makers were?" I said. "They could send an asteroid millions of kilometers at the perfect trajectory to safely land in Earth's orbit, and even *they* couldn't defeat two ships. Apparently no military or weapon was sufficient. The fireteam was the best option."

More silence.

I looked at Luther. "I know it's risky, but what else can I do?"

"Not die?" he said.

"Luthe—"

"I know you're the Astounding Fireteam, but this plan . . . it's too much for one person, and outrageously dangerous. You might as well jump into a volcano."

"I know," I whispered. "But I don't know what else to do."

"Let's mull this over dinner, shall we?" Howell said brightly.

Everyone muttered agreement and began to shuffle from the room. Luther glanced back at me before leaving. I just stood there, already feeling half-dead.

Only the thinker could use the tokens of the slain team members. Clearly the token-makers had considered casualties likely. If at least one out of five was expected to die, what was the probability that one out of one would survive?

I wasn't as strong as Ruthless. I couldn't produce as much armor as Jack Havoc or shoot as often as Code Blue. My techno token was weaker than at first, and I clearly couldn't plot as well as the Wild Card. I longed to counsel with Wilder. I glanced at him as he left and reminded myself how he'd laughed at me when he'd shot off Fido.

I turned to Howell.

"I just want to remind you that GT's son is still walking around free."

"I sent away everyone I couldn't trust with my life," she said.

"Yeah, and you're crazy."

Howell giggled. Straight up giggled. "But Miss Brown, wouldn't I have to be?"

I shouted after her as she walked away, "What does that even mean?"

I ate dinner in the lab with my dad and Luther. Dad was chatty with the whitecoats, going over the robot suit, hypothesizing about whether the interior of the ship would be solid as well. He seemed so upbeat, but I detected cracks in his gusto. Sometimes he looked at me like Luther did—as if seeing me already dead.

For the first time since getting Ruth's token, I didn't want to eat.

"What if you stay on the ground?" asked Luther. "What if you watch where the pink ghosts go and don't only shoot havoc at it but direct missiles and balefire, Maisie, we could try a nuke, right? There's no reason—"

"The missiles won't work. I don't know why, but I have to listen to whatever subconscious data the thinker token is uploading to my brain."

"I wish . . ." He took a deep breath. "I wish none of this had happened."

When the others went to bed, I stayed in the lab. Wilder wasn't there, but I knew he would come. Since the lockdown, there was nowhere else for him to go except his lonely little room, and he hated being alone. Only child. Missing mom/absent father. He came to astronaut boot camp with an entourage of friends, even though he had nefarious plans. He tried (succeeded?) to get together with me, and who knew how many other girls. The boy needed company. And I wanted a full confession. The question and presence of Wilder was distracting me from my mission.

I was fiddling with the mini-trooper suit when I sensed him at the open door. I spoke before he could try to slink off again.

"Why does Howell trust you?"

"Because I didn't kill Mi-sun."

"You told me you did."

"I was lying."

"Brutus said—" I stopped. I hadn't thought of it since getting the thinker token and suddenly felt like a fool. Brutus had said Wilder killed Mi-sun. He could have meant GT Wilder. His testimony was questionable. I threw it out.

"Did you know we were going to kill Ruth?" I asked.

His tone was cautious. "So, are we talking now—"

"Did you know we were going to kill Ruthless?" I asked again, turning.

"Yeah, I knew. I knew other things too—that no one would stop her but us. And she'd do a lot of damage first. Killing her quickly was one option; the other was to let her rage and raze until we were forced to kill her anyway."

"You didn't have to kill her. If you'd—"

"No. She wasn't going to fight for the team anymore, and we needed the token back. Without all five, we'd fail, and my nanites were constantly screaming that our mission would be colossally important."

"It was all an act," I said. "You made me care about you so you could use me." I wished my voiced hadn't quavered. That weakness goaded me, and I shouted. "You perverted worm, you nonhuman, you're a hundred times worse than your father!"

He trembled. "I didn't make you do anything! Besides, *that* wasn't my plan. The *you* part."

"You lied and manipulated me into going after Jacques—"

"The other part! The part where I fell in love with you."

I felt as if I'd been slapped.

"Shut up."

"Make me," he said, then laughed at his own absurd joke. Because, of course, I *could* make him.

Enough confession. I pronounced judgment in a calm, even voice that made me proud. "You are a murderer and a liar, and you're so far gone, you don't even care."

He matched my gaze as if it were a contest. "So, what are you going to do with me?"

I couldn't stand to have him around anymore. Every time I looked at him, my heart hurt all over again. Besides, the way he'd sat there like a vulture while I was paralyzed scared me. Handing him off to the police was ridiculous. Everything we were, everything we'd done with these tokens, it seemed apart from the rest of the world.

"I'm the general now, and you're not welcome here or anywhere near people I love. Leave HAL tonight and don't come back."

I turned and got to work on my suit. He stayed for fifteen seconds more. I counted his retreating footsteps till he was gone. Then I sat down, elbows on knees, my face in my hands. I was glad my body had waited for his absence to start shaking.

Instead of relief I felt a loss. I wanted to curl up in a dark room next to Laelaps and sink into numbing sleep. But Wilder had dumped new data on me, and I couldn't relax till I'd examined it and organized it on neat little shelves in my brain.

Ruth. I hadn't been the thinker when I'd known her, and I had to admit, his analysis of her seemed right.

Mi-sun. The evidence indicated he'd killed her, but I couldn't be one hundred percent sure.

But Wilder couldn't lie his way out of trying to kill me. He most definitely aimed blue shot at my person and tried to—

I dropped my hands from my face. He'd aimed. And missed.

I hadn't understood before, but aiming was so easy with the shooter token. My eyes were the weapon's sights—I looked and there my ammo flew. I could shoot someone in the eye, no problem, especially from only a few meters away.

Okay, but he did destroy Fido.

Then again, he could have shot those havoc knives at my torso or head. Instead he hit the only place that wouldn't make me bleed. I'd assumed he'd made mistakes that night, but what if everything he did was on purpose? Maybe he took an overdose of potassium or something *intending* to stop his heart—a self-execution. Why would he want to die in front of me?

So his tokens would leave his body. So I would be there to take them.

But neither of us could have known what I was beginning to guess—when his heart stopped and the tokens began to shut down, I leaned over him and the electricity of my three tokens must have drawn his nanites back to their base. I'd pulled them away before he was fully dead, and so I'd been able to revive him.

He'd shot my Fido arm, even knowing that without it, I wouldn't be able to call for help. Help for *him*. He walked into that building believing he would die. If I didn't question that he was the bad guy, then I'd let him.

The thought was so sharp, so sad, I fell back into a chair.

He wasn't the thinker anymore. I shouldn't have been able to sense him, but I thought I could. He was above me. The upper floors were closed. What was he doing?

I remembered him in the cafeteria, turning to me, arms open, inviting me to kill him. I'd wondered then if he didn't want to live.

Wilder was on the roof.

CHAPTER 49

I ran. Too hurried for stairs, I scaled the outside of the building, leaping onto the roof. Wilder was standing near an edge. With the building in lockdown, now that he was out, there was no exit but down.

I walked closer, and he startled when he heard the gravel slide beneath my feet. I'd never seen Wilder startle before. He used to know when I was near. He used to know everything.

"Tell me again." I stopped a few meters away. "I'm going to try to listen better."

He blinked surprise. "Yeah?"

"Yeah."

"Thank you." He began to pace a short track in the roof's gravel top. "Okay. Everything? Um . . . my dad found out about the tokens and Howell's plans. He made sure I would be one of the recipients. We had only a vague understanding of what the tokens were and what they would do, but Dad knew they would be valuable. I knew it'd be a risk, but when I heard that the tokens might make me stronger or smarter, Dad didn't have to work to convince me.

"Dad intended to use me as his little spy and help lure the rest of the token holders into his employ. 'We'll be more powerful than anyone can imagine,' he'd say. 'We'll do whatever we want, own whatever we want. We'll be a team.' A few years earlier, I might have really believed that once I had a token my daddy would *wuv me*," he said in a baby voice. "I knew better than to be completely sucked in by his promises, but still, he would *notice* me, and at the time, that was enough."

He glanced up as if expecting I would walk away. I stayed. He looked back at the ground.

"I chose you at boot camp because of your arm."

"What do you mean you *chose* me?"

"I'd agreed with Dad I would stay single at boot camp because Howell might choose anybody, and I didn't want to complicate matters with a potential teammate. The plan was to secure everyone's loyalty for Dad, and if anyone didn't side with us . . . Dad might have to . . . you know . . . get rough. I did hook up with a couple of girls at boot camp, but I knew they wouldn't be chosen because they weren't too bright. I got bored with them. You didn't qualify as not too bright, but I was sure Howell wouldn't pick you because of your arm." He looked at me, grimacing. "How am I doing on the hate meter? Rising up to ten?"

I shrugged. I didn't want to pass judgment yet.

He couldn't seem to hold my gaze, looking down again. "When your name was on the list, I was . . . wow, I don't know that I've ever been so angry. At Howell, at you, at myself. It wasn't until then that I realized I actually liked you, and how much I thought that weakened me."

I nodded, and he seemed encouraged to go on.

"Dad didn't want you loyal to me—he wanted you loyal to him alone. I was a terrible thinker. I could feel that urgency to unite the team and train us for what was coming. But I wanted to use that brain power to show my dad I was worth the gamble. I wanted the world, and I wanted him to see me get it. And it all backfired in Ruth. I should have seen what was wrong with her before she blew."

"So you decided she had to die."

He nodded, still looking down. "I convinced myself I was a hero who could stop a killer. It wasn't until we were on the boat that I knew she'd die. I felt sure that only the thinker should salvage her token—but you took it first."

"Sorry..."

"Yeah, you're kind of grabby." He tried to smile. "So... you left, and when you did, my ability to keep the team together broke. Jacques and Mi-sun went home—or so I thought. I didn't trust Howell, so I left too, and it was then I realized GT had killed my mom. I wanted to punish him. I didn't want him dead—I wanted him alive and eaten away by remorse.

"But the pull of the fireteam interfered with revenge. I felt like half of a person without you... you guys. And I was convinced something really bad would happen if I didn't re-form the team. So I made a plan, and it started with you. After Dad visited your house, I gassed you out to make you feel in danger."

"It *was* you."

He laughed ruefully. "I know, this just gets better and better. Are you sure you—"

There was an angry hum followed by a loud crack. I ran to the edge of the roof. The north wall was splitting, chunks of concrete falling loose.

"Speak of the devil," Wilder said, crouching beside me.

"He's determined to get these tokens, isn't he?" I said.

"He'll never stop."

I called Dragon.

"I'm on the roof," I said.

"Yeah, electric fence down and something is attacking the north wall," he said. "You stay put and stay low, Brown. They're here for you. Don't give them a target."

"My dad—"

"Those suckers are not getting through our wall. We have a few surprises." He disconnected.

The turrets were showing their bristling firepower, weapons lighting up the night. I saw a swarm of aerial droids take off from HAL, zipping down the line of a searchlight. The wall continued to crack.

"Laser gun?" I asked. After sporting alien technology for half a year, a laser gun trying to break a wall seemed practically mundane.

"Quiet, less likely to draw outside notice," said Wilder. "GT tried to paralyze you and take you away. That failed, so he won't try it again. He doesn't know that the tokens won't stay put in gravity. So this time he's here—"

"To kill me." I nodded. "So go on. I can multitask."

He smiled. "Okay." We were whispering now, both of us crouched and keeping an eye on the commotion. "So my plan was to get you isolated from everything and make you believe I was your one lifeline. But while you were in Florida—"

"You knew where I was?"

He shrugged. "Sure. I . . . uh . . ."

"You put a tracker in my necklace," I said.

"And risk your discovering it? Give me some credit. No, I monitored Luther's computer activity, hacked that Japanese site, and, after you posted, followed your IP trail. But I didn't lead GT's guys there. I didn't know he had your dad—"

"I know," I said. "Go on."

Wilder took a breath. "So, GT had recruited Mi-sun and Jacques straight out of HAL. They were especially susceptible to my dad's manipulations. The nature of the tokens made them want a team, a leader—but after Ruth, they didn't want *me* anymore. Dad had them take out some of his old enemies, partly just to get them in so deep they'd feel like they couldn't leave. Jacques went shopping for a 'hitman wardrobe.' Mi-sun . . . got weird. I pretended to join up with Dad so I could figure how to get Jacques and Mi-sun out. After a while Mi-sun agreed to leave with me.

"I think she hadn't really processed what she'd been doing for Dad until she had a choice to stop. We were at Dad's, and she was heading to her room to pack when she started to scream. I heard her in the hallway, but before I could get to her, she pulled a ring off her finger and shot it at her own chest. Maybe she was aiming at the token, but she hit her heart."

I shivered.

"Dad picked her up and felt for a pulse. Brutus and some other guys saw it happen, but they didn't know about the blue shot. It must've looked like Dad was choking her—and maybe he did, to make sure she was dead." He squeezed his eyes shut. "Then he's hollering at me to come take her token. It was coming out of her chest. Whatever we were made for, we would need every token. But I hesitated.

"Jacques was there too, and he leaped for her. I kicked him back and took it myself. Better me than him, that's what I thought. Until the pain hit." He took a breath. "It only lasts a few seconds, but it feels like forever, doesn't it?"

I nodded. In the distance we heard shouts, zaps, a helicopter. Still crouching, I bounced on my heels. I wanted to be helping, not hiding.

"How did Jacques feel about that?" I asked to distract myself.

"He armored up and declared his intention to take both my tokens. I actually thought about killing him and claiming his instead. But the memory of pain was so fresh, I couldn't go through it again. I don't know how you did it, Maisie."

"I wanted to die," I whispered, looking out. No movement beyond the wall. The landscape was steeped in darkness. "Taking Jacques's token, choosing to go through it a third time? Like shoving a knife into my own chest."

"It had become clear that Jacques was as lost to the team as Ruth had been. But I couldn't kill him. I mean, I *could* have." He smiled.

"Yeah, yeah, I know, you're so tough."

"But Dad rightly became suspicious of me. He gave the order to kill me, but I escaped, went into hiding. It's funny that doesn't bother me anymore. Maybe it was inevitable, father wanting to kill the usurper son."

"It's so Greco-Roman."

"Am I Jupiter still?"

"You've always had a god complex."

Something exploded in the courtyard. Smoke billowed outward. Dragon and the security guys in gas masks ran into the haze. The breeze shifted, and I made out figures fighting Howell's guys.

I was in a perfect sniper position. No matter Dragon's orders, I had to attack.

Forming flat havoc pellets, I began to precision-fire on invaders as I saw them, like punching them from a distance. Quickly I depleted the electrons stored in the shooter token battery. Mi-sun could store more electrons than I could, my shooter token tangled with four others. Yet another weakness.

I kept firing, pulling electrons from the gas molecules in the air around me. I could feel my hair rise, the hairs on my arms standing, the air molecules pulling on anything to replace the electrons I'd stolen.

"We're maintaining the perimeter," said Dragon on the headset. "Stay back, Brown."

"Careful," said Wilder. "They're trying to draw you out."

I moved to steal electrons from a new patch of air. I aimed at a guy just as he turned to aim at me. He must have fired first. I heard that familiar whistling noise. Needles.

CHAPTER 50

I pushed Wilder down, hitting the roof beside him. There was another explosion. This one bright—a light bomb maybe, something to blind us.

We huddled flat to the roof, Wilder's arm over me. I opened and shut my eyes, but everything was orangey-white, my eyes dazzled. I felt for Wilder's head and traced my hand over his skull and chest, giving him a havoc helmet and breastplate.

He whispered, "Does this mean that you don't want me dead?"

I almost laughed.

"I'm sorry, Maisie," he said.

"You didn't mean to be a complete douche bag to everyone you knew," I said flatly. "You were trying to accomplish something impossible, and you had to play tough in order to win."

"It sounds absurd when you say it out loud."

"It didn't feel grand at the time either," I said quietly. "You should go back in."

I heard him knock on his helmet. "Naw, I'm good."

"You're as stubborn as your dad."

"It just feels good to explain. I don't mean to excuse myself. Maybe there's no good reason for all I did. When I had the thinker token, it seemed so clear. And now . . . nothing's clear. Almost nothing. Is your sight coming back?"

"Yeah." I could make out shapes in the dark. The humming and cracking started again. If the HAL forces had destroyed one laser cannon, another had taken its place.

"So it's . . ." Wilder rubbed his face harshly. "It's been torture this past year trying not to care about you. Because I am—*was*—the leader, and I couldn't let what I felt get in the way of what I would do. I meant what I said—falling for you wasn't the plan." He didn't seem the least bit shy declaring this. "I felt like trash every time I lied to you. You were willing to leave your parents because you were worried about Mi-sun. If you'd known she was already dead, would you still have come? I believed I would fail without you. But I was just scared you would hate me if you knew. That she was dead. That I had her token. That I'd lost a second team member.

"When we confronted Jacques that first time, I was half hoping he'd tell you he thought I'd killed Mi-sun. If you hated me, it might make it easier to . . . to take your tokens too. But he didn't say it. And I couldn't bear to. In Philly, in the *lair*, lying next to you, holding you . . ." His exhale was nearly a sigh. "Full confession: after that night, I made sure we didn't find GT and Jacques too quickly."

I gasped. That made him smile, though it faded quickly.

"For weeks I believed I would have to kill you. The techno token was buried under the brute token. I would have to unite them with my thinker token or the fireteam would fail. Here I was trying so hard not to be my dad, and in order to be a hero, I would have to be a murderer."

I thought of his e-mails. He'd sweet-talked me into a death trap.

"Then when you came to Philadelphia, this wall I'd been bricking up just crumbled, and I knew I couldn't . . . well, *kill* you. But the Purpose pressed and insisted that all the tokens be together. I didn't know how. My head hurt trying to find a way out, and I couldn't and couldn't until . . . you were beside me, asleep, and I thought, she would be a better thinker than I am. And like that I realized I could kill myself instead. It's ludicrous I didn't realize that before, but maybe it was a safety function of the thinker token— survival above all else. The moment I overrode that, everything changed."

Another swarm of aerial drones buzzed over us, heading for the night beyond the north wall. One of the turrets there was gone. It must have been destroyed while we were blind. I sat up, hugging my knees to my chest, too anxious to lie flat.

"Did you ever read the book by that guy who was hiking alone when a boulder fell on his arm?" Wilder whispered. "For three days he was pinned, trying to get the boulder off, believing he was going to die. Then it occurred to him—he could cut off his own arm. He said when he realized that, he felt profound relief. That's how I felt. It was the night after we kissed—you remember?—and you slept next to me, and I watched you sleep for hours—is that creepy?— but I watched and thought and realized I could cut off my own arm—I could kill myself—and give you all the tokens. I woke up unafraid for the first time in months."

"I remember that morning," I said.

"Yeah, me too." His smile was more real now. "For whatever reason, you and I handled the tokens better than the others. Our brains took the changes without imploding. And you were a better candidate for the thinker. After you learned about Mi-sun and took off, I had to figure out how to get you to take my tokens. I knew you'd try to save me if you could, but if you believed I was evil—"

Another light bomb. I shut my eyes just as Wilder pulled me down, piercing shrills passing over our heads. Those weren't just numbing needles, I was pretty sure. Those would kill us if they could.

We flat-crawled across the roof, away from the attack. Above us the south turret's searching eye was still, staring motionless in one direction. I glanced around—the other searchlights were twitching, human hands moving them, looking for and finding targets.

I called Dragon. "I think no one's in the south turret. We've got a blind spot."

"Sending someone," he said. "Stay put."

I crept to the edge of the roof. Below, the south courtyard was blacked out. I heard scraping, a mumbling drill, and then from a hole beneath the wall a figure dressed in black crawled free. All that on the north wall was a distraction. Here was the real danger.

I formed a hollow havoc ball and shot it, knocking the figure flat. A second came through the hole. I went to shoot this one too but the first—injured but conscious—shot at me, a swarm of needles. I dropped.

"Dragon, tunnelers under the south wall," I called on Lady. "They're packing needles."

"Don't—" Wilder started.

I leaped down. I wasn't wearing impact boots, but a few stories didn't bother my brute body. I landed near the tunneler and havoc-banded his wrists and ankles. Then I covered the hole with havoc armor, bonded to the concrete around it. Fast. I had to find the other ninja dude before he found Dad and Luther.

I ran around the side of HAL, armoring myself as I went. A high whistle. I dived to the ground, the needles going over my head. A black shape disappeared around the corner. He was hunting me. I knew that. I should have been running away.

There was a small explosion. I rounded the corner to find the door blown off its hinges. Inside the corridor was empty.

I looked up. The ninja dude was clinging high to the wall. I shot a fist-sized havoc shield just as he shot needles. They met in the middle. My needles-studded shield crashed to the floor.

I ducked behind a wall, breathing hard. The dozen poisoned needles had nailed straight through my impenetrable havoc shield. My armor wouldn't protect me. He was waiting for me around the corner. And now I heard soft footsteps from behind.

CHAPTER 51

I couldn't let myself get trapped between two bad guys. I leaned out to shoot at the ninja dude again but he was gone. I hurried out, looking. Around the corner. Up on the wall. Nothing.

Come on, Maisie. If you need to take down an entire hostile ship, you should be able to stop a couple of regular creepos.

I heard a *zap* and startled back.

Around the other side of the wall, the ninja was still standing, his needle gun aimed at where I'd been. He fell to the floor. Dragon came from behind me, a fancy Taser gun in his hand.

"Those needles can go through walls," Dragon said.

Of course they could go through walls if they could pierce my armor, but I hadn't thought fast enough.

"Thanks," I said.

"Don't try to soften me up," he said, kicking the needle gun away from the unconscious guy. "You put yourself at risk against my express orders, and I intend to stay grumpy with you."

"Understood." I felt pretty grumpy with myself.

"No other breaches," Dragon said. "Threat on the north wall contained for now. Keep your precious hide inside."

He glared so hard I didn't go up to the roof for Wilder. I was on my way to check on Luther and Dad when I ran into Wilder in the corridor. It was as dark as outside. He stood alone, hands in his pockets.

"I just checked on them," he said. "They were asleep. The bunkers are soundproof."

"Thanks." I looked at my hands. I was holding Dragon's Taser gun, a little thing that had proved more effective than my whole fireteam self.

Wilder reached up to rub his hair, forgetting he was wearing a havoc helmet. I went closer to crack the armor and ease it off his head and chest.

His face was expectant. I took a step back.

"Growing up, whenever faced with a problem, I would ask myself what my dad would do," he said, turning the havoc helmet over in his hands. "But these past few months, that's changed to you. I wish I knew—right now—what you would do."

His smile was so sad, but I didn't know how to sum up the whirling and thumping and knotting inside me. The shouts of command from outside dimmed, the dark numbing everything outside of us. I lifted my hand to my chest, so aware of the five tokens I could practically feel their weight, their heat. Now that they were joined, I couldn't imagine losing a single one.

"Does it feel hollow there?" I asked.

"A little . . ."

I let my hand drop. "I understand why you did all you did." I wouldn't have done it the way he had, but I understood. "You could have told me days ago."

"I tried. But you wouldn't have believed me anyway if I'd told you before you asked."

"Took me a long time to ask, didn't it?"

He groaned in agreement.

I felt suddenly shy and turned away to go into the lab. Finishing the jet pack felt more urgent now than ever.

My techno-token-inspired brain came up with an idea for a battery that would store electrons for me and have a higher capacity than my swamped shooter token. It would take a few days to build. After tonight's attack, I doubted I had the time to spare. If only I wasn't the lone fireteam member.

An hour passed as I worked, aware of Wilder beside me, watching, tapping notes on a tablet.

"What will you wear when you attack?" he asked. "You can withstand the cold of the upper atmosphere, I think, but probably not the decreased pressure."

I nodded. "I don't want to end up like Ruth. I'll wear a pressure suit."

"And havoc armor too? It just seems wrong—risky—to depend on our own technology somehow. I remember thinking that, back when I could think better."

"Yeah, I agree."

I'd decided not to say what I'd been thinking when I suddenly changed my mind. The idea was too big, too stark and sharp to stay inside me. I whispered it.

"Wilder, I don't think I'm strong enough to do this alone."

He didn't say anything for a minute.

"A ship, Wilder. A massive, flying, city-sized ship. I couldn't even . . . Dragon had to . . . one guy in black clothes with a stupid needle gun, and I couldn't—"

"Maisie," he said in such a way that I looked up. "I don't know if I mentioned it, but I'm pretty smart."

A laugh surprised me in my throat.

"And I used to be even smarter, you know," he said. "With my brain plus a thinker token, my superpowered conclusion was, Maisie Danger Brown is the best—the only—person who can do this. You, Maisie, can do this."

It was a nice pep talk. But I was the thinker now, and I knew the odds of a one-person fireteam were frighteningly small.

"Maybe I could take the drug you took to stop your heart and dislodge the tokens," I said. "And when the tokens leave me, you could take one or two, and Luther too, and give a couple back to me somehow after you revive me so there'd be three fireteam members—"

His frown was as sad as his smile had been. He didn't have to say it wouldn't work. It was a fantasy. All five tokens were stuck together now. When Wilder's two had come out into me, there'd been no way to separate one from the other.

"I know," I said.

"If you want me to, I'll take them. I'll be the fireteam for you. But—" He shook his head. "What if we can't revive you?"

"It's okay, I'll be the fireteam," I said. "I just thought—"

"I know," he said this time.

He did know. He was the only one in the world who could.

In silence I kept working, he kept watching. And I found myself examining his story for holes, weighing his actions one by one, still hesitant to trust him again.

When at last I thought I could sleep, I fell onto one of the lab cots. Wilder was occupying another. He rolled over. He looked at me. This boy who had been a fairy tale, a figment, now was next to me and almost real again. I wanted to lift my arm. I wanted to touch his hand.

The idea was too much. I closed my eyes.

◆

It seemed only moments later I woke up. Howell and the PhDs were stumbling in. No one had slept much after laser cannons and explosions. I sat up, saw Wilder beside me, and couldn't remember if I was supposed to scowl or smile.

Wilder must have detected my uncertainty. "I'm pretty sure you revoked my banishment last night."

"Did I?"

"If you can't remember, then my answer is yes, absolutely. You begged me to stay and swore unfailing, eternal love."

Dad and Luther came in, and I blushed, remembering what Luther had said. *Promise me you won't choose him.*

Howell was arguing with the whitecoats about whether or not to abandon HAL.

"Think GT will give up after last night?" I asked.

"That little skirmish? He was just testing our defenses."

"When will he be back?" I asked.

Howell and Wilder looked at each other.

"He needs time to regroup," he said. "Less than a week, I'd guess."

"Then we end this first." I was surprised by how confident I sounded. My stomach felt like dry ice on water.

"You have a plan, oh great and terrible thinker?" Wilder asked.

"I don't know what you did to this thinker token, but it hasn't been magically implanting foolproof plans into my head."

"Maisie." Dragon was holding a cell phone. His expression was cautious. "Our team in Florida. They found your mother."

Dad sat upright. Luther put his hand on my shoulder, as if to shield me from bad news.

Dragon held out the phone. I took it with my left hand. It was noticeably shaking so I switched to my cyborg hand.

"Mom?"

"Hola, Maisie. ¿Dónde estás?"

Her voice! I bounced on my toes and smiled at Dad. Dragon set the phone to speaker so everyone could hear. I glanced at Howell, who I knew spoke Spanish as well as a dozen other languages, and she shook her head. I understood she didn't want me to reveal my location, just to be safe.

"I'm with Dad. Are you okay?"

"Yes, I am fine," she said in English now. "I had dinner. I had meat for dinner."

What? Was she trying to speak to me in code or something, afraid bad guys were listening?

"The people who found you are helping me out," I said. "You can trust them."

"Do you still have that token? You're still strong?"

"Yes . . ."

"Dígame dónde estás. Exactamente." She was asking again where I was. Why wasn't she asking about Dad? An idea began seeping through me, cold.

"Um, what did you have for dinner?" I asked.

"Meat. It was tender. Very easy to chew."

"Nothing like tender meat," I said slowly. "Did you salt it?"

"Oh yes," she said. "Plenty of salt to bring out the flavor."

My cyborg hand was shaking too. I looked at Dad. His frown touched his eyes, wrinkled his forehead. He was confused. Wilder wasn't. His look confirmed my fear.

I wished Jacques were alive to express in his ear-singeing way exactly how I felt about the *bleepity-bleep* aliens who had claimed my mom.

CHAPTER 52

Are you hurt?" I asked Mom. "Are you sick or injured at all?"

"No. Where are you, Maisie?"

"Mom, I'm going to come get you, okay?" I said, trying to keep my voice neutral. I didn't want to say anything that might lead the alien inside her to figure out that I was at HAL.

"*¿Dónde estás, mi hija? Dígame.* I'll come to you."

"That's not safe. Stay with the guys who found you, and I'll be there soon."

I ended the call. Dad was staring at me. I wished the nanites made me immune to sorrow. I didn't want to cry, so I clenched my jaw and stared hard at the wall, my chin vibrating like a rabbit's nose.

"Don't say it," Dad begged.

"I don't know how to help her, Dad," I whispered to keep from crying. "I don't know what to do."

"Frakking flatscans," Luther muttered.

Wilder cursed in Russian.

"Apparently, while fleeing GT, she'd gone into a quarantined town a couple of hours from where you'd been staying in Florida," said Dragon. "Our team rescued her from the town, but I told them to stay put with her for now."

"She must have gambled that GT's guys wouldn't pursue her into the quarantine," I said, my voice dry. "She didn't know that the Jumper Virus was an alien infestation."

Dragon stepped in front of me, his shoulders straight, his arms at his sides.

"Tell me what to do, Brown," he said. "Give me an order."

I knew—with a surety that felt like a thousand knives in my stomach—that my mother was no longer controlling her own body. I didn't know if it was even possible to boot out the alien and reclaim her. The thinker token didn't just upload facts into my head. I had to actively think something through and test out its trueness.

"So Howell's guys went into a quarantined town after your mom and came out still ghost-free?" said Luther. "Sounds like the ghost-men are trying to ferret you out. They want to find you through her."

I nodded. "Mom's ghost-parasite has access to her mind. We should assume the ghostmen now know everything she knew, including that her daughter was a member of the fireteam. If we bring her here, their ship can track her and then master-blast us to a crater. They don't seem to care about frying host bodies. The ghosts inside just rejoin the ship."

"Any way to move her without the ship knowing where she's gone?" Luther asked.

I shut my eyes and thought, demanding every kilowatt from my nanites.

"Dragon?"

He nodded, eager for anything I would say.

"Tell your guys to sedate her. And capture and sedate as many possessed people from the quarantine town as they can manage—all at once, before any of them have a chance to report back to the ship. Wilder might have some tips on gassing a building. The ghosts inside become dependent on their hosts for their senses. I think when their host bodies are unconscious, the ghosts can't communicate with the ship or each other. Bring Mom and the other sedated host people here."

"I will." Dragon smiled, his teeth startlingly white. "Brown, I'd take a bullet for you."

He pointed at me as he left. Wilder followed him out.

The lab was quiet for a time. We ate lunch. Dad and I held hands. I bet the last time we'd held hands, my preferred fashion style had been pigtails and pajama pants.

We talked about Mom. We used present tense verbs. I was glad I'd never told him about the bodies I'd seen piled up, gnawed by stray dogs.

Wilder returned to report that Dragon's team was on their way to Florida.

"We need to be ready by the time they get back," I said. "All I'm sure of is I need to destroy the ship. Odds are it wasn't near that diner when I went in, but the ghostmen must have communicated with the ship and it arrived fast enough to blast our helicopter. The only way to identify its location is to see an escaping ghost get sucked into it. So we need to boot a lot of ghosts, one after another, giving me a trail to follow."

"So," said one of the PhDs I'd nicknamed Sparky, "it's looking likely we'll need to—quickly and humanely—kill several possessed humans."

Everyone groaned.

Sparky lifted his hands up innocently. "I don't *want* to! But is there another option?"

"My mom is one of those possessed humans," I reminded him.

"So not her," said Sparky. "Save her for last."

More groans.

"Hey, don't shoot the messenger!"

"Seriously," said Luther. "You need to shut your mouth."

I was wincing. "Let me think . . . I need . . ."

"You need ideas to try out," said Wilder, "see which one feels right."

I nodded.

"So . . ." The speed of Wilder's pacing increased. "We could expose the possessed humans to extreme temperatures—cold or heat—or sound vibrations, loud or unique sound waves might shake them loose. Or photons of light of varying shades and intensity."

I shook my head. None of those ideas clicked in my mind.

"They react differently to gravity, right?" said Luther. "How about sending them to space? Shoot them up farther away from Earth's gravity and see if they pop out."

"A Beanstalk pod isn't big enough for all the ghost-ridden passengers we'd need," I said.

"Yeah, and once they're in space," Luther said, "it would be much more difficult for you to follow their trail."

"Could you invent an antigravity chamber?" asked Howell. "It's about time the world had one."

"That would be double-plus good," Luther said wistfully.

I considered, the techno-tokened parts of my brain rolling the idea around. "It's too complicated, and it would take forever to manufacture."

"What about . . . pressure," said Dad. "High pressure."

"That would kill the human bodies too," Howell said.

"A hyperbaric chamber?" said Wilder. "They use those for treating scuba divers with decompression illness."

I ran to a computer and looked up how hyperbaric chambers worked. My thinker-nanites approved, my techno know-how perking up. I started to scribble notes. "If we modify them . . . the pressure from the chamber would temporarily make the body inhospitable to the ghosts. Dad, I think it might work."

I smiled, trying to exude more confidence than I felt. He gave me a thumbs-up, and I had the impression he was trying to buoy me up in return.

By dinner we had two hyperbaric chambers in the lab. Cylindrical, made of glass, they looked like high-tech coffins for Snow White. I gave my gaggle of whitecoats instructions on their adjustments and returned to my jet pack. If the ship was in the upper atmosphere, the jet pack would have to be very powerful. And while I was at it, I attached it to an improved robot suit. If you've got the chance to build a flying robot suit, why ever turn it down?

Dad was off pain meds and was alert enough to ground me to my room that night, making sure I got rest. Lately my mind refused to sleep more than three hours at night, though I was always tired, exhaustion sticking to me like a greasy film.

Luther stayed near me the next day, chatting away while I worked, which helped rest my brain. Luther's possessiveness kept Wilder from approaching me. I didn't have the energy to sort out what I felt about him.

And with Luther and Dad, I forced myself to view the alien video again. They held my arms as I fell into the images, following the ships through space, and then plunging toward the planet before flying into the ship itself. I spent hours at it but still couldn't make sense of the fireteam's actions.

At last I shut my eyes, curled up on the carpet, and despised myself as I cried.

"Whoa, Maisie, are you okay?" Luther asked.

"Lock the door, Luther," Dad said.

I heard Luther click the lock of Howell's office door.

"I'm okay," I said from behind my hands. "It's just . . . the images do this. I'm not really—"

"Maisie," Dad whispered. He leaned over from his wheelchair, put his hands on my head. "Maisie, we're leaving. Now. There's nothing we need to pack. They can't stop us, Maisie. They can't stop you."

"But Mom—" I started.

"Would want you safe." His voice shook. "This is . . . this is ludicrous, what they're asking of a child. You don't have to do it."

"I do," I said.

But then I looked up at him and almost changed my mind. The way he looked back at me—if I'd ever been unsure before, I had no doubt now that my dad loved me more than the world.

But at that very moment Dragon and his team were loading Mom and fifty unconscious possessed Floridians into two jets. A few of them were newly possessed members of Howell's own team. They'd shot through a number of attacking mini-troopers but hadn't been fast enough to save three of the guys. Mom and Howell's crew would arrive by morning. Since GT might attack any day, I'd decided to assault the ghostmen ship tomorrow.

The other reason for the rush I kept to myself. Every day I could lift less weight, hold less shooter token charge, make less armor. The token-makers hadn't intended for all five to coexist inside one person. I couldn't afford to waste any more time. Tomorrow I'd either stop the invasion or die trying.

"I do," I said again.

Dad looked defeated.

"I have more work," I said, getting up. "Luthe, look after Dad, okay?"

And I left quickly. Because if Dad called me his little girl and took my hand and promised we could just run away again and everything would be okay, I might give in. And I couldn't bear to live hidden away somewhere, useless, while the Purpose screamed inside me. I couldn't bear to fail Mom.

I locked the door to the lab and worked alone. My suit was finished. I triple-checked the hyperbaric chambers. Soon I had nothing left to do but twiddle wires.

Tomorrow, I thought. *And tomorrow, and tomorrow . . .*

I hopped out a window and scaled onto the roof. Wilder was there. Lockdown didn't seem to hinder him. He'd laid out a blanket on the gravel top as he had last summer. There were no binoculars and only one pillow.

"Your dad try to talk you out of it?" he asked.

"But you won't," I said.

"Wish I could, but—"

"You'd make the same choice I am."

He nodded. "That Purpose rides with razor spurs." He looked at my neck. "You're wearing the necklace."

"One of the four gifts Jupiter gave to Europa," I said, fingering the tanzanite.

"I managed to give you the javelin that never misses too."

He gestured toward my chest—the shooter token.

He put his hands in his pockets. I put my hands in mine. Far from the light pollution of a city, we had a front-row seat to the galaxy, the sky drenched in stars. A breeze found us, the cool, sweet smells of nearly spring twining between us, connecting. He was only a few paces away but it felt like kilometers. I came closer. He didn't look at me, as if not to startle away a wild animal.

I reached out and touched his chest above his top button—smooth, no sign the tokens had ever been there. I looked because I was curious; and I looked because I wanted to make contact with him and didn't know how. His hand caught mine and held it pressed there.

"Maisie . . ." His face struggled as he searched for words. He shook his head and let go.

I held out my hand. "Let's start over. Hi, I'm Maisie Brown."

He shook my hand.

"Thank you," he said. He didn't let go this time. "Thank you," he said again.

"You're welcome," I said.

I wanted to lean into him. I wanted to rest my head against his shoulder. I wanted his arms to go around me and how safe that would make me feel, even if it was an illusion. I wanted to lift my face and let him kiss me, and kiss me more. I wanted our bodies wrapped together and kisses faster than breaths, and my mind drugged by the emotions, turned off and humming, my body yearning and content, and how kisses can douse the rest of the world and make everything a single moment of touch. I wanted Wilder to love me. I wanted to not be afraid.

I was the fireteam. I took one step back. He let go of my hand.

I thought about going down to my room and my cold pillow, but there would be plenty of time tomorrow for solitude. So I sat on his blanket, my back leaning against the stairway door, and Wilder sat beside me.

"May I put my arm around you?" he asked.

"Yes please," I said.

"I promise to be a good boy," he whispered, and I laughed.

I let my head relax against his shoulder. We looked up. The stars were out. The whole galaxy was out.

"I've been lonely," he said.

"So have I."

I was tired. My body seemed to melt. Soon I was lying down, Wilder beside me. Every moment closer. My head rested on his arm. My knee against his leg. His neck touching my forehead. My arm over his side. His eyes closed first. I watched for a time, glad that he could sleep beside me. Soon I was scarcely aware that I was asleep, only that I felt peaceful.

I woke at first light. I was on my side, Wilder's chest pressed to my back, his arm over mine as if to keep me warm.

It should be the other way around, I thought. The air was chilly, and without his tokens, he must be feeling it. But Wilder was deep asleep.

This might be my last morning on Earth, I thought, and I tried to feel the reality of that.

I turned over carefully and watched Wilder's face get bright with dawn.

CHAPTER 53

Mom's hand was warm. A loose eyelash lay under her eye. I touched it with my fingertip and brushed it away. She had tiny freckles on her cheeks, just a few but more than I'd noticed before. Her chest rose and fell with breaths, but her face didn't so much as twitch with a dream. Asleep I couldn't see any wrongness in her eyes. Asleep I couldn't tell that there was a ghost inside her, trapped by her unconsciousness, ready to scream warning to its ship the moment Mom woke.

"Get out of her," I whispered to Mom's ear. "Get out or I'll find a way to end you. You don't know who you're messing with. I *am* dangerous."

Mom didn't rouse when I carried her from the plane to the bus. I settled her gently onto a seat in the back near the hyperbaric chamber. I put on her seat belt, tucked loose hair behind her ears. Kissed her cheeks. I patted the chamber as I walked off the bus as I might pat Laelaps.

I'd hoped as soon as I saw her, I'd just know if she was still whole, that once the alien left my *mami* would remain. But I wasn't sure. Ice in my gut warned she might be a breathing corpse.

Howell had two charter-sized buses, each carrying one of our souped-up hyperbaric chambers, over two dozen unconscious passengers, and the remainder of the whitecoats to stick them in for sessions that would hopefully pluck out their alien parasites. I'd decided it wouldn't be safe to conduct the extractions at HAL. Too easy a target for the ship's master-blasts. The buses would stay in motion. And to allow more erratic mobility we fit them with monster truck tires so they could stay off road. Yosemite Sam would pilot one and Hairy the other. Dragon would stay at HAL in case GT attacked.

"Dad, you and Luther get into HAL's bomb shelter."

"I'll stay with your mother," he said.

"Dad—"

"I'll stay with her."

I sighed. "Okay."

If the ship master-blasted the buses, I'd be losing both parents today.

"Luther—" I started.

"I'm staying too," he said.

Both parents and a best friend. I didn't argue with them. The Purpose was a scream inside me, shaking every cell of my body, urging me up.

"Maisie, it's not too late," Dad said. "You don't have to do this."

"I love you too," I said.

He nodded, sad and afraid, but also, I think, proud of me.

Hairy helped Dad up the bus steps.

"Hey, Dad! Make sure they save Mom till the end. And if anything goes wrong with the others, don't let them—"

"I won't," he said.

I turned and rammed into the wall that was Dragon.

"Let me come with you," said Dragon.

"The jet pack will only support my weight," I said.

"I'll wear a space suit. Fly the Speetle. Ram it into that ship and join you inside it for whatever mayhem awaits."

The idea made me smile, but I shook my head. "I don't think this is blind fear—I think it's nanite-enhanced intuition. You *can't* help. I have to do it alone."

He nodded, but his expression was as sad as I felt. He trudged back inside the complex.

Wilder was going to stay with Dragon, but for the moment he just stood there in the brush outside the battle-scarred walls, watching me.

Covered in havoc armor, I stepped into my pressure suit. Wilder came closer to help me do up the straps. I sighed. "It was supposed to be a team."

Wilder nodded. "You shouldn't have to be alone."

"I can do this," I said. I didn't really believe it. But I would try.

He nodded and headed after Dragon.

"Luther," I called. He looked out a bus window.

"When you go home again, if your parents weren't miserable missing you, toss 'em to the curb and take mine."

"We'll share them," he said, his expression stern.

"Sure." I was wearing the sunglasses Dragon had given me. I took them off and handed them up. "I'll want these back."

Luther put them on. "I'll keep them warm. Don't be long or I'll come after you."

"*HAL crew is in position,*" Dragon said in my headset.

"*Bus Alpha in position*," said Yosemite.

"*Bus Beta in position*," said Hairy.

"Wait." Wilder jogged back toward me. "I just—" He looked me up and down, put out his arms, and tried to embrace me. I was dressed in four layers: clothing, havoc armor, pressure suit, and robot exoskeleton—much more cyborg than girl.

"Beep-beep hug Wilder," I said in robotic monotone.

"Hug enacted," he monotoned back.

He lifted my havoc-covered and gloved Lady hand and kissed it.

"Kick some transparent booty."

"With pleasure," I said. And for a moment, I meant it, my stomach tingling not in fear but anticipation.

I watched the buses drive off in opposite directions and spoke into the headset. "Fireteam is go."

"*Okay*," said Howell on Bus Alpha. "*Our first subject is in the chamber. I am turning it on . . .*"

I could hear a hum. I held my breath.

"*I'm not sure if—*" Howell began.

"It worked!" I shouted. I could see a pink ghost coming up through the roof of the bus. "It worked immediately! Proceed with the plan! Go, go!"

I turned on my jet pack and shot up into the air like a rocket, chasing the first Alpha ghost. The air felt harder than armor, like swimming through solid rock. Soon I could see a few more pink specks rising up below me. According to the plan, Teams Alpha and Beta would alternate releasing a ghost every ten seconds. If they were able to exorcise a ghost out of each infected human, I'd have about seven minutes' worth of incoming ghosts. Seven minutes from the time the first one entered the ship till the last. Seven minutes to try to get inside it myself. *If* the ship stayed put till all the ghosts were in.

The jet pack had two exhausts tied to the backs of my legs, belching fire past my feet. I maneuvered by moving my legs, like the tiller of a boat. I kept my head tilted back, my arms at my side, speeding to reach the ship at the same time as the first ghost. This high up, oxygen was getting spare, so I was breathing from a tank in the robot suit. I wanted to save my twenty minutes of held breath for when I'd really need it.

I was only a couple of kilometers up when I thought of Ruth, shooting up through the water as I now did through air. I was wearing a pressurized astronaut suit over my havoc armor, but what if . . . ? I didn't know what the rest of the question was, but I'd learned to trust these nanite-induced intuitions. The only place on my body that wasn't havoc-armored was my face. I grew an ultrathin layer of armor over my eyes, only a few molecules thick, hopefully enough to maintain my internal pressure should something happen to my astronaut suit. I could see through it like sunglasses. I extended the armor over the rest of my face, leaving just a hole for my mouth so I could breathe from the oxygen mask.

I didn't dare look down and slow my ascent. Were more ghosts coming? Was one of them from Mom?

"Can you hear me?" I asked in the headset.

I didn't know if there was an answer. The rush of air was deafening.

Just ahead of me, the first ghost disappeared. The ship had arrived. I followed at full speed, hoping to break into the hull of the ship with the force of my impact.

But before I hit the spot where the ghost had disappeared, I passed through some other barrier. Electric needles of pain pierced my skin, digging, fingering my nerves. I screamed. And my astronaut suit, robot suit, oxygen tank, and jet pack shredded and fell away.

CHAPTER 54

In a second everything but my body and havoc armor was torn apart. Even inside my armor, I felt Lady tremble and twitch, savaged perhaps by the ship's barrier. I havocked the small breathing hole over my mouth, sealing myself completely in. At last I understood why the tokens resisted gravity just like the ghosts—nothing but ghostmen could get close to the ship, and so the tokens had to be created from the same stuff. Dragon in the Speetle. Metal bullets. A nuclear missile. Nothing would have made it through the ship's barrier.

I survived because I was bonded with the tokens, my armor made by them. My pressure suit had not made the cut.

Not to mention I was now several kilometers above the ground without a jet pack.

The momentum of my flight kept pushing me up for a few more seconds, and I used that time to extend my right arm with a meter-long havoc hook and swing it with all the force of my body. Just as the second ghost disappeared, my hook hit something solid. The ship. I seemed to be dangling from an empty sky.

Don't look down, I thought.

I looked down. Freezing panic shot through me as if new tokens were burrowing through all my limbs. I could still see the shreds of my equipment falling toward Earth, and I seemed to be falling with them, the ground hurtling toward me.

Vertigo. Just vertigo.

I blinked hard and focused on the pink ghosts rising up. As soon as the last one entered, the ship would probably take off, maybe into space. I had to get inside first.

Dangling from my right arm, I shot havoc pipes from my left at the invisible shell of the ship. Something cracked. What had seemed empty air now showed silver-white lines.

Waves of white energy flowed from the ship, rolling over my armor. I could feel heat and a sharp tingle, especially against my eyes where my armor was the thinnest. The ship was attacking me. Perhaps it couldn't directly master-blast me here, so it sent a localized blast. The wave of energy didn't breach my havoc armor.

My oxygen tank and mask had been lost, my face was armored, my breath was held. The twenty-minute count had begun.

I formed a pick tool on my left hand, and I tore away chunks of the ship's hull. I widened the crack into a Maisie-sized gap.

I bet the *bleeping* token-makers could fly, I thought.

Below me I could see the end of the line of ghostmen, the last little pink one that perhaps had come from Mom. The ship didn't wait. It moved. Dangling, I whipped around.

I swung up, catching the edge of the hole with my armored toes, pulling myself in feetfirst. Beside me the last ghost entered. I rammed myself forward.

The interior of the ship was solid with the same nougat stuff as the interior of the mini-trooper—white, halfway between soft and stiff, like slightly stale marshmallow. I was curled up in the hole I'd hacked. I pressed the nougat, and it compressed with the shape of my hand. I was inside a giant candy bar. The only way forward was to dig.

I formed a scooper over one of my havoc-lengthened arms and a machete over the other. I started to dig and hack my way through the nougat.

I felt a rush in my belly. The ship was moving up.

I dug and hacked, and dug and hacked some more. I didn't form ammo to shoot myself a passage. I had to guard my resources.

The brute strength was essential. Normal Maisie would have tired quickly. If I'd had the whole fireteam, I would've had Jack Havoc make machetes for Ruthless and sent her through first.

I thought over the design of the mini-trooper suit. Most of it was filled with nougat like this, with controls in the center.

I dug toward where I thought was the center. And hoped it was the right direction. The farther in, the darker it was, the only light coming through the hole I'd made, now far behind at the beginning of the narrow tunnel I was digging.

My throat was dry. My pouches of water were gone with the rest of my gear. At least I had a bellyful of carbon nuggets. I'd swallowed three handfuls of the rough-diamond–like pebbles. My lab groupies had helped me enhance the concentrated carbon with oxygen, nitrogen, and hydrogen. Was I ever glad now. I had no air to breathe, no water to drink, no other way to get the elements I needed to make havoc tools and ammo.

I dug. Everything looked the same. The ship was huge, and I had only twenty minutes of air. No, make that eighteen.

Ghosts drifted through the nougat. The solid stuff was a passage to them. It seemed ghostmen could no sooner move through empty space than people could move through walls. One ghost stopped at the edge of my tunnel, trembled, and then dived at me, swooping right through my body. I felt the sting of its presence, like the prickles of a limb falling asleep. It passed through, entering the nougat on the other side of my tunnel. Another dived at me. And another. Stinging chills made my chest hurt. But they couldn't claim token-protected me. I kept digging.

Poems dodged in and out of my brain like ghosts through the nougat. I clung to Robert Frost, desperate to have a companion here at the end of the world.

They cannot scare me with their empty spaces
Between stars—on stars where no human race is.
I have it in me so much nearer home
To scare myself with my own desert places.

Humans were nothing to the ghosts. We were candy wrappers, apple cores, something they would toss aside. You'd think with all those millennia to grow up, the ghosts wouldn't be so selfish. Maybe it was the brevity of life that forced humans to mature. Life is precious because it's finite.

I didn't want to think about the brevity of life anymore.

Between stars—on stars where no human race is . . .

I kept digging.

I was so deep, no more sunlight reached into my tunnel. Nothing to orient my trek. I blindly hacked at the nougat with my machete, breaking the stiff stuff. With my scooper I pulled the loose nougat apart, then trampled it under my armored feet, compressing it enough to give me space to walk forward. One step at a time, my shoulders hunched. The nougat felt harder than it had before. Maybe my muscles were tiring.

I couldn't see the pink ghosts now, only feel them gathered around me, dozens or hundreds, swooping, diving at my chest. My token firewall rejected them, but they kept trying. Every time one passed through me, it felt as if someone wriggled a finger inside my backbone to stroke my spine. I shivered uncontrollably.

They can't scare me, Mr. Frost.

My havoc machete bounced off something. It radiated a soft white light. I pushed back the nougat around it, exposing a glowing fiber, like a vein running through flesh. I followed the fiber, cutting my tunnel alongside. The ghostmen swarms thickened. I swatted uselessly.

Faster, Maisie. Ruth wouldn't have tired. And Wilder would have known what to do.

There was a hum followed by a crackle, and the fiber lit up lightning bright. I shielded my eyes. The ship vibrated, and then the fiber dulled again.

Had the ship just master-blasted a bus zipping around on monster truck tires? I shook my head. If ever I needed to be robot Maisie, it was now.

Adding teeth to the havoc machete, I sawed through the fiber. It was a pointless gesture. My tinker-and-techno-self concurred that cutting just one such fiber wouldn't prevent another master-blast. There might be thousands of them. But I also suspected the fiber converged somewhere important, so I followed it deeper.

I dug, clenching my teeth against the burn in my arm muscles and the horrible feeling of all those ghostmen reaching inside me. My held breath, my armored face, the tiny space of the tunnel— everything seemed to press against me, long to squish me, end me.

I don't think I can do this, I thought.

Don't be such a frakking wuss, Luther would say.

I didn't want Luther to think I was a wuss, frakking or otherwise. I kept digging.

The fiber reached a bulbous sac, also glowing. It made me think of a lymph node or a gland nestled inside a body. The nougat didn't touch it, leaving about a half meter of space around the sac, the only empty space I'd seen inside the ship.

That, I thought.

I had an inkling that the stuff inside would hurt me, so I hacked past it to a safe distance and then shot it with a havoc dart. There was a wet explosion. The goo melted the nougat around it. I waited to feel the ship react. Nothing changed.

Time was definitely getting to its sticky end. I wouldn't have breath and strength to dig my way to all such sacs. If only there were four other teammates. I pushed myself harder.

The fiber continued past the now-empty sac. I kept digging.

Suddenly my machete hit nothing and I lurched forward. My tunnel met up with a spacious chamber.

They cannot scare me with their empty spaces . . .

I pushed my way inside, spilling clumps of nougat into the chamber. The ghostmen that had been clinging to me couldn't follow into the hollow center of their ship and stayed stuck in the solid nougat behind me.

The chamber was low but as expansive as several soccer fields. The ceiling was nougat, the floor was gray and firm, and around the sides dozens of empty mini-trooper suits waited. In the far distant center of the chamber glowed something blue.

It was the size of a hearth fire. It moved like kelp underwater, twinkled like a galaxy. The fiber I'd been following ran along the ceiling and converged with many others above the blue thing. The ceiling arched high right above it, as if the nougat couldn't get too close. If the techno token was a person, it would have been screaming at me. That was the power source for the craft. That was what I needed to destroy.

In that moment, two thoughts thundered through me:

1. My shooter token might not be able to fire something that far anymore, not with as much force as I guessed it would require.
2. If I broke that, the ship would go down. My jet pack was gone, so I'd go down with the ship.

I'd calculated that survival was a long shot anyway, but I'd still harbored a small, hard diamond of a hope. That now dissolved like the carbon nuggets in my belly.

I removed the havoc machete from my left arm and formed a large havoc dart. If I'd been a true robot, I would have tried the shot without hesitation. Instead, crouching under the low ceiling, I ran forward. I was too conscious of my mortality, I guess. I was aware that this was a moment like Sydney Carton walking to the gallows; like Samson, his hands on the building's support pillar just before he pushed. Who knew if there was a part of me that never ended, like the ghostmen themselves? I'd climbed the Beanstalk and found space. Maybe there wasn't anything else to find.

My own desert places, between stars, on stars . . .

I wasted five precious seconds in order to linger, to savor, to say *adiós, la vida.*

A suit moved off to my left. I turned and shot a havoc pellet through it, watched the pink ghost inside rip free and flail into the white ceiling. By the time I turned back, I couldn't see the blue hearth. All the mini-trooper suits were live, blocking the way, and moving toward me.

I shot them rapid-fire, downing one after another, sometimes several in a row as the havoc darts I formed shot clean through suit after suit. I turned, shooting all sides, till a wall of wrecked suits formed around me.

There was one mini-trooper different from the rest. It was holding a weapon. I turned to face it. Turned my chest toward it.

I shot it just as its weapon fired with a burst of white, striking me in the chest. I slammed against the wall, leaving an imprint of my body in its softness.

I looked down. Something was leaking straight through my chest armor. Not blood. It was the tokens, squeezing through, dripping free.

CHAPTER 55

I would have expected pain, considering how the tokens felt going in. But I watched as the five tokens emerged from my chest, and I felt nothing.

They were gray now. A dead color. They fell on the floor with a wet slap.

I scooped up the tokens in my hand, praying for them to light up, willing them to reenter me. They oozed through my fingers—a shapeless, lifeless goo.

Cold touched my back, and I flung myself away from the wall, where pink ghostmen stuck out limb-shaped parts. My token firewall was gone. Pink bits reached from the ceiling too, and I dropped to my belly, shaking on the firm floor.

I have it in me so much nearer home . . .

The chamber was alive with clicks and whooshing as the mini-troopers worked a way through the piles of downed suits. I had been the only thing standing between Earth and the aliens, but there was no more fireteam.

I expected to die immediately, but my lungs weren't convulsing for air yet. Maybe the tokens had left so quickly that most of the nanites remained in my body? Would they keep working without their tokens? I kept shooting havoc pellets at the mini-troopers, but after a time the shots barely pinged their armor. I tried to form a sword and there was nothing left.

I have it in me . . . The havoc machete I'd removed from my hand lay on the floor. I dived for it and slashed at the swarm of mini-troopers. My brute strength was lasting longer than blue shot and havoc. As I hammered cracks into the suits, their ghosts whisked back into the ceiling. The lifeless suits piled up around me, creating a temporary barrier between me and the onslaught.

I remembered Samson now with desperate respect, tearing down the building over his own head.

Yes, I thought. Yes, I'll do that. Please let me do that.

But the goal seemed impossible. I crawled forward, stabbing wildly, pushing aside the damaged suits on my way.

I touched the one with the weapon.

They cannot scare me with their empty spaces.

The white burst of power the weapon had fired reminded me of when I first held the techno token, how it had lit up to my touch. This weapon had been created to destroy the tokens. And the tokens were made of the same stuff as the aliens.

I grabbed it, sensing the mechanics of the weapon, the remnants of my techno token still live enough to teach me to slide my fingers along the side, to cup my hand around a bulbous part and apply pressure. It fired. Mini-troopers flung away with the force. More were coming in, but for a split second I had a view of the blue thing in the center of the chamber. This time I didn't hesitate.

I fired.

My white blast struck the blue hearth. The motion of firelike tendrils stopped. They quivered. Then they melted. Sloppy blue sludge poured out, pooling on the hard floor. Where it dripped, holes sputtered through. The air began to crackle. Mini-troopers hung where they were, vibrating.

Victory. It was victory. Wasn't it? Not the Death Star exploding in spectacular violence perhaps, but I thought I'd done it.

The room was sizzling, hissing, crumbling.

As one, the trembling suits panicked. It was a mad rush for the walls, ghostmen abandoning their suits for the safety of the nougat. The crackling reached right through my havoc armor and raised the hairs on my arms. The hole around the blue sludge lengthened, crumbling my way.

I crawled across the floor and wormed back into the tunnel. The white foam I'd cut had already begun reconnecting. I swiped at strands like thick spiderwebs, scrambling on my knees, my heart pounding. There was nowhere to go. But whatever was left of techno-sense in me warned to get away from the chamber as fast as I could.

A parachute. I need a parachute, I thought.

Forget the parachute, *chica*. You're not going to find anything that resembles a parachute on a ghost ship.

A havoc parachute! I thought, before remembering. I could no longer havoc anything.

Even if I got out of the ship, I was going to fall a long way, and I was going to die. It was pointless, but I kept crawling. My skin inside the armor felt tender, my knees ached. I was not the same person who had come this way only minutes ago.

The crackling behind me got louder, lightning striking lightning, electric and angry. A pulse convulsed through the whole ship,

knocking me flat. My lungs took a useless breath, somehow anticipating what would happen next before it did.

And what happened was, everything fell.

The ship had lost power. It was falling to Earth. I could hear
tearing, the ship a meteor, breaking apart, burning. Falling, me falling with it, my body pressed to the top of the tunnel I'd cut. Falling
hard, too hard to breathe even if there had been air. I was conscious,
though, so my cells must have still retained some oxygen from my
last breath.

My last breath had been so long ago—ten minutes, fifteen.
Twenty?

I was nearly blind in my little tunnel, seeing little, feeling nothing but falling. And I wondered if the ship would hit the ground
and splatter like a clown's whipped cream pie, whatever pieces of
me that remained smooshed into the white gunk.

I managed to turn my head a few centimeters to one side and
saw the tips of ghosts dipping into my tunnel, shivering as they circled and circled through the nougat. The ghosts were falling too,
stuck inside the ship, nowhere to go. I had no more token firewall,
they could have entered me. But they didn't bother. That scared me
like a knife at the throat. Even they knew I was about to die.

CHAPTER 56

Booming sounds, crackles and cracks, and then suddenly there was no more ship. The floor beneath me broke apart. The hull ruptured into pieces. The nougat crumbled. And gravity claimed us all.

All except the ghosts. Their safe, solid ship was gone. Gravity rejected them. I looked up as I fell and saw thousands of pink shapes falling the other way, going up into the black to be claimed by the vacuum of space. The ghostmen would just keep going, I thought. With no ship, no form, their momentum would send them hurtling through outer space indefinitely. They'd never be able to come back.

I did it, I thought. But I didn't feel the victory. I could only feel the fall. Every cell of my body seemed to scream with it, every atom spinning faster and faster, trying to escape the fact that I was going to die. And that I was being given a few minutes to know it first.

Horror, horror, cannot compute this, Maisie.

While I was inside it, the ship must have moved up very high. I was still in Earth's gravity but so close to space I thought I could reach out and touch it. The sun was bright and colorless, and through the scant atmosphere I could see straight to blackness. The stars twinkled down at me, all unsympathetic innocence. Just then, I hated the stars.

I was falling in a cloud of nougat dust and ship pieces. Even at full brute strength, I wouldn't be able to survive a fall this high. There was almost no air up here to stabilize me, no friction to slow me, and I sped faster and faster the farther I dropped. I was flipping, my arms and legs flailing, trying to swim or fly maybe. I clawed at the nothing, pathetic as a fish on a bank.

And I just kept hurtling down, though the distance was so great, the Earth seemed no closer. The thin layer of armor over my eyes started to crack. I covered my eyes with my hand.

My stomach hurt, seemingly yanked from my body over and over again. My heart was pounding at machine-gun speed, my head pained to cracking, my muscles so tense I wondered if my skin would split open. I vaguely realized my body must be overdosing on adrenaline, higher brain functions shutting down and primal brain functions taking over. All I knew was fear and panic.

This was the part of my life when I *should* have gone robot. But I didn't want to anymore. Even battling terror like being strangled in slow motion, I wanted to *experience* it. This was life, these few minutes were all that I had left. I didn't want to die halfway down. I wanted every single second I had left. I yelled at my brain to work.

Mom and Dad, I thought.

Mom and Dad. And Luther, my best friend.

And Jonathan, I thought.

I meant Wilder, but with its last electrical fizzing, my mind called him Jonathan. The whooshing feeling, the terror of falling, the lightning in my belly, the frantic pounding of my heart—all reminded me of how I felt when I kissed him. And when I didn't. And when I'd lost him, and when I almost had him again.

Falling in love and falling to your death feel about the same, I thought. And I almost laughed.

And still I fell.

There was a crackling sound. Heat. I'd hit the lower atmosphere now, the friction of gas molecules slowing me slightly, the speed of my passage sparking fire across my armor.

When my body splattered, would a soul—my soul—come rising out of it, like a ghostman fleeing a useless body? Would it rise up, drift through space, pause in nebulae, moving from star to star? Would I be sucked up into a God-touched place with billions of other souls? Or would I simply cease to be? Mom believed, Dad did not. I didn't want to simply choose to believe or not believe; I wanted to *know*. I had no answers, and at the moment this seemed a catastrophic hole in my education.

I seemed to be falling for hours, though surely it was only two or three minutes. I let my hand drop from my eyes. I was back under a blue sky again—*in* a blue sky. The world was air and blueness and patches of color below.

And then I saw a road.

Until then, it hadn't felt completely real. I was falling, I was thinking, I was sure I would die, in an abstract way. But seeing that road was like a gut punch. The ground wasn't distant. There was a highway. The green speckle of trees. *So much nearer home, so much nearer home, so much nearer . . . scare myself with my own . . .* Where was I? The ship could have moved over Australia or China or anywhere. When I hit there'd be nothing to identify, no way for my parents to even know what had happened. If they were still alive.

Mom and Dad, Mom and Dad, Mom, Mom, *Mami*, please . . .

My face armor was pierced with cracks, and I tore off a piece now, sucking in any air I could, the oxygen in my cells depleted at last. My lungs battled the air, losing. I flipped myself over, my back hitting the hard rush of air.

Land charged closer. There appeared to be a huge black crater, but maybe I imagined it because black dots were rushing in from the side. When all the black dots converged, I knew I'd lose consciousness. I didn't want to fall asleep. Desperate for every moment. Black dots. White lines. Green speckles. Patches of color. Indistinct becoming distinct.

An object was moving toward me, fast, coming up at an angle. Imagined? I was barely conscious now, breathing in small hurried gasps. The rushing seemed to fill me, my ears full of air as thick as water, my chest a windsock.

An object charging at me.

You're hallucinating. You're crazy in your last moments. *O, Mami, por favor* . . .

I didn't believe the thing was real until it slammed into me with the roar of a jet pack. My left shoulder and arm cracked at the impact, and the pain made me feel more alert. The jet-packed person clung to my back, falling with me, while shoving me around midair. I thought about fighting back, but what was the point? That tree down there seemed so close, I almost thought I could reach—

There was a gut-wrenching yank. It took me a moment to realize what had happened—the person in a jet pack had strapped a parachute to my back and pulled the cord, letting me go. My plummet slowed with sudden force, and the little air in my lungs was thrust out. I managed a few grateful breaths before realizing the parachute was too late—the ground was too close, and I hadn't slowed enough.

I hit feetfirst with a crunch in my legs, the rest of my body following, slamming down into a rock pile, my havoc armor shattering. The parachute gusted away, an urgent jellyfish. I was dragged along with it. Rocks scraped my now-bare face and arms.

Release cord, I thought airily.

My head slammed into a rock. Sound and sight changed, as if I were underwater and a carnival blazed in the distance—merry-go-round music, distorted and slowed. I kept blinking but couldn't focus my eyes. There was blood. It was mine.

I wasn't dragging anymore. The parachute had caught on something or else the wind had stopped. But that hadn't improved the situation.

I lay there, my whole body feeling like a rock pile. The carousel music transformed into a hard, uncomfortable rhythm, and I realized it was my own shuddering gasps.

Here's the part where I die, I thought.

I was almost glad it had arrived at last. So much buildup.

Still I clung to consciousness as if to the ledge of a skyscraper. Even pain was better than nothing.

There would be a few more minutes of agony and then I'd slip away, and maybe I'd find out if there was some part of me that went on. My scientific soul—unquantifiable, unprovable, intangible? It wasn't going to be a pleasant few minutes, but they were *my* minutes.

And then something went and spoiled it all—a loud, angry noise, like a swarm of giant insects. That kind of freaked me out, because for all that they're the most prevalent creatures on the planet, giant ones would be enormously creepy. I tried to sit up, but things were broken inside me. I think I screamed.

The insects kept coming. I could see them now. Alien ships, I figured. Maybe I only destroyed the first wave, and now the real destruction would begin. The insects were brilliant, shooting beams of light into my eyes. I could feel cold tears leaking down my cheeks. It was one thing to linger in pain and pass away, but another to go like this, attacked by alien insects, and me broken and crippled and unable to fight back. And I'd failed after all. It wasn't over. Mom wouldn't be okay.

I knew it would hurt, but I tried again to get up. Again, broken bones slid, and I screamed.

"Stop that!" A hand on my forehead, the voice in my ear. "Hold still, would you?"

"Why is she—"

"Look, her tokens are gone."

"She hit the ground without—"

"Big bugs . . ." I said. My jaw cracked and hurt like crazy.

"Helicopters, Maisie," said Wilder.

He smelled metallic, electric, like ozone. His hands were ice cold. He was wearing a black helmet and something bulky on his back.

"You made an extra jet pack," I mumbled without moving my jaw. He'd been the thing that put the parachute on my back.

"Just in case. I tried to match your design, but mine wouldn't go as high. I wish I could've transferred it to you midair—"

"Shouldn't wear it . . . not designed for normal people . . ."

"A little third-degree burn on the backs of the calves never hurt anybody," he said.

I moaned sadly. I'd liked his calves.

"Stop trying to move," he said.

His voice sounded wrong, false somehow. I realized he was terrified. He thought I was going to die. I couldn't blame him.

The hands that had been checking my pupils and pulse now folded me in half, kicked me a few times, and threw me onto a stretcher. In truth they were probably very gentle, but that's not how it felt. I screamed. I had no choice.

Someone put an IV in my arm, and it must have included some serious painkillers because the pain in my body became slick like sausages. Then I was trying to hold a handful of greasy sausages, but they kept squelching out of my hands and falling, and falling and falling into nothing. The sausages part was a dream, I'm ninety-nine percent sure. And I was glad for it. Now that I wasn't officially dead, I wanted to stay unconscious for a long time.

CHAPTER 57

I woke. Mom was there. Alive. Or else we were both dead.

"You're *not* dead," she said as if she could read my mind. And she touched my face to prove it. Her hand was warm. My face was cold. Neither of us felt like a ghost. I tried to feel relief, but I couldn't seem to feel anything. Numbness was the new happiness.

I looked her over to see if she was different after playing host to an alien infestation. She was looking me over, I guess searching for signs of how much I'd changed since becoming the fireteam and destroying an alien ship. Her eyes seemed the same. I wondered if mine did too.

I was in a hospital. A real one, not the lab at HAL. That's when I suspected HAL was gone.

"GT or aliens?" I asked my mom through my wired jaw. I felt barely human, casts and bandages and monitors. I remembered vaguely waking before to a doctor explaining that I had six cracked ribs, a cracked skull and jaw, a cracked pelvis, broken arm, fractures in all six leg bones and many foot bones, not to mention a ruptured spleen, crushed kidney, and punctured lung. The doctor had said

I should be dead. He'd said it with a smile, as if I should be over-joyed by that news. I'd probably passed out after.

"Both," said Mom. "GT attacked first. Howell believes the attack drew the ship's notice away from the buses—so in one way, GT was actually useful. There were flashes of white light, and then HAL was gone."

"Sucks . . . ," I said.

Mom didn't like that word, but she didn't correct me.

"The blast also consumed most of GT's attacking forces. He was not among them."

I had so many questions I wanted to ask. I blinked hard, attempt-ing to wake up, but then couldn't get my eyelids to open again.

"That boy with the jet pack was awfully slow to find you."

"He got to me just in time," I mumbled, moving nothing but my tongue and lips.

"I would have preferred his arrival a little sooner." She lay a hand on my mummified leg.

I licked my lips, afraid to ask the next question. "Was anyone inside HAL?"

"Some . . ." Mom sniffed. That was as close to crying as she ever got.

"Dad?" I squeaked. "Luther?"

"They're fine. They were on the bus with me."

I relaxed and felt myself sinking again, darkness rising up over my head. "Laelaps?"

"Alive and slobbering."

I tried to smile but it hurt too much. Sleep was nicer.

CHAPTER 58

I woke again, chased out of a dream by the image of Jacques, skinny and nearly dead under his armor.

"Mmmff," I said, which meant, I haven't eaten since I don't remember when and I have to eat all the time or I'll deplete into nothing like Jacques so whoever is nearby hurry and bring me a cheeseburger on the double if you please.

Then I remembered I was tokenless. Everything hurt, including my eyelashes and toenails.

"Mmmff yourself," Luther said. He was sitting beside my bed reading *Popular Mechanics*.

"Mmmaff," I replied, which meant, please hand me that little sponge-on-a-stick so I can wet my mouth because my tongue feels like roadkill frog three days dead.

"Good Trog," he said, patting my head. "Nice Trog."

"Shut up," I managed before falling back asleep.

I dreamed about falling. I kept expecting to hit the ground but I never did. Is it possible to fall forever? That's where the ghostmen were now, falling through space, on and on and on . . .

CHAPTER 59

Howell was beside my bed. I looked for Mom. She was reading in a chair in the corner. Well, sort of reading. Mostly watching Howell. It made me feel kind of cozy that Mom didn't trust Howell. She was here now. Someone was looking out for me.

Then I noticed what I should have noticed immediately, which made me even more alarmed about the general health of my brain and eyes: Howell was bald. Her head looked alarmingly tiny without her bouncy frizz. I almost laughed, but there was something so pathetic about it that my throat constricted. Maybe I guessed that it meant something very bad.

"Hello, Miss Brown," she said. "Thank you for saving the world."

She placed a trophy on my belly. There was a little woman in gold plastic with a fist raised in the air, a stance of victory. The plaque on her pedestal read:

MAISIE DANGER BROWN
1ST PLACE
SAVING THE WORLD

In my periphery, I could see Mom roll her eyes.

"Thanks," I croaked. "Your hair?"

Howell nodded, and no curly Afro bobbed with the motion. "I shaved it off. I'm in mourning."

"Who?"

I thought I could take it. After all, loss was expected in a war.

But then she said, "Dragon."

"He was in HAL?" I asked.

She nodded again. Her tiny pink face scrunched up and she started to cry. Cry hard, cry like a small child cries, with uninhibited, anguished sobs.

Mom came over. She put a hand on my forehead. She cried with both of us.

CHAPTER 60

I slept a lot. The doctor said that was normal. My body needed all my energy to stitch back together and had little left over for consciousness.

It wasn't until I overheard Dad talking with a doctor about my "skydiving accident" that I realized the doctors didn't know that I'd fallen from the stratosphere. I was grateful for the lie. Explaining my defunct superpowers to the broader world sounded exhausting.

Mom and Dad practically lived with me in the hospital. Luther went back to his parents, who seemed genuinely elated by his return. I think they probably always liked him as much as they liked his sisters. They just needed a reminder.

Inez. Inez Aguilar Lugo. My mom's real name. She seemed pained to speak the words, and yet relieved too.

She told me about being a small child, waiting for the cars to come back after another protest, another attack, and counting heads to see how many of her community had returned that time. And if her parents would be among them.

"My parents never asked me to pull a trigger. But I would

have—for them, I would have done anything. And after they were killed, I tried. But *mi gente* stopped me. The whole community took care of me, got me a new name, set me off on a new life. The Paraguayan government grouped me with the rest of *la Bandera Amarilla*, and I was convicted of the murder of soldiers in abstentia, so I could never be Inez again."

"That's why we've lived as we have."

"I hope you weren't unhappy," she said.

I'd pull a trigger for you, I thought. I'd live a small life for you.

"Your father and I swore we'd never bring children into a fugitive's life. But you came anyway, *la Peligrosa*, and you made everything better. We would have had a dozen more of you, if we dared."

"So . . . it wasn't because of my arm?"

She looked confused. "Your arm?"

"GT said you were afraid that if you had another child, it might be like me . . . born without a limb."

Mom straight up laughed. "No, *la Peligrosa*, it wasn't because of your *arm*."

She tilted her head and smiled, her eyes accusing me of being silly for asking such a question.

CHAPTER 61

After my crash landing I didn't see Wilder.

"The FBI want him, now that they've arrested GT," said Dad.

My stomach felt hollow. "Why do they want him?"

"To testify against his father. They have Wilder in protective custody."

"When is the trial?"

"It's not set yet." Mom tucked a piece of my short hair back into my head bandage. "These things can take a long time, Maisie. The officer told me it's likely he'll be in witness protection for years, and possibly forever."

I stared out the window. It faced the backside of another building. *I miss you.* I thought those words like a message, words everyone should hear sometimes. I missed him, with a clean, brilliant, sidewalk-after-the-rainstorm kind of longing. No twitch, no sick need of a teammate for the thinker. I just missed *him.*

"Are you in pain, *mi hija*?"

"No," I lied, because I didn't want any more pain medicine. It muddied my brain.

Mom must have guessed that in fact most of my body felt as if I were caught in a combine, because she turned on the TV for me. Way better than nasty pain meds. I watched this guy show how you could live off the carcass of a camel. And then a marathon of *Xena: Warrior Princess*.

Nothing in the news mentioned an alien invasion, but there was plenty about the Jumper Virus. Howell was credited for discovering the cure: a simple session in a modified hyperbaric chamber killed the virus, she claimed. Her group traveled the world, curing the infected—for free in poorer nations (with plenty of media to document her philanthropy) and for a nice sum in others.

The newscaster interviewed people in a small Texas town who had all recovered.

"I don't remember a thing," said a busty, big-haired blonde. "Five months of my life, just wiped out. I feel fine, 'cept I gained thirty pounds. That's not going to be a treat to lose!" She laughed.

Others could not manage to be so chipper. They spoke of family members missing or dead, their bones found rotting in the street. Of small children who were taken away, now returned, no longer recognizing their parents.

Behind one interviewee, I recognized the boy who'd been devouring chocolate cake in the diner. He was with a group of boys, jostling one another for room to get in front of the camera.

I followed the Jumper Virus story over the next few weeks, mostly because I never turned off the TV until the day my doctor released me.

"Your recovery was speedy, considering the shape you were in. Extraordinary, really," he said, shaking his head as he left.

Mom and Dad looked at me. I shrugged.

"Maybe when I got zapped and lost the tokens, the nanites couldn't return for reassignments, so they just shut down. It wasn't like when I got the brute token and it overrode my techno nanites. This time some of the changes the nanites made in me remained, at least temporarily. The powers I'd had for the least amount of time—blue shot, thinker, havoc—diminished pretty quickly. But the brute enhancements stayed longer, so when I hit the ground . . . it wasn't as bad as it might have been."

"And your technology intuition?" Dad asked.

I glanced at the notebook by my bed and away again. The moment in the ship when the tokens slid out of me, I'd had a techno-nanite–inspired idea. It'd hit me like night lightning, so sharp and clear I didn't forget on that long fall or through my long sleep. As soon as I was able to hold a pencil, I'd jotted it down. But I wasn't ready to share it.

"It's mostly gone," I said. "Though when I watch tech shows, my mind feels more alive."

Howell didn't come to see me discharged, but she chartered a plane to take me home, since I wouldn't be able to sit up for another three months or so. Howell was currently in Sri Lanka with one of her Team Rescue groups, and we talked on the phone. She was surly about not making more money off the aliens. She'd found and collected debris from the crashed ship, but it was just scraps and nothing useful. The one mini-trooper suit I'd liberated had been destroyed with HAL. All she had to show for it were the plans for the inventions I'd made, tucked safely away on offshore servers.

"Go to college," Howell told me over the phone. "Study something useful, and then come see me about a job. I am applying for patents on your jet pack design. Try to sue me and I will win. No

whining. I paid off your parents' mortgage, had your mother's iden-
tity properly sponged, and created a college fund for you—enough
to cover an advanced degree, as well as living expenses, food and
rent and books, computers, phones, private lab rental, research supplies, solar paneling . . . the basics."

"I didn't whine—"

"And you won't, because I'm hanging up."

And she did, before I could ask her how she was doing, but I
already knew. She missed Dragon. I guessed she always would.

I spent a few weeks in a hospital bed in our living room. Mom
and Dad got a TV to help ease me through my convalescence. After
being starved for TV most of my life, it took me months to finally
reach the "enough" moment—the day I turned it off because I was
really and truly sick of it.

Soon after that I started walking with crutches and could sit in
a car, go to a movie, eat out at the noodle place.

The world was normalizing. There'd been a burst of chaos right
after the mother ship broke apart, and I guessed that the remaining
pink parasites had been angry and rampaged in their human hosts.
But then they got gassed and decompression chambered, and their
unwilling hosts woke up with limited amnesia. I had no idea how
many out-of-the-way towns were still body-snatched, but Howell
would get to them all eventually.

TV off, casts off, weather great, I stopped paying attention to
the rest of the world. I was about to get really busy. I was enrolling
as a junior in high school.

CHAPTER 62

First-day jitters are probably normal. Maybe everyone gets that buggy excitement in the belly and an obsessive need to keep looking in the mirror. We converted my hacked-off hair into a pixie cut, and I think I prefer that style after all.

Luther picks me up in his hideous 1989 Ford Fiesta—a two-door hatchback, zero to thirty mph in one minute flat. He loves this car way more than he thought he loved me. Lately his cuticles are black with grease because he's constantly taking the engine apart and putting it back together. The radio doesn't work, so we drive to school sans soundtrack.

"Why are you so twitchy?" he asks.

"I'm nervous, I guess," I say. "Aren't you?"

"No."

He'd better be nervous. The high school thing is his obsession all of a sudden. My heart feels fluttery, my hands shake a little. I put on the sunglasses Dragon gave me. They're my last piece of armor.

We enter the front doors of West High School, and I hold my breath, half expecting a gang of mean girls and football guys to accost us and mock our nerdish ways and handless limbs.

I'm wearing Gidget. It's a prototype Howell's crew built based on Fido's design. Gidget is a far cry from Lady and even farther from Fido. But I love her. I'm rethinking my whole astronaut goal. If I were an engineer, maybe I could develop an affordable, mass-producible robotic arm.

"Ooh, look at the lockers!" Luther says as we walk down the hall. "And everything smells just like I imagined."

"Like bleach and sweat?" I said.

He nods, his eyes shining.

His excitement is catching. Only partly teasing, I chant "high school, high school," and dance down the hall.

"Stop that. Don't get me labeled a geek-by-association on my first day. Besides, I don't want your sorry dance moves burned into my brain."

"Now, by *sorry*, do you mean smokin' hot?"

"I've measured your hotness and passed. I kissed you once, remember?"

"Yep."

"Wait, you were supposed to forget!"

"Forget what?"

"But if I ever *had* thought I wanted to be your boyfriend, it was just because you were the *only* girl I knew. Don't go thinking you're some kind of dream girl. You're already in danger of getting conceited, what with being the hero who saved the human race from slavery and extinction."

I shush him, but still no one is paying us any attention. We are invisible in our inconsequentialness. I like it.

"See you at lunch, best friend!" I shout after him, super cheery.

He squints at me before entering his calculus class.

I've decided to be super cheery with Luther all the time. It actually takes less energy than admitting to him that I'm exhausted. That all night, dream after dream assaults me. That I still feel broken up and not sure if I'll ever heal.

But don't let me get dramatic. I survived a fall from the stratosphere. I can handle a few nightmares and a little loneliness.

I go down the wrong hall, finally arriving at College Prep Chemistry as the bell rings. The teacher is at the board, squeakily writing, and I scan for an empty chair. There's one in the back. Next to a guy in a gray T-shirt.

The guy in gray stands up to look at me. He's still wearing the woven leather wristband his mother gave him. I'm still wearing Dragon's sunglasses, but I pull them off. I can't seem to breathe. There's that sloshy feeling, my head like a bag of water minus the goldfish.

I say, "Jonathan."

The teacher is looking at us. Everyone in the class is looking at us, two idiots standing there, looking at each other. It's way too much *looking* all around, but I can't seem to do anything else—besides say, "Jonathan," which seems to surprise him as much as it does me.

His gray T-shirt says FBI in yellow letters, and I wonder if it was a gift after months in hiding. His hair is longer, and a little lighter too, bleached by the sun. And he is looking at me in a way that reminds me the heart is a pump that works very hard.

"Is something the matter?" the teacher asks.

I shake my head and with an effort break eye contact with Wilder. With Jonathan.

"No, sorry, we just . . . know each other."

"Congratulations," says the teacher.

Jonathan watches me cross the room. He waits until I am in the chair beside him before he sits.

And he doesn't say anything. And I don't say anything. And we sit through all of chemistry not saying anything.

It has been six months since he donned a jet pack and stuffed me into a parachute before I crunched to the ground. Six months since I lay on the rocks, a heap of broken bones and bleeding organs, Jonathan holding my hand.

The bell rings, and I still don't know what to say. Maybe Jonathan doesn't either. A year ago at astronaut boot camp he was calling me "stone-cold fox." Now he stands in silence, his hands in his pockets, his shoulders hunched a little.

"Hi," I say, holding out my left hand. "Maisie Danger Brown."

"Jonathan Ingalls Wilder," he says, and shakes my hand.

We hold on, looking at each other. I can't help smiling, and then he does too, and then we laugh. The classroom is clearing out, but I'm not in a hurry.

The teacher is the only one left. She slips us glances, and I know she's trying to guess our story. Good luck.

He switches his left hand for his right so he can hold my hand and walk beside me.

He's holding my hand.

Jonathan Wilder is in Salt Lake City, Utah, walking beside me and holding my hand.

"So, your dad's trial . . . ," I say.

"Will go on for years. But it turns out I'm not an ideal witness. My sordid background, my grudge against my mother's killer. He wasn't very cautious once he started going after you and the tokens, so they had enough crimes on him without my help."

We find Luther by his locker.

"Maisie, did you see—" Luther stops, his gaze frozen on Jonathan. "Craptastic."

"Hey, I know you thought I was a jackass," says Jonathan.

"Thought?"

"And you want to protect Maisie from my jackassiness. I respect that. And I'm sorry." Jonathan holds out his hand as if to shake. "Truce?"

Luther squints at Jonathan.

"You know I think you are a ridiculous entity."

"Understandable."

"And I think she's worth ten to the tenth power of you."

"Aww, that's sweet," I say.

Luther's glance switches from Jonathan to me, and a miserly smile takes his lips.

"I know how these things work. You take some sports team to state and run for student body office and freshmen girls swoon as you walk by. So follow through on that, publicly claim me as a friend so your star power rubs off on the nerd boy, and it's a truce."

Jonathan nods.

Luther shakes his hand. "Okay. But I'd better have a girlfriend before winter break. And if you two ever, *ever* kiss in front of me, the truce is off."

I slug Luther in the shoulder with my Gidget hand. He fakes like it hurt, and Jonathan moves in as if to protect Luther from me. Luther cowers behind Jonathan, I say some old-timey gangster lines like "Why I oughta . . ." and it's all stilted as if we're following a movie script. But Luther's laugh sounds real.

Jonathan walks me to world history class. After, he's waiting for me in the hall, and my heart startles, as if I hadn't been sure yet that he was real. I think of the Keats quote, "Nothing ever becomes real till it is experienced." I think it hard, taste its truth like a peppermint on my tongue.

He's wearing basketball shorts that hang past his knees. I can see pink scars on the backs of his calves. Jet pack burns.

On the way to English, he asks me on a date for Friday, but I'm busy all weekend. It turns out I have an uncle and a couple cousins. Now that Mom isn't in hiding, I'm going to meet my dad's fam.

"Then . . . tonight?" he asks. "We could—what do normal people do? Go to dinner and a movie?"

There was a time when, if someone had told me one day I'd go on a date with Wilder, I would have flat-pellet-shot them in the face. Generally speaking, if a guy breaks your jaw and leg and cuts off your robotic arm, you file charges and get a restraining order. The only exception is when subtle machinations are needed to save the world from a massive, catastrophic alien takeover. But in *no* other circumstance.

I think it'll be my first real date.

After school Luther and Laelaps come over. We do homework. I love that the highest expectation I'm currently facing is to write an essay.

Mom has office hours at the university all afternoon. Dad hasn't found work yet. He's gone grocery shopping and brought home five different kinds of cheese. When I insist my love of the stuff was mysteriously knocked out of me somewhere between the stratosphere and the troposphere, he makes endless puns. ("Cheddar is as gouda cheese as you can hope to try. But it's nacho cheese, so leave my provolone.") I laugh because I want to.

Mom and Dad nix the dinner—they want to eat as a family and hear about my first day—but they okay the movie, so I text Jonathan, and he responds immediately. I don't think he gets many calls. He's lost his family, his old friends, his home. He's legally emancipated and living alone in a tiny apartment I plan to call his lair.

Later, Jonathan pulls up in a powder-blue Camaro that's seen some hard living. It's not a convertible. Mom and Dad watch me go from the front stoop.

"Nice wheels," I say as he opens the passenger door for me.

Jonathan shrugs. "It was the right price."

"So, I take it you're no longer burdened with your daddy's obscene fortune?"

"All seized by the FBI. A judge allowed me a trust fund to get me through college. After that . . . well, Howell offered me CEO."

I laugh. "Oh man, you and Howell are way too close to evil genius to make that pairing comfortable."

We've been driving in silence for a few minutes when he asks, "Nightmares?"

"Yeah," I say. "You?"

He nods. "Mi-sun mostly. Killing Ruth. Almost dying."

"Usually Jacques," I say. "But also Ruth. Pink ghosts sticking to me till I suffocate. Lots of falling. Dragon waving to me from a window when HAL vaporizes."

Jonathan is looking forward, his voice a little shy. "At least I'm not in your nightmares."

"Oh yeah, I forgot you! I'm hiding in the dark up in the rafters, and you're shooting at me."

He winces.

I rub his hair as if he were Laelaps. "It makes me feel a little more chipper knowing you have nightmares too."

"Schadenfreudist."

"Neologist."

"Gesundheit," he says. "So, you have some left?"

I know what he means. I nod.

We're at a stoplight. He picks up a coin and shoots it from his fingers. I catch it in my palm. The impact is so light, it wouldn't have hurt even if I wasn't still a little bit tougher. I'm surprised he can do that without the shooter token acting as a battery. Maybe his whole body is a battery of sorts now.

"The effects will probably fade with time, maybe disappear entirely when our brains mature," he says.

I'm not brute strong, but I can do a lot of push-ups. And in the notebook by my bed are plans of how to make an external token. Most of the nanites must still be inside me, and remnants inside Jonathan too, all in standby mode since losing their tokens. I think I could reactivate the nanites. If I needed to.

"You know what's amazing?" he asks.

I nod. I know lots of things that are amazing. But he specifies.

"I've never gotten bored with you."

"Thanks," I say, the word a flat thud.

"Aren't I a charmer? I mean, I get bored with everything. But I'm not bored with you. And I don't think I ever will be."

"As far as compliments go, I give it a three."

"I used to be better at this, didn't I?" he says. "You know me better than anyone in the world, and somehow you still like me."

"Who says I like you?"

"You do. You say it with your *eyes*." Stopped at a red light, he looks at me, all mock-mystery, and presses his forehead to mine. We stare at each other super close till I laugh first. The light turns green.

I remind myself that teen brains haven't developed the areas that are capable of lasting emotional commitment. But if I don't start forming all the connections I can now, didn't Howell say it'd be too late? I'm alive. I don't want to wait to start living.

We park across the street from the theater. He opens the car door for me, and we stand on the curb. The traffic stirs up wind.

"Ooh, you know what sounds good?" I say. "Licorice."

"I pledge to search the world over and bring you back licorice."

"It'll probably be at the snack bar."

"We can try there first, before scouring the world over."

"That's thinker logic hard at work."

"I prefer black licorice myself," he says. "They're wrong somehow, an anomaly—"

"Like edible dark energy."

"Exactly."

Without thinking about it first, I put my arms around his neck. His arms go around my waist, as if they belong there, and he sighs a little. He is warm from the car ride, his skin and clothes all summer and noon in the fall evening. He feels new.

"I do like you," I say.

"I'm so glad you do."

There were times when I thought I loved him. But I see now that I didn't really. Attraction, infatuation, and consternation do not love make. I don't know if I love him now, but I like him so much the joy is exquisitely painful. And this, too, is new.

I put both my hands up in his hair, my arms lifted. The posture makes me feel vulnerable, exposed, but inviting too. I stand on my toes, and I kiss him. He leans in, grateful, and kisses me. I do not count the kisses. We are not spinning, not flying or floating. Our feet are firmly on the Earth. My fingers curl. His hand rises to my neck, exploring the ends of my short hair. His other hand presses against my back. I am a part of something good.

There's a break in traffic. He holds my Gidget hand. We are running across the street toward the theater, headlights pointing at us, white against black like the sun in space. And I think this is my favorite part. Not the part where I saw Earth from above, or the weeks blissfully ignorant in the lair. Not the part where I swam through the guts of a ghostman ship, or when rocketeer Jonathan Wilder caught me.

This part. Jonathan and I holding hands and running with nothing chasing us, the after-rain street shiny as Christmas ornaments, the night behind us, the theater ahead. My right hand is in his left, and Jonathan turns to look at me. Looks at me for no other reason than he wants to.

And this is where I'll end, before I know what happens next.

ACKNOWLEDGMENTS

I would have floundered without the extraordinary help of early reader feedback; *muchísimas gracias a* Dean Hale, Victoria Wells Arms, Gabe Janke, Megan Whalen Turner, and Barry Goldblatt. You guys are seriously cool. All the folks of Bloomsbury gave a lot of hours to this book, including Michelle Nagler, Hali Baumstein, Rachel Stark, and Kaitlin Mischner. Thanks to Ava Cabey for inspiration. *Gracias a* Rebecca Allred Clyde. ¡*Rohayhú* Paraguay!

Super cheers to Kindra Johnson, without whose childcare prowess I wouldn't have finished a book since 2006. Extra awesome babysitting help courtesy of Kayla Huff and Maggie and Amy Thatcher.

All the research was fascinating, but one standout title was *The Canon: A Whirligig Tour of the Beautiful Basics of Science* by Natalie Angier. I also appreciated Arthur C. Clarke's *The Fountains of Paradise*, the first novel featuring a space elevator.

Profound thanks to Dr. Bart J. Kowallis, Dr. J. Ward Moody, Dr. R. Paul Evans, and Dr. Summer Rupper. I love scientists! And I'm not as smart as they are, so any mistakes are mine. Fist bumps to Heather Moody and Abigail and Eli Rupper, who know what it's like to have scientist parents.

I should also acknowledge my outstanding high school English teachers who showed me how to love poetry: Kathryn Romney, Paula Fowler, and Aisha Barnes. Hugs for high school counselor Lori Hargraves, who taught me teen survival skills.

Works quoted include Edgar Allan Poe's "A Dream Within a Dream," William Shakespeare's *Macbeth*, the correspondence of John Keats, W. B. Yeats's "The Second Coming" and "Brown Penny," and Robert Frost's "Desert Places."

Thanks to my readers for being willing to go on this new adventure with me. *Besos y abrazos.*

SHANNON HALE is the author of twenty novels, most of them for young readers, including the Newbery Honor–winning *Princess Academy*; its sequels, *Princess Academy: Palace of Stone* and *Princess Academy: The Forgotten Sisters*; and the Ever After High series, all of which are *New York Times* bestsellers. Her first book, *The Goose Girl*, was an international favorite; her adult novel *Austenland* is now a major motion picture starring Keri Russell. Shannon cowrote the acclaimed graphic novels *Rapunzel's Revenge* and *Calamity Jack* with her husband, Dean Hale. They live with their four small children near Salt Lake City, Utah.

www.shannonhale.com
@haleshannon

Explore the world

of SHANNON HALE